Witch King

The Cloven Land Trilogy, Book 3

Simon Kewin

Witch King – The Cloven Land Trilogy, Book 3

Copyright © Simon Kewin 2016

STORM
CROW
BOOKS

ISBN: 978-1-9993395-4-8

CROW•24

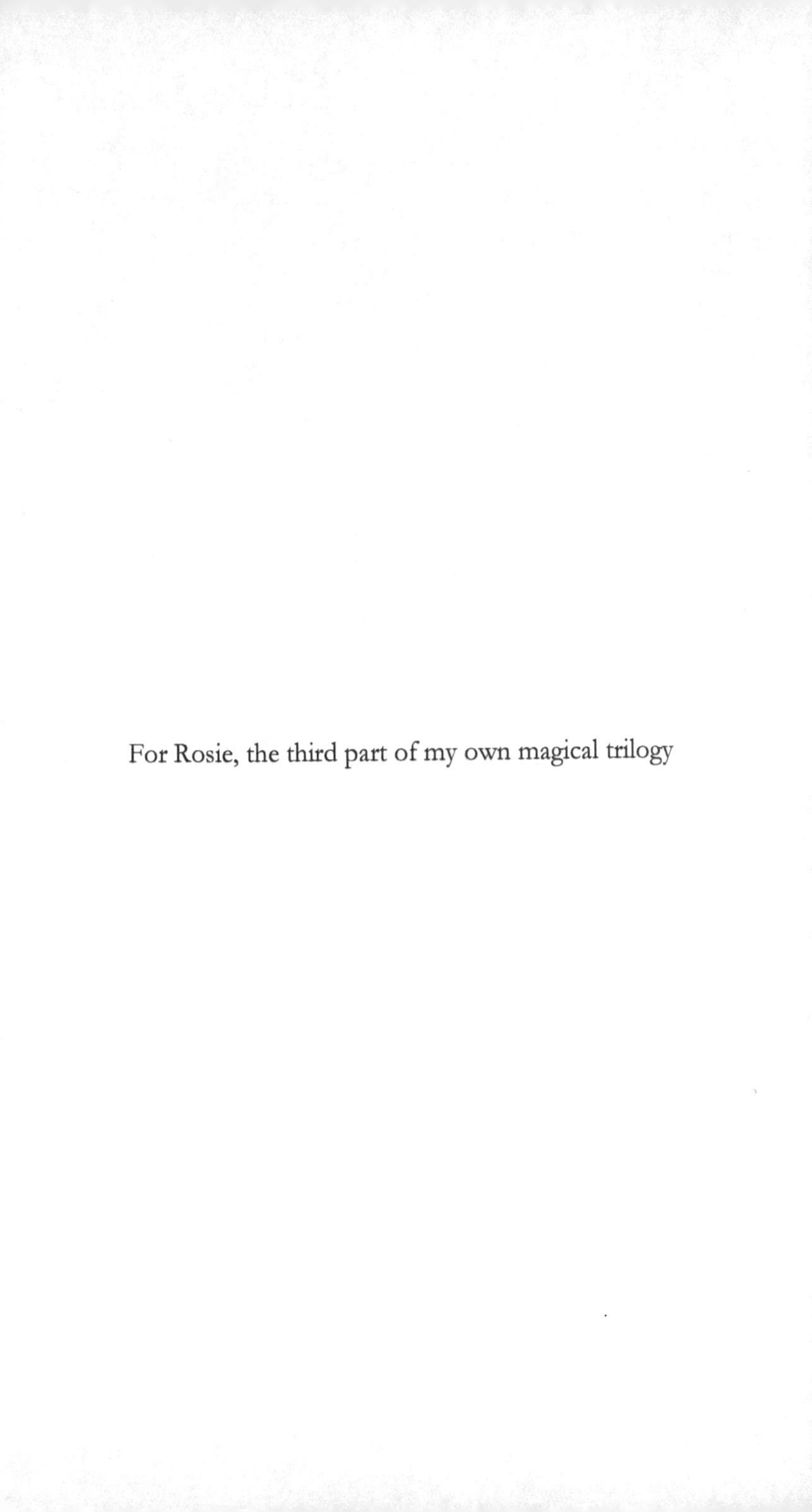

For Rosie, the third part of my own magical trilogy

CONTENTS

		Page
1	Howl Hill	1
2	Witch Hunt	9
3	A Single Word Different	23
4	Bethany Weerd	35
5	Hyrn's Oak	45
6	Smoke on the Water	55
7	The Lord of Misrule	67
8	The Ice Fair	79
9	Blood on the Ice	89
10	Hyrn's Oak	103
11	The High Walls of Caer L'dun	119
12	Voices in the Dark	135
13	To the Centre of the City	149
14	The Shadow Town Hall	167
15	A Maze of Streets	177
16	Leviathan	195
17	Unquiet Spirits	205
18	Xoster	219
19	Crashing to the Ice	231
20	Across the An	243
21	Witching Hour	259
22	Witch King	275
23	Ran	283
24	The Fate of More Than One World	291
25	The Orchard of Witches	307

1 – HOWL HILL

Andar

Hobbe stepped into the blur of the snowstorm. The wind from the north cut through him despite all the fur and cloth he'd muffled himself in. The hard, cold air took his breath away, hurt his lungs. The first true blast of winter. The mountain peaks around him were invisible, their lines wiped away by slanting snow. Even Howl Hill, its bulk towering behind his ramshackle hut, was gone.

He waded rather than walked through the snowfall. It was already up to his knees. He'd known for months a hard winter was coming. You didn't live in the wilds of the north without getting a feel for the place. Summers were dazzling in their beauty, but winters were brutal. They were the price you paid. A price he'd met happily for many years, enjoying his solitude. He could sit for a whole day and watch the shifting light washing across the waters of the An, and no one would disturb him. He could wander the woods for hours and see only fleeing deer, hear only the racketing, chattering birds in the treetops.

But winters, now. Winters were to be endured. When the light faded and the cold came, his old bones ached. Sometimes, when he tried to rise in the morning, he felt like he'd frozen solid overnight. He hoped he'd collected enough provisions to last through to spring. He'd gathered twigs and sticks from the evergreen woods all summer, as he always did. Enough to keep his log fire smouldering through winter days and nights.

Water, at least, would be plentiful.

If he stayed healthy, and didn't slip on the ice and smash leg or arm, the only problem he had was finding enough to eat. Again, over the years, he'd learned to stock up during the long, warm weeks of summer, the brief fruitful days of autumn. He had a barrel full of apples plucked from his stunted little orchard. He had a larder hung with salted meat: fish pulled from the An and even a few rabbits or martens caught in the woods. He'd cooked up cauldrons of bilberries and hurtleberries to make a sticky purple paste. A precious taste of sweetness for the darkest days. He had honey and roots and even some hardy green vegetables that could grow through the winter if he kept the worst of the snow off them.

Yes, he was well-stocked. But he couldn't afford to take chances. It only took an extra month of cold weather to make all the difference between surviving and dying a lonely death. He was old. Some day he'd have to leave the log cabin he'd built with his own hands. Leave his little garden and his orchard and the place he sat to look out over the waters. Put it all behind him and head south to civilisation. To Guilden, most likely, the city he'd been born in. Teeming, troublesome Guilden that he'd fled as a young man, vowing never to return.

Once a year he had visitors from the city. Three bearded and bedraped mancers would drift up the An, their boat moving against the current without sail or oar to propel it. They always came ashore near his little hut, and set up their brass telescopes and astrolabes on the flat table of land at the foot of Howl Hill. Despite his love of solitude, and despite the pang of alarm that still rang through him when he saw them coming, he'd grown to look forward to those brief visits. The mancers were stern and talked little, but he could get news from them, find out what was occurring in the wide world. He found it pleasing to know that the hubbub of life was going on and that he was isolated from it, safe from it. That no one cared, also, who or what he was.

There'd been a young mancer this year who'd been unusually talkative. He'd stood apart while the two older men – and they were all men of course – took their careful readings of the advancing snow line on the slopes and consulted their battered black books of charts and tables. Hobbe and the young mancer – Ash? Ashen? – had fallen into a halting conversation while the older mancers bickered over something in their observations.

"Why do they argue?" Hobbe had asked.

The young mancer was tall and spindly beneath his robes and cloaks. His long hair was wild, like a dandelion's seed-head. His expression was amused as he replied. "They can't agree what their readings mean."

Hobbe had glanced up at the peak. Howl Hill was a constant presence in his life and he'd grown used to its moods. In the old days only the triangular peak was dusted with white at the autumn equinox. This time half the mountain was under snow. He'd already seen two or three avalanches exploding off distant slopes.

"The weather is changing," said Hobbe. "A hard winter is coming. Don't need to consult charts to see that."

"How hard do you think?" asked the young mancer. A clear note of concern coloured his voice.

"Hard enough to freeze the An for miles out. Each year I have to walk farther and farther to reach open water."

The young mancer looked thoughtful for a moment.

"Perhaps you should come south with us. Come to Guilden for the winter at least. There's room enough on the boat."

Hobbe shrugged. "I like it up here."

"But how do you even survive? The winter must be cruel."

For a moment, Hobbe nearly explained. A part of him longed to tell someone what he'd done, why he'd fled the world. He'd been about the same age as this young mancer, studying, like him, the arcane arts. But Hobbe had done terrible things. Everyone knew the ancient tales of the necromancers of Angere and what they'd achieved. As a boy Hobbe had been fascinated by old tales of the creatures walking across the ice in the high north. Ignoring the sternest warnings of his elders, he'd researched the ancient magics. Dabbled.

There were said to be many old books kept at the Witches' Isle that might have helped, but he had no access to them. Instead he'd pieced together what few scraps of lore he could, filling in the gaps for himself. His attempts to reproduce Ilminion's work had gone hideously wrong. The young woman he'd worked on hadn't died by his hand, but the screaming, bloody creature that returned to life, begging for release from her agonies, had been his doing. Even now, decades later, he woke from nightmares, soaked with sweat, panting as if he were being chased.

But in that moment he'd seen himself through her eyes. Felt the horror, the hate. In disgust at what he'd done he'd turned away from it. Given the poor girl the release she begged for. Burned his notes and books. Then fled north for a life of solitude. An exile, a punishment.

All this he very nearly confessed to the young mancer. Instead, looking away, Hobbe simply said, "I like the peace."

The young mancer nodded, a thoughtful look on his face, but didn't reply.

Of course, the mancers only came to discover whether

the winter would be cold enough for an Ice Fair on the river at Guilden. Once the ritual had served another purpose, a more serious purpose. The people had needed to know if they'd be safe from nightmares creeping south in the dead of winter. Now the mancers' ceremony was merely a part of the Midwinter festivities. They came and took their readings and, if it were cold enough, they'd announce to the cheering people that there would be a fair.

Hobbe well remembered the festivities from when he was a boy: those magical few days when arenas and stalls and games and races were set up on the ice and people set aside their old lives for a time. Heady, wild days when laws didn't apply because they celebrated in a place that wasn't a place – the river – and in a time that wasn't a time – the gap between the end of the old year and the start of the new. One year, an uncle had been voted the Lord of Misrule, and Hobbe and his cousins had been at the head of the bonfire procession, assigned a series of jokes and tricks to play on people over the three days. And then, when it was over, the good folk of Guilden went back to their lives and became the people they were for the rest of the year.

Shaking his head at these memories, Hobbe worked his way down the slope to the river bank. In the summer it was alive with the chirrup of invisible insects. Sometimes a bright purple butterfly would flit around, sipping at the tiny yellow flowers. That was gone. The slope was a sheet of snow, treacherous to descend. He took it slowly. If he broke a leg here he'd struggle to crawl back to his hut. He had his stoutest fishing-pole with him. These days it was as much a staff, a crook, to keep him upright as he worked his way forward. Once out onto the ice he would head for open water. Fish caught now meant a day or two more he wouldn't have to dip into his supplies.

He reached the edge of the river without mishap. This was the place the mancers had left after their fortnight of observations, climbing into their miraculous boat to float back to Guilden. Only the young one had looked troubled, constantly glancing around him as if expecting attack, peering into the frozen north or westward across the An. Hobbe had watched them leave with something like regret. If his life had gone differently, if he hadn't made the mistakes he'd made, this might have been him. A wise, revered mancer of Guilden, bearing glad tidings to the rapturous crowds that there would be an Ice Fair. But it could never be. That bridge had been swept away a long time ago.

He stepped onto the ice, adopting the foot-sliding walk he always used on frozen ground. He'd find the water and see if he could pluck out a fish or two. He slid along for an hour without coming to the edge. Occasionally he reached out with his pole to tap, terrified of stepping onto thin ice and crashing through into the An. The river remained as solid as stone. How far out was he? How deep was the water beneath his feet? He tried not to think about it.

There were serpents in the depths. Colossal creatures that would drag down any boat attempting the crossing. Even the mancers, when they sailed from Guilden, clung to the banks, following the line of each inlet and headland so they could stay in shallow waters. Were the monsters there now, rolling through the depths beneath his feet? The thought sent a shudder through him. Still there was no end in sight to the ice. He kept sliding forward, part of him wanting to turn around, part of him hating wasting all that effort for no gain.

He walked for three hours before finally deciding to turn back. There was no sign of open water. Numbness had crept through his toes and turned his legs to ice. He wasn't going to find any fish. He suddenly felt very exposed, very alone. A cold, old man alone on the frozen waters of the An, many miles from the safety of land.

He turned around, and it was then he slipped. His frozen limbs, refusing to work properly, locked into place, overbalancing him. There was a moment of disorientation as he fell. A sickening thud of pain thumped through him, and ice filled his brain.

When he woke it was dark. How long had he lain on the ice? Panicking that he might be frozen into place he pushed himself upward. His head swam for a moment at the effort. A patch of darkness marred the place where his head had rested. He touched his temple and found the wound. The blood had frozen solid.

As he struggled it came to him that he'd had enough. He should have given up and gone south with the mancers when he had the chance. He was too old and frail for such a hard life. Next year, if he survived the winter, he would sail with them to Guilden where it was safe and warm. Perhaps he would admit his crimes. There wasn't much they could do to him now. But, one way or another, he would find some peace. He'd paid for what he'd done, even if he'd punished himself. Surely that counted for something.

He stood. A full moon hung low in the western sky, lighting the ice with a misty silver glow. He breathed more mist when he exhaled. The mountains of Andar were visible in the distance behind him, a faint saw-edge line of peaks against the hard stars. How far had he come? The ice stretched westward as far as he could see, moonlight reflecting dully off it. It didn't seem possible. There would be no more fish this winter.

He was about to turn away, begin the long trudge back to the banks of Andar, when he caught a glimpse of something out on the ice. A faint light from the west, flickering yellow. How could that be? No one else would be out there on the frozen river in the middle of the night.

Hobbe stood and watched as more lights twinkled into existence. A line of them, stretching upriver and downriver as far as he could see, countless in number. The lights bobbed and flickered.

Torches. Behind them, rank upon rank, came more

torches, and yet more.

Panicky now, half-running and half-sliding, Hobbe headed for Andar. But he knew it was useless. In a few moments he could hear them: the clanking metal, the huffing breaths, the stomp, stomp of their feet. The ice shook to the sound of their passing. He glanced over his shoulder and saw them. This was no Midwinter tale, no legend from the old days. The undain of Angere were coming. An army of them. A vast, wide army.

He stopped. He was already exhausted. He would never reach the banks before they overtook him. He would never set foot in the beautiful woods of Andar again. Perhaps it was justice after all this time. Retribution for his ancient crime. It occurred to him that maybe this was what he'd been seeking all along. Perhaps he'd simply sought judgement from the sorcerous creatures that he'd tried, in his vanity, to create.

Hobbe slumped to the ice and waited for them to reach him, knowing he would be the first of many to die in the invasion of Andar.

2 – WITCH HUNT

Manchester, England

Clara Sweetley fixed each member of Genera's Board with a questioning stare, waiting for each to be cowed into silence.

The boardroom occupied the entire top floor of Beetham Tower in the centre of Manchester. The clutter of the city's roofs and the hills and plains beyond were visible all around. On rainy, foggy days they lowered the flexible screens and showed video from various Genera feeds around the world. Scenes of war, riot, fleeing refugees. Today, with the sun shining on the city for once, they'd make do with their spreadsheets.

When the wind blew from the right direction, the shape of the building sent an eerie moaning, a banshee keening, across the city. People said it was a mistake in the design of the structure. It was nothing of the sort. It was a touch Genera had insisted upon.

Finally there was silence in the room. Clara made a mental note of who had shut up immediately and who among the twelve had chattered and laughed for a time. She had to keep an eye on any sign of disrespect, any challenge. The board members were all expendable, naturally, but there was a cost and a difficulty to replacing any of them. They all had some inking of the true nature of Genera, knew some part of what was really going on, and anyone removed from the board became an immediate security risk. Sometimes a simple secret held over them bought their silence. Sometimes they had to be killed. She'd been amused to read her own file on ascending to her position. The secrets Nox had planned to blackmail *her* with should she ever part company with Genera. The detail, the lengths they'd gone to, were impressive. That file was now destroyed, and expunged from all back-ups and archives. No one on this world had power over her any more.

"Shall we begin?" she said. "Karla, would you kindly give us a summary of the global situation?" It was eight days since her audience with Menhroth. Eight very busy days. Plans were in motion the world over. She'd slept little, but that was what you had to do to stay ahead of the game.

Karla Simonov, Head of Global Operations, cleared her throat and instructed everyone to open the spreadsheet with its columns of figures: tonnages, extraction rates, all the key indicators of the Genera operation. She raised a perfectly sculpted eyebrow and glanced around the room to make sure everyone was doing as instructed. Clara nodded at her to begin.

Half an hour later, Karla completed her talk and asked for questions. She glanced around the sullen faces in the room but mainly, Clara noticed, at her. That was good. Karla understood whose opinions really mattered. And the woman hadn't attempted to sugar-coat the effect their increased Spirit extraction rates were having on the world. There were those among the board members who opposed what Clara had ordered: one or two who, perhaps, calculated they could take over when everything went badly, when chaos and death skyrocketed. Clara understood that. Once, not so very long ago, she would have been making the same calculations. Anyone playing down the effects of Genera's actions might be hoping Clara overcompensated, upped the rates to the point where nations began to fail. Karla, it seemed, was not one of those.

"Thank you, Karla. Very illuminating. If I may summarise, our Spirit extraction rates are currently averaging 210% of where they were a week ago?"

Karla nodded. "250% in some parts of the Far East and Africa, ranging down to 190% in Northern America and Western Europe."

"A good start. But we still have more work to do. We have to ensure rates rapidly move to 350% of the levels they were on our baseline date." Menhroth had specified a tripling of the rate. The extra 50% was entirely her own invention. It always paid to build in a little leeway. She stared around the room, making sure she caught the gaze of everyone of them. "So, suggestions, ladies and gentlemen? Observations?"

She said the last word as if it were a mere afterthought, intending to lure any dissenters out with a pretence of valuing their views and advice. Anyone who didn't understand they were present to implement her orders clearly shouldn't be there.

Buckley, Head of Extraction Strategy, cleared his throat. "Clara, Ms. Simonov's excellent report spells out the effects of our activities in South/Central America. I think we can go a lot further there." He was a man she had many doubts about. Fortunately he was also a man with many secrets. For a lay Minister of the church, he had a surprisingly voracious appetite for illegal substances and bought women. When it came to it, his silence could certainly be guaranteed.

"Go on," she said. "You think we can extract more Spirit?"

Buckley glanced around as if seeking support from his

fellow board members. No one, she noticed, met his gaze. He swallowed, his Adam's apple bobbing, before he pressed on. "I do. Extraction rates have been upped to 225%, but they were, I believe, disproportionately low in the first place. It's true there has been a wave of brutal killings in central America, as well as riots in Brazil and Venezuela, but not very much more than the region is used to."

"Interesting," said Clara, nodding her head as if appreciating his sage advice. "So what rate do you think we could sensibly push to in that region?" Give them enough rope, that was the way.

"I believe 400% is achievable for a short time, a month or two. Given that there are some regions we want to keep on a lower rate – those where we happen to live, of course – I believe we will have to exceed our target average in others."

"And if we run at extraction rates that high for two months, what effects do you project?"

"Riots, civil unrest, the breakdown of order in the larger cities. Death rates will undoubtedly rise as banks fail and governments struggle to maintain order. Health care systems will be overrun and suicide rates will soar. But I believe in time, six months or so, some sort of normality will be restored, possibly with the assistance of the military."

Clara nodded and gave him her *thoughtful* expression. She already had detailed projections for all regions on the planet; she'd calculated them herself, taking the greatest care on the figures. Hitting 400% in South America would tip the whole continent into meltdown. Border disputes would escalate as populations tried desperately to flee the growing panic. Food production rates would plummet. Central America and then the USA would be in the firing line, triggering a massive reduction in global extraction rates. And thus ensuring she, Clara Sweetley, would incur the wrath of their masters on the other side of the portal.

Buckley's efforts were, she had to admit, nicely done. 400% was certainly high but not very much more than the maximum rate she had calculated. He was no fool. But he had badly miscalculated.

"I am only concerned that we hit our targets, of course," said Buckley, nervous of her silence.

"Naturally," said Clara. "Well. Can we take this offline? Talk to me after the meeting. I wanted to discuss another matter with you anyway. Certain … reports that have come my way, matters we don't need to trouble everyone with."

Buckley looked like he'd been struck. He grasped, immediately, that he'd misjudged her, overstepped the mark. There was something of the startled rabbit about the look he gave her. Really, she almost felt sorry for him.

"Of course," he said.

"Very good. We'll carry on upping the rates toward those you suggest. We'll get to 350% and see where we are, shall we?"

A murmur of assent rippled around the room. They all knew what had just happened. No one wanted to follow Buckley.

"Excellent," she said. "So, turning to matters closer to home, Williams, can we have your initial report on the events at Glastonbury yesterday?"

Williams, her Chief of Security, stood hesitantly before he began to speak, like an errant schoolchild. They had failed badly at Glastonbury, and Williams clearly expected he would be held accountable. Which, in truth, was exactly what was going to happen.

Williams began, covering events at the concert at the G-Mex centre, the strange reappearance of the criminals as they stole an electric guitar from the band one of them used to play in. A turn of events Ms. Sweetly still did not understand. Why a guitar? It made no sense. It couldn't be mere sentimental attachment. The women – the *witches* – from this world as well as the one from Andar and this guitar player had risked their lives. They'd very nearly been caught, too. It was her very good fortune that an undain lord had apprehended them – and then been defeated. That gave her some small amount of wriggle room with the White City. If her people had been to blame it would have been the end of her. Unfortunately for him, such leeway didn't need to extend to Williams.

"So they fled to Glastonbury with this guitar, pursued by our operatives?" she said.

"Indeed. Units were scrambled across England. We elected to follow them, surround them, rather than attempting to apprehend them in the sight of so many people." Of course he was attempting to illustrate how sound his reasoning had been. It made little difference. He'd lost the trail of the people they'd pursued, all save the one who'd died at Glastonbury. It was a failure that couldn't be tolerated.

"And what is your summary of events on top of the Tor? Of how the end of our little witch hunt unfolded?"

"It is … hard to be completely sure of the facts," said Williams. "Certain very unusual weather conditions – a thick fog – hampered our attempts to retrieve the people we were pursuing."

"The wrong sort of fog?" said Clara. "I believe we have technology capable of seeing through a bit of mist these days."

Her words did nothing to make Williams look any more comfortable. He picked up his pen from the table, twisted it around in his fingers, then laid it down again. "Yes. Of course. For some reason none of them functioned. No doubt some effect of the, of the … magical power our quarry was able to bring to bear."

"No doubt."

"Our … colleagues from beyond the Portal were present as well, of course. They, too, were hampered by the fog. It appeared to have a certain, well, solidity to it, as if it was a physical wall." Williams, too, was attempting to pass the blame onto the undain. Exactly as she knew he would.

"I believe there was a fifth individual as well?" she said. "The driver of the car?"

"Yes."

"An individual we have monitored previously, someone the criminals were known to have contacted upon their arrival in Manchester?"

Williams looked for a way out but couldn't find one. "Yes. He worked at an Indian restaurant. That was where they went to see him."

"Do we know what was said?"

"No."

"A shame. I believe there are indications, also, that our communications have been compromised? That these ridiculous witches from a place where they don't even have electricity were somehow able to direct a highly sophisticated cyber attack on our systems?"

She thought he was going to turn and run there and then. Instead he said, in a small voice, "That is correct."

She held his gaze for a moment, watching him squirm. She would speak to him afterward, too. His period of usefulness had come to an end. Unfortunately, he appeared to have led a blameless life, a devoted husband and father, no habits beyond a passion for one of the Manchester football teams. For him, alas, the only way to ensure his silence would be to explain to him the extent of the danger his beautiful young children would be in should he prove untrustworthy. Either that or arrange his suicide. She hadn't decided which yet.

"So," she said, "you believe those we pursued escaped into the other world?"

"Yes, that's our working hypothesis. When the mists finally cleared, there was only the dead woman, Fiona Weerd. The others were gone."

"And you obviously scoured the area for signs of them?"

"We did."

She nodded. Although, in truth, she had her doubts. The people they sought were resourceful, powerful. She'd make sure Genera carried on looking, just in case Williams had missed something.

"And there was no sign of the book either?" She spoke more quietly, almost gently. No one else in the room made a sound. Not all of them knew why they were pursuing the women, but everyone had heard something about the book. Rumours. Gossip. The Witch King coveted it. Nox had lost it and been replaced. Now she had lost it, too. She caught the briefest flicker of pleasure on Buckley's face. She added it to one of her mental lists.

"No sign," said Williams. "The book and the criminals were gone. We recovered the car, of course, but that's all."

She nodded. They weren't to know that the other witch, the girl Cait, was in Angere, in the land of the undain. She hadn't yet been apprehended, but the word from the White City was that it would only be a matter of time. And Clara had made it clear to her masters that, to the best of her knowledge, Cait and Nox had the book with them, that there was certainly no sign of it in this world. Whether that was true or not she didn't know, but it was enough to keep her safe. For a time.

"I see," she said. "Then I think we're done. Buckley, Williams, if you could come and see me in my office for a little chat please? The rest of you, same time tomorrow, yes? Let's make sure we hit our targets."

The smiles of relief on the faces of all but Buckley and Williams were a delight to see.

Fifteen minutes later, Buckley stood with his head bowed in front of her. He would be allowed to stay on in Genera, carry out some meaningless role that would pay him enough for him to survive without having any power. She had shown him all the evidence they had against him. His shock and horror were enough to convince her they could rely on him to remain quiet. Nevertheless, they would keep an eye on him. Just in case.

When he was gone, gaze still cast down to the expensive carpet, Williams took his place.

"I'm afraid there is a price for failure," she said to him, watching him from across her desk.

Unexpectedly, a spark of anger flared in his eyes. It was more than she would have given him credit for. He shook as he spoke. "And what of your failures, Ms. Sweetley? What of the mistakes you made when that schoolgirl escaped the refinery? Or were they even mistakes? Is it possible you let her go to inconvenience Mr. Nox? Those security systems looked like they'd been deliberately deactivated to me."

He'd been saving these accusations to hurl at her. He'd made a mistake to speak them now. As it happened he was absolutely correct, and that was a fact no one could ever find out.

She smiled at him. "Serious allegations. We must report them immediately to our undain masters."

He looked surprised at her words. "We must?"

"Oh yes."

She pressed a button to summon the creature from Angere. Such a shame about those beautiful young children, but there it was. The board room was no place for the weak and foolish.

When the door opened, a look of triumph flashed across William's features. It turned to alarm when he saw the ravening, snarling creature that strutted into the room, teeth bared.

Williams took a step backward. "No! I promise I won't…"

After that there was nothing intelligible from him, only wordless cries and screams. After a few moments they died out, too.

When it was done, Ms. Sweetley pressed another button. "Cleaning Services? Could you send a *special team* to my office please? There are some stains that need removing."

Fer, Catherine and the wise man known as the Lizard King walked in a line through dense woods, weaving their way among the boughs. The ground was soft beneath their feet, springy with a carpet of pine needles, and the only sounds were the chatterings of birds. No one had spoken for an hour or more. They were all exhausted, numb from events on the Tor.

Fer wasn't entirely clear what had happened on that strange, conical hilltop. Fiona had worked strong magic, it was clear, protecting Johnny while he tried to play his way back into Andar. She and Catherine had offered what help they could. Then the undain had broken through and everything had become confused. Her memories were mainly of snarling teeth, flashing claws and screams. Then some sort of explosion had picked them up, tossing them around, scattering them. Either she'd knocked her head in the chaos, or else she'd fallen into some sort of fugue as a result of the magic she'd worked, but in any case she'd lost her senses.

When she came round, she thought for a moment she'd been carried back to Andar, some effect of Johnny opening the portal with his guitar playing. It soon became clear that wasn't right. The Lizard King showed them the signal on his phone. They were still in England, yet somehow they'd been transported a distance from the Tor. A mile away, the Lizard King said, studying his screen.

"Fiona's doing," said Catherine. The shock at the loss of her daughter filled her mind, painful to see. Fer tried to think of something to say to help, but there was nothing.

"We'd better keep moving," said the Lizard King. They spoke in the language of Andar so Fer could understand. The wise man had learned the tongue from his years of eavesdropping, and Catherine had been taught it by Jaiin in the library. "If Fiona did hurl us away as far as she could, she did it to protect us, give us a chance. We can't throw that away."

He was right, of course. Catherine nodded and they hiked away, nursing their aching, cramping limbs, following pathways through the trees that would take them far from Glastonbury.

Now, as they trudged along, Fer tried to think about what they should do. Of the five who had set out from Andar, only she and the archaeon remained. Seleena had died in the Tanglewood. Ran had fallen into Angere with Cait. Johnny had – seemingly – made it back to Andar with the book. She was alone in this strange, confusing world save for Cait's grandmother, the Lizard King and the bookwyrm. Catherine was kind, resourceful, but not particularly powerful. The loss of her daughter and worry about Cait flooded her mind. Fer knew very little about the wise man. He'd come to their rescue, but his magical abilities were limited. He could occasionally glimpse events through the eyes of others but could do little to intervene. Still, at least he and Catherine knew how this world worked. That would be some help, perhaps. The bookwyrm, too, if the creature could be persuaded to assist. She wasn't completely alone, but with the forces of Genera and Angere ranged against them, it seemed pretty hopeless.

"What are we going to do?" said Fer when they stopped to rest. They walked among oaks now, the trees' leaves beginning to turn to yellows and oranges. Clouds had slid over the sky, and a light drizzle pattered down onto the treetops.

"We may still be needed," said Catherine, all colour gone from her voice. "We should go back to Manchester in case Cait needs us somehow."

"How far is it?"

"Two hundred miles or so."

Fer considered, worrying mainly about Catherine. She didn't see what they could do for Cait. "I think we need to rest. We're in no state to go back. I think we should hide for a time until we're ready for the journey. Perhaps we'll hear something across the aether about what we need to do."

"Hide where?" said Catherine. "We're in the middle of nowhere."

"I think I might know a place," said the Lizard King, frowning as if recalling faint memories. "Maybe twenty miles from here. Used to be a witch lived there, kept herself to herself. She died five years ago but I might be able to find it."

"Who lives in her house now?"

"Possibly no one. I stopped seeing when she went, of course. But even in her day it was a ruin. Four stone walls and only half a roof to keep the rain off. There was a tree, I remember, growing in the middle of one of the rooms, right through a hole in the ceiling. She used to tie decorations around its trunk and burn little candles in its hollows."

"And perhaps it's been bought and converted into a luxury home since then," said Catherine.

"Perhaps. But it was remote, half-way up a hillside. A barn or a cattle shelter or something. It's all I can think of. If we get that far, and if it's not safe, then I guess we can just carry on north."

Catherine nodded her assent. She clearly had no strength for an argument. "Shame we can't drive. We could be back home in a few hours."

"Too dangerous," said the Lizard King. "We dare not hitchhike or take a train or anything. They may believe we ended up in Andar, but we can't be sure. We have to assume they're still looking for us."

"Can you see anything through the eyes of others that might help?" asked Fer.

"I will keep trying. The visions ebb and flow. I have very little control over them."

"What about your phone? The bookwyrm?"

"I'm almost out of power. Unless you can work some magic to recharge it?"

"I have no idea how to do that," said Fer.

"We'll try this ruin," said Catherine. "Twenty miles is a long, weary walk, but maybe we can make it before nightfall."

None of them speaking further, Fer, Catherine and the Lizard King threaded through the trees, Fer looking constantly around in fear of pursuit.

3 – A SINGLE WORD DIFFERENT

Andar

They met on the green grass of the orchard of witches: Cait and Danny, Ran and Nox, Johnny, Ashen and Hellen. In the middle of the circle were two identical books: the same red leather cover, the same etched diagrams of skeletons and skulls, even the same old stains. It was weird to see them side-by-side. The left and right hand halves of Ilminion's Grimoire, one brought from Cait's world by Johnny, the other stolen from the Witch King by Cait. Both of them originally stolen from the enemy by Nox.

They'd made landfall in Andar early the previous day. Ilyrn had rowed through the night, never speaking, never pausing despite his age and seeming exhaustion. When they'd stepped out of his little boat he'd simply rowed off, back into the mists. Apparently he wasn't a man but some sort of woodland god. He looked pretty wrecked for a god. He reminded Cait of someone she'd met or glimpsed in a dream. She couldn't recall the details. She was just glad to be in Andar. Not safe ground, exactly, but safer. For now.

Johnny had been waiting for them on the banks, his

dazzling, brightly-painted boat moored nearby. *Smoke on the Water*. That, in turn, had brought them down the An to the mouth of a river called the Gleaming which in turn led to Silverwater Lake and the island of the witches that she'd heard so much about.

It was good to see Johnny again. He'd explained everything that had happened back home as they floated along. Everything Cait's mum and gran and Fer had said and done. How they'd recovered his guitar and been hunted by the forces of Genera. And then how Cait's mother had died at Glastonbury Tor to give him a chance of returning to Andar. He hadn't known she was dead until Hellen, hearing word across the aether, broke the news to him.

"She gave me a message for Hellen," he said. "Told her to save you, use the book or whatever was needed. But just to save you. That was all she cared about."

Cait thought about that for a time, staring over the quiet waters of the An. Losing her mother so abruptly was still impossible to understand. It was like a coldness inside her. Now she'd lost both parents. How did you come to terms with something like that? So many things had been left unsaid. "But my gran and Fer survived?"

"So Hellen says, although communication with our world is patchy. They'll obviously still be in a ton of danger, but it looks like your mother managed to magic them away from Glastonbury before ... the end."

Cait nodded, not trusting her voice to work in reply.

At the island they'd been met by Ashen. He was tall and wiry, apparently taking after his dead father, the wyrm lord Borrn, but she could see something of Hellen in his face. *A lot going on behind those eyes*, Cait thought. She liked him immediately.

"I've heard a lot about you, Cait," he said as they walked up from the jetty. "What you did was wonderful. Incredible."

"Couldn't have done it without you. Your mother

explained how you sent the message about the bridgehead to Phoenix."

"Yes. With help."

"We'd have been lost without that."

"It was a small thing. The least I could do."

"You did what was needed," said Cait, thinking that she suddenly sounded like her gran. "That's all that matters."

Now, they sat in the silence of the orchard. A sharp chill hung in the air. Grey clouds billowed toward them from the north, following the line of the An, bringing the threat of rain. There was a heavy, orange tint to some of them, as if they bore a weight of snow. Cait hadn't understood why they couldn't sit in the round, echoing space of the Wycka. It was open to the elements at the top but would at least have been warmer. But apparently the spirits of the dead witches lingered here, taking up residence in the trees. Spirits that liked to contribute to discussions. The crooked old boughs surrounded them, like the skeletons of proper trees, all twigs and knots.

Fer had described a gathering like this to her when they'd first discussed what was to be done about the book. Now it was her turn. Her and Danny's. He, alone, didn't speak the language of this world, so she would have to translate for him. The gift Phoenix had given her, the gift of voices, meant she could follow everyone's words with ease.

She huddled closer to Danny for warmth. Fortunately someone had lit a crackling fire of fallen branches. Not for visions from the stones that Ran wore around his neck, but simply to keep the chill off. Sweet-smelling wood smoke filled the air.

"So," said Hellen. "Here we are. Now we must decide what is to be done about the book. And everything else, come to that."

"Is there any way we can fight the undain without using the death magic?" asked Cait.

"How big was the army you saw?"

"I don't know. Huge. There were thousands of them."

"Hundreds of thousands," said Nox.

Hellen cast a glance at Ran. "And there are only a thousand or so wyrm lords."

"But there must be other armies in Andar," said Danny. "Other defenders?"

"Not really," said Ashen. "There are a few watchmen in Guilden and the other cities. Then there are the wyrm lords and the witches. That's about it. We've grown complacent. There's never been war in Andar. The events of five hundred years ago are distant, an old story. Or maybe that's what people like to think. But we won't be enough, not nearly enough. I was at Howl Hill at the equinox, I saw what the coming winter will be like. For all we know, the invasion may have started already, up there in the high north."

"So then we have to use the book?" said Cait. "Turn their own magic against them?"

"You don't like the idea?" said Hellen.

"It feels wrong. I don't know, bad."

The air buzzed with a murmur of half-heard words. The voices of the dead witches in the aether.

"There are many here who would agree with you," said Hellen. "But is it so different from what you did at the White City? That was magic many on the Witches' Isle would have shunned. Sometimes, I think, we have to get our hands dirty."

"Still," said Cait. "I don't like it."

"We have to use all the weapons at our disposal," said Nox.

"We may not have to work the magic Ilminion did," said Ashen. "Perhaps, if we understand the rites, see why Menhroth wants the Grimoire so much, we'll find a weakness we can use without having to work any death magic ourselves."

"Is that likely?" asked Cait.

"Perhaps," said Hellen. She pulled another book from

the folds of her skirt, this one smaller and black, its cover plain. "This is Akbar's journal, brought to Andar with your ancestor, Cait, and held at Caer D'nar ever since."

"It says something?"

"No one has been able to make sense of it these five hundred years. Fortunately, we now have someone who can."

"The bookwyrm?" said Danny. "I thought the creature was all over the internet in our world."

"Yeah," said Johnny. "It is. But I brought a copy of it in my phone when I came here." He waved his mobile around as if to prove the point. "Before the battery died we managed to transfer the wyrm into the journal. Back from pixels to ink and paint."

"And it can read Akbar's words?" asked Cait.

Hellen smiled. "You know what the creature is like. It tells me that the handwriting is extremely difficult and the language all-but forgotten, but that it is, thankfully, wise enough to interpret it."

"And what has it found?"

"It's still working its way through Akbar's writing," said Ashen. "But one passage has emerged that is of interest. Before he split the Grimoire in two, in what little time he had, Akbar studied it. He noted that there were two different versions of the Ritual used by Ilminion to resurrect the King."

"Two different versions?" said Cait. "How do we know which one was used?"

"We don't. But it is interesting Ilminion set down a second."

"So he made a mistake with the first version," said Cait. "That's not so strange. You should see my schoolwork."

"It might have simply been a mistake," said Hellen. "Or, then again, it might not."

"Can we even tell how the two differ?" asked Danny.

Ashen threw another branch onto the fire, flaring it briefly into life. "Akbar said they are almost identical. Only a single word different."

"I don't see how a single word can make much difference," said Cait.

"Perhaps," said Hellen. She looked thoughtful as she spoke. "Or perhaps it makes all the difference in the world. Depends on the word. If we can recreate the Grimoire then maybe we'll be able to make some sense of it ourselves."

"Are we able to do that?" asked Nox.

"Not yet," said Ashen. "But once the archaeon has finished translating Akbar's words we might be able to get somewhere."

"Only a mancer could unwork Akbar's magic," said Hellen. "Fortunately we have Ashen here to attempt it." The pride on her face as she spoke was clear.

"The book may not be a weapon," said Cait. "There may be nothing there we can use."

"True enough," said Hellen. "In that case it makes little difference. All we can do is fight and hope that somehow, by some miracle, we prevail."

"OK, so," said Danny, "while Ashen gets on with that, what about the rest of us?"

"I've been thinking about it," said Hellen. "I have an idea or two."

Cait caught Danny's eye and had to look away for fear of bursting into laughter. They'd privately agreed that Hellen would say almost exactly that. Nox frowned at them.

"Go on," said Johnny, covering for them.

"Five hundred years ago," said Hellen, "the witches of Islagray Wycka marched north to the ice, to bring the An into flood and so sweep the great bridge away. Witches and mancers on both sides worked together to seal off Andar. Now I think it is time to repeat that march. The snow and ice will be creeping south. I think we have to move north to meet it, everyone save a few to continue singing the Song. Wherever the undain choose to attack, they need the frozen river to do it. We should go and try and stop them. At the very least warn people of what is coming."

"What chance will we have?" said Cait.

"Very little," said Hellen. "At best I think we can try and delay them, give Ashen and the witches who remain here at the Wycka more time. The dragonriders will defend Caer L'dun, and they, too, may hold out for a while. We have to hope Menhroth takes each city and town as he moves south rather than racing directly here."

"You said the witches melted the ice in the old days," said Danny, Cait still translating for him. "That they flooded the An. Can't you do something similar again? Melt the ice under the feet of the undain?"

Hellen shook her head. "It is beyond us. There are so few of us, and what was done five hundred years ago, great as it was, was simply to hurry along the thaw that was going to happen anyway. Mountainsides of ice and snow slide into the An every spring, thankfully not all at the same time. Even the witches of old couldn't have melted ice up the length of the river."

"OK, so," said Danny, who'd clearly been thinking about this, "What about the serpents? You said they smash up any ship that attempts the crossing. Why can't they break through the ice and drown the army?"

"There is something in that. But the serpents are Hyrn's, as I think you know, and he is far gone, weakened by everything that has happened. The effort of rowing us back to Andar may have finished him off. And even the serpents may struggle to break through the ice when it is ten feet thick. But … perhaps they can be persuaded to play their part."

"We have to at least warn Guilden," said Ashen. "No one there has a clue. The city will be thronged with revellers for Midwinter. I tried to tell them but they wouldn't listen."

"They might listen to me," said Hellen. "So I will go

north, along with most of the witches and wise men of Islagray. We may not be able to do much but we will do what we can. The rest of you should stay here. Cait especially."

"Why?" demanded Cait.

"Because it is safer. Because I was given a solemn duty to look after you, and I'll carry that duty out as best I can."

Not so very long ago, Cait might have crumbled and gone along with Hellen's wishes. Not any more. Not after everything that had happened. "No. It's no safer here, not really. I'm coming with you. Perhaps I can help slow them down. I've fought them before, remember. The only witch here who has."

Hellen studied her for a moment before replying. "And what would your mother say to such a suggestion?"

"She'd sigh and complain about headstrong Weerds and then let me go."

With clear reluctance, Hellen came to a decision. "Very well. Come if you must. At least I can keep an eye on you."

Hellen peered around the circle to the others. "And what will you all do? Ran, I think you, at least, should be spared this journey. You have suffered much, by fire and sword. You have watched over Fer and then Cait, done far more than I could ever have asked. We could leave you at Caer D'nar as we head north."

Ran shook his head. "No. I will go with Cait."

Hellen frowned but appeared to be aware it was pointless trying to argue. "And you others? Johnny? Nox? Danny, it seems, can hardly be separated from Cait."

All three indicated they wished to travel north, although Johnny looked distinctly alarmed by the prospect as he nodded his head.

"Good," said Hellen. "I think we can allow ourselves a few days rest. We've all been through a lot. But winter is drawing on, and we must reach Guilden soon. Find warm clothes and good boots for the journey. We'll need them."

"One other thing," said Cait. "It just occurred to me.

When we were in the White City we saw cartloads of Spirit being wheeled along after the army. Vast amounts. They must need a constant supply of it for the invasion."

"A lot of it will be coming through the pipe from the refinery, no doubt," said Danny. "Bled from the people of our world. Perhaps we should try and disrupt the flow, do something to the pipeline. We talked about trying it before, when we were back home. It'll be dangerous, obviously."

Hellen considered, the dead witches of Islagray Wycka joining in with the conversation. After long moments Hellen replied. "Perhaps it is for the best. We have the book now, so even if Fer or Cait's grandmother are captured Menhroth won't be able to complete the rites. It is a hard thing to say, but perhaps now the risk is worth taking."

"How do we get the message through to them?" asked Cait.

"I will attempt it," said Hellen. "As you know, the aether is disturbed thanks to the Tanglewood and the aethernal dwelling within it, but perhaps I can get word through. If not, we'll have to hope they work it out for themselves. Now, let's all get some rest. There may not be much chance in the days and weeks to come."

When everyone was heading away, Hellen came up to Cait and placed a hand on her arm, drawing her aside.

"Cait, there is one thing I would like to ask you while we are alone."

"Oh?"

"The truth is I didn't only try to dissuade Ran because of his injuries. Are you sure you want him to come with us?"

"Why wouldn't I?"

Hellen gazed at the disappearing figure of the rider. She spoke quietly. "I don't know. I wonder about him sometimes. He's so hard to make any sense of. The riders all are."

"You were happy enough for him to go with Fer to my

world."

"I've learned a little more about the events of five hundred years ago now, thanks to Akbar's journal."

"What have you learned?"

Hellen took a moment to reply. "Nothing detailed, nothing definite. Rumours and suspicions. Maybe only folks' fear of the riders and what some of them did."

"But what rumours?"

"Only that the riders aren't really to be trusted."

"That's mad. He's always protected me and fought for me. I thought you were the one who always dismisses such talk."

"Yes, I did. I do. But still … he's never done or said anything, I don't know, odd?"

"I have no idea what *odd* means any more," said Cait. "Everything is odd."

"But you trust him? You were with him all the way across Angere. And in your world."

Cait considered. There were times when they'd been separated, but that had never been at Ran's suggestion. She tried to recall everything the rider had said and done. It was hard; he was basically always *there*, saying nothing, standing in the background. Did she trust him? A damn sight more than she trusted Nox. "Ran always did what he could to protect us. You've seen his injuries."

"Yes," said Hellen. "I have." She considered Cait for a moment, as if peering into her thoughts, then relented. "Good. Nothing more than unfounded fears. My apologies, nothing seems certain or clear to me any more. If we can't trust each other then we truly are lost."

Cait left Hellen and headed down the green slope toward the spire of the wycka and the huddle of huts and shacks the witches lived in. She called to Danny, Johnny and Nox. They turned to wait for her.

"Listen," said Cait. "None of you need to come with me, you know. It's all very noble and heroic, but I'm not sure there'll be much any of you can actually do."

"And you will?" said Nox.

"Perhaps, I don't know. But you might actually be more useful here, Nox. You could get involved in the plans for defending Andar. Isn't that the sort of thing you do?"

He considered her words for a few moments, eyes narrowed. "No. It's too late to be of much use. And somehow I don't think they'd listen to me if I started ordering them around. I'll come north. Might be able to do something to hurt the undain."

"OK, so you, Johnny. I know you're not keen. You've done so much already. Perhaps it's time to get back in that boat of yours and sail away south. No one would blame you."

"Tempting, I'll be honest," said Johnny. "Don't think I haven't considered it. But, nah. I wanna see how this story ends. Besides, if it's true what they say and the An is an endless circle around this whole world, I'd just end up back in Andar anyway. I'd like to be sure it's still here before I set off."

"Looks like you're stuck with all of us," said Danny. He took her hand, interlacing his fingers through hers.

Cait frowned, as if she were cross with them. Although, secretly, she was delighted and very, very grateful.

4 – BETHANY WEERD

That night, lying in the utter darkness, Cait closed her eyes to find Bethany, the dead witch-girl whose spirit she carried inside her.

Sometimes it was difficult to find her way to that mountain lake. Sometimes she could only wander alone through an endless fog, no sign of Bethany except for a distant whisper. But sometimes the girl was easy to find, the lines of her face and body hard and clear, as if she were real and alive. It was like that tonight. Cait waited on the mossy banks while Bethany moved through the cold lake, water streaming from her hair and the plain white dress she wore, and the little ragged doll she always clutched to her.

Cait was never completely sure how much Bethany knew of events outside in the real world. Or how much she understood them. Bethany only saw things through Cait's eyes or felt things reflected in Cait's thoughts. But she often missed out on detail, didn't know where Cait actually was in the world. Perhaps she sometimes slept, or faded, or did whatever dead spirits did. Perhaps she could only sense something threatening was near because of the fear buzzing through Cait, without really understanding what the danger was. It had to be confusing and frustrating. Sometimes Bethany was a little girl, childish, not understanding, and sometimes she was old and wise and weary. The trouble was she was both, of course. A young girl who'd been dead for hundreds of years.

"Hi, Bethany," said Cait.

"Hello, Cait." The girl sounded girlish today, much more so than the last time they'd communicated in the dungeons of the White City. "You haven't brought Danny with you this time, then?"

She hadn't told Danny anything of what she was about to attempt. "No, he's asleep."

"That's a shame. Such a fine-looking lad. And we've left the other land? Where the Masters were?"

"Yes. We've travelled to Andar, across a vast river. Still in great danger, but it isn't so close."

"The Masters are distant," said Bethany, looking into the sky as if she could glimpse them. "Distant but hungry, as they always are. Angry too, after what we did."

"I wanted to thank you for that. For showing me what to do. It saved us."

Bethany giggled, as if they were both playing some childhood game, but didn't reply.

"I wanted to ask you about something, too," said Cait.

Bethany began to play with her doll, rearranging its tatty white clothes. It appeared to make very little difference. "Go on."

"You know Phoenix gave me the gift of voices, so I could understand people from Andar and Angere?"

"Yes."

"So, he said he needed your help to do it, and I was wondering if you'd got the gift at the same time. If *you* could understand people from this world now."

Bethany shrugged without looking up. "I suppose."

Cait pressed on. "And you know you said it's only possible for me to carry your spirit around within me because we're related?"

"Yes."

"Well, does that mean you could inhabit another of our relatives instead?"

"I suppose so. Why, Cait? What are you thinking? Don't you want to be my friend any more?" For a moment Bethany looked like a very little girl, forlorn at being rejected.

"Of course I do," said Cait. "I don't know how I'd have managed any of it without you. And to know I've always had a friend to turn to has been a life-saver, really. But, the thing is, there's someone else, another relative who maybe needs your help even more. I mean, we're both in great danger, but I have more friends around me than she does now."

"Who? Not some dull old person I hope, full of rules and complaints?"

"It's Fer. She's trapped in our world. I think my gran's with her, but other than that she's alone. She must find everything pretty strange and confusing and I wondered if you could go and help her. Not necessarily with magic and stuff I mean. But with how the world works. Just, anything she might need to know."

"That world is strange to me, too. We hid from it for so long. Hid as well as we could."

"Yes, still. You'll have more idea about things than she will. She's smart and powerful, but she'll probably get confused between a green light and a red one and get squashed by a bus or something."

Bethany didn't reply for a moment. She bobbed up and down, sending out circles in the water. "I could probably help her," she said at last. "Does she know about me?"

"No. I've only told Danny."

Bethany giggled again, as if that were highly amusing. Then her seriousness returned. "Fer's stronger than you, much more practised in the ways of magic."

"Yes I suppose she is. Does that matter?"

"You were easy to slip into. You didn't have a clue. You're better at defending yourself now, and it will be a lot harder with her, too."

"But you could do it?"

"I could try. She might think I was attacking her, I'd have to be careful. But it would be nice to be home. All the others will be so lost and confused without me. Some of them were just children, you know."

Cait remembered their raging fury as they attacked the rider at Empire Towers. "Yes. I know. There is a bigger problem, though. We're obviously on different worlds and the aether lies between us. I don't really understand such things. Is there any way you can make the journey? Being, you know…"

"Dead."

"Yes. Dead."

"The aether is a cold and lonely place," said Bethany. "I've glimpsed it occasionally. It's endless, endless nothingness. A place you can get lost in and never find your way home from. The universe is mostly darkness, you know. Endless night with only a few tiny, tiny flames of light here and there."

"The thing is there's a wood there," said Cait. "Like, in a bubble all of its own. Fer used it to reach Manchester. The doorways are closed, now, but I thought, maybe, you could use that as a guide, from the outside I mean. A pathway through the greyness to get back home."

Bethany didn't reply for a moment. She sank into the waters a little as if shrinking from Cait's words. "Such a long, cold journey."

"Yes. I wouldn't ask, it's just that I think Fer needs help. And, also, there's a message I'd like to send her, and I don't know how else to do it."

"What message?"

Cait hesitated. This part might well put Bethany off completely. Understandably so. "You remember the refinery?"

"The bad place where the fog suffocated you and you couldn't think or speak."

"Yes. That. The thing is, we want her to go there."

"Why would anyone go there?"

"It's complicated. That place, it sucks out peoples' spirits, collects them all together to send through a big pipe to the city where we freed all the trapped souls."

"I heard them," said Bethany. She seemed to recede a little as she spoke, as if moving away. "When we were there. So many voices. Voices in the pipes, crying out. So many people, lost and confused."

"That's what we need to try and stop," said Cait. "I don't know how, but if Fer could get there and somehow stop them, at least interrupt them, it might make all the difference. There's an army coming, you see. An invasion. And if they run out of Spirit they might, I don't know, crumble or die or something."

"Yes," said Bethany.

"You'll do it?"

"No, silly. I mean they'll crumble and die."

"So, will you go? I'll be sorry to lose you, truly."

Bethany still fussed at her doll. Then she sighed and looked up at Cait. "Yes, I'll go. I don't like it here. Neither side of the river is safe, not safe at all. I want to go home."

"Will you go now?"

Bethany's arms fell to her sides. "Yes. I'll go now." She began to sink into the waters, her eyes closed. "Good bye, Cait. It was nice to meet you."

Cait wondered if she'd ever talk to the girl again. She suddenly didn't want to lose her, be without her, but there was no choice. "Good bye. Thanks for all your help."

In a moment the waters closed over the dead girl's head, leaving only widening circles to ripple across the lake.

Bethany floated, clutching her doll to her chest. Below her, the girl she'd lived within, Cait, lay on her bed, eyes closed. Bethany looked at her for a moment. It was strange to see her from the outside. She was so young. But she'd grown, too, in these few weeks. And she had friends. That was important. But she was in such terrible danger that Bethany knew she might never see her again. She was jealous of Cait in some ways, jealous of her life, but she wouldn't swap places with her even if such a thing were possible.

"Good bye," she whispered, although there was no one who would be able to hear. "Be careful, Cait."

She floated away, through walls, over trees. A round tower stood nearby, and beyond that stood a lake of silvery water, shining in the moonlight. She'd glimpsed it through Cait's eyes. It wasn't like home. She did want to get home.

She drifted around the circular tower for a time, trying to find a way into the greyness between the worlds. A gap, a flaw. She'd slipped inside the aether before, more than once, but only as a sort of accident. It was like going to sleep. She tried to make the young ones she looked after go to sleep sometimes. She didn't really know why, but that was what you did with children. Sometimes it was easy, it just happened. But if you tried to make it happen it became impossible.

She floated for some time before the voice came for her.

"And who are you, girl, flying around our island in the dead of night? No one from this world I think?"

"I'm Bethany. What's your name?"

"I'm called Hellen. How did you get here?"

"I came with a friend."

"Oh? And who might that be?"

"Her name is Cait. Do you know her?"

"Yes, I know her. I didn't know she brought you with her."

"It was supposed to be a secret."

"I see. So she carried you within her?"

"Yes."

"Ah. Full of surprises that girl. I had no idea. So to do such a thing … you're related?"

"Yes. My mother came from this world many years ago."

"You're Bethany Weerd."

"Yes I am."

"What wonders there are in the world. You survived all this time without fading away or finding release?"

"I was so angry! I died, you see. Me and others. We were so young, and it wasn't fair."

"No, it wasn't. I'm sorry for what happened to you, Bethany Weerd."

"It's not your fault, silly."

"No. And what are you doing now?"

"I'm trying to find my way home, to help someone else in trouble."

"Cait has asked you to go to Fer?"

"Yes. The other girl needs my help. It's very important."

"Yes, it is."

"You know Fer as well? You seem to know lots of people."

"It's helpful to know about people, I find. If I help you, can you give Fer a message from me?"

"About the Spirit? And the refinery? I'm already going to tell her that. Cait said."

The old woman who was speaking to her laughed, but it was a kind sort of laugh. "Very good. Her mother's daughter, that one. And her grandmother's granddaughter."

"How can you help me anyway? I'm trying to find a way into the greyness. There's water all around and I can't fly over it so I'm stuck."

"Let me show you a road to take," said the voice of the woman. "I can open up a way for you. You intended to follow the shadow pathway the Tanglewood lies upon?"

"Cait said it will take me home."

"Yes, she's right, but be careful. And don't go into the woods. There's a creature there that might … consume you."

"I'll be careful."

"Good. Here is the opening. Slip inside. See the pathway? Stay close to it. Don't stray or you'll be lost forever."

"Yes, I know," said Bethany. "I'll be careful. Good bye! And thank you, Hellen. You're nice."

"You're welcome," said the voice of the old woman, the little laugh in her voice again. "You're nice, too. And thank you. For everything."

Once inside the aether Bethany paused. It was cold there. Not the cold of water or ice. That didn't trouble her. This was a cold that slowly leeched away your mind, your spirit. If she stayed there for long there'd be nothing left of her. She had to hurry.

The pathway was a silvery line, very faint, like a cobweb in the moonlight. You had to look at certain angles to see it. Sometimes it disappeared completely. Sometimes it crossed other lines. It was difficult, but she could see the wood Cait had mentioned. A smudge of shimmering green. Hunger emanated from the monster living within it. An insatiable hunger. Bethany didn't need to be told not to go near. She'd lived her whole life, and her whole death, avoiding creatures like that. Monsters who wanted to hurt her and consume her.

Beyond the wood, the silvery line continued through the endless grey. Here and there were tiny lights like stars. Only they weren't real stars. Instead of being above you they were all around, in every direction. The shimmering line she was following led to one of them. That was her way home. She'd be safer there. She could find the others, the little ones she'd looked after all this time, and make sure they were all right.

There was something else, too. A decision Bethany had

come to. Perhaps it was Cait who had given her the idea. Cait had been so frightened so much of the time they'd travelled together, and she'd lost so much. But she hadn't given in. She fought back. What they'd done at the city of white walls, the way they'd taken on the Masters instead of hiding below ground. It was terrifying, but also wonderful. And that was what Bethany was going to do, too.

She didn't know how, yet. But it was time she and the others, all the trapped spirits in Manchester, came from their cold graves and took revenge on the Masters.

She reached the light the silvery line led to. Beyond was her home.

Yes. Sometimes you had to hide away beneath the stones, cower until the bad people had gone.

And sometimes you had to stop hiding and fight back.

5 – HYRN'S OAK

Six of them climbed into Johnny's dazzling, painted ship in the early morning. A smoke-like mist drifted across the surface of the Silverwater, lit up into a pearly glow by the first rays of the sun. Cait pulled the woollen shawl she'd borrowed closer about her shoulders. It wasn't a look she'd have gone for back home, but right now she didn't care. She shivered in the cold air. The boat rocked as Danny stepped over to sit beside her.

She held out her hand to steady him. It was good to have him there, his warmth beside her on the boat's little bench. It felt weird not having Bethany's presence inside her any more. She hadn't slept well; she'd tossed and writhed through confused dreams in which she'd wandered inside a deserted house, passing from room to room in search of someone who wasn't there.

"Why are we sailing anyway?" asked Nox, sitting opposite her, his knees brushing hers. "Can't we fly or something? It'll take days and days by boat."

Hellen was by Johnny on the bank, apparently conversing with the golden figurehead that housed the spirit of the mancer.

"*I* could," said Hellen, casting a glare at Nox. "Possibly even Cait could. I think the rest of you might struggle though."

"I thought time was short," said Nox. "Can't you work some spells and give us all the power of flight?"

The scowl on Hellen's face was terrifying to see. "Yes, I could do that if I wanted. And then I'd arrive in the north exhausted and utterly useless."

Either Nox hadn't seen her expression, or he was immune to it. "But we have to sail south before we can reach the An and head north."

"True enough. But we can sail upstream quicker than the other witches can walk along the road. We'll overtake them soon enough. The earlier we reach Guilden, the better. Besides, I want to travel the river. See for myself what's going on. Andar is wide and beautiful, but most things of interest happen along the An, I find."

Ran stepped into the boat with an easy grace, despite the pain his wounds and burns had to be causing him. He settled down beside Nox, eyes narrowed as if wary of attack. He looked like a caged animal in the narrow confines of the boat. He laid his serpentine sword on the planks at his feet. He'd polished it until it shone. It was beautiful in its own way, finely decorated, but Cait didn't like it at all. A blade like that could slice into you far too easily.

Once Johnny and Hellen were aboard they cast off. A couple of Islagray witches pushed them from the bank, but they weren't really needed. *Smoke on the Water* glided forward by its own means, floating through the wispy mists rising from the Silverwater. The six of them – Cait, Danny, Johnny, Hellen, Nox and Ran – watched in silence as the spire of Islagray Wycka faded into the fog behind them. Cait, fingers entwined through Danny's, wondered if any of them would ever see it again.

They reached Forness, the place Hyrn had left them, a day later. *Smoke on the Water* had brought them rapidly down the Gleaming, then turned right to head up the An. They sailed against the great river's flow, slowing their progress. Spumes of spray flew off the boat's bows as they chopped through the oncoming stream. Most of the time they clung to the curves of the bank, staying in shallow waters, although occasionally they darted across the mouth of an inlet rather than following its bend. No one spoke much, everyone worrying about what was to come. Cait spent a lot of time peering north, terrified of seeing the undain army again, marching down the river bank toward them. Or she gazed westward, across the An. The undain that had attacked Fer had flown across the river from Angere here. And the wyrm lords had said they had reports of other undain making the impossible journey.

Cait felt very exposed in the little bobbing boat on the open water. Would the undain come for her, too? They saw no sign of attack from either upstream or across the river. Mostly they saw people hurrying north on the road that ran beside the river, save where it looped around a hill. Heading for the Ice Fair, Johnny explained. Cait wanted to call to each of them, tell them to turn around, flee what was coming. But she doubted they'd believe her.

Once they'd landed at Forness, Ran and Danny went off to forage for what late berries and fruits they could find in the forests. Hellen came to stand beside Cait. "This is the exact place the undain landed. The point on the river they found Fer and she destroyed the winged one."

Cait looked around, trying to imagine the scene. Everything seemed so peaceful. The river gurgled by. The last leaves of the year, dropped by the trees that overhung the banks, floated by like a flotilla of fairy boats, yellow as sand, red as blood.

"Why here?" she said. "Why does it always come back to here?"

"Forness is the closest point to the other land. This is

where the ancient bridgehead was. This is why that's there." She indicated the tower of Caer L'dun behind her, its top peeping over the treetops. Its crown shone, sunlight shining off high windows set in a circle.

"And do you know how Fer did that? When I fought the one at the Duke of Greygyle's I did it by finding a tiny spark of its former self within it, showing it what it had become. But Fer did something else completely. By the sound of it she ripped the creature to pieces."

Hellen gazed over the waters, her forehead furrowed. "I have no idea. I wish I did. Clearly she wielded some power over the undain – something perhaps you, as another heir of Ilminion, could use as well. The two of you are the only ones ever to have fought and defeated an undain with witchcraft."

Johnny wandered up to them, scratching the stubble that had formed on his chin. "That, ah, that reminds me of something actually."

"It does?" asked Hellen. "Go on."

"When we were in Manchester getting Mr. Shankly back, we were caught by one of the baddies as we were escaping. A powerful lord, not some mindless zombie. The one that caught you, I think, Cait. It *had* Fer. But then she spoke some words. Like a spell I guess. The effect on the undain was incredible. It sort of writhed and melted and after a few moments it was just a heap of bones on the floor."

"What words?" asked Hellen with sudden interest. "Can you remember them? Their sound?"

"It was no language I've ever heard," said Johnny. "They sounded, I don't know, *sharp* somehow."

"She didn't tell you what she'd done? What words she'd uttered?"

"No. Muttered something about a family secret when I asked."

Hellen cocked an eye at Cait. "And do you know anything about this particular secret?"

"Not a clue," said Cait truthfully. "Fer never told me anything about it."

Hellen looked thoughtful. "So she spoke these words and the undain died?"

"Yeah," said Johnny. "Wait. No. There was something else. She spat at it too."

"Spat at it?"

"Yeah. I was kinda surprised, but the whole scene was pretty mad. The weird thing is I think she spat blood."

"Blood?"

"Must have bitten her tongue or something. It hit the undain bang in the face. I could see the red in it."

"And then it died?"

"Yeah. Like, *imploded.*"

Hellen looked troubled. "This disturbance in the aether is bothersome. I need to speak to Fer, find out what she did. Some memory must have come back to her. Or she worked something out."

"Like what?" asked Cait.

"Hard to be sure. Ilminion … he must have made plans. Passed the words down to his daughter, explained something. But how? Weyerd was only a baby when she was brought here. She was too young to understand." She was talking to herself more than Cait and Johnny now. "He must have suspected something might happen. He feared the King, feared some treachery, and he would have wanted to be sure those who came after him understood. Somehow his words reached Fer, down the generations. But where did he write it down?"

"Fer mentioned something about a locket," asked Johnny. "A family heirloom, she said. You know she had that jewellery, all those chains."

"A chain!" said Hellen brightly. "Yes, that might do it. The account said the baby had a chain around her neck. That has to be it. There must have been a locket attached to it. Perhaps only one of Ilminion's line could open it."

"Wait, wait," asked Cait. "You think Fer knew the

words of Ilminion's rite? You think she spoke them here, and again in Manchester, and that was what destroyed the undain?"

Hellen didn't reply for a moment, lost in her thoughts. "It's possible. She may have known the sounds to speak if not their meaning. There was blood on the ground when I came here the first time. I suppose it could have been hers."

"But why wouldn't she tell us?" said Cait. "Why keep a thing like that from us?"

"I suspect because she didn't know," said Hellen. "She had no memory of what occurred here. All she knew was this shameful family secret passed down from mouth to mouth over the centuries. The words of a charm or a rhyme, as she saw it, that came to her when she was in great danger and that turned out to mean something. Or perhaps I'm wrong and I'm seeing patterns where there are none again."

"So we need to find out," said Cait.

"Yes. I'll keep trying to reach Fer. Although none of it matters if Ashen can't put the book back together. We need to understand what Fer's words were, what they mean."

Ran and Danny returned ten minutes later, a few bruised apples foraged from the ground in their arms. They set off in the boat once again. They were soon passing underneath the tower of Caer L'dun. The dragonriders' fortress stood upon a rocky outcrop jutting out into the An. They all peered up at it. It looked utterly indestructible, built from massive stone blocks, a sheer face of rock on the river side, broken only by the circle of windows at the top of the spire. The watchtower, Hellen had called it. Where the wyrm lords looked out over the river for the coming of the undain.

"I will go there," said Hellen. "Drop me off upriver. I need to tell them what more we've learned. They probably won't listen, but there we are." She glanced at Ran as she spoke. The dragonrider remained impassive. "In any case," she continued. "I might be able to learn something from them. Find out how their plans for our defence are proceeding."

"Should we wait?" asked Cait.

"No, no. Speed north. I'll catch you up soon."

"And how will you do that?" asked Nox.

"By flying, of course," said Hellen. "How else?"

They saw their first chunk of floating ice three days later. It drifted out of the mists, silent and huge. Its sides were blue, and a dusting of snow coated its top. It was hard to work out how big it was, how far away. No one spoke as they watched it. Cait half-expected to see someone appear on its top, some Angere horror riding down the An.

It soon became common to see icebergs, big and small, drifting by. Winter was coming on fast, the year in Andar and Angere older than it was back home. The air grew sharper with cold, and Cait was glad of the woollen clothes she'd borrowed. It snowed too, coating every surface with a fine dusting of white. In the mornings the trees lit up by the sun were ghostly and beautiful, gilded with sparkling frost.

Larger and larger towns appeared along the river. For the first few days they'd camped upon the banks, huddling around a fire for warmth while they ate and slept. Now they were able to find shelter or even a bed for the night in a tavern or one of the Wayhouses set aside for travellers. Many of the places they passed were filled with visitors, crowds gathering for the Midwinter festivities.

"They must think we're a pretty weird sight," said Cait to Danny as they floated past another village that ran down from wooded slopes to the edges of the river. "Not just the boat, but *us*. There's only Ran who's even from Andar."

"Wouldn't worry about it," said Johnny. "We all look

the part. Besides, people get used to strange sights and travellers from afar when there's an Ice Fair. They won't bat an eyelid."

Everyone they met in Andar was certainly welcoming enough. Ran no longer had to forage in the wilds. Either they bought food from stalls and shops, or else people simply gave it to them, inviting them to eat at the long tables set up in town squares. Midwinter was still weeks away, but it seemed people were starting the celebrations anyway. Although, despite Johnny's words, Cait more than once caught a wary look in the glances cast their way. Especially at Ran, it seemed.

The dragonrider appeared not to notice. But at times it felt a little like they were spoiling the party, like they were a shadow in the corner when all else was light and laughter. Perhaps she imagined it, but the people appeared relieved when they moved on in the morning.

Cait agonized over what she should say to the people they met. How to warn them about what was coming. But what could she tell them that they hadn't already heard? They'd lived in Andar all their lives. They had to know. And where could they go? Perhaps if Hellen had been there it would have been different. But, then again, perhaps it wouldn't. The people looked like they were too determined to have fun to worry about nightmares emerging from old stories.

It wasn't only Guilden that had an Ice Fair. They began to see that smaller towns had their equivalents, lights and stalls set up on the patches of ice that crept across the bays of the An. Decorations became more frequent, too: garlands of greenery or brightly painted streamers were hung in the trees. Sometimes it seemed whole forests had been festooned. At night, a thousand fairy lights twinkled from the windows and doors of the towns they passed, the sight a delight to Cait, lifting her spirits. They often smelled cooking food, heard the sounds of people cheering and laughing before they sighted habitation around a curve in the banks.

On the fifth day of their journey they rounded a bend to see a large town, yellow and red stone houses jumbled up the hillsides of a half-moon bay. A single, vast oak stood at the water's edge in the centre of the curve, the buildings arranged around it.

"Hyrn's Oak," said Johnny. "I stopped here on my way southward. Good crowd."

There was still no sign of any attacking undain army. From over the water came the sounds of music and the din of the Midwinter revelries.

6 – SMOKE ON THE WATER

"Hyrn was here?" asked Cait as they drifted into shore beneath the outstretched arms of the titanic oak tree.

"It's just a name I think," said Johnny. "When the floods hit five hundred years ago, the inhabitants climbed into the branches of the tree to escape the rising waters. It was, like, only a village back then. But they all survived, so people figured the oak had magical powers. You know, Hyrn's protection. Since then the place has grown a lot. Only Guilden is bigger."

Hyrn's Oak was clearly a fishing port, too. To one side of the bay, a wooden wharf stretched into the waters. Many flat-bottomed skiffs were moored there, nodding up and down in the swell. They were the sort of vessels she'd seen all along the coast, trawling the shallows for darting fish.

The wood of the wharf was slick with the silvery flesh and red, wormy guts of the catch. A sweet, rotting smell filled the air. Rock-salt used to preserve the fish crunched underfoot as Cait and the others stepped ashore to join the crowds.

Rings of tables were set up in the cobbled space around

the wizened oak, its wide branches splayed like an upturned hand, its trunk gnarled and misshapen. The people of Hyrn's Oak clearly revered the tree. There were no leaves left on it so late in the year, but many brightly-coloured streamers had been woven among its branches, and countless glasswork pendants glinted from its twigs.

When Cait and the others had eaten and drunk, Johnny repaid the gathered crowds of the town by singing songs underneath the tree. He'd left his guitar at Islagray, but borrowed something that might have been a lute. He soon had the throng cheering and singing along. Once or twice he dropped in an acoustic version of a Screaming Machinery track, casting a knowing smile at Cait and Danny as he did so. The people of Andar danced to these, too. Cait felt safer and more at ease than she had at any time since leaving Islagray. It was hard to believe anything could endanger these laughing, happy people.

Once Johnny had finished playing, she wandered away from the bright lights and merriment, wanting to clear her mind before settling down for the night. Wanting some time to herself. It was cramped on the boat even with only five of them.

"Don't wander too far," Nox called after her.

Annoyed at being told what to do, she set off into the jumble of stout, stone houses that made up Hyrn's Oak. The streets twisted and turned at random, and without being able to glimpse the glittering tree between the buildings she'd soon have become lost. She kept the river to her left side as much as possible, thinking that she only had to do the opposite to find her way back. The streets were busy with couples walking with arms around each other, as well as rowdier groups of people carrying bottles and tankards, singing and shouting. Everyone was in a good mood. Perhaps, somehow, their unquenchable optimism and jollity would prevail, and the invasion from the Angere would come to nothing. It was a pleasant fantasy to lose herself in.

She reached a point on a small rise where much of the town was laid out before her. Lights still blazed around the central tree. Whoops and roars of delights, hushed by the distance, came to her through the cold night air. The windows of the houses glowed red with the log-fires burning within, the smoke from a hundred chimneys filling the air with a woody, comforting scent.

In one of the squares of the town, large numbers of revellers were cheering as archers took turns to fire arrows at a series of targets set up in a row. From what she'd seen, many people in Hyrn's Oak carried bows. Johnny had told her people made a living hunting in the woods as well as fishing in the shallows of the An. The archers of Hyrn's Oak were famous throughout Andar.

Beyond the edge of the town she glimpsed the naked flames of another fire. Concerned that some outlying building had caught ablaze she set off to investigate. She soon saw that it was a bonfire, set beside the road leading out of Hyrn's Oak. Two figures stood beside it. Most of Hyrn's Oak was on a round island, connected to the mainland by a series of wooden bridges that arched over the Teem, the stream that surrounded the town before emptying into the An. The figures were guarding one of the bridges.

Intrigued, she crossed the bridge, the wooden surface echoing hollowly beneath her feet. A bell had been set up on the far side of the bridge, attached to one of its pillars. The guards' fire crackled and spat. It was good to feel the heat coming off it. The woman and man by the fire greeted her warmly, inviting her to join them in drinking some warmed, spicy drink. As well as swords, they each carried bows. Iron stands embedded in the ground held a plentiful supply of arrows.

"You aren't celebrating with the others?" asked Cait.

Glances passed between the two. "We're watching the road," said the woman.

"In case the undain come?"

There was another pause, as if this were an uncomfortable subject. "We take turns to keep watch," said the man. "Us and others." He sounded older than the woman. His eyes glinted in the firelight. "Not everyone sees the danger but some of us like to keep a watch."

"And if the undain do come?"

"Then we'll be ready. If we ring the bell people will come running to defend the town."

"You're a witch aren't you?" asked the woman. "From Islagray?"

"I … yes," Cait replied. It seemed too complicated to say anything else. "My name is Cait."

"I'm Venn," said the woman. "This is my father, Torven. So what do you think? Do you believe all these dire warnings we keep hearing?"

How much should she tell them? Andar was so unprepared, but there wasn't much that could be done about it now. Perhaps it was better if people enjoyed themselves while they could. But she said, "Yes. I've seen what's coming."

"A lot of folks don't believe it," said Torven. "Say they've heard it all before. Say we're just superstitious."

"This time it's real," said Cait. "Believe me."

More silent looks passed between the man and the woman. "So what should we do?" asked Venn. "We can fight, of course, but we may not be a match for them. We're fishers and hunters, not warriors."

Cait wished she had answers for them. It felt weird, them asking her for advice. She was only a girl. "We'll all fight them as best we can. And you're not alone. There are the dragonriders as well as the witches. Perhaps, between us, we'll be enough." She didn't sound convincing even to herself.

"Aye," said Torven, "perhaps we will. Although I wouldn't trust those dragonriders far as I could throw them. Menhroth's men, some say. Worms in the apple."

"Come on, Dad," said Venn. "That's idle gossip. We

can't afford to be choosy, we need all the help we can get."

"Aye, well," said the man. "Perhaps."

"How many of you are there?" asked Cait. "Guarding the bridges, I mean."

"Ten, twenty," said Venn. "There's usually more, but at Midwinter things break down a bit." She shrugged. "You know how it is. If we ring the bell they'll come, although they might have trouble shooting straight."

"I'll walk a little farther," said Cait. "Will you be here when I come back?"

"We'll be here," said the woman. "Mind how you go. I know you're a witch, and all, but still…"

"I'll be fine," said Cait.

She walked a couple of hundred yards around a bend that shadowed the line of the An. Night time creatures racketed around in the undergrowth. She found a gap between the trees to stand overlooking the waters, the ice gleaming in the silvery moonlight. Could she do any of this? The odds were overwhelming. The archers' words had filled her with doubts. Hellen and Ran and the rest of them gave her hope, but what chance was there really? Sometimes she wished she could simply get back home. Abandon Andar to its fate and return to her own life. But she wouldn't be safe. Because of who she was, she could never be safe while the undain survived.

She shivered. Time to get back to the others. Get some sleep. One way or another it would all be over soon.

She only became aware of the undain as it rushed at her. The absence where its aura should have been loomed suddenly clear to her mind's eye. She flinched and screamed, but it was too late. A weight thudded into her, bowling her over. Thin, wiry fingers found her throat, squeezing tighter and tighter. Panicky, Cait writhed and elbowed at the weight on her back. She couldn't dislodge it. The bony fingers squeezed tighter, hurting her. She tried and failed to breathe. One of the undain was there in Andar, attacking her.

Her lungs screamed for air. In desperation she tried to reach into the creature's mind, repeat the trick she'd used in Angere. It was no use. Her brain was full of fog, the world already fading. She couldn't make the magic work. In desperation, Cait threw herself backward against a tree, hoping to dislodge her attacker. The undain hissed in a halting little voice as if it were laughing but didn't loosen its grip.

Cait fell to her knees.

A blast of cold wind slammed into her, sending both she and the undain reeling to the ground. Immediately the grip on her neck loosened. She scrabbled at the ground to get away from the undain. She gasped raggedly at the air, coughing and spluttering, her throat raw and bruised. She looked up to see who had unleashed the magic.

"There you are girl," said Hellen. "Out for a little night-time stroll?"

"No, I…"

"You can explain your stupidity to me later. We need to get away. I've slowed that thing down, knocked it senseless, but I can't kill it. Not if you can't." Hellen pulled Cait to her feet. "Come on, back to the town."

"Hellen…"

The hissing sound in the darkness froze them both. They turned, Hellen striking a werelight to illuminate the scene. The undain stood in the road, a short, skulking creature, slight and bony like something made from waterlogged sticks. A body well-suited to sneaking through forests. It hissed again as it stepped forward and then there were words in its voice.

"Now you will die, old witch. And you, heir of Ilminion, you will come with me across the ice."

Its body was already changing, bulking up, becoming more like the voracious dog creature Cait had seen in the basement of the library, although this one had much larger teeth.

Hellen put herself in front of Cait. "That family secret

of Fer's. Are you absolutely sure you don't know it?"

"I wish I did, believe me," said Cait. Desperately she looked around, hoping the two guards by the fire would have heard the fight and come running. There were no shouts, no ringing bell. She and Hellen were alone.

"Best try something else then, girl. Or we'll both be dead before the night is out."

Cait reached into the undain's mind, looking for the spark of light, the glimmer of what the creature had once been. If she could show this one the truth, release that trapped fleck of its former self, perhaps she could turn it upon itself.

The creature laughed once more. It appeared to know exactly what she was doing. "Ah, you think that will defeat me, witch? You think I don't know what I am? I accepted my status gratefully many hundreds of years ago. You have no power over me."

The creature leapt at Hellen, mouth wide as it went for her throat. Hellen unleashed another flurry of ice. It hit the undain but succeeded only in knocking it aside. The creature caught Hellen's arm, raking her with its sharp, scratchy talons. Hellen, crying out, stepped back. She hurled another bolt but it passed through the undain without harming it.

"Pathetic witch," the creature snarled. "Let me hurry you to your grave." It prepared to leap at Hellen again. Cait stepped forward to unleash her own cold magic. As with Hellen, there was no effect. The undain lunged.

The serpentine sword flashing out of the darkness caught it mid-chest, skewering it. The creature writhed and screamed, its voice piercing and inhuman. Try as it might it couldn't free itself. It tried to reach its attacker, warping into a different body shape with longer claws. But its strength was already failing, the sword-blow fatal to it. After a moment it gave up struggling and collapsed into a tatter of bones and flesh on the road.

The rider holding the sword stepped from the gloom.

Cait thought it was going to be Ran, but it was no one she knew. He was old, his leathery face wrinkled, hair thin. It was hard to be sure in the low light, but the tattoos on his face looked to be red.

"Hellen," he said, his voice little more than a rasp. "I came as soon as I could. Forgive me."

Hellen didn't reply for a moment. She was panting heavily. Finally she stood, arranging her hair into some sort of order with her fingers. "Well, well. It's about time you came back, Borrn."

The old wyrm lord, Ashen's father, kicked at the remains of the undain. "I've tracked this abomination south for many miles. It seems our old rider blades have some power against them after all. That is good to know."

Hellen walked up to him, studying him in the glow of the werelight. "So here you are, alive after all. And all this time you've been too busy, have you? Too preoccupied to even visit your son?"

Borrn held out his hand. It was shaking noticeably. "I ask you again to forgive me. I have travelled far and wide. I have seen much and suffered much. I was unable to return any sooner. I have been … imprisoned."

"We scoured the aether for you."

"It is a long tale, Hellen, but I give you my word. I would have come back if I'd been able. Tell me, how is Ashen?"

"He's alive and well. Gets his looks from you and his sense from me."

"He's near?"

"He's at Islagray. A mancer of Guilden now."

That surprised the old wyrm lord. "Truly?"

"Truly."

"Then, as soon as I've reported to Caer L'dun I must seek him out."

"Yes, you must."

"Will you come south with me?"

Hellen shook her head. There was something in her

face Cait had never seen before. A tenderness as she looked at this ragged, battle-worn dragonrider. A tenderness despite her apparent anger at him. "I wish I could. But we're heading north to face the undain."

"To *face* the undain?"

"To face them or slow them as much as we can. The riders will defend Caer L'dun. It's up to us to protect Guilden and Hyrn's Oak and every other town down the An."

"You will never succeed," said Borrn. "I've been watching for them in the high north, far beyond the borders of Andar. I've seen them coming. There are too many. This one was only a spy, scouting out the land for the main army."

"I know," said Hellen. "It is hopeless. Still, we have to try. Make your report to Axana, give them what guidance you have. Then you should go to the Isle to see your son. While you can."

Borrn stepped closer. He touched Hellen on the side of her face. "And you?"

To Cait's surprise, Hellen didn't sweep his hand away. "Perhaps I'll get back there too. Perhaps I won't."

Borrn nodded, as if this were exactly what he'd expected. His weariness seemed to weigh him down for a moment. "Very well. I am happy to have seen you at least one more time, Hellen Meggenwar. All these years I have thought of you and Ashen often."

"And I you."

The rider lingered for a moment longer, a faint smile on his face. Then, with a nod at Cait, he turned to lope into the shadows of the trees.

Hellen kicked the remains of the undain into the river. "Well," she said after a moment. "You just never know who you're going to bump into on the road do you?"

"He's a fine looking man," said Cait. "In a rugged, outdoorsy sort of way."

Hellen narrowed her eyes as she studied Cait. She

looked like she was about to say something scathing, but changed her mind. "We'd better get back to the boat. We both have more important things to worry about, don't we?"

"How did you even find me?"

"I found the others by the tree and they said you'd wandered off for some fresh air. Don't do it again. At the very least take Ran or someone with you. Haven't you noticed it's not safe in Andar any more? Not for any of us but especially not for you."

Six of them in the boat once more, they set off from Hyrn's Oak the following morning. Hellen spoke little, lost in her own thoughts. Whether it was because of Borrn or because of her conversations at Caer L'dun, Cait didn't know. She had overtaken the other witches the day before, along a wooded section of the road hidden from the river. The boat would get to Guilden first.

The blocks of ice they encountered on the river soon became so numerous that they took to weaving around them to make further progress. The biggest chunks were out in deeper waters, but soon the shallows were covered with sheets of ice, and all they could do was plough through. Their progress slowed.

"Surely we could move into slightly deeper waters?" said Nox. The inactivity of the journey hadn't suited him, and he'd grown more and more irritable. "We're getting nowhere cracking through this ice."

Hellen, lost in her own thoughts, didn't reply.

"Too dangerous," said Johnny. "If we go any farther out we'll risk the serpents. With all this ice it's hard to make a dash for the safety of the shore."

"You know that for sure do you?"

"Not at all," said Johnny. "But fortunately *Smoke on the Water* does."

"We're never going to get there at this rate. How far is it to Guilden anyway?"

"Two, three more days."

"Great," said Nox, muttering, but loud enough for them all to hear. "What an enjoyable trip this has turned out to be."

Soon the ice became so thick that they ground to a complete halt. The eyes on the golden figurehead closed, as if it were exhausted. "So what now?" said Danny. "We walk the rest of the way? Might have to backtrack a little so we can reach the bank."

"Actually," said Johnny, "I think there's a better way. This is a magic boat, right? It might be worth everyone getting out for a moment."

"Why?" said Nox. "What's going to happen?"

"You'll see."

Hellen climbed out first, Ran leaping over the side to offer her a steadying hand. She scowled at his presumption but took his hand anyway. Cait trod warily, she and Danny holding on to each other, testing the ice with each foot before putting any weight on it. The cold crept through the soles of her feet. The six of them stood in a huddle, watching the boat, waiting for something to happen.

"So, what?" said Nox. "We stand here and admire the paintwork?"

"Watch," said Johnny.

The boat jerked and shook. Cait could feel the magic fizzing through it. Grating, harsh magic, utterly unlike anything she could work. The boat jumped once more, then flew fully round in circles, faster and faster, a blur of green.

When it stopped, it had changed. Two metal blades ran the length of it, resting upon the ice. It was no longer a boat, but a sledge. The eyes of the figurehead were wide once more.

"Cool," said Danny.

"Oh yeah," said Johnny. "Now we can move more quickly. Reckon we'll be in Guilden late tomorrow."

"Very good," said Hellen. "Unnatural magic, but

handy, I'll give you that."

They set off again, the babble of water replaced by the hiss of ice. Cait still peered forward constantly, reaching out with her mind, expecting the undain to be revealed around each twist and turn of the river. More and more she stared into the west, conscious that the army could come for them from that direction too.

They slid north all that day and the next, encountering nothing on the ice save the occasional long-legged bird padding around as if confused at where the water had gone.

The sun was setting once again, heavy and red in the west, when they saw a cloud of billowing smoke around the next bend. Hellen stood, peering forward. The smoke was tinged orange by fires as it rolled over the ice toward them. They could hear its crackling, and the cries and screams of many people.

"Guilden," said Johnny.

7 – THE LORD OF MISRULE

Cait and Hellen pushed their way through the teeming streets of Guilden.

They'd been there four days now. Cait had imagined Guilden burning when they'd approached. That the undain were already there, destroying the city, slaughtering the people. But the smoke and flame they'd seen were from one of the huge conical bonfires set along the edge of the river. Each evening, to cheers from the gathered crowds, they lit another, a count down to the Midwinter festivals now only a week away. Already the ice on the bay was covered in stalls and tents and raised stages and arenas for games, all arranged into streets as if the city itself had spilled onto the river.

Tall iron braziers, ornately decorated and set upon wooden platforms to keep the heat from the ice, had been positioned along the rows for illumination. Each evening there were more and more people out there, many on skates, whizzing along in groups or lines, taking part in races whose rules Cait couldn't begin to understand. Others sipped at hot, spiced wine or danced and cheered as groups of musicians performed a dazzling variety of musical styles.

No one seemed to be remotely worried about the threat of the undain.

The city was so crowded there were no beds to be had anywhere. A village of large communal tents had been set up on the ice to help house the hundreds of visitors flooding into Guilden. Taverns and hostels were completely full, as were all the wayhouses in the surrounding area. Fortunately, Hellen had the key to Ashen's quarters, three rooms at the top of a leaning, creaking wooden house near the docks. It was basic but had enough room for the six of them to sleep in. They laid out what bedding and matting they could find, although Ran seemed perfectly happy to sleep on the hard floor.

It was a frustrating time for Cait and the others. They spent the first few days trying to warn people of what was coming, trying to make their voices heard. But the people of Guilden seemed too intent on enjoying the festivities to listen to dire warnings of their imminent destruction. Some simply shrugged as if to say w*hat can you do?* Others nodded as if they understood, explaining that, once Midwinter was out of the way, they would turn their attention to the threat. Many were simply too drunk to listen. In many ways, it was tempting to join in with the celebrations. The crowds in the streets were so good-natured, so intent on having a good time, it was hard not to get caught up in it all.

On the third evening, Cait and the others gathered in their garret room to discuss what they should do. Shouts of laughter and the sing-song cries of the street-vendors provided a background chorus.

"I will speak to the Doge," said Hellen. "I've sent word to him, although there's been no response yet. These city rulers like to play their games. They think their little empires are the whole world. Tomorrow I will go there and make sure I'm heard."

For once, Ran spoke up. He stood by the window, glancing outside repeatedly as if he expected danger to threaten at any moment. "I will head north, out of the city, see if there is any sign of the undain army."

Hellen considered for a moment. "Will you take anyone with you?"

"Best I go alone. I can move quietly and quickly. If I see anything I'll return with word. It may give us some warning."

"Very well," said Hellen. "Johnny, you know people here. You should go out there and talk, listen for news and rumour, find out anything that might give us a clue about what the undain are doing."

Johnny lay ragdolled across some sacks of straw scattered on the wooden floor like cushions. He looked up with clear alarm at her words. "You think there might be Angere spies here?"

"Could be. We know some of them can alter their appearance. Both Cait and I have seen them do it. For all we know there are hundreds out there now, reporting back to Menhroth on how best to take Guilden."

"But, you know, can't you and Cait spot them with your voodoo powers?"

"It's hard," said Cait. "Trust me, I've tried. The streets are too crowded. Even with the seeing stone, by the time you line up people with their auras, they've moved on and ten other people have got in the way."

"But you've seen them?"

"It's hard to be sure."

"It's not only undain spies," said Hellen. "There'll be people here arriving from the north all the time. Maybe you can pick up word of something. Anything might be useful."

"Network," said Johnny. "Got it, I'll try. Danny, want to come with?"

Danny nodded. He and Johnny had struck up a close friendship, bromancing around the fair together while Cait worked with Hellen.

"And what do you have planned for me?" asked Nox.

"You're good at strategy," said Hellen. "Guilden clearly isn't ready for an attack, but perhaps you could assess the state of its defences, see where the weakest spots are?"

Nox nodded. "Shouldn't take long. What about the others from Islagray? Where are they?"

"They're here. There aren't many of them, but perhaps they'll be able to do something when the moment comes."

"Yeah," said Nox. "Perhaps."

"Well," said Hellen. "Then, assuming we survive the night, let's see what tomorrow brings."

Cait and Hellen crossed the wide, cobbled square that lay at the heart of the city. In its centre, a round fountain sprayed water high into the air. When the coldest weather came the water in the fountain froze completely, a column of ice that the mancers lit up with a thousand dancing, glimmering lights. Ahead of them, the palace was an ornate stone building, its many towers making it resemble a vast crown, windows glowing red and blue for jewels. The entire square was called the Golden Square because of the palace's gilded spires. In the centre of the façade, thirty feet up, she could see the jutting balcony where the mancers and the Doge appeared for the Ice Fair pronouncement. Cait imagined the whole square thronged with revellers earlier that year when news of the snows came. The scenes of delight Ashen had described.

The square was busy enough now even though it was still early. The background chatter of a hundred conversations filled the air. Did no one understand what the coming of the ice meant? No one seemed at all concerned. Queues of customers snaked up to the stalls selling spiced breads, the smells delicious.

Hellen was not in a good mood, cutting through the crowds as if they were little more than annoying bushes in her way. At the Palace gates guards blocked her, demanding to know her name, her business. Hellen gave them short shrift, glowering as she told them who she was and pushing on through. Cait followed in her wake.

They found themselves in an echoing hall that was just as crowded as the square outside. A line of red-robed secretaries sat at desks upon which were set out enormous ledgers. The secretaries were attempting to field shouted requests from the crowds of gathered merchants and travellers, occasionally scribbling things in the ledgers with quill pens. Many of the supplicants held out rolls of parchment which they banged on the desks to attract the attention of the secretaries. Handfuls of coins were exchanged, sometimes slammed onto the tables, sometimes slipped across discreetly as the merchants and performers vied for the best sites for their stalls and pitches.

Hellen pulled Cait past the hubbub, ignoring demands for them to join the queues and await their turn.

They climbed a flight of wide stone steps to reach a grand hallway, sunlight slanting in to light up gilded pillars. More guards stood there, holding wooden staffs with curved blades attached to them. They wore extravagant gleaming helmets, feather plumes curving from them. Hellen didn't hesitate, walking into the hall before anyone could stop her.

The columns held up an ornate roof where a map of the whole of the city of Guilden had been painted. Cait peered upward as she and Hellen crossed the hall. The detail was incredible: each street and house visible, each boat on the An, even the people and dogs in the streets. By some magic everything moved. The tiny people flowed through the squares and alleys and smoke rose from flickering braziers. Birds soared across the scene. She searched for a miniature Danny and Johnny somewhere in the throng but couldn't pick them out.

Two thrones sat at the far end of the hall, both occupied. In the larger one, highly decorated and set with jewels, sat the man who was clearly the Doge, his dress ornate, all finely stitched purple and gold. A crown like the palace in miniature sat atop his head. Cait couldn't help wondering how heavy it was.

Next to him, in complete contrast, sat a ragged man on a rickety, lopsided chair. He wore patchwork clothes and a crown in the same shape as the Doge's, but fashioned from twigs and straw. Instead of jewels, stuffed birds and fish eyes adorned it. Where the Doge carried a short golden staff, the symbol of his power, the other carried what looked like a dried fish of a similar size. Both men studied Hellen and Cait as they approached.

"So," said Hellen. "Which of you is the Doge and which the idiot Lord of Misrule?"

Hellen had explained it all to her. For the period of the Midwinter, for the solstice and the day either side, the Doge formally handed control of the city over to the Lord of Misrule, whose role was to oversee the merriment and chaos. For those three days, the Lord's word was law, not the Doge's. In the week beforehand, the Lord of Misrule shadowed the Doge, poking fun at all the ceremony and pomposity, making his preparations for tricks and games and celebrations. The Doge was elected for a period of ten years but a different Lord or Lady of Misrule was chosen from the people each year.

It seemed like a good system, maybe one they should try back home. According to Ashen, Guilden was a completely safe, law-abiding place for the rest of the year. Allowing people to let their hair down for three days appeared to help keep the peace the remaining time.

The Doge leaned forward, a disapproving expression on his face. The ragged Lord beside him mimicked the Doge's movements, copying also his sombre glower.

"Well, well," said the Doge. "The famous and terrible Hellen Meggenwar. It is rare indeed for the Queen of the witches to visit us here in Guilden. How may we be of assistance?"

"I am no queen," said Hellen, "as well you know. And you know also why I'm here, I think."

"You've come for the celebrations?" asked the Lord of Misrule. "Come to join in the dancing and debauchery?"

"Dancing and debauchery would suit me very well," said Hellen, "if it wasn't for the undain army marching across the ice from Angere to kill us all. I find mass slaughter spoils a celebration. Don't you?"

The Lord of Misrule laughed at her response, as if she'd told a good joke. The Doge, however, simply shook his head. "It seems you've been listening to the dire warnings of one of the mancers. Strange for a witch. Ah, but of course, that one is actually your son, isn't he? The son of a witch and an Angere wyrm lord."

"This has nothing to do with Ashen," said Hellen, "and everything to do with the ice on the An. Most likely it has already frozen from bank to bank farther north. Tell me, how far have you walked out? How far west does your ice stretch?"

"Surely not all the way to the Lost Land."

"You know that do you?"

The Doge looked thoughtful for a moment, and Cait thought he was going to relent. "Eldest," he said, "we of Guilden may, regrettably, have little time for the old ways, but it pains me that you disapprove of us so much."

"I don't disapprove of you. You have every right to carry on like idiots. I'm simply trying to stop you being slaughtered."

The Doge stood. "Will you walk with me? From the top of the tallest tower you can see much of Andar. It is a good place to consider the state of the world, I find."

"Happily. Lead the way."

The Doge glanced at Cait. "And your companion? Do you have your own underling to mimic you, too?"

Hellen spoke before Cait could get a word out. "Cait is a witch from another world. She has suffered much, battled much in our defence. She has crossed all of Angere, and the An too, to be here. She has faced death and horror. She is no underling, Doge."

Instead of taking offence at the clear irritation in the Hellen's voice, the Doge dipped his head to Cait. "Forgive me. We are honoured and delighted to have you in Guilden, Cait." The Lord of Misrule, standing beside him, bowed also, so low that his crown fell to the ground, scattering sticks and feathers to the floor. He proceeded to scoop up the scraps and stick them back in, dropping two more for each one he retrieved.

The Doge took no notice of the fool beside him. "Then, if the two of you would like to accompany me, the Sun Tower is this way."

They walked together from the throne room, the Doge leading the way, the Lord of Misrule following, swigging from a bottle of wine. They climbed more stairs, winding in a helix, until they emerged in a bright, airy room, circular in shape, diamond-paned windows all around. It reminded Cait a little of a lighthouse. A narrow balcony ran round the outside. The Doge ducked through a low doorway and held it open for them to follow.

Outside, the wind was immediately strong, gusting at them from all directions. The city of Guilden surrounded them, streets arcing out from the central square just as the painting in the Hall depicted. Muffled by the distance, Cait could hear the background roar of the throng, their conversations and shouts and footfalls. Occasionally the breeze brought with it a scent of cooking meat or spice. Beyond the city on one side lay the frozen An, the temporary town of stalls and tents. On the other side, evergreen forests swept away to climb the foothills of the distant mountains. It was beautiful, the air so clear it seemed to bring everything into sharper focus. Looking at it, it was truly hard to believe anything could threaten it.

The Doge gazed out over the Ice Fair. "Tell me, Eldest, do you know how long Guilden has stood here?"

"Long enough," said Hellen.

"Let me tell you. I know the wicca don't write things down much, but if you knew your history, you'd know this city has stood here for over six hundred years. In that time we've had fires and floods and storms strong enough to topple our towers. But we're still here. Guilden will always be here. A bit of ice won't finish us off. Nor will some fairytale monsters from the Lost Lands."

"And how will you keep these *fairytale monsters* at bay when they attack?"

"We have defences. We have guardsmen and watchmen. See the line at the edge of the city? Those walls are solid stone and ten feet high."

"And will they be manned during the revelries?"

The Doge smiled. "The guards *may* be a little less assiduous it is true. But the walls will remain as strong and tall as ever I believe."

"I see. And if the undain choose to march from the west, on the river side where there are no walls?"

"Even if such a thing were possible, which of course has never happened before, we still have our defences. Do you see that clear line arcing across the bay? The Line of Fire we call it. A channel containing black powder and fish oil has been cut into the ice, enough to blast right through should any sort of attack come. We need only ignite it, and we'll have open water between us and the main river."

Hellen gazed out, considering. "Ingenious. How wide?"

"How wide what?"

"The channel – how wide a gap will it give you?"

"Twenty feet."

"And you think that much water will stop the undain?"

"It's well known that running water defeats sorcery."

"And how many guards do you have in total?"

"Hundreds. And many of the citizens can be called up as militia if the need arises."

"Even if they are lying drunk in the gutter?"

"Even then. During the three days things are different, of course. People are free to do as they wish. But if there were an attack" – his tone made it quite clear he thought such a thing unlikely – "I'm sure they'd want to come to the defence of Guilden. It would be a brave invader who tried to interfere with the revelries of the Ice Fair."

Hellen didn't speak for a moment. She walked around the circular balcony, gazing over Guilden, the wind making her grey hair lash about.

When she returned to the Doge she said, "You seem to know much about witches and sorcery. However, let me point out one or two small mistakes. Firstly, Guilden has been here for only three hundred years. There was a city six hundred years ago but it was ten miles farther north and was swept away by the great flood. I know that because it is written in the records at Islagray. As it happens I do know a bit about our history. I also know that the undain will laugh at twenty feet of running water and simply leap over. Just as they will leap over or smash through walls ten feet high. When they come a few hundred guards, a few thousand city folk will be able to do nothing at all. We of Islagray will do what we can to help, but it won't be much either. If you want my advice, you should abandon the Ice Fair and start organizing people into a proper army. As I've suggested to you before."

The Lord of Misrule, standing beside the Doge, put his hands to his ears, feigning horror at Hellen's words.

The Doge also appeared to be unconcerned. "You really believe that all this, mighty Guilden is in danger?" He indicated the scene with a sweep of his arm. "The city is vast."

His words amused Cait. Guilden might be large by Andar standards, but it was nowhere near the size of cities back home. "I've seen the undain army," she said. "Seen their numbers, seen what they're capable of. Hellen's right. Your walls and ditches will be utterly useless. Your people will die."

"Half of Andar has conveniently gathered here to be slaughtered or enslaved," said Hellen. "You have to do something."

The Doge smiled at them both as if they were amusing

children and shook his head. "Well. I'll be sure to discuss your concerns with the captains of the Guard. Now, unless there's anything else, perhaps you'll excuse me? Regrettably, an Ice Fair doesn't organize itself. And do, please, enjoy all that Guilden has to offer while you are here, yes?"

Hellen began to turn away from him, but then she stopped. "You know, you still haven't answered my question."

"Question?"

"When I came in I asked which of you was the Doge and which the Lord of Misrule. I'm afraid I'm none the wiser."

She turned and strode away, Cait following closely behind.

8 – THE ICE FAIR

Cait found Nox by the northern wall of Guilden, scowling at the scene around him.

"Come to man the barricades?" he asked.

"Would it help if I did?"

Nox shrugged and called to one of the men upon the wall, directing him angrily to move farther along. Nox had taken control, started organizing the defences, arranging formations. He looked stressed and exhausted. He also looked like he was enjoying himself immensely.

"You found some people to order around then?" asked Cait.

"A few. Not enough. Ninety percent of the people in this city are too busy enjoying themselves to care. Maybe five percent believe there's an invasion coming and are willing to stand and fight."

"What about the other five percent?"

"They're the real idiots. They believe the undain are coming *and* they welcome it. They're like Andar goths, embracing the darkness. You know, kids like you and Danny."

She ignored his gibe. "So how are the defences looking?"

"They'd look a lot better with some modern weaponry. If I had a tenth of the arsenal Genera keeps at the refinery we could slaughter the undain before they reach the walls. As it is we have swords and spears and all sorts of other weapons that are basically pointed sticks made from metal."

"Don't you still have your gun?"

"Oh, sure. Just no bullets to fire from it. At least we'll get some warning of attack now. I've posted forward guards, manned with horns to raise the alarm."

"And then?"

"We'll fight as best we can. Now at least the defenders are all singing from the same hymn-sheet." He flashed a grin at Cait, like he knew a really exciting secret. "Plus there are the barrels of black powder I unearthed in the cellars they laughably refer to as the *armoury*. Most of it was for fireworks or the Line of Fire."

"Black powder?"

"It's basically gunpowder. Although quite how a society invents gunpowder but not cannon or rifles escapes me."

"You can still use it on the undain?"

"We're setting up fire pits we can explode under them as they approach. Hellen's witches will come in handy. Apparently some of them can send a spark shooting through the air to set the barrels off. Spells used to light ovens and log fires that we can put to a better use."

"You can't bury gunpowder in the ice."

Nox scratched the stubble on his chin. Somehow, despite their situation, he had managed to keep it fashionably short. "True. We've got more guards with horns to raise the alarm if anything comes that way. If they do, the witches and mancers will start blasting them with, you know, fireballs or whatever nonsense it is you do."

"You should put witches who can sense the undain with the forward guards. Might give you a little extra warning."

He nodded his head, like he thought she'd actually said

something sensible for once. "I'll talk to Hellen, see who's available."

"And will it be enough?" asked Cait. "Can we keep them out?"

Nox shrugged. "Do you want me to be honest or do you want me to be wildly optimistic?"

The following day, a procession of fire snaked its way across the ice from Guilden. The Lord of Misrule led the way, waving to the gathered crowds with exaggerated self-importance. Seemingly oblivious, a dog lay on the ridiculously long cape he trailed behind him. It barked at the crowds with enthusiasm as it was pulled along.

Behind, a long procession of revellers walked onto the ice, many carrying smoking torches that filled the night air with scents of pine-resin and honey. Some wore skates on their feet, metal runners like those *Smoke on the Water* had sprouted. Others had tied metal frames to their shoes with lines of little spikes underneath to give them grip. Everyone was muffled up in layers of wool and fur, but their eyes were bright, reflecting the thousand lights of the torches and lanterns of the Ice Fair.

The processions walked toward a line of unlit bonfires, rising like a small mountain range along one bank of the bay. Each district of Guilden built their own fire, a competition to discover who could create the biggest and who could decorate theirs with the most outlandish effigy. The crowds cheered as the Lord of Misrule walked down the line, setting each bonfire alight. Flames licked up the sides of them. Some were truly enormous, fifty or sixty feet tall. Several had an effigy of the Doge in a golden chair on top but others were crowned with exaggerated monsters that were, perhaps, their builders' idea of the undain.

Cait stepped back from the fires as the flames took hold, the raging yellow lighting up the faces of the assembled crowds. It was strange and troubling to be surrounded by so much merriment. She wished she could enjoy it all. Wished she could lose herself in the celebration and forget what was coming. They hadn't managed to persuade anyone that the threat from the undain was real. The people of Guilden were too busy having fun to notice their world ending. Ran had returned from the wilds two days previously to report no sign of an approaching army, but it had done little to reassure her.

Danny, holding her hand, stepped back with her. "Any sign of the others?"

"Nox is still at the walls, ordering people about. I saw Johnny a while ago. He was supposed to be watching for trouble, but someone had given him another lute and made him start playing. He didn't look too upset."

"Apparently the minstrels compete for the crowds too," said Danny. "The one who writes the catchiest Ice Fair song, the crowd favourite, is crowned as the king of something or other."

"It is all pretty crazy," said Cait. "Wish we could have come and just enjoyed it."

"Yeah."

There had to be thousands on the ice now, people of all ages, the entire population of Guilden seemingly. A hubbub of voices filled the night air: shouts, laughter, the occasional scream. Cait wondered if they were screams of delight or terror. Each time she thought it had to be the start of the attack, but each time it turned out to be nothing worse than drunken revellers chasing each other.

"Have you seen Hellen?" She had to almost shout in Danny's ear to make herself heard above the roar and crackle of the fires.

"Not for a while. She said she had to commune with the powers that be."

"What powers?"

"Haven't a clue. You know what she's like."

Arm-in-arm they walked away from the fires to the main street of the Fair, a wide, straight road with the other streets curving off it. *Mainway* it was called. They walked past a fire-breather, billowing great clouds of red flame into the night sky to roars of appreciation from a crowd of onlookers. He was no mancer; like any fire-breather back home, he spat out sprays of some oily, flammable liquid to produce his flames. The brief warmth on her face was very welcome.

"Drink?" said Danny. "Something hot?"

"Something hot would be good," said Cait.

A spice merchant had set up next to the fire-breather, doing a roaring trade in cups of steaming liquids of various descriptions. Mulled wines and ales were doing particularly well. A sign above the stall declared the owner to be *Merdoc, Supplier of spices to the Witches' Isle*. There were copper vats set along his stall from which he dispensed his drinks to the crowds.

"Something to keep the cold out," said Cait to the merchant when it was their turn. "But we need to keep clear heads."

The merchant considered his stocks. "The fireseed and lovespice cordial is very popular. The spices come all the way up the Spice Route, thousands of miles from the distant lands of Azandia."

"Lovespice?"

"So-called because it is so sweet, like a lover's touch, yes?"

"Uh, yes," said Cait. "I suppose so. We'll take two."

As the merchant poured their drinks he looked up into Cait's face and stopped for a moment, looking puzzled.

"What is it?" asked Cait.

He resumed pouring. "Nothing, nothing. Forgive me. You reminded me of someone. Someone I met on the road here."

"Who?"

"A wicca called Fer. I don't suppose you know her?"

"Yes. A distant relative."

"Ah. Tell me, is she well? She did me a great service,

protected me on the road. But when I last saw her she was in a bad way, lost to the world on the Witches' Isle." Merdoc leaned in closer so no one else would overhear. "We were attacked by one of the undain. Can you believe it? Flew clear across the An. Never seen the like."

"The last I saw her she was fine and well," said Cait.

"Ah, good. Is she here?"

"No. She's gone off on a long journey."

"I see," said Merdoc. "A shame. I hope to see her again one day so I can thank her properly. And that Hellen Meggenwar. Very kind to me, she was, very proper. I don't care what folks say around here. Lots of them laugh at the witches and all the old ways but I'll hear none of it."

"Then … you've heard the warnings about Angere? The coming of the undain?"

Merdoc nodded. "I've heard them. Who hasn't?"

"Yet you're still here?"

"If the stories aren't true then I can't afford to miss out on the Ice Fair. And if they are, well, I suppose it doesn't make any difference one way or another does it?"

"No. I suppose not." Cait sipped at the liquid Merdoc had poured her. It was delicious: fruity and spicy at the same time. She could feel it warming her insides as she drank.

"That's wonderful, thank you. How much do I owe you?"

"Please, my treat," said Merdoc. "Any relation of Fer and so on, yes? Now you take care out here. No knowing what goes on out on the ice, yes? And I'm talking about the people of Guilden, not the undain."

"We'll take care. Thank you, Merdoc."

They sipped at their drinks as they walked farther from the land. A line of ice sculptures had been carved there, beautiful ghostly figures in the shapes of trees and dragons and men with deer-antlers growing from their heads. Like the fountain in the Golden Square, the sculptures had been lit with thousands of tiny sparkling lights that seemed to be frozen within. Cait and Danny walked around them, marvelling at their beauty.

A runaway horse and cart, spooked by some fire or explosion, came thundering down Mainway then, a cloud of ice crystals flying off it like white flame, the people crying out in alarm to jump out of its way. The cart clipped one of the ice sculptures, a model of the Doge's palace, sending it crashing to the ground. The lights within it continued to twinkle on the ice, like a trapped constellation of stars. Thirty yards behind, laughing as he followed, the Lord of Misrule approached, a flaming torch in his hand. Spooking the horse had been his doing. He bowed low when he saw Cait, then raced off to cause more mayhem.

A little farther down Mainway, teams of people were competing to hurl flaming iron balls attached to chains, seeing who could throw them the farthest. Danny, eyes wide, clearly fancied his chances. "Most of them are drunk out of their heads, look."

They watched as one competitor, swivelling his flaming ball wildly, overbalanced and sent the object flying into a nearby tent that housed a company of dancers performing for a small crowd. Screams of panic and amusement competed as the dancers scattered from the burning tent.

"Have a go if you want," said Cait.

"You don't sound very enthusiastic."

"It's just, you know, all this. Everything that's going to happen."

"Doesn't your gran always say to live for the moment, that you never know what's around the corner?"

"Suppose so, yeah."

"There you are, then."

He turned out to be good at it. A small crowd gathered as he competed against a tall, powerful man, the muscles of his arms bunching as he practised his swings. The man looked on with amusement as Danny lifted his flaming iron ball and swung it around, trying not to get tangled up in it. They took it in turns to hurl the spheres farther and farther onto the ice, each throw greeted with great cheers. In the end the man won, sending the iron ball high into the night sky like a shooting star, farther than Danny could hope to manage. Unable to speak the language, he bowed in defeat, to the delight of the crowd.

"Didn't know you could do that," said Cait.

"It's all in the timing. Done something similar at school. That guy was amazing, though. See the muscles on him? Maybe with people like him on our side we'll have a chance after all."

"Maybe."

They walked on, past jugglers keeping four, five, six flaming torches in the air at the same time, past stalls selling roasting chestnuts and meat from spit-roast animals and more hot wine. There seemed to be very little trouble, although occasionally a laughing youth weaved headlong through the crowds, pursued by some shouting, red-faced merchant.

They walked farther still, through swept drifts of snow that crunched and cracked beneath their feet. The crowds began to thin out and the stalls become more scattered. Overhead, the stars blazed down in the cold night, reflecting so perfectly in the swept ice that it felt like they were walking through the air, depths beneath them and gulfs above. They reached a line of the iron braziers and, thirty yards beyond, the ropes and the wooden slats that covered the Line of Fire. In the distance, a guard paced about for warmth, no doubt wishing they were having fun at the Fair like everyone else. A chill wind had picked up, making Cait's cheeks sting. She'd run out of Merdoc's hot drink. They had to be nearly beyond Guilden Bay, out on the river proper, its vast waters surging beneath their feet. Anxiety fizzed within her.

"We should stop," said Danny. "Head back in case Hellen needs us."

Cait turned to survey the scene behind them. The twinkling lights from the Fair and, beyond, the houses and palaces of Guilden, windows aglow with candle fire. Some of the black powder had apparently been salvaged for a firework display after all. As she watched, bright globes of stars blossomed over the scene as rocket after rocket was launched into the sky. A second after each explosion the rattling bang hit them. They could hear the whoops and roars of delight over the background jumble of voices.

She turned away again. Westward, apart from the stars, it was fully dark. For some reason she wasn't ready to go back just then, "Let's go a little bit farther." Perhaps she wanted to know if the ice really did stretch all the way across.

"Sure?" asked Danny.

"Yes. I think we should."

They walked for ten more minutes, alone on the ice, until they saw the line of bobbing, twinkling torches moving across the ice toward them. At the same moment, the mournful cry of warning horns from the sentries set by Nox wailed through the night air.

9 – BLOOD ON THE ICE

Cait and Danny ran for the land. More horns echoed as other watchers picked up the call. The lights of the Fair seemed distant as they slipped and skated along, holding onto each other for support. She expected attack at any moment. She tried to find the presence of the undain in the night behind them, look for any speeding forward at them. She could sense only a huge, unfocussed cloud, like a storm massing in the night sky.

"Nearly there," said Danny. He sounded badly out of breath. He still hadn't recovered from being imprisoned beneath the White City. There was a clear edge of panic to his voice.

The line of braziers marking the Line of Fire was up ahead. Still the undain hadn't broken rank to intercept them. They had to reach the safety of the Fair and the city. Hellen's witches and Nox's defenders would give them a chance. Out here they were alone.

A spark of light flared in the corner of Cait's eye. At the same moment she heard a roar like an express train powering through a station as the spark became a raging fire rushing at them, suddenly searing hot. The ice beneath her feet rumbled and shook. Lumps of ice crashed through the air, hurling the two of them backward.

The Line of Fire had been ignited, a wall of flame rising up to obscure Guilden. She and Danny were on the wrong side of it.

They scrambled to their feet. The smell of burning oil filled her nostrils. Toward Guilden, the black powder had blasted a wide crack in the ice. If they'd been a few yards nearer, jumping over as it was ignited, they'd have stood no chance. The fire raged, wood and straw bales coated with oil burning with an angry red flame. Many floated on the water where the ice had been blasted away. She could see no way to reach the safety of the other side.

They turned to face the undain. The Angere army was perhaps two hundred yards away. In the glimmer of the torches the undain carried, she could make out individuals. The glowing blue of the giant dragonriders and, behind them, other more hulking shapes. The ice reverberated with a weird metallic noise, echoing to the tramp of their feet. Danny glanced at her in wide-eyed terror, then back to the undain.

Cait stepped backward, but the raging fire at her back stopped her. They were trapped. She reached out with her mind's eye, hoping against hope to find some gap in the ranks, some flaw she could exploit.

She saw then who walked at the head of the army. He was suddenly clear in her eye: the stooped old man she remembered, unarmoured and unarmed, the large key around his neck. Charis walked at the head of the army. Walked directly toward *her*.

Another figure appeared on the ice then, arriving from nowhere, to stand mid-way between Cait and the approaching army. She could discern only a silhouette from the light of the undain's torches.

"Is that Hellen?" said Danny.

Cait's mind found the stranger. Not Hellen. Another old man, another she recognized. The rower who had brought them from Andar.

The undain army stopped as Charis raised his right hand. The only sound was the roar and crackle of the flame and, beyond, cries and shouts from the Ice Fair. Cait watched as Charis walked forward to meet Hyrn. Both figures looked so frail and weak it seemed ridiculous they should be there. Her mind's gaze hovering in the air above them she heard the words they spoke to each other.

"This is not your domain, Hyrn of the Green," said Charis, his voice the weak quaver Cait recalled. "Go back to wrapping your arms around your trees while you still can."

"You and your army of death can go no farther," said Hyrn. It was the first time she'd heard him speak. His voice whispered like the leaves of a forest in a high wind. "Return to the Lost Land."

Charis laughed a dry little laugh. "We are the gods now, Hyrn, not you. You are faded and broken, You do not matter any more. The wild woods of Angere are gone. Hadn't you noticed?"

"Woods can grow again. It takes only a few tiny seeds and a little time."

"But you have no time. Andar is ours. You should be grateful to us. You've lain wounded and broken these five hundred years. Now we will do what you always wanted. We will reunite the two halves into a whole. All of An under the control not of Hyrn, but Menhroth."

Now it was Hyrn's turn to laugh, a thin creak of a chuckle. "I never controlled these lands. I never wanted to control them. Your mind is so full of hate and conquest and destruction that you don't see it, thing that was once Charis. All I ever did was walk in the green spaces of the world and feel the sun on my face."

"Then run and find what greenery you can. Your time is over."

Hyrn seemed to consider Charis' words for a time. "No, I think not. Because it isn't only me. The land rises in revulsion at what you are. I am old and weak, it is true, but the lifeblood of An runs strong and true even if all of Angere is lost."

"And what do you intend to do, Hyrn? Tie us up in brambles and ivy so we can't walk? Make the flowers bloom at our feet and hope we will be distracted?"

Hyrn shook his head. "I could do all those things, but it would achieve nothing. Besides, I don't intend to do anything to stop you. I don't need to. There are others who will."

Charis hesitated, and Cait saw the briefest moment when understanding flashed into Charis' eyes. Then the ice behind him, the ice the undain army stood upon, exploded.

She'd seen glimpses of the serpents on their crossing of the An, slopes of grey flesh in the mists. Now she understood their true scale and ferocity as they smashed through the ice, giant heads like wrecking machines from back home, roaring and lashing as the ice splintered around them. Perhaps twenty or thirty of them: their coils lashing so that it was hard to know where one of the creatures stopped and another started. The An boiled with their fury. They reminded Cait of the mind she'd touched in Caer D'nar. Xoster, the mother of the dead dragons.

Many of the undain were hurled into the seething waters of the An. The others fled, breaking rank to run for the shallower waters where Cait and Danny cowered, or away upstream and downstream. But always there was another serpent rising through the depths, mouth like a pit gaping wide to snap and crush them.

Some among the dragonriders tried to fight back. One leaped onto a serpent, as if determined to become a wyrm rider once more. Straddling the serpent's coils, the rider hacked away with their sword, the creature's blood spattering the ice. The serpent, roars so deep Cait felt them in her chest rather than heard them, dived, taking the rider into the depths.

In their hundreds, Cait felt the undain disappearing in the aether, blinking out of existence. One or two were crushed or cut in half by the serpents' teeth. The waters of the An took most of them. Magic couldn't cross running water, and being submerged in the flow of the An meant destruction for the sorcerous undain. In a few minutes of roaring and screaming chaos, the entire undain army was gone, scattered to the waters.

Charis, still standing apart, stepped backward from the carnage as one of the serpents, head lashing, came for him. Hyrn was gone, disappearing as abruptly as he'd arrived. She could feel Charis beginning to work some magic, the power of it building within him. He clutched the key about his neck, as if he planned to banish the serpent through some portal into the aether.

"Cait, do something." Danny, still standing beside her.

For the moment, Charis' attention was focussed on the serpent towering over him. Could she work the magic without Bethany to guide her? She reached for the familiar well of coldness within her. As Phoenix had once promised her, it came to her more easily than it ever had. Perhaps it was just easier because she was standing upon ice. Suppressing any troubling thoughts of the effects too much power would bring, she unleashed a gale of cold directly at Charis' back. She wasn't powerful enough to defeat him, she knew. She might be able to knock him off balance for a moment.

The cold blast hit him, sending him reeling to the ground. He rose, puzzled, and looked back at her with his white eyes. There was a moment, the briefest moment, when he recognized her, knew what she'd done to him. And, she knew, Menhroth saw as well, watching through Charis's eyes.

Then the serpent's head smashed down, taking Charis and a wide circle of ice with him. The ancient undain was gone. Silence washed across the ice as the last of the vast creatures slipped beneath the waters.

"I don't believe it," said Danny at last. "We defeated them. You and Hyrn defeated them. Even Charis."

Exhaustion filled her as she waited for another attack, for Charis to rise from the waters and come for her like some end-of-level monster in a video game. Nothing moved. "Yes. I suppose so."

"I mean, just like that. Andar is saved."

"There's still the Witch King."

"Not much use without an army is he?"

"I suppose. Come on, let's get away from here."

"Yeah."

Supporting each other, they hobbled back to the Line of Fire. The flames were all-but burned out now, but the gap of water was there, just as the Doge had promised. It was too far to jump. Neither of them fancied a dip in those freezing waters.

"Jump," said Cait. "I'll boost us over."

"You can do that?"

She nodded. "I can't manage flight yet but I reckon I can do this. Not sure I can give us a soft landing though."

They ran together, holding hands, and jumped. She gave them a little kick as they left the ground, the pinch of pain within her slight. They flew alarmingly through the air, arms and legs flailing, to land hard on the other side, sprawling in a heap.

"Anything broken?" she asked.

"Don't think so. Let's get back to the land."

The Ice Fair looked as though a hurricane had swept through it: tents and braziers and stalls were strewn to the ground, knocked flat by the crowds fleeing in their panic. The ice sculptures were all smashed, a sea of tiny lights glimmering among the shards. They passed Merdoc's stall, flattened to the ground, drinks from his copper vats staining the ice red and purple. The people of Guilden finally believed the invasion from Angere was real. Only a few individuals milled on the ice, those too drunk to understand what was happening. The Lord of Misrule was among them, walking with his arms wide as if he'd staged the whole thing as a huge joke. His big finale.

When they reached the shore, Hellen came hurrying out of the crowds to meet them.

"There you are, girl. And Danny. You saw what happened?" She looked alarmed, her hair wild. She looked, as Cait's gran would have said, like she'd been dragged through a hedge backward.

"We were out there when the attack came," said Cait. "On the ice."

"What were you doing out there? Do you never listen to anything I say?"

"The serpents rose and killed them all," said Cait, ignoring Hellen's question.

"Did they? That's good." She didn't sound particularly surprised.

"That was your doing wasn't it? When you said you were communing with *the powers that be* you meant Hyrn."

"Half of Andar is here at Guilden. It seemed the obvious place to defend."

"But I thought the serpents couldn't smash through the ice?" said Danny. "That's why this hard winter is such a big deal."

"They wouldn't have been able to if the ice had been any thicker," said Hellen. "But the biggest and oldest of them were able to break through. Hyrn shepherded them to this one place. It left the rest of the coast undefended in case of other attacks, but there we are."

"Other attacks?" said Danny. "What do you mean? The whole army was just swallowed up by the An. We've beaten them. Andar is saved."

As if to answer him they heard more horns then. Many of them, their mournful cries echoing across the city from the north.

"The wall," said Hellen. "The other half of the army is approaching. I think Charis intended the two to strike at the same time."

"The other half?" said Danny.

"Charis is gone," said Cait. "A serpent took him."

Hellen's eyes widened in surprise. "Good. No loss to the world that one. Just leaves his army to deal with. Come, we must hurry to the walls to see what we can do."

The streets of Guilden were thronged with panicking people. No one laughed and joked now. People ran from blind terror, one or two screaming as if they were pursued by the undain. It was a struggle for Cait, Hellen and Danny to fight their way through the crowds. Everyone seemed to be going in the opposite direction, save for one or two trying to press through to the northern wall, clutching what weapons they could find. Some seemed to have no idea where they should be going, darting first one way and then the other. Bells rang out from the towers and domes, but no one seemed to have any idea what they meant.

In the end, Hellen had to hold out her hand and blaze a great light before her, enough to make people shield their eyes and shrink away. Even so, it took them twenty minutes or more to push through the throng to find Nox.

He stood observing the defences from a guard tower on the northern wall. He was bellowing out orders to anyone who could hear. Beyond the wall, a sloping plain covered with evergreen trees led to the rocky foothills of the mountains. Many of the trees were decorated with garlands and baubles for Midwinter. It was a weird sight. Black powder explosions bloomed among them here and there as Nox's traps were triggered. In between, the undain soldiers were clearly visible: thousands of them, a force even larger than the one that had marched across the ice. They'd crossed farther north and marched south on this side of the river. They stood unmoving, waiting.

A line of perhaps a hundred defenders stood scattered along the length of the wall. As Cait watched, a few of them broke ranks and fled rather than facing the undain onslaught. Despite Nox's commands it was clear order was breaking down among them.

"The undain will push through easily," said Nox. "There's nothing I can do. A few minutes at most."

"Are there any more barrels of black powder buried in the ground?" asked Hellen.

"Some. See the trees with only red streamers? They mark where the barrels are. Zap those when the undain get near, and we'll take a few out."

Cait could see only six or seven trees with red streamers. It wouldn't be anywhere near enough. "What do those bells mean? Are they summoning help from somewhere?"

"They just mean there's bad things happening," said Nox. "Far too late to be telling everyone. Unless the riders have come north from Caer L'dun, there is no one to help."

"They're also telling people to leave, abandon the city," said Hellen. "Escape into the wilds. The longer we can hold on here, the more time we'll give them to get away."

Cait joined Hellen and a few other witches at the wall, climbing stone steps to stand behind the crenulations that gave the defenders some protection.

"Can you fight them off with magic?" asked Cait. "Can we touch them?"

"We'll do what we can. Don't know much about spells for the battlefield. Mostly it's easing people's pains and persuading rain clouds to go elsewhere. We'll do what we can."

Hellen was a weatherworker, so she'd explained, and she fought by whipping up squalls that whirled and smashed into the undain. It slowed them down but in truth did little to harm them. Cait joined in, sending ice shards lancing into the nearest attackers. Delving into their minds and breaking them one by one as she had in Angere would clearly take too long. The witches laboured away for ten minutes, all of them grunting with the effort of each spell woven. Most of the undain still hadn't moved, only small groups setting off to cross the wooded plain.

"Why don't they attack in force?" asked Cait. "They could overwhelm us easily."

"Ignorance," said Hellen. "They don't know how many of us there are, what strength we have. It seems the vigilance of Borrn and the other wyrm lords has prevented Menhroth's spies from reporting back." Hellen unleashed a red flame that flew toward one of the red-garlanded trees. The explosion that followed shook the ground. A small group of advancing undain were blown to pieces.

"In any case," said Hellen, "I think their commander is testing us, sending a few of his soldiers forward to draw our fire, see what we're capable of."

"That's terrible," said Cait.

"So far as they're concerned these foot-soldiers are expendable. Hideous, yes, but it also makes them hard to fight."

From behind them, Nox bellowed something, an urgent note in his voice. Peering through the smoke of the explosion, Cait tried to grasp what was happening. Then she saw. The undain commander of the northern army had clearly decided enough was enough. A mass onslaught was running at the walls.

The undain moved across the ground with such speed that they were there in moments. A few final explosions caught the second and third ranks, but not enough to slow them down. The undain leaped onto the walls in a line to hack and slash at any defenders daring to oppose them. There were suddenly thousands of them and only a few scattered defenders.

Cait screamed and almost fell from the wall. An undain soldier stood over her, sword raised to strike her and Hellen. The older witch was preparing some powerful magic, working in conjunction with the other remaining witches. But there was no time left. Desperately Cait tried to blast the undain backward from the wall as the creature swung its sword. But in her panic she couldn't get her jumbled thoughts into line.

The undain stopped in mid-swing. The tip of a sword appeared through the front of its chest. The creature looked down as if wondering what it was. Then he slumped to the wall and rolled back to the ground.

Ran stood there, out of breath, sword in hand. He'd been scouting in the north and must have raced south one step ahead of the army. A look of purest alarm, almost panic, twisted his features.

"We must flee," he said. "There are too many of them. Far too many."

Hellen and the others of Islagray worked their magic then. A wall of fog swept forward, so dense it was almost as solid as the stone of the wall. It pushed outward, sweeping the attackers from the walls, obscuring them completely. Cait could feel the power of it. She could sense, also, the mounting fury of the undain attackers as they battered at the grey walls the witches had crafted.

Exhaustion was clear on Hellen's face as she turned to Cait, Danny and Ran. "That will hold them for a little time. We must go. There's nothing more we can do here."

They had to fight their way through the screaming, panicking crowds on the streets. The Golden Square was crammed with people, many of them gathering to demand the Doge or the mancers do something. Or simply because they felt safer in the press of the crowd. Pushing through proved to be impossible. Fortunately Nox appeared to know which back streets to take to get around the worst of the crush.

"Always pays to have a good map, even if you have to memorize it," he said.

A heaving mob had developed at the southern gates as people tried to force their way through onto the road. People were starting to use their fists to beat off those in their way. Panic rose in the air like a cloud. Fortunately they didn't need to go through the gates. Guilden was completely open to the river on its west side.

Lines of boats lay ice-locked in their moorings. Some people were there, desperately trying to hack vessels free to push them southward to open water. One or two coaxed huge carthorses on the ice, the great beasts leaning into the effort of hauling the boats free, slipping on the ice despite their spiked ice-shoes. One great black beast, crashing to the ice, went right through into the water with an alarming scream. It thrashed around, white eyes panicky, until it managed to right itself. It tried to swim for the shore but the ice stopped it.

"We have to help," said Cait.

"No time," said Hellen. "They've all been warned often enough. Now they're on their own."

Other people, forgetting about the ice-locked boats, were simply skating south, only using the land to work their way around the gap in the ice blasted out by the Line of Fire.

Cait and the others went that way. The thought they were abandoning Guilden and its people to their fate gnawed at Cait. But what could they do? If they stayed they would only be caught again, enslaved or killed.

"We have to flee south," said Nox, apparently thinking the same thoughts. "Live to fight another day."

Hellen nodded, her eyes narrowed as she stared into the sky, as if seeing answers written up there. "Agreed. We can go no farther north. It's time to turn back and retrace our journey. This time we'll have the undain snapping at our heels."

Smoke on the Water lay half a mile offshore, Johnny waiting inside. They'd calculated that most people leaving Guilden would cling to the banks as they fled. The other witches would go with the refugees while Cait, Danny, Hellen, Johnny, Ran and Nox slid across the ice in the sleigh. One after another they climbed inside. The golden figurehead opened its eyes in readiness.

"South," said Hellen.

"To where?" said Johnny. "I mean, what's the point now?"

"We'll see about that," said Hellen. "But we've made

some progress, and learned something, too."

"I don't see what."

"We know for sure what we're up against now. We've seen the scale of the attack. We've destroyed some of them, too, mainly thanks to the serpents. The death of Charis was an unexpected bonus."

"And now?" asked Nox

"Perhaps we can delay them again at Hyrn's Oak and the other towns," Hellen replied. "But Caer D'nar is our only real hope. And then, after that, Islagray."

"And if that's not enough?" asked Danny.

"Then it doesn't much matter any more. There will be no one left in Andar to know what's been lost."

They were about to set off when they heard shouts from the ice. A single figure shambled toward them, limping from some leg wound.

Cait expected it to be the Doge, fleeing the city he'd once ruled. Or perhaps the Lord of Misrule. Instead it was Merdoc, lumbering across the ice as quickly as he could.

"I saw you leaving the city. I beg you, is there room for one more?"

The look of horror on his face was familiar. She'd seen something similar on many of the people.

"Step in," said Hellen. "And then we must flee."

"My thanks to you once again, Eldest of Andar. I am in your debt."

"Good. Then I'll expect some very good prices next time we buy from you."

"You think there'll be a next time?"

"There might. I see you had enough presence of mind to bring your takings with you?" A leather pouch, heavy with coin, dangled beneath Merdoc's cloak.

"I salvaged what I could," he said.

"As it should be," said Hellen. "I think that's all any of us can do now."

Smoke on the Water jerked forward as if being hauled by invisible horses. They picked up speed, heading south.

Everyone on board watched in silence as, behind them, the tallest tower on the Doge's palace, the Sun Tower, came crashing to the ground in a ball of dust and smoke. Flames raged in Guilden.

"Well," said Johnny after a moment. "That was an Ice Fair they won't forget in a hurry."

10 – HYRN'S OAK

Word of the sacking of Guilden had reached each town and city they came to on their flight south. At least people no longer doubted that the warnings of invasion were real. Word had passed rapidly through the aether from hedge witch to wise man. *The undain are coming with the ice. Andar is invaded.*

Hyrn's Oak was a very different place now. They could see no revellers, no cheering, laughing crowds as they approached. The Midwinter festivities had been forgotten and no music played. Up in the arms of the great oak, guards holding bows scanned the river. No fairy lights flickered among the branches.

"We'll stop here," said Hellen. "Perhaps we can delay them further." They were back in open water, but a crust of ice covered the An, crunching and squealing as *Smoke on the Water* cut through it.

"Do you think we're ahead of them?" asked Cait. There'd been no sign of the pursuing army on the banks, and her attempts to sense them through the aether had revealed nothing.

"I think they'll take their time to deal with the people of Guilden."

"You mean … to kill them?"

"Eventually. I suspect for now they'll be taken back to the White City to be imprisoned until they can be dealt with by Menhroth's clerics. That Ritual of theirs takes time to perform, and it must be many years since they had so many to deal with. The dungeons you were kept in will be full for a time."

Cait didn't reply, imagining being back there, imagining the people of Guilden hauled screaming up those steps one by one and not returning. She felt so powerless. There had to be something she could do.

"I was thinking," she said. "You remember we were attacked by an aether creature in Angere."

"An aethernal."

"The thing is, if they can survive in the real world, why don't we try and summon one and unleash it on the undain army? I mean, then we'd have an aethernal to face, sure, but that seems preferable right now."

"I've thought about that," said Hellen. "I don't think it would work. Why do you think you met the creature in the far north of Angere?"

"Because … that's where all the normal, living people and animals are?"

"The undain have no life, no spirit to drain, save for the occasional spark like those you've glimpsed. An aethernal would be too dangerous, most likely it would ignore the entire undain army and come for us."

"So, will Hyrn's Oak be any different from Guilden?"

"Perhaps. At least we won't have to persuade them the danger is real. Hyrn's Oak doesn't have Guilden's high walls, but they proved no barrier anyway. What it does have is running water all around it. The Teem on three sides and the An on the fourth. We might be able to work something with that. If we can keep the waters flowing we might hold them up for a time. Nox had a chance to look around on the way north, too. Apparently he has plans.

"Do you really trust him?"

Hellen glanced sideways at her, a sparkle of amusement in her eye. "About as much as you do. But from what I've seen of his thoughts, he genuinely wants to defeat the undain. They annoyed him, and he wants his revenge."

"I didn't see any black powder he could use when we were here before."

"No, but there are those archers of theirs. They might be able to inflict some damage."

"I don't think a few arrows are going to bother the undain much."

Hellen nodded in agreement. "Perhaps. But a shattered knee can at least stop one walking for a time."

"It seems so hopeless," said Cait. "They're marching across Andar and there's nothing we can really do."

Hellen nodded her agreement. "We should have been more prepared. People don't like to hear dire warnings, that's the problem. They see the sun rising in the morning, as beautiful as it was the day before, and refuse to believe anything could change."

A group of armed townsfolk waited for them on the wooden quay as they drifted nearer. Most held bows and while none had arrows knocked, Cait was under no illusion they could fire in a moment if they wished. Wary eyes studied them as they docked. Johnny leaped out of the boat to help tie up *Smoke on the Water*. He, at least, seemed to put the townsfolk at ease. Clearly there was more than one there who'd enjoyed his performance on the way north.

Venn and her father pushed through the group of archers. Both wore the same grim expression, the resemblance between them clear in the light of day. Venn's hair was nut-brown where Torven's was wispy and grey, but they had the same sharp nose and keen eyes. They carried their bows in their hands: long, gently curving spars, highly polished. Both had leather bags full of feathered arrows strapped to their backs.

"Guilden is lost?" asked Venn.

"It is," said Hellen. "Are you ready here? Have you stopped drinking and dancing long enough to prepare your defences?"

Venn looked too exhausted to quarrel with Hellen. "We've done what we can. The children and the sick and old left this morning for the deep woods. There are glades and caves higher up in the hills where they might be safe for a time."

"Who's left here?" asked Nox. "How many archers?"

"Perhaps three hundred of us."

"All armed?"

"All are hunters of Hyrn's Oak. Some of the witches who came north from Islagray are here, too, awaiting your return, although a couple left with the children."

"Have you destroyed the bridges?" asked Hellen.

Venn looked puzzled. "No. Why would we do that?"

"You'll have more chance as an island. How can you live in Andar and not know magic doesn't like to cross running water? The flow sucks it away, drains it. A little trickle like the Teem won't stop the undain, but they might choose to wait a day or three for it to freeze before they come for you. That won't be long now given how cold it is. But if there are bridges, they can just walk across, can't they? Same as you can."

Glances passed between Venn, her father and the others in the group. There was no Doge in Hyrn's Oak, no one was in charge, so Johnny had explained. The town ran itself, any disputes handled by verderers' courts that met every month. The archers were the closest thing they had to authority. After a moment, without a word being spoken, the group on the quay appeared to consent.

Venn nodded. "We'll see to it immediately. Will there be other witches coming to our aid?"

"No more from the south. One or two fleeing from Guilden, perhaps."

"Won't they need the bridges to reach us?"

Hellen shook her head. "The risk is too great. They'll

take their chances. If they arrive ahead of the undain horde we can send boats over for them. Most likely they'll spend their time holding up the advance in whatever way they can. In truth, I doubt any of them will reach us."

They took axes to the wooden bridges that crossed the Teem, including the one Cait had crossed on her first visit. The hollow sound of the blades chopping into the stays reverberated off the boughs of the trees, thirty of forty yards beyond the far side of the river. When they were done, the archers manhandled the detached bridges downstream with wooden staves to reach the An. Hyrn's Oak was an island once more, separated from the rest of Andar by ten yards of water.

The central course of the Teem flowed quickly, the waters gushing off the mountains, but it looked a meagre defence to Cait. A crust of ice crept from both banks, joining up in places, the gurgling waters rushing underneath. When she dipped her fingers in, the chill was intense. Hellen was right, with the ice creeping south it wouldn't be long before the Teem froze, too. Every branch and twig of the trees lining the far banks was coated in a heavy frost, sparkling gold where the sun struck.

Nox spent his time walking the defences, helping them organize. He came to stand with Cait for a time, muttering about the archers being too used to hunting alone to act together as an army. He was good at what he did, though, she had to admit. She'd worried he'd start barking orders at them, throw his weight around and get an arrow for his efforts. He was more subtle than that, though. Hyrn's Oak was different than Guilden. She watched as he suggested and hinted to the archers, pointing out to Venn and the others how they might arrange themselves, asking whether this or that approach might be a good idea. Most of the time, she saw, the archers thought they'd come up with the suggestions rather than Nox.

Within a couple of hours he had them set up in groups

all the way around the circumference of the town, each cluster of archers within sight and arrow-flight range of each other. Their arcs of fire covered the whole perimeter. He'd made sure each group had a bell, too, so they could raise the alarm when the attack came. He'd worked out a whole language of rings, allowing the defenders to pass round details of sightings, attacks and all-clears even in the dark or the mist. There was no wall around Hyrn's Oak, but they assembled what barricades they could for each group: lugging stones to build sections of wall tall enough for the defenders to hide behind, vertical slits built into them to shoot through.

It was impressive. Perhaps a third of the archers were left in reserve, away from the front line, ready to rush to any point on the periphery when a concerted attack came. The town had a plentiful supply of arrows: cartloads of long, heavy bolts, metal-tipped. Venn demonstrated to Cait how far they could fire the arrows as well as how destructive they could be when they hit, splintering wood and shredding targets with ease.

While the archers prepared, Cait, Hellen and the other witches from Islagray met to prepare the magic they would use. They could try and bring down individuals, but there were too many undain and nowhere near enough witches. Instead they'd use the Teem. Hellen still thought it likely the undain would wait for the ice to fully form before they attacked rather than allowing the rushing waters to drain them. Her plan was to wait for that moment, then crack and melt the ice under their feet. Throwing them into the running waters would drain them or even destroy them.

"The witches of old brought down mountainsides of snow into the An to bring it into flood," she said. "I'm sure we can manage a bit of ice on this stream."

"It will only work once," said Cait. "Once they see what we're doing they'll attack, jump across the river."

Hellen nodded. "Most likely. Their ignorance is our defence. They don't know how strong we are, how many of us there are. If they knew, I don't think they'd bother waiting. They'd ignore the running water and overwhelm us."

They waited three days for the attack. Long, cold days, Cait alternating between boredom and terror. The all-clear call clanged again and again from across the town, the sound mournful. She walked the banks of the Teem with Danny to keep warm, reaching over the waters with her mind's eye to try and detect the approaching army. Each bird clattering into the sky, each breeze ruffling the branches sent her heart fluttering.

Snow swirled repeatedly over Hyrn's Oak, obscuring the world beyond, coating ground and buildings in white. Cait sat for hours, mesmerized by the spell of the endlessly falling flakes. The waters froze over on the second day and on the third day the air was icier still, all memory of warmth gone from it. It sucked the heat straight out of Cait's body as she sat and watched the snow.

In the end it was one of the archers who raised the alarm. They'd sent a few scouts out to ghost through the trees, watching for the approaching undain. One appeared suddenly on the far banks, chest heaving, eyes wide. At the sight of him, the archers rose as one, flexing the muscles in their arms and fingers, drawing arrows in readiness. Bells began to ring out, passing Nox's messages around the defences.

Cait could feel them now: a tide of the undain rolling forward to engulf Hyrn's Oak. They'd waited for the ice as Hellen had thought. The scout slid down the snow-coated bank onto the frozen Teem, slipping her way across, casting alarmed glances backward all the time. She reached the near shore and was being pulled up the bank by Venn when the undain emerged from the tree-line behind her.

The archers unleashed their first volley, the arrows flying almost horizontally to slam into the attackers. A line of the creatures went down, limbs and faces broken by the heavy wooden bolts. There was no screaming from them, though. That was almost the worst part. That and the way they rose again if their bones and muscles worked well enough to permit it. One or two were so shattered they stayed down, writhing uselessly on the floor or crawling forward as best they could. Those that stood over them reached down to place a hand upon them and drain the Spirit from them, taking it for themselves.

More volleys of arrows flashed from the defenders and more undain crashed to the ground. Each time most but not all rose again. As at Guilden, the undain appeared to be assessing the defences of Hyrn's Oak, working out what they faced.

Then at some unheard call the mass attack came. Once again they moved with blinding speed, covering the ground between the trees and the Teem in the blink of an eye. Thousands of them: normal-sized soldiers and huge muscled giants, all carrying swords and shields. There were others who loped along on all fours, part-human and part-animal, teeth bared in snarling mouths.

From the trees, a wall of arrows slammed into the defenders, arching over the top of the attacking forces. Where the hunters had relied on accuracy, choosing targets carefully, the undain simply tried to overwhelm with the sheer number of their shots, one or two managing to find their way through the narrow slits to send defenders spinning to the ground.

The giant undain, meanwhile, hurled boulders with a terrifying force, smashing down the hastily assembled walls where they struck. Each time the defenders were exposed to a rain of arrows slamming into them. The archers of Hyrn's Oak returned fire as best they could, aiming and shooting in a blur, some standing despite the arrows protruding from bloody wounds in their legs or chests.

The reserve defenders raced up to help plug the gaps where the assault was heaviest. Venn dodged around, calling out orders, reeling off arrow shots. Cait caught glimpses of Nox, too, watching over the scene from atop one of the stone buildings, occasionally bellowing out orders to the archers to cover a point where a breach in the defences looked possible.

Cait stepped back from it all, horrified at the slaughter, screams and cries filling her ears. The snow, once so pristine, was trampled and stained red. The calls of the bells were a constant cacophony, ringing from all directions, all meaning lost. There were too many of them. Far, far too many. She watched as Torven, peering out to unleash an arrow, was thrown backward to the mud, four or five undain bolts in him. He didn't move.

Hellen grabbed her by the shoulder. "Come. We have work to do."

The witches of Islagray assembled in a small square behind a row of houses on the edge of the town, shielded from the arrows of the undain. It was one Cait had walked across on her first visit, the place the archers had set up targets for their archery competition. The screams from the defenders were muffled only slightly by the distance. Venn stood by Hellen, a curved hunting horn in her hand. Her eyes were wide and she panted hard. At a nod from Hellen, she winded the horn, the piercing sound cutting through the cries and clash of the fighting. The retreat. The defenders began to appear, limping through the gaps between the houses, many of them wounded, supported by others.

Cait, Hellen and the other witches formed a rough ring, and between them they began to work the magic they'd arranged. Closing her eyes, Cait caught glimpses of events outside on the Teem through her mind's eye.

The undain, seeing the defenders fall back, were pressing forward, marching onto the ice. Ranks of quick-moving, child-sized undain hurried to the front. They were lightly-armoured, carrying only knives, but there were thousands and thousands of them and they were light enough not to crack the ice. Perhaps they were children; it was hard to tell beneath their armour. Best not to think about it. In an instant the Teem was thick with them, skipping lightly across the ice.

At a word from Hellen the witches poured what magic they could muster into the river. Some threw heat and flame at it, trying to melt the ice beneath the undains' feet. Others stirred up the waters beneath, Cait among them. She thought about the river serpents, the way the An had boiled as they rose at Guilden. The image helped her form the magic she wanted. The pain of what she was doing pulled at her stomach, seeming to stretch her guts, but she didn't relent. She was aware of gasps of pain from the witches around her but none stopped.

The waters of the Teem frothed as they wove their spells, throwing up spumes of water as the ice cracked and melted. The front ranks of the attacking undain were already on the near shore, flying up the banks to launch themselves with abandon at Hyrn's Oak. But behind them, the cracking ice heaved and then tipped the attackers into the seething waters.

The effect on them was immediate. They screamed high-pitched screeches, floundering in clear agony is if the waters were boiling. Archers on the roofs of the buildings along the river popped up and shot at both the floundering undain and those that had managed to make the crossing. In only a minute or so the Teem was clogged with a raft of lifeless bodies. With a final cry of pain, the assembled witches threw one more wave of their strength at the stream, keeping the waters flowing to sweep the lifeless undain away into the An.

More than one witch collapsed to the ground, exhausted at the effort of what they'd done, clutching themselves as if physically wounded. Hellen nodded at Cait, her mouth set in a line, but both were too out of breath to talk.

The archers in the square busied themselves picking off those few undain that had made it through, defending the circle of witches. Some of the creatures were killed outright by a hail of arrow-shots to their heads. Others were incapacitated by hits to their limbs. These were quickly finished off by the hunters' knives. Ran was there, too, sword busy as he made sure no undain made it near Cait or any of the other witches.

When it was done, a silence washed across Hyrn's Oak, broken only by the groans of those injured by the onslaught. And then, echoing off the stone walls, the all-clear call.

The archers and the witches filed out to the water's edge. The undain were gone, retreating into the darkness of the woods as quickly as they'd arrived. The ground was strewn with all those that had been felled, arrows protruding from their misshapen bodies. A cheer in the distance was picked up by the nearby archers and soon Cait and even Hellen were joining in.

They'd done it. For the moment they'd beaten the undain.

When she'd made sure Danny and Johnny and Merdoc were OK, Cait went to find Nox to thank him. His plans and defences had worked flawlessly; quite possibly they couldn't have defended Hyrn's Oak without him. She felt bad at doubting him all the time when, in truth, he'd done everything he could to help after being cast out by Genera. He'd given them the two halves of the book, and he'd helped her, in his own way, to cross Angere. She wanted him to know how she felt. Despite their history, she wanted him to know she was grateful.

She found him propped against the wall of a stone building. She felt annoyed at him for not bothering to seek her and Hellen out, for not telling them what he planned to do next. It was just like him.

But then his blood-soaked chest showed her the truth of it. Four of the undains' arrows sprouted from his chest and two more lay on the ground beside him. He panted little breaths as if anything deeper would hurt too much. Despite the pain he had to be in, he managed to grin as she approached.

"See what you've got me into now, Cait."

She kneeled beside him, studying the ugly, ragged wounds that dribbled blood down his chest. "I … I'm sorry. I didn't mean this to happen."

He shook his head and spoke in short, broken sentences. "Everything was going so well, you know. Until that day at the library. You just walked past me. A schoolgirl carrying a book and everything changed. If I'd stopped you, everything would have been different. Instead, here I am. I was going to be immortal, Cait. Now I'm about to die."

"You're not about to die," she said. "We can heal you. The witches…"

He shook his head. "These injuries are too bad. I've inflicted enough on others to know the signs. Too much blood lost. Perhaps if Andar had modern hospitals with proper medicine it would be different."

"I didn't mean this to happen," she said again.

He looked amused. "You hate me really."

"At first, yeah."

"And now? You can be honest. It hardly matters."

"Now, I guess I don't know. You've done so much for us, giving us the book. Then everything in the White City and Guilden. I came here to thank you. Still, I remember the way you hunted us in Manchester. When I look at you I remember how much you enjoyed doing it, too."

He nodded, as if these were fond memories. He licked his lips. "You asked me if I blamed you for what happened to me. Perhaps I do a little. But you can repay me by beating them, Cait. By destroying them completely. Promise me you'll do that."

"I'll try."

"Good. See, I've stopped underestimating you now. I know you can do it."

There was something she'd been meaning to admit to him. It seemed now would be her only chance. "Nox, you remember when we first arrived in Angere, and we climbed that hill from the stone circle?"

He nodded his head but didn't speak.

"There was a dead crow on the ground. Later I … I think I saw it fly away to raise the alarm. You asked me about it but I said it was nothing. But I think, maybe, that was why the undain came to Greygyle's for us. I should have told you."

He looked amused. "See. We're not so different. You have plots and secrets all of your own."

"Tell me," she said, "if you had a chance, if the undain would take you back, give you immortality, you would, wouldn't you?"

"No. I told you. They pissed me off." But he sounded like he was mocking her, and there was a spark of amusement in his eyes.

"But if they offered you Genera again, let you run it instead of Ms. Sweetley, you'd bite their hand off."

"You want to watch her, you know. She's dangerous."

"But would you?"

He closed his eyes and shook his head. "What do you think, Cait?"

What did she think? It always seemed like Nox was playing a double game, or a triple game. Hedging his bets so that it looked like he was helping both sides in the war.

"Sometimes I think you're a friend," she said. "Sometimes I don't trust you at all. I don't know whose side you're really on. So tell me, if you even know yourself, which is it?"

But when she looked back down at him, his eyes were closed and his ruined chest had stopped moving. He was gone.

Unexpected tears came to her eyes. She had feared and hated this man, but somehow it was no longer that simple. The lines between good and bad weren't always as clear as the river separating Andar and Angere. Menhroth said he trusted Nox to do only what was in his own best interests, yet Nox had died trying to defend Andar. Perhaps that had been nothing more than a way of surviving as he awaited his chance to turn against them. She'd never know, now.

Danny found her ten minutes later, still kneeling in the dirt beside Nox. Danny held her close, saying nothing. He, too, had reasons to despise Nox, but also to thank him. They crouched there together for a time.

"We should go," said Cait eventually. "Before they attack again."

"Hellen says we have a little time. The Teem is still flowing. Most likely the undain will wait until the waters freeze again tonight. We've held them off for now."

"What shall we do with him?"

"Put him with the others, I guess."

The archers carried the dead of Hyrn's Oak to the quay. The skiffs moored there for the winter were normally laden with gulping, flapping fish but now they were given another use, loaded with a very different cargo. When the bodies had all been lifted aboard, the boats were doused with oil and pushed into the An. There was still open water in the bay. The sun sank in the west, seeming to melt into the waters of the river as it shaded to orange and then blood-red.

The dwindling band of defenders lit the tips of oil-coated arrows and aimed them at the boats. Venn was among the archers, the body of Torven on the skiffs. At a cry, a volley of flaming arrows arched into the sky with a roar. Most found their marks, igniting the oil on the boats. Soon they blazed with an orange light. No one spoke as the burning boats drifted away, taken by the current of the great river to jostle with the ice floes in deeper waters.

After a few moments, Cait could no longer tell which fire was Nox. It occurred to her she didn't know if he had family or even friends back home. If there was anyone who'd miss him, puzzle over what had happened to him.

She wondered, also, who else she was going to lose before the end.

Hellen came to stand beside Cait. The flames from the burning boats flickered in her eyes as she stared out to the river. "They'll come in the night," she said quietly. "The undain. There are more of them all the time. Do you feel them? There's an anger to them. There's nothing more we can do here. They know our numbers, now. The night will be cold enough for the Teem to freeze once more and I don't think it will unfreeze again before the spring."

"We've held them back for a while," said Cait. "We've bought a little time for those who fled for the woods and hills."

Hellen nodded. They both knew it was a small victory. "Their tree didn't save them from the flood this time."

Back at *Smoke on the Water*, Cait sat next to Danny while Johnny and Ran untied the ropes. Merdoc glanced around nervously, fiddling with the drawstrings of his leather purse. Hellen conversed on the wharf with the remaining archers. Venn and the others would retreat into the forests, too. They'd harry the undain with ambush and trap before slipping away into the deeper woods. It was all they could do. Perhaps they could survive by hiding away, living like wild animals. Hyrn's Oak, like Guilden, would fall to the undain. Their victory had been glorious, but brief.

Once Hellen was aboard they pushed off to follow the course taken by the burning boats, south for Caer L'dun. It was only after a few minutes that it occurred to Cait she'd left an empty space for Nox to sit beside her.

11 – THE HIGH WALLS OF CAER L'DUN

Cait shivered in the blast of the cold wind blowing through the open windows of the watchtower. The wyrm lords were too tough, too heroic to notice the chill. From what Hellen had said they probably enjoyed freezing to death. But she, Cait, felt like a block of ice. She'd been offered furs, which she'd refused on principle, although she was regretting it now. Her fingers were numb, fizzing unpleasantly when she touched them to something. Surely they could light a fire, as Phoenix had at the top of his tower in Angere?

It occurred to her she was now the second person, after Ran, to climb to the top of the dragonriders' two towers: Caer L'dun in Andar and Caer D'nar in Angere. The second and probably the last person. The walls of Caer L'dun were high and strong, built from the remains of the ancient bridge she'd been told, but it seemed unlikely they could withstand the undain onslaught.

Hugging her woollen clothes about her for what warmth they offered, she returned to gazing out of the window. There was no movement, no flow to the waters of the An, now. The river was finally frozen this far south, the light gleaming dully off its solid surface. They'd been there a week, waiting for the attack. It wouldn't be long.

A lone bird, black against the white and grey, flapped toward them from the north. For a moment she thought it might be another chough like those of Caer D'nar, its beak bright red. But, no, this was a crow. It flew directly for the tower and Cait, touching the creature with her mind, saw what it really was.

A minute later she stepped backward to allow the bird access to the tower. There was a swirl of movement, twirling wing-feathers becoming cloth and it was Hellen crouching there on the worn wooden floorboards. Cait's mother had done something similar outside the factory when Nox cornered them. It was a trick Cait really had to master.

With Cait's arm for support, Hellen climbed to her knees, then her feet, brushing dust from her clothes. For the briefest moment, the beady black eyes of the crow looked back at Cait, looking weirdly like Menhroth's, and then Hellen was fully herself again.

Barion, First of the gold dragonriders, marched over from his table and his maps to demand a report. He was a squat, powerful man, and completely bald. "Well, did you see? Are they close?"

Hellen nodded as she smoothed her grey hair back into shape, pinning it into place with long needles. "I saw them. All the armies that crossed north of here have met up into a single force. They will throw everything at Caer L'dun. There is no reason for them not to."

"How many are they would you say?"

"I told you I thought there might be a hundred thousand undain."

"You did," said Barion. The room had gone completely silent as everyone stopped what they were doing to listen.

"Well, I may have been a little out. On the other hand, we have managed to account for a few of them, especially with the river serpents. And I suspect there will be another column coming directly at us from the west, although I can't separate the smell of them from those remaining at the White City."

"How many?" asked Barion again, folding his arms across his chest.

"It's hard to count with the brain of a bird, dragonrider, but I'd say eighty thousand of them. They spread across the land north of here like a flood, like spilled ink spreading across that map of yours."

"Moving toward us?" asked Barion.

"Oh, yes, marching now. They'll be here by the end of the day."

Jenath, the young chief of the green dragonriders spoke up from the table. "Well, that's not so bad. It means only eighty undain for each wyrm lord rather than the hundred we feared. How can we lose?"

Barion paid no attention to his Green Wing counterpart. Jenath's words were probably the closest the wyrm lords got to humour, and Barion clearly didn't do humour. He continued to quiz Hellen. "What formations were the soldiers in? Are there giants among them? Are there flying creatures? Tell me everything."

"I've no eye for such things," said Hellen. "I can tell you they march in square ranks, some down the road, some along the An. Most are foot-soldiers, the normal ones that did most of the fighting at Guilden and Hyrn's Oak. There are giants among them, too, powerful beasts the size of two or three normal people. I saw the quick-moving, swarming ones, as well, the sort that could flood your defences in a wink. There are also packs of bestial undain running along on four legs."

"The carts bearing the tanks of Spirit?"

"Trundling along safely behind, and very well guarded. Impossible to say how full or empty they are."

"And the flying undain?"

"None in the air but they were there, also hauled along

in carts."

Barion nodded thoughtfully, looking as if he were slotting this information into the plans he held in his mind. "The creatures they construct in mockery of the dragons are broken, clumsy horrors," said Barion. "But they'll be unleashed when they are near. We'll have to fight them off, too."

"And will you be able to?"

Barion scowled, making little attempt to restrain his irritation. "You clearly don't think we can."

Hellen's eyes narrowed slightly, almost as if she were studying Barion through her crow's eyes again. But her voice was calm when she replied. "No, truly, I think you're our only hope to slow their march southward."

"To slow but not to stop."

"I'd be delighted if you proved me wrong," said Hellen.

"What of your plans?" asked Axana, her red tattoos bright upon her cheeks and neck. She stood next to Jenath at the table, poring over maps of Caer L'dun and its surrounding areas. "Do you still see hope in the ancient book and the spells of the necromancer?"

"That remains to be seen," said Hellen. "I've spoken through the aether to those remaining at Islagray, and they are still working on the ancient text, trying to decipher it. They have no answers yet."

"Do they know when?"

"No. Ashen simply asks for as much time as we can give him."

Barion snorted, the sound somewhere between amusement and disdain. "Then we will have to rely on the swords and spears of the dragonriders. We'll have to hope the high walls of Caer L'dun can withstand the undain, won't we?"

"We will," said Hellen.

Thirty minutes later, Cait stood with Hellen, Danny and Ran behind the gates. Den, the First of the blue riders was there also, mounted on a gleaming black horse, saddle and bridle inlaid with swirling blue lines like Den's tattoos. Behind him, two hundred mounted riders waited in silence, horses snorting steam and raking the ground with their hooves.

Borrn was adjusting the bridle of Den's mount while Hellen watched him work.

"Horses make a poor substitute for dragons," she said.

Borrn nodded without looking at her. "The beasts are swift and intelligent but their ability to fly is somewhat limited. Still, the riders of old rode horses. A rider learned to fight on dragonback by first performing the moves on their horse."

"Makes sense. Less far to fall if things go badly wrong." Hellen's tone was different when she talked to Borrn. She didn't order him around like she did everyone else.

Cait let her gaze wander among the assembled troop behind Den. They were from all four wings: the best riders in each according to Barion. Their mission was desperate, possibly even hopeless. They would charge from the fortress before the undain army arrived, attempt to circle around and, before anyone knew what they were doing, attack the Spirit carts. It would have no immediate effect, but might restrict the army's options after a day or so. If any riders survived the attempt, they were to attempt to cut directly through the enemy lines back to the fortress. The undain ranks would be well armoured and defended at the front, but might be easier to split in two from the rear.

Cait caught Den's gaze as he adjusted his leather gloves and the straps on his boots. She said nothing. Den was well aware his chances of returning were slim, but she could see no fear in him, his face as expressionless as Ran's always was. Den held his chin up in a way that suggested a fierce pride. At last he was riding out to face those who had shamed him and his people.

Ran, beside her, watched with eyes narrowed as if he were imagining himself riding among Den's cavalry. But he'd been assigned to stay close to Cait, protect her in the battle to come. She was very glad of his presence. She and Hellen would play their part, working what magic they could when the attack came.

Danny, Johnny and Merdoc had been instructed to hide within the central tower and not show themselves. *The riders will have enough to worry about without trying to protect you*, Barion had said. Danny had looked worriedly at Cait as it was explained to him, but Johnny had been hugely relieved, as if he'd been afraid someone would hand him a sword and tell him to fight. He'd surely be more danger to the defenders or himself than the undain if he were given a blade to swing.

The gates of Caer L'dun were hauled open by rattling chains. Den's cavalry clattered off, horses whinnying in their excitement, metal armour and weapons shining as the column cantered out. Half the horses had been shod with spiked ice shoes to circle west on the river. The others would move east and north, following woodland trails well known to the riders. If all went to plan they would meet again in two hours as they swooped on the undain rearguard.

When the last horses had passed through, the gates were hurriedly closed. Reinforced wooden bars were lifted into place to secure them, further trunks angled against the gates to buttress them against any attack. Hellen, touching the wood with her outstretched fingers, worked some magic into the grain to further strengthen the doors.

The onslaught began half an hour later. This time there was no feint, no attempt by the undain to measure the strength of the Andar defenders. Instead the army streamed forward, moving with its inhuman speed up the slopes of the rocky outcrop upon which Caer L'dun stood. The defenders could only unleash a single volley of arrows before the undain reached the foot of the walls. It was immediately clear that the riders were a different prospect to the watchmen of Guilden or the archers of Hyrn's Oak.

The wyrm lords were highly-trained fighters, moving as one, a line of them ducking to reload while another fired over their heads.

Cait watched with Hellen from one of the lower towers. A few surviving witches of Islagray, those that had managed the trek southward, were scattered around in the other towers. They were well above the fighting, but near enough to hear every piercing scream rising above the clatter of battle. Most of the cries were from the undain as a rider's arrow found its mark. The sounds surprised her. Were there, perhaps, living humans among the attackers? She swept her gaze across them with the seeing-stone but could see no sparks of life.

She began to work what magic she could, flinging ice at the largest attackers she could see, trying to copy Hellen by whipping up whirlwinds to knock them backward. The effect was limited in the closely-pressed ranks of attackers.

Their tower protruded from the line of the walls, allowing the defenders to shoot arrows across at any attackers. She watched as nimble, child-like undain, something like those they'd seen crossing the river at Hyrn's Oak, jumped onto the walls from the throng, managing to climb the sheer rock face with splayed hands and feet. The riders on the battlements and in the flanking towers rained down arrows and tipped over pots of molten oil in response. But the undain relied on their overwhelming numbers, and each time one of the climbing undain fell, another was there to take its place.

Cait stopped attacking the army on the ground and turned her spellworking to the walls instead, sending a frosting of ice from her fingertips. It had the effect she'd hoped for. The climbing undain, unable to find grip, either fell backward or hung where they were to be picked off. The riders, seeing what she'd done, stopped tipping over the boiling oil for fear of melting the ice. Mustering her energy, Cait unleashed more cones of ice, trying to cover the whole width of the wall. It became harder and harder as the distance grew, each spell hurting her more. She stuck at it. It was better than being down on the battlements where the riders waited with their swords.

Pausing to rub the tearing pain in her sides, she caught sight of Barion, watching over the whole battle from the turret of the tower opposite, his bald head unmistakable. He nodded his head as if in appreciation of her efforts, then turned to bellow out more orders.

Back on the ground, a rank of the giant undain were lumbering forward, wading through the undain army as if it was water, not caring if their smaller brethren got out of their way. They carried ladders: long wooden poles with many crosspieces attached, like the spines of some impossibly tall creature. The ladders were long enough to reach to the battlements. As the undain swarmed up, the giants held shields aloft, protecting the climbers for the first part of their ascent.

Again, the undain relied on sheer numbers to attempt to flood the defenders. They had more luck this time. For every ladder the wyrm lords managed to push from the walls with long wooden poles and send crashing back into the ranks on the ground, another admitted a stream of attackers onto the battlements.

Each time, Barion's defenders were ready, rushing to meet the attack with a knot of dancing, sword-wielding defenders. Hellen, Cait and the other witches did what they could, but it was tricky to pick out undain from wyrm lord in the confined space of the battlements. Wyrm lords began to die, overwhelmed by attackers, hacked down by their swinging blades. The sight was sickening. She'd seen many of the undain destroyed in Angere, but this was much worse. Living men and women were falling, writhing in agony or flopping dead over the walls.

The defenders beat back the attacks, but each time there were fewer of them left standing on the battlements. The overwhelming numbers of the attackers would soon be too much.

From among the ranks of the undain on the ground, fizzing balls of fire began to fly at the defenders, jinking through the air as if they were alive and seeking out individuals. The undain had spellworkers of their own. Cait saw Barion go down as one of the flaming spheres slammed into him. Ran, beside her, sheathed his sword and lifted a shield with both hands, ready to bat away any fireballs coming for her.

"Help me block them," said Hellen. The old witch was summoning walls of fog once more. Cait did what she could. She lacked the skill for the spell but lent her strength to the effort, leaning against the castle wall for support as she grimaced. She could feel the other witches adding their voices to the magic. The fog, when it formed, was thin, misty, but it had the desired effect. Fireballs flew into it, lighting up streaks of red, but none passed through.

In response, the undain threw even greater numbers at the walls, hauling up more ladders, trying to overwhelm the witches' ability to slick the walls with ice. Some of the giants even began to hurl small, snarling undain directly onto the battlements. Hand-to-hand fighting raged all the way across the fortress. The tide of undain showed no sign of abating.

Then blaring, metallic horns sounded from the distance. In an instant the undain stopped fighting and fell back from the walls. The horns sounded again, calling a descending note, and the undain raced away like a receding tide, answering some urgent summons.

Cait, badly out of breath, the stitches in her side making it hard to move, tried to make sense of it. Barion, scorched and cut but still alive, limped up. "Den. He has reached the carts. The undain rush to defend them."

Cait knew little about war and battles, but she remembered enough from history lessons to know armies had to maintain their supply lines. Without the reserves of Spirit the undain were doomed. The defenders slumped to the ground, exhausted, or else they tended to the wounded, winding bandages around tattooed arms and legs. Hellen added her magic to that, too, healing and soothing where she could. A strange silence washed across the walls, broken only by the grunts and cries of pain from the wounded. Everyone waited, staring over the An and the woods to see what would happen next.

Cait, reaching out with her mind, felt Den and the other cavalry die. She saw glimpses of screaming, bucking horses, of riders falling to the ground, grimaces of pain, blood spraying from wounds. She saw, also, the cartloads of Spirit that the wyrm lords had managed to reach. More than one was overturned, sent smashing to the ground, their precious cargo soaking into the earth. Cait felt the surge of relief in the aether as the ground drank the spirits from each spillage.

The sensation was repeated again and again as more of the carts were upheaved. The horns sounded once more, an angry buzzing. Cait caught more glimpses of desperate fighting, of horses crashing wide-eyed to the ground. Then it stopped. She could sense no more living riders, no more horses. Den and his cavalry had been destroyed.

The renewed attack came a moment later. The undain surged forward once more, streaming up the slopes of the hill. More ladders were laid against the walls while more undain climbed the walls. In a few moments, the screaming, crashing battle resumed with full intensity. Perhaps Den had achieved something and the undain were throwing everything at the fortress while they still could. If the wyrm lords could withstand the assault for a while longer, perhaps there was a chance.

For another hour, or more, the onslaught continued. Wave after wave of the undain surged up the walls. Each time they were repulsed, but each time the line of defenders grew thinner and thinner. Barion, Jenath and Axana, the surviving Wing chiefs, walked among the riders, calling out encouragement, wading in with sword and dagger when the attacks came.

The riders fought with calm, controlled discipline, attacking, defending, attacking. More than once, Cait thought they would succumb to the numbers of attackers. Each time, incredibly, they fought back. The violence and death went on and on, and it seemed there would never be an end to it.

Then flying undain flapped through the tatters of Hellen's fog. They were ugly, ungainly creatures, their movements clumsy and halting, something like the Bone Harvester she'd seen in Angere. It seemed incredible the creatures could fly at all. Their bones were visible through their tattered flesh, as if the person creating them hadn't bothered to complete their work. Each bore three or four attackers on their backs, ferrying them to the walls.

Fer had destroyed one of these sorcerous creatures, unleashing her secret magic to break it apart. Cait wished she could do the same, but she had no idea how. She tried to hit the creatures with ice, to freeze their joints from the inside as she'd done in Angere. At the same moment the riders' arrows and spears hit, pinging and skittering off the undain. One, a wing-joint mangled by a well-aimed spear, spiralled to the ground, the undain riders upon it falling onto the attacking hordes. But the other flying creatures lurched to the walls. They crashed rather than landed onto the battlements or fully inside the fortress.

Riders rushed to swarm around each, their organized formations in stark contrast to the desperate lashing and swinging of the undain. Again, the attackers relied on numbers rather than skill.

Desperate fighting broke out all around Caer L'dun. Barion had kept a small group of defenders back in the central tower. These he now unleashed, sending them running into the courtyard to fight the flying undain and their passengers. The riders on the battlements, meanwhile, were attacked from all sides: from those scaling the walls, from those undain who had crash-landed in the courtyard behind them, and even from above, as those flying in fired arrows or dropped rocks.

Barion and Jenath still fought alongside the remaining riders. Cait could see no sign of Axana. The desperate fighting raged on and on, the ferocity of the undain matched by the grim determination of the riders.

Ran and Borrn fought together on the steps of the tower that Cait and Hellen worked their magic from. The scuffling and clanging from their combat echoed up the stone stairway. Impossible to know how many were trying to force their way up, who was winning. Cait tried to ignore the danger and focus on the battle before her, hurling out ice into the ranks of the attackers where she could. Her efforts were weakening. She had little strength left. More than once the world seemed to recede from her as she unleashed some bolt of ice, dizziness washing over her. Hellen, too, was struggling, her face a mask of pain as she worked and worked at her magic.

Then, again, the horns blared across the battlefield. Once again the screaming hordes retreated, undain falling from the walls to scurry or crawl away. The attack had been repulsed. Borrn and Ran reappeared, both bleeding, Borrn breathing heavily from his exertions.

"They're retreating," said Cait. "We've actually beaten them."

But Borrn, walking to the open windows, stared westward, across the river, alarm clear in his blue eyes. Cait turned to follow his gaze, see what he was seeing.

The mist had closed in, now, so that sky and fog and ice were one uniform greyness. But something was emerging from the gloom of the An: three vast, trundling contraptions, their approach making the ice rumble. All the fighting ceased as wyrm lords and undain together stood to watch the fresh assault Menhroth was sending against Caer L'dun.

Cait had the impression of huge skeletons as the veils parted: A-shaped frames of interlocking bones lashed together upon moving platforms. They were huge: as tall as a three or four storey building. The frames held pivoting arms, as if the devices were a nightmarish cross between a child's swing and a see-saw. Human-sized undain swarmed over each, winding cranks and turning wheels, or else simply standing to watch the tower of Caer L'dun coming into view, like sailors on the deck of a sailing boat.

They were machines, siege-engines. Catapults. She'd seen something similar back home, on weekend trips to mediaeval fairs, but never anything on this scale. A brown tail snaked out behind each, leading back into the mists. Pipelines. The bone catapults were being fed Spirit directly from the White City, fuelling their movements.

The detail puzzled Cait. Why did the undain need to employ necromancy to build siege-engines? Instinctively she reached out with her mind's eye to study the trundling machines.

She saw immediately: the machines were alive. There was a mind in each of them, a controlling intelligence. Somewhere in each latticework of bones were those of the single person who had been transformed, remade into one of these hulking, creaking contraptions. Fer had described something similar in the flying undain she'd destroyed on the banks of the An: bones from many bodies cut and lashed together, necromancy and mechanics combining to make a new life form.

Cait could feel the seething malevolence coming from each, the glee at seeing Caer L'dun. They had been constructed for one purpose, the destruction of the wyrm lords' fortress. She wondered who they'd been, these three individuals. Had they accepted their fate with delight or horror? Many more bones had been added to their bodies, lashed into their structure. Some of the additions were huge, perhaps even dragon bones. There'd been remains that large in the crypt beneath Car D'nar.

The great machines stopped their advance. The undain riding along on them leaped off, teams of them moving to turn wheels that drilled spiral anchors down into the ice.

At the same time the great arms of the three machines began to tilt backward, straining against thick sinew-like ropes. At the end of each arm was something like a hand, cupping a single, round boulder the size of a car. Spirit energy fizzed through the machines as they prepared to fire. Cait caught glimpses of the devices' thoughts, weighing up distances and trajectories.

"Can you reach them?" asked Cait. "Will arrows fly that far?"

Borrn shook his head. "They're out of range of our weapons, as they must have known. Can magic not destroy them, cripple them?"

She reached into the mind of the middle of the three machines. Perhaps she could confuse it, disrupt it. Even persuade it to turn, send its boulder crashing into one of the other machines rather than at the fortress. She could see no other way.

The mind in the machine laughed at her, dismissive. It was far too strong, fuelled by all that Spirit. Cait tried again but it was like battering against walls of glass or ice. Gasping from the effort of it she staggered back, the walls of Caer L'dun about her once more. She shook her head as Borrn raised a questioning eyebrow at her.

The first of the catapults unwound. The undain leaped from the device as the great arm shot forward with alarming speed, stretched ropes pulling on it as the Spirit pumping into the machine pushed. The contraption shot backward despite the anchors, part of the A-frame buckling from the weight and strain of hurling the boulder into the sky.

The partial collapse of the catapult made little difference. Cait watched as the huge rock arched toward them, graceful and silent, looming larger each moment like a new moon in the sky. It soon became clear the machine's aim was true. To cries of alarm, the boulder smashed into one of the walls of Caer L'dun, striking it at its base, punching a ragged hole clean through.

Dragonriders tumbled as the breached wall crumbled, spilling the helpless defenders on top of it to the ground.

The undain army roared as it prepared to flood into the castle.

12 – VOICES IN THE DARK

England

Fer was standing in the dark of a moonless night when the attack came.

She'd had trouble sleeping, pursued in her dreams by nameless, faceless horrors, forever reaching out to touch her as she fled from them. She'd left Catherine and the Lizard King snoring in the tumbledown stone hut they'd made their home for the past two weeks and stepped outside, hoping the cold night air would bring her to her senses and drive the phantoms from her mind.

The world was hushed, the night moonless. She liked the feeling of the darkness enfolding her, but she worked a werelight to stop herself tripping on the rough ground. In its pearly glow a pair of white eyes shone from the night, but she knew from the slow, panicky mind behind them it was only one of the sheep that roamed the hillsides. In the distance, the agonized cry of a fox cut through the night air.

Fer breathed deeply, savouring the peace, the safety. This strange world unsettled her with its noise and speed and flashing lights. She felt more herself in the wilds and woods, far from road and city. But they were never truly safe. They often saw gleaming machines flying high and silent overhead, or else clattering away in the distance behind the trees. There was danger everywhere. Sometimes she thought she was losing her mind, unclear whether the voices she heard were her own, or those of lost spirits in the aether, or whether they were the words of the disembodied voices that spoke from their machines.

She hugged herself tightly against the cold. She'd had a bad dream; she was spooked, that was all. The inactivity wasn't good for her.

They'd seen no pursuit since their flight from Glastonbury; it seemed Genera genuinely thought them either dead or in Andar. Catherine was a little better, too, a little more her old self, although Fer still caught a look of bleakest despair in her eyes from time to time. Understandably. The old witch had lost her daughter and probably her granddaughter. There were no words Fer could speak, no spell she could work, to make that any better. Still, they'd begun to discuss the future, talk about taking up the fight against the enemy once more. In truth there was little they could do, but it would be good simply to do something. Do *anything*. Keep busy, keep her thoughts about Andar and her family and the people she'd grown up with at bay.

Her thoughts often turned to Seleena, the witch who had set out with them on the journey to this world and who had been killed in the Tanglewood. That could so easily have been her, Fer. Perhaps it was best not to think about such things. She thought about Hellen a lot, too. The old witch had annoyed her with her meddling and her instructions, but Fer found herself missing Hellen now, wishing she were there. They needed all the help they could get.

The assault on her mind that hit her threw her into desperate panic. She'd let her defences slip a little, lulled by the quiet of the night. She fell to her knees, hands clutched to the sides of her head as if to press the intrusion from her mind. The presence from her nightmares was still there, in the real world, sending its tendrils over her, tasting and feeling, tapping and pressing to find a way inside.

With a cry of effort, Fer cast the creature back, making the walls around her thoughts strong again. She would not let them invade her. She knelt on the wet ground, panting heavily. She waited for further attack but the presence was gone, like a night time creature startled at being seen. She began to breathe once more.

She had to be more careful. There were undain everywhere in this world and they were looking for her, always searching. She'd learned to keep her thoughts guarded, of course. Everyone in Andar did so from a young age, even when they were sleeping. But she had never needed to resist such unrelenting attack. She had to get better at keeping her enemies out of her mind. She wondered if Cait, if she were even still alive, was learning to do the same. Her cousin was so untrained, so open.

Something touched Fer on the arm and she gasped in alarm, scrambling backward to escape. Her werelight had gone out in the attack, and now there was someone in the darkness. It gripped her tight.

"Fer, it's OK. It's me." The voice of the wise man, the Lizard King. He'd come out to find her when he heard her cry. "What happened?" He took his hand from her arm.

Fer flared the werelight into life again, making it sputter above her head. "I was attacked."

"Attacked magically?"

"There was a presence seeking for me, sniffing me out."

The Lizard King didn't speak for a moment as he searched the aether for the enemy Fer had described. "I see nothing now. It feels like we are alone." The Lizard King's face was lined with concern. "Are you sure it was an attack?"

Fer rose to her feet and began to brush the dirt from her clothes. "Of course I'm sure. What else would it be?"

"I don't know. It's just … there is something I recognize in the air. Like an echo of a familiar voice."

"Whose?"

"I'm not sure. One I've heard before I think."

"It was still an attack."

He nodded, his forehead furrowed. One of the lizard tattoos that adorned the skin of his neck tilted its head as if it were studying Fer.

"Sometimes," he said, "when I slip into the thoughts of others, the person sees it as an assault and reacts as you have."

"As they should. You can't invade the mind of another like that. It's repulsive."

She caught the flicker of dismay that crossed his features and regretted her words. She knew he had grave doubts about what he did. He was a good man, honourable enough to be troubled by his abilities. And she should be grateful to him. His intervention had saved them outside the concert hall.

He didn't reply, only nodding his head as if he agreed with her.

"Forgive me," she said. "I didn't mean you. I know you only act when driven by need. But there was nothing gentle or subtle about this attack. Someone or something tried to force their way into my mind. It has to be the undain or Genera."

"I suppose," said the Lizard King, although there was a note of doubt in his voice. "You kept them out?"

"Yes. But whoever or whatever it was knew I was here. We may not be as safe as we thought."

The Lizard King paused before he spoke as he often did, as if he consulted with invisible presences in the aether. "Then I suppose it is time we returned to civilisation as we discussed. I've been thinking Catherine might be up to the journey now. At least if we're moving we'll be harder to trace."

"You mean back to Manchester?"

"The city is at the centre of things in this world. Genera has its headquarters there."

"Perhaps it's the worst place to go then," said Fer. She wished more than anything she could have gone back home with Johnny. Andar needed her. "They won't let you simply go back to your old life."

"I know," said the Lizard King. "I'm not sure anywhere is really safe. But perhaps we can antagonize the enemy somehow when we're there, deal them a blow when their attention is turned to the other world."

Fer sighed. "Perhaps. It seems pretty hopeless. Angere is so powerful and we're so weak. What difference can a few little spells, werelights and a bit of ice, really make?"

"If there's one thing I've learned from all my eavesdropping it's that everyone is vulnerable, everyone is flawed. We all have secret weaknesses."

"Hard to see any weakness in *them*."

The Lizard King looked thoughtful. "It might be something small, so insignificant they've overlooked it. It might be something huge, so big they haven't even seen it. But it will be there."

"Well, we can try at least," said Fer. "How do we get back to the city?"

The Lizard King smiled in the glow of the werelight. "Walk, I suppose."

They made their way north for a week, trailing across fields and woods, occasionally chancing a short journey by bus or train. For much of the time they navigated using the map and the lodestone – the *compass* – built into the Lizard King's phone. Or, to preserve battery, they used the sun and stars to guide them. Catherine showed Fer how to find the North Star in this world. A figure that resembled a ladle or a pan with a bent handle pointed the way. The shape was a bear, supposedly, but Fer couldn't see it. By day they simply kept the low winter sun to their backs. Or sometimes, if the sky was a uniform grey, the Lizard King found north by studying the scattered houses and farms they came across.

"How can you tell which way is north from them?" asked Fer. "Some sort of magical divination?"

The Lizard King shook his head at her words. "Ah, no, not that. It's the satellite dishes. They always point south."

Mostly they slept out of doors, huddling inside sleeping-bags bought by the Lizard King at a large roadside shop, but on some nights it was too cold, or too wet, and they had to chance a night at a convenient Wayhouse. A *pub* as Catherine called them. The woman was tough, and never complained, but winter was coming on quickly, and it was clear from her stiffness each morning that the cold wasn't good for her joints. Fortunately the Lizard King had come prepared with a plentiful supply of paper money to pay for what shelter and food they needed. The warmth and comfort of a proper bed was always welcome, even if Fer always lay awake listening, heart pounding at each night time thump and scurry.

Every excursion into civilisation was a risk. Each day they had to cross numerous roads, Fer always feeling very exposed. The cars and lorries roared by so quickly she didn't have time to study who or what was inside. When it was dark, the machines' blinding lights seemed to pick Fer out, pin her in place. If a vehicle slowed down her stomach fluttered in alarm. Cait and Danny had been pursued by riders on two-wheeled machines. *Motorbikes*. Fer kept a special watch out for those, although fortunately there seemed to be few of them about in the winter.

Whenever they were in public, she and Catherine worked magic to alter their appearances, enough to fool casual glances thrown their way. Maintaining the glamours was an effort, one they could only sustain for an hour or two at most, and Fer was under no illusion the undain would be deceived. As the days went on, it seemed inevitable she and the others would be spotted at some point. The intrusive attacks on her mind continued, but she was ready for them and kept them out.

Despite all the dangers they managed to remain undetected so far as they could tell. They'd kept the Lizard King's phone charged, and the bookwyrm reported to them no sign Genera knew where they were, no chatter about them on the mysterious *network*. It was possible the creature didn't see all the messages of their enemies for reasons Fer didn't fully understand, and Fer spent her days searching the world around her with her mind's eye as well. So far as she could tell, no one was following them or lying in wait for them.

One evening, as Catherine lay snoring in her sleeping-bag, Fer sat with the Lizard King beside the small fire they'd allowed themselves. The wet sticks smoked and spat in their little circle of stones, but they gave off a welcome warmth. The weather was changing, colder than it had been. That morning, the ground and leaves had sparkled with a thick frost. By the look of the hard stars in the sky it would be the same tomorrow.

"Have you suffered any more attacks?" the wise man asked.

"A few," said Fer. "So far they haven't broken through."

"That is good."

"Yes, I suppose." In truth it was a small victory. What chance did they really have against the monsters of Angere, their servants in this world with their terrible machines? She and Catherine and the Lizard King were walking to their own deaths. They had little choice, they had to try, but she was under no illusions. It wouldn't be enough.

If only the people here had fought back, done *something* over the years. Most of them happily accepted their subjugation. No, that wasn't it. It was worse in a way. Most of them didn't even notice. They lived with this terrible weight upon them, the vile machines leeching away a portion of their souls, and they didn't even know. Why hadn't they rebelled, raged, refused to be broken down? Anger at all of them flooded through her. The people of this world had allowed Angere to become what it had, and now everything would be destroyed. Andar would be destroyed.

She wanted to hurl these bitter accusations at the man sitting quietly beside her, poking his stick into the fire. She held her tongue, making herself breathe. She had no right to criticize the inhabitants of this world. People at home were just the same: peaceful Andar slumbered, its people refusing to see the nightmares at their door. That was how folk were. They dealt with the small things, the things they had some control over, and by those means navigated the treacherous quest from dawn to dusk one more time. It was as if some dangers were simply too big to see or comprehend. The weather was changing, and the nightmares drifted across the An to trouble the sleep of those in Andar, but few had paid any attention.

She caught the gaze of the wise man, suddenly alarmed he might be able to read her mind, see her troubled thoughts. His mild expression gave nothing away. She had no right to be angry with him. He had lived his life under the rule of Angere, knowing what was going on but unable to do anything about it. He had willingly sacrificed everything to help her, twice now, risking his life to do what he could. And in truth she wasn't angry with him, or anyone in this world. She was tired and frightened. She was angry with herself, at her own powerlessness, her own limitations. The light was fading and there was nothing she could do. Her own people were fleeing and dying and she had escaped the slaughter. It would make little difference in the end, but still she felt like she'd betrayed them, left them to their fate.

In the end all she said was, "We should get some sleep."

The Lizard King nodded in reply but didn't speak.

Manchester was an orange glow spreading across the horizon when they stopped for a final night's stay on their journey north. They stood on the lip of a steep hillside. In front of them, the land dropped sharply away to the plain upon which the distant city and its outlying towns lay. The scale of the habitations in this world still dazzled Fer, but at least it might mean Genera would have trouble finding them.

The rain they'd trudged through earlier had lifted, and a few white stars glinted above them. A crescent moon hung low in the western sky, lines of cloud barring it as if someone had attempted to scribble it out. Fer sneezed, the sound loud enough to be heard for many yards. At some point on their journey they'd all picked up colds, which hadn't made sleeping in the wilds any more enjoyable. Her nose and throat were prickly and raw and her legs felt like they were made of heavy wood. Still, it had to be worse for Catherine, although the older witch never mentioned it.

Fer turned to Catherine and the Lizard King to suggest they seek a place under the trees to sleep for the night. The wise man had said there were caves in the rock around there. Perhaps they could lay out their sleeping bags in one to keep the rain off.

But as Fer turned she saw the Lizard King slump to the ground. He curled up in a ball and began to make little snuffling sounds as if he were shivering with cold. Catherine knelt beside him, placing a hand on his shoulder, her eyes wide with concern.

Fer crouched, too. She'd been so busy keeping their enemies out of her own mind that she hadn't noticed the wise man being assaulted. Despite his abilities he was weak when it came to other forms of magic. "Is it the undain?" she asked. "Have they found us?"

"No," said Catherine after a pause. She stroked the Lizard King's hair. "Just a vision I think. It can be like this for him sometimes, when the eyes he's borrowing are far away or hard to reach."

"What do we do?"

"All we can do is wait and watch over him. Make sure he doesn't harm himself."

A car sped by on the nearby road, lights briefly illuminating the skeletal trees. It didn't stop.

"We're too exposed out here," said Fer. "We won't be able to move him if anyone comes."

"There's nothing we can do," said Catherine. "We'll be safe enough if no one knows we're here."

Fer placed her own hand onto the Lizard King, as if she could calm him with her touch. His muscles were as hard as wood, tense as he shook and whimpered. The tattooed lizards that adorned his skin also had their eyes closed tight. They clung to their ink branches as if enduring a howling gale, some shaking and swaying.

"It must be hard for him," said Fer, "having blackouts that come upon him unbidden like this."

"Yes," said Catherine. "I wouldn't want his gift for all the tea in China."

She had no idea what that meant. "Does he get any warning?"

Catherine sighed. "I don't think so, no. We're fortunate one didn't come upon him when he was driving."

"Yes."

Slowly the Lizard King's shaking and breathing began to calm. The muscles in his shoulders and neck relaxed. A lizard opened one of its purple eyes.

"It's passing off," said Catherine. She still stroked the wise man's hair, as if he were a sick child. After a few moments, the man's eyes flickered open. He looked puzzled for a moment, perhaps unsure of where he was and who he was with. Then he spoke.

"Sorry. It came upon me suddenly."

"Are you hurt?" asked Catherine.

"No, no, I don't think so. Bit my tongue, that's all."

"What did you see? Where were you?"

"Andar," said the wise man. "I was with Cait."

Catherine gave a little gasp of joy. "She's still alive? She made it across the river?"

"Yes. She was with friends. Hellen was there. Ran and Nox too, and also the boy. Danny."

"Danny's alive as well?" said Catherine.

"Yes."

Catherine closed her eyes for a moment, absorbing the news, drinking it in. "Thank the stars. Oh that's wonderful."

"What about Johnny?" asked Fer.

"I didn't see him, but he was somewhere around I think. Getting back to him was in Cait's thoughts."

"So he did make it through to Andar."

"I think so," said the Lizard King. "But there was danger all around. Cait's fear burned brightly."

"Where were they?" said Fer. "What was happening?"

"A city of tall towers. The streets and squares were thronged with thousands of people. Some sort of celebration, but everyone was fleeing in panic, fighting to escape."

"Guilden," said Fer. "The Ice Fair."

"The undain army was attacking. Cait and the others had inflicted a blow on them, destroyed some of them, but it wasn't enough. The city was about to be overwhelmed."

"Where was Cait going? What were they doing?"

"I don't know. Her mind was filled with alarm as they battled through the crowds."

"South," said Catherine. "All they can do is flee south. Hellen must have taken them north to try and defeat or slow the undain but they weren't powerful enough."

Fer met her gaze. "If they're at Guilden it won't be long before the rest of Andar falls. Time is running out." She sat back on the damp grass. It seemed hopeless. Minute by minute, her home was being destroyed and there was nothing she could do. She was so far away, so powerless to help. Despair flooded through her and she couldn't hold it back.

In that moment of vulnerability, the being that had harried her and attacked her all the way north found its opening. Before Fer could summon the strength to repel the attack, the presence entered her, its voice a cry of glee and hunger in Fer's mind.

Fer cried out and covered her head with her arms, as if that would keep her attacker at bay. The presence of another being inside her own head, her own thoughts, was sickening; it was the worst sort of violation. She fought back, desperate to be free of the mind rampaging through her thoughts, assaulting her. She was aware of Catherine nearby, her words of concern, but Fer ignored them.

In her mind, she saw a blazing light that was the alien presence. It was blinding to look at, painful, but she threw herself at it. She had to defeat it, expel it at all cost. If it were one of the undain lords the fight would be grim and perhaps too much for her. She didn't hesitate. She had the words of the family secret; she could use them once more. If she didn't, they'd take away everything she was, strip her of herself. Make her one of them.

A shape began to emerge from the light, its form warping and shifting as if glimpsed through the air above a fire. Fer stopped and waited, steeling herself for the battle to come.

The figure wavered and became solid. But instead of one of the undain, a young girl stood there, hair lank, dressed in a stained white robe that reached down to her ankles. She clutched something to her chest. A tatty rag doll something like the one Fer had played with as a girl.

The girl swept closer without appearing to walk. "Hello, Fer," she said. "My name is Bethany. Cait sent me to find you and give you a message. I've been trying to talk to you for such a long time." The girl grinned, as if the whole thing were a game.

Fer paused, confused, caught between revulsion at the intrusion and sympathy for the lost young girl before her.

"You were inside Cait's mind weren't you? I … I caught a glimpse of you."

"Oh yes. I travelled with her for a while, but now I've come home."

Fer stepped closer, studying the girl's face. Cait hadn't understood how this union, this *haunting*, was possible, but Fer knew how it worked. "You're one of us. You're related to Cait and you're related to me."

The girl giggled. "Of course. My family came from Andar, but I'm from here. I helped Cait in the other world, and now I've come to help you in this one."

The girl looked around, as if inspecting her new home. There were suddenly trees there, tall boughs, red and brown and grey, illuminated by the dappled light of summer. A carpet of white flowers. The woods of Andar in Fer's mind.

"Oh good," the girl said. "Much better than icy water. I think I'm going to like it here. Are you ready to begin? I think I know what we have to do to hurt the Masters."

13 – TO THE CENTRE OF THE CITY

"We have to get safely into the centre of the city," said Fer. "We have to reach the Shadow Town Hall. Once again we need your help, oh wise and noble archaeon."

Fer waited for the bookwyrm to respond, letting it play its little game of feigning boredom. As before, the creature dwarfed her, although its appearance was very different now. In the Tanglewood it had resembled a dragon from the old tales of Angere. Sulphurous smoke had drifted from its scaly snout as it lay curled in its cave. Now its smooth lines glinted like polished glass, as if it were fashioned from some silvery, molten metal. When it opened its eyes she saw, instead of her own tiny image reflected in the black depths, lines of glowing letters and numbers scrolling rapidly upward. The rough stone of the cavern walls had been replaced by bare metal, polished and reflective, making it hard to see what was real and what was image. Although, of course, the whole thing was an illusion, a game.

The bookwyrm had taken up residence, *uploaded* itself, to the internet of this world, and there found more knowledge than it had absorbed in centuries of life in the tomes and scrolls of Andar. In the process it had changed, transmuted, become an altogether different form of life. It lived in the machines as it had once inhabited the thoughts and ideas within the old books. It had also multiplied, making thousands – perhaps millions – of copies of itself, so that it could occupy all the computers at the same moment. And, seemingly, converse with itself when it wanted to.

Fer didn't understand much of what any of that meant. Cait and Danny had tried to explain it to her, but she lacked knowledge of even the words they used. She did know that many things in this world were controlled by these computers, and that many of them were connected to each other. This allowed them to converse, to exchange news and instructions and *data*. It all seemed magical, especially as she could see nothing connecting the machines. The words and voices and pictures simply appeared on the screens of the phones they carried. Appeared from *somewhere*. She'd been assured it wasn't magic at all, but secretly she had her doubts. Or, at least, thinking it was magic helped her understand. If she assumed computers and phones were basically a form of witchcraft, they made sense to her.

The archaeon lifted its head to study her with its glowing, computer screen eyes. "You are mistaken, little witch. There is no such place as a *Shadow Town Hall* in Manchester. Perhaps you misunderstood what was told to you?"

Fer tried her best to ignore the creature's mockery. "The Shadow Town Hall is a very well kept secret," she said, "but I'm assured it is real by one who has been there. It is a gathering place. Unsacred ground. The only ones who know about it are the dead, and they tend not to write much down. Or to upload things to the internet."

"The dead, little witch?"

"Not all of them you understand. The restless ones. The angry ones. Their quiet voices fill the air of this city whenever there is a moment of calm. I was aware of their grim chorus as soon as I arrived."

The dragon exhaled, filling the air with smoke. Instead of the stench of sulphur, the smell was more acrid, like burning plastic or metal. "And you converse with these dead?" asked the bookwyrm, amusement clear in its voice.

"Bethany is as real as you, bookwyrm. Perhaps more so: at least she lived and breathed once. At least she was more than lines on paper or dots on a screen."

"Ah, Bethany is it?"

"So you know of her?"

"No, no," said the dragon, closing its eyes once more. "It simply sounds like the sort of name someone would invent for a – forgive me – imaginary friend."

Fer resisted the urge to punch the ridiculous beast on the nose. The wyrm was simply taking pleasure in riling her. It would surely know about the sprits of the witches in the orchard on Islagray, and many other instances of people lingering after their deaths.

Fer forced herself to speak calmly. "So would you like to meet my imaginary friend?"

One eye opened slightly, revealing a few lines of the scrolling symbols. "Oh, I'd like that very much, little witch. By all means summon her. Do wake me when you've finished your necromancy."

Was such a thing even possible? Bethany was a ghost that haunted her, a shape in the aether, without physical form. And the archaeon was – what? Something similar. The cavern Fer stood in didn't really exist. It was the dragon's idea of itself. Perhaps it was in her mind, or perhaps it was an island in the aether like the Tanglewood. Whichever, she couldn't see why Bethany and the bookwyrm shouldn't be able to meet. It had to be worth a try.

Fer closed her eyes to find the whisper of the witch-girl. The presence of the other within felt uncomfortable, irritating, like a thorn embedded deep in her flesh. There was nothing to be done about it now. She wondered how Cait had borne it for so long.

Speaking softly, trying to ignore the troubling thought that she was looking for a dream within a dream, Fer set about coaxing Bethany into the light.

It took several minutes, during which time the archaeon affected a deep, rumbling snore. When Bethany appeared, little more than a sketch of faint grey lines, her eyes were wide with fear. To her, dragons were no different to the undain or the Masters who had made her young life such a misery, or the boggarts and goblins whose stories had been told to her. They were all monsters.

Moving slowly, Fer took Bethany by the ghostly hand and led her from the shadows of the passageway toward the great creature. Bethany held back, reluctant, but she responded to Fer's reassurances and allowed herself to be brought forward. In a few paces the two of them stood before the head of the wyrm.

Fer cleared her throat and spoke in a loud, clear voice. "This is Bethany Weerd, noble and wise archaeon. She is my relative and forebear from centuries past. I'm afraid she is dead, but she would like to speak to you nevertheless."

The archaeon opened its eyes once more. For a moment Fer thought the dragon, seeing nothing, would roar its laughter at her. Instead the creature, studying Bethany, tilted its head to one side, like a dog trying to understand human speech.

It sniffed. "Hmm, interesting…"

Fer, Catherine and the Lizard King crept warily into the city early the following morning. The two witches took turns to maintain the glamour about themselves as they trudged along. They were well-enough practised at it now.

Fer tried hard not to look nervously around at every car, every passer-by. Traffic was already building up, making snaking lines of cars crawl along the roads. Each time one slowed nearby, moths fluttered in Fer's stomach. At every moment she expected shouts, the grasp of a hand on her arm.

The plumes of choking smoke from the cars and buses made her cough and splutter. No one else seemed to be affected. Most people on the pavements had their gaze cast to the ground, or else they stared into the distance as they listened to music from one of their machines. Fer tried to maintain the same attitude of bored indifference. She had to resist the urge to check her reflection in every shop window they passed, in the glass of every car as it crept by.

The background chorus of sighs and moans that she'd heard – or felt – in the aether on her previous visit mounted as the streets grew busier. Perhaps it was the city's equivalent of the Song. The sound's volume mounted the farther into the city they walked, seeming to sing from the red bricks and the stone ground. Fer cast a glance at Cait's gran each time the noise stepped up a notch, but the old witch appeared to be unaware of it. Perhaps you really didn't hear it if you lived in the city all your life. And perhaps if you were like the Lizard King you had to learn to blot the sound out to stop yourself from going mad. At times, the noise took on a shrill, keening edge that sent a shudder through Fer's bones.

When she could, Catherine led them off the wide roads onto narrower side-streets. They still had to cross the main roads, though, and Fer saw several sets of cameras peering down at them from tall buildings. The Lizard King said they were mostly there to watch the flow of traffic, but Fer wasn't convinced. She could *feel* the devices watching her. They had to hope the bookwyrm was doing what it had promised, removing their images from any pictures the cameras captured. She'd hoped the glamours would deceive the machines, but apparently that wasn't the case. The cameras saw the three of them as they really were.

What was worse, the machines could scan whole crowds of people and identify individuals with ease. Why did people allow it? The phones everyone carried could be used to track their movements, too. Again, the bookwyrm assured them it was perfectly capable of stopping that happening. Again, Fer was unconvinced. Her nervousness increased with each step. She found she was clenching her jaw tight, making her cheek muscles hurt. She breathed deeply, trying to make herself relax.

Ahead of her, Catherine stopped suddenly. "Oh. That's not good."

Up ahead, the road they were on was blocked by three ruined cars, one on its side. All three had been set on fire and were now little more than heaps of smoking brown metal. The road was strewn with rocks and sparkling shards of glass. The police were there, clad in bulky uniforms, keeping people away. The stench of plastic and metal in the air reminded Fer of the bookwyrm's smoke.

"What has happened?" asked Fer.

"More trouble," said Catherine. "A riot by the look of it." Fer began to pick out more details: the smashed glass of the houses' windows, doors that had been battered into splinters.

"Genera," said the Lizard King. "The Spirit extractors."

"It's getting worse," said Catherine. "If we don't stop them soon, who knows how bad it will get."

"It isn't normally like this?" asked Fer.

"No." Catherine sighed, and the lines on her face were etched deeper than usual. "I mean, there's unrest occasionally, but I haven't seen it this bad in a long time."

From somewhere nearby the wailing of police cars or ambulances filled the air. The sound was angry and mournful at the same time, echoing off the houses and walls so that its direction was impossible to work out. Fer's heart raced as the sound grew louder, reached a blaring peak … and then faded away as the vehicle sped elsewhere. She couldn't shake off the suspicion it had been looking for them.

"We have to do what Cait told us as soon as possible," she said. "Perhaps we'll be helping both worlds."

Catherine nodded, her gaze fixed on the burned-out husks of the cars. "Yes. Let's backtrack, find a different way into the centre. Those might be normal police up ahead, and they might not be."

They'd only just started moving again when the Lizard King's phone made an urgent buzzing sound. The wise man looked puzzled as he pulled the device from his jacket pocket and studied the screen.

"Someone contacting you?" said Catherine. "I thought no one knew the number."

The tattooed man studied the screen through narrowed eyes. "It's OK. It's the archaeon getting my attention." He lifted the phone to his ear and listened for long moments, saying nothing. Occasionally he nodded his head, his expression mournful. Finally he slipped the device back into his pocket.

The tattooed lizard on his neck slid out of sight to hide underneath his collar as the man spoke. "The bookwyrm says we've been spotted. Genera know we're here."

"How?" said Fer. "Didn't it hide us from their machines like it promised?"

The Lizard King shrugged his shoulders. "It says it kept us perfectly hidden but that one of the undain must have spotted us." He peered upward. A flock of raucous birds thronged overhead, dark against the brightening blue of the dawn sky. Beyond them, lit up gold by the rising sun, one of the flying machines let out a straight line of smoke or steam as it flew to who-knew where.

"They're all around us," said Catherine, her eyes shut as she concentrated. "I've been aware of them for a while."

Fer quested with her mind's eye and soon saw them. Hundreds, thousands, of the undain, pitch pools in the darkness. The monsters were all around, apparently watching and waiting. "Why don't they come for us? It makes no sense."

Catherine's eyes were troubled as she replied. "I think *they* think we're heading for the Library, to try and reach the Andar portal. Where else would we be going? Clara Sweetley is herding us. She must have set a trap which she's letting us walk into. She must know now that Cait has succeeded in reaching Andar. With Fiona gone that only leaves me and you, Fer, with the blood the undain crave. They won't risk spilling it. They'll wait until we're in their power, safely out of sight in the basement of the Library, and then they'll show themselves."

"You don't think they know about the Shadow Town Hall?"

"I think it's a well-kept secret. I've never heard of it."

"How far is the Library from the Town Hall?"

"They're next to each other," said the Lizard King.

"Then … this might actually work in our favour," said Fer. "If they let us reach the Library they might not realise where we're really going until it's too late."

"Perhaps," said Catherine, although the haunted look didn't leave her face. "For now, I think we should go back to the big roads. Being in plain sight is our best defence. There are still plenty of normal people in Manchester. I did plan to stop in the grove where Cait and Danny found me, but now I think we should hurry on. We don't want Menhroth growing impatient and coming for us."

"Are you up to it?" asked Fer. The long walk had taken its toll on Cait's gran. She was moving stiffly and Fer had seen her wince more than once as she put weight on her right leg. A grim determination had come over her since the events at Glastonbury, and she spoke little as she plodded relentlessly forward. Her shoulders were more stooped than they had been.

"I'll be fine," said Catherine. "Don't worry about me."

"We could find you a cup of tea."

"Later. Not now."

"Why don't you head to the grove while the wise man

and I carry on to the centre?"

"Because I don't want to," Catherine snapped, her voice strained almost to breaking. "Now enough talking and let's go."

Her exhaustion and pain were making her cross. Fer thought about insisting she rest, then decided against it. Catherine had every right to be involved, to do what she could for Cait. To do *something*. Perhaps it was the only thing keeping her going.

They limped into the city centre, Catherine moving more and more slowly. The undain massed around them but kept their distance. Fer tried to pretend she hadn't seen them, hadn't caught glimpses of fang or claw from the corner of her eye. If she reacted, if she turned and ran, the spell would be broken. The undain would guess what they were really up to and attack. For now they had no choice but to dance their slow dance.

They worked their way up the long, straight road they'd walked down when first coming to Manchester, when Johnny had led them to the Golden Palace to meet the Lizard King. Its name was Oxford Road, a fact that amused Fer. Back home, there was a muddy crossing on a nearby stream referred to as the *ox ford*, and, indeed, there was a track to it from her village that people sometimes called the *ox ford road*. It was very different indeed from the snarled-up, stone street they trudged along.

They had to stop again and again for Catherine to get her breath back, but the woman refused to give in. Each time, with a nod, she set off once more. At one point they stopped outside a large shop whose windows were filled with many television screens, all broadcasting the same pictures of a shattered city somewhere, its buildings sagging to the ground, its streets nothing more than a jumble of debris and wreckage. And, here and there, a grimy child's face peeping out into the light. Large, ugly vehicle like guns on wheels lumbered along the streets. Whether there were people inside, or whether they were just machines, Fer couldn't tell.

Following that there were pictures of boats, crowded with standing people bobbing upon a rough sea. The people held out their arms, pleading for something. Some jumped or fell into the water. Then came images of bodies washing up on a beach, nothing more than flotsam in the foam, rolled onto the sand by the waves.

Was it all to do with Genera, the global extraction of Spirit? The sights filled Fer with bitter sickness. Perhaps it was like that back home, too, in Guilden and Hyrn's Oak and Woodhavn and every town and city she knew from her childhood. Perhaps there were, even now, boatloads of terrified people on the An, shivering children hugged close by their wide-eyed parents. If the river hadn't already frozen completely over.

"I see it all over the world," the Lizard King said as he looked at the screens. "A rising tide of misery, louder with each passing hour." He seemed to be talking to himself as much as them. When he glanced up at Fer she could see the horror in his eyes. He had to live with listening to that, seeing it through borrowed eyes. No, she didn't envy him either.

Fifteen minutes later they reached the city centre. She had never actually seen the Library from the outside. She and Johnny and Ran had escaped through the tunnels, following the witch-marks Catherine had left on the walls. It was a white, round building, huge like a fortress, glowing in the dawn light. A line of columns at its doors made Fer think of a row of teeth in some monstrous mouth.

Nobody tried to prevent them approaching. Hundreds of the monsters were there, gathered on the streets behind them like an audience at a mummer's play or a crowd at an execution. She couldn't identify living people among them any more. Although, up ahead, there was a beggar sitting against the wall of the Library, head down, huddling under rags. He, at least, was alive, the light from his mind in the aether flickering and pulsing oddly.

Turning to study their pursuers, she caught clear glimpses of the monsters' true selves among the human shapes in the crowd. Their trap about to be sprung, the undain were letting their masks slip. Tongues flicked across wide mouths of needle-sharp teeth. Red eyes shone from porcelain faces. Deep growls thrummed in the air. They were there on the tops of the buildings, too, watching and waiting for the final act.

Fer, Catherine and the Lizard King walked to the entrance of the Library, the spot where, according to Cait, she'd dropped the Grimoire at Nox's feet and everything had started.

"When I give the word, run," said Catherine, her voice a hiss.

"*Can* you run?" asked Fer.

"With that lot behind me, yes."

"You're in pain. You can barely walk."

"Then I'll hobble really quickly."

"Which way do we go?"

Catherine indicated with a nod of her head. "Follow the wall of the Library around. You'll see the Town Hall on the other side."

Bethany had explained that the Shadow Town Hall was a cavern, a void deep beneath the foundations of the real building. Fer wondered if there was a way to reach it from the tunnels they'd taken beneath the Library. Possibly not, the place was apparently sealed off to human access. A bad thing had happened there many years ago. Bethany was vague on the details, but people – children – had died and that had been the start of it. Slowly, over the years, others had arrived, seeping through the rock like rainwater. The cavern pulled in the dead from the cold earth for miles around, attracting them like moths to a dark flame, enticing them with its shared well of anger and loss. It was a place only the dead could enter.

And that was where she had to go.

The beggar was rocking his head from side to side, as if

trying to dislodge troubling thoughts. Then he looked up sharply at Fer, his gaze piercing. For a moment he looked puzzled. "You? Here? No, no, that isn't right. You mustn't be here. You have to flee, before they eat you. The hunt is coming. Can't you hear them sharpening their knives? Can't you see their staring eyes? Run and hide, run and hide!"

Catherine walked over to kneel beside him on his reeking, stained blanket. "It's alright, Tom." The man's gaze didn't leave Fer as she approached. Behind her sat a heavy wall of silence, as if the undain had stopped moving and were waiting for the word to make their move.

The beggar – Tom – looked to Catherine and then back to Fer, his cracked lips working as he tried to find the words to speak.

"Tom," whispered Catherine. "We need your help. Perhaps there's nothing you can do, but you were powerful and clever once, before the horror filled your mind."

"Help?" said Tom, his voice hesitant.

"That's right. The monsters behind us think we're going into the Library, but it's a trap. We're going to try and open the door to the Shadow Town Hall instead."

Tom looked so alarmed at that Fer thought he might burst into tears. "No, no," he said. "Run and hide, run and hide. Don't go there."

"Tom, please," said Catherine. "You've sat here all these years. Perhaps … perhaps you've been waiting for this moment without knowing it. I'm sorry to ask, truly, but we need your help. We are going to try it. They'll see immediately what we're doing and come for us. Please, remember what you once were and try and stop them. A few moments might make all the difference."

"The monsters?" He looked puzzled, grappling with difficult concepts.

"Yes," said Catherine. "We're going to try and stop them, stop them all."

There was a moment, brief, when understanding

flickered in the man's eyes. "Stop the demons?"

"Yes."

Tom looked back to Fer and the light went out of his eyes. "Monsters," he said again. "Run and hide, run and hide, run and hide."

Catherine sighed and stood. There was only despair on her face when she looked at Fer. "Well, it was worth a try. And now I think it's time we ran."

She turned and hobbled off, moving surprisingly quickly, away from the entrance and toward a high-sided canyon between the curving wall of the Library and the adjacent building.

Fer and the Lizard King bounded after her. And from behind, the wall of silence broke like a dam and the screaming horde of the undain threw themselves forward.

Fer knew they had no chance. True, most of the undain were behind them, arrayed in an arc around the entrance. They hadn't foreseen that Fer and the others weren't trying to get into the Library, which meant that their escape route was momentarily clear. But it wouldn't take long for the creatures to cover the distance. Fer glanced over her shoulder. The snarling, snapping throng was already at the entrance to the passageway, only paces behind.

Then a light blazed in the space between the two buildings, bright enough to make Fer flinch. Thrown off-balance by it, she stopped running and turned to see.

The silhouette of a figure appeared in the light, arms outstretched, cape held out wide. At first she thought it was one of the undain, a Lord maybe, come to claim them.

Then the light dimmed and she saw who it really was. The cape wasn't a cape; it was a tatty, smelly blanket. This was no undain; it was the beggar, Tom. He was screaming, but not from fear or pain. There was something like jubilation in his voice. Red light flared from his fingertips.

"Who *is* he?" asked Fer, watching in wonder.

"One of us, once," said Catherine from beside her. "Things went badly for him and he lost his way, but he was remarkable. It's a sad story."

"And what's he doing?"

"Holding back the flood. Come on, he's bought us the moments we need."

Fer turned away as seething shadows began to wind around the light that was Tom. He surely couldn't hold them back for long. She didn't wait to find out. Running beside Catherine and the Lizard King, they emerged around the curve of the Library onto another wide square, stone-flagged and lined with more high buildings on all sides.

Catherine turned right and led them past one building, across a road, and then along the front of an ornate edifice, as grand as anything in Guilden. Fer thought there'd be guards on the doors, but they entered the building without anyone barring their way.

"Which way?" asked Fer. The interior of the building was more dazzling than the outside, every surface decorated, the stone carved, the floor patterned, the glass of the windows coloured, the ceilings painted with golden stars. The occasional beauties of this world still surprised her. Everywhere, for some reason, were images of bees, like some magical rune worked through the fabric of the building. If she understood it properly, this was where rules were made, where the equivalent of the Doge sat. But it was an older, stronger, deeper power they sought.

"Downstairs," said Catherine. "Follow me."

They clattered down stairs that spiralled into the ground. Occasionally they passed startled denizens of the Town Hall who clutched papers to their chest as they threw themselves out of the way. Some shouted angrily, but they were people rather than undain and didn't try to stop them. More cries and howls echoed from above and Fer knew, without needing to see, that these were the monsters, in pursuit of their quarry.

They reached a grey metal door. Catherine translated the words painted upon it. *No Entry. Authorized Personnel*

Only. From what little Fer had seen of this world there were doors like this everywhere, and it was through them that the truly interesting things were to be found. A little box of buttons and blinking lights was affixed to the wall beside it.

"Can we open it?" asked Fer.

After a moment, Fer heard the tinny voice of the bookwyrm. "Yes, yes, just a moment. I'm working on it." This time, however, the voice was coming from a tiny grille on the lock rather than the phone.

Puzzled, Fer looked to the Lizard King for an answer. "The creature jumped between the machines?"

"It's in both, the phone and the security systems of the building. Different copies of itself. It's everywhere."

She was still having trouble understanding how such a thing was possible. "Yes. Of course."

"Hurry, please," said Catherine, peering upward as if she could see through the stone ceiling. "They are very near."

"Then stop interrupting me," said the creature. "Their security is good. It will take even me a few more moments. It's fortunate I can pull in processing power from all over the net to brute-force their encryption."

Fer looked to Catherine for an explanation. The older witch shrugged.

There was a silence filled only by the sound of running footsteps, louder each moment. Then a metallic *sproing* came from the door and three lights lit up green on the lock. The Lizard King pushed and the door swung inward.

"Can you lock it once we're through?" asked Catherine, speaking loudly as if she had to for the creature to hear her.

"Obviously," said the voice from the lock. "But then you're on your own. There are no electronics inside and the phone signal's almost gone."

They stepped into the darkness, slamming the heavy, metal door behind them. Catherine sent a hissing werelight into the air. Instead of bricks or tiles it revealed a passageway hewn from bare rock leading downward. Strange to think of all that splendour built on top of it.

Crouching, they shuffled forward. The air tasted of clay. Here and there the floor was patches of red brick, worn and crumbling, but mostly it was cold mud. No one talked as they descended. Catherine panted heavily from the effort but she wouldn't stop.

They reached another door. This one had no lights, no buttons. Instead it was bare wood, tattered and rotten, held together by lines of iron nails. There were marks etched upon it, standing figures she couldn't quite make sense of, a repeated spiral scratch. The wood looked like it would crumble to the touch, but when Fer tried to push it open it resisted as if it were made of rock. She tried again but the door remained utterly strong. Warding magic had been worked through it. She wondered if it had been set there to keep something in or out.

Bethany? Can you open it?

It will yield for me. I am one of them. Place your fingers on the door.

Fer did as she was told. The sensation of magic flowing through her skin, magic that wasn't *her*, sent a shiver through her. Then the door creaked open, and they were through.

We must set the seals back in place, said Bethany. *The monsters must not be allowed entry to this place. Place your hand upon the door again.*

When it was done the three of them stood side-by-side, the rock and the door to their backs. Fer caught the scents of roots and worms and seeping water, but there was something else there, too. Something about the echoing space reminded her of the building they'd hidden within before retrieving Johnny's guitar. The cathedral. There'd been whispers there, too. She heard them again now, insistent, angry. Somehow they knew not to strike a werelight. Not, even, to talk. A watchful, brooding presence filled the air. A cowering fear that crackled with a burning resentment.

Faint, bobbing lights began to appear in the darkness, white and yellow like candle flames. More and more of them lit up, like thousands of ghostly stars appearing in the night. Except, they weren't only overhead. The lights were all around, surrounding Fer and the others. Some blazed brightly while others were nothing more than dim smudges. The hard wall at their back was gone. Perhaps they were no longer in a cavern beneath the ground of Manchester.

Soon the whole space glowed with the lights. Did she really have the right to ask them what she wanted? She'd promised to do what she could to help the lost and broken spirits of this world. Cait, too, had made a promise. Perhaps this would do it, give the spirits peace. Or perhaps it would be a start.

Fer's voice echoed hollowly in the cavernous space of the Shadow Town Hall. The ghosts wouldn't be able to understand her, but she wanted them to hear her voice. Bethany would translate.

"My name is Fer. Bethany Weerd is my relative and my friend. Please, we've come here to ask for your help."

14 – THE SHADOW TOWN HALL

Fer sat on the cold ground while the ghosts of Manchester thronged around her. A constant breeze blew on her face, bringing with it musty smells of cobwebs and age. In the shifting light it was hard to be sure but the echoing cavern felt huge, no ceilings or walls to be seen, no sense of the rock pressing in on her.

It was surely too vast to be a real void in the ground beneath the towering buildings on the surface. The ghosts' home had to be something like the archaeon's cave or the Tanglewood: separate from the real world, a place apart, an island or a bubble in the aether.

If the scale of the place wasn't enough to make that clear, the appearance of Bethany did. As in the bookwyrm's cave, her dead relative was a girl of flesh and blood here, not merely a whisper and a giggle in Fer's mind. All the dead were visible, flickering lights no more. They were children mainly, but one or two among them were fully grown.

Most of the ghosts were as solid as Bethany: girls and boys and women and men. To Fer's eye the dress of one or two looked modern, not very different to those of the real people on the streets. Those recently lost to the world, unquiet in their graves. The majority of the dead, though, were clearly from earlier ages, their clothes like Bethany's: simple cloths, grey smocks, patched rags.

They walked and talked in the Shadow Town Hall despite shocking injuries to their bodies. A woman with long, golden hair stood nearby, face calm as she listened intently to Bethany's words, one of her arms dangling from her shattered shoulder by shreds of flesh. The limb waved and spun as the woman moved. It didn't appear to trouble her at all.

Next to her stood a young lad who had clearly been crushed to death, his body badly deformed, his ribs caved in so that their teeth-like ends poked from his chest. Again, it didn't stop him joining in with the shouting and arguing. In truth he seemed to be enjoying himself greatly. Fer had the impression their visit was the most exciting thing that had happened to him for a long time.

Others among the gathering were less solid, glowing palely or threatening to flicker out completely at any moment. Fer watched several shrink back from the hubbub of the gathering, their translucent eyes wide as they slipped into their own private shadows. Some among the host were barely there at all, mere windblown shreds of memory and emotion, bodies drifting in and out of existence within the crowd.

As she studied them, Fer tried to set aside the troubling thought that she was little better than Hellen, giving everyone their orders at Islagray. Fer had summoned the lost spirits of the great city and now with Bethany's help she was cajoling and persuading them to do what she wanted. How was she any better than Hellen? She'd shunned the coven and its rules all her life, hated people telling her what to do, and here she was, trying her hardest to do just that.

She could see little alternative, but that didn't make her feel much better. The arguments raged on around her. Fer felt the touch of the ghosts again and again, like tendrils of fog creeping into her bones. The spirits' words made little sense to Fer, but the Lizard King translated as best he could, trying to keep up with the flow of the debate.

Bethany called for hush as the cacophony of voices rose to a crescendo. Many of the spirits clearly knew her, Bethany addressing them by their first names. When there was quiet, she set about explaining at length all she'd seen on her journeys in the other world. The lands of Angere and Andar. The great river. The undain. Then she explained about the Masters' machines, and the refinery and the pipe and what it was all for, what it was doing to people. Finally, she repeated the words Cait had given her. They had to try and stem the flow of Spirit from their world into the other. If the undain army were deprived of the stolen life-force, even for a time, it might help Andar. It might make all the difference. They had to try. The other land was a beautiful and peaceful place, and it would be crushed and burned. They had to do something.

A stick-thin girl, half her head gone from some terrible slicing injury, pushed her way through the crowd to stand directly before Fer and Bethany. Her lack of half a face, half a skull, didn't stop her talking. "No. We mustn't go outside. We're safe here. They leave us alone here."

Bethany kneeled so that her face was level with the girl. "This might be our chance to defeat them, Abigail. To make them pay for everything they've done."

Other voices murmured their agreement. But a fury blazed in Abigail's one good eye. "But I don't want to go outside. I don't want anything to do with them. You should never have brought those three here. Now the living know about us and everything will change." There was an edge of panic in the girl's voice as well as anger.

"The wards on the doors are back in place," said Bethany. "They can't touch you."

Abigail shook her cloven head. "No. Can't you feel them? The Masters and the monsters, battering at the doors? They followed you here. They *hunger* for these two witches. They'll devour us all because we're in the way. Because they *can*. Because we've annoyed them."

Worry clouded Bethany's face. Were the girl's words true? Perhaps. Perhaps Fer had damned them all by coming here. She could think of nothing to say to the girl in reply.

A boy who might have been nine or ten when he died spoke next. His body looked whole and unblemished, his hair an unkempt tangle. "Why should we help them other people? No one helped us when the pit roofs caved in on us, when the machines grabbed hold to chew us up."

Bethany put out a hand and stroked the boy's black hair with clear fondness, trying in vain to smooth it into some order. She spoke as a parent might to a troubled child. "I know, Ethan. I thought the same once, you know I did. I even told you we had to hide away. But now I've seen sunrises and woods. I've smelled the flowers and felt wet grass on my feet in the morning. I've dipped my hand in cool, running water. Cait gave me that, Cait and now Fer. And I've decided I don't want to hide any more. That was all taken from us, and we need to get it back. And if we can't, then I think we can at least stop others having it taken from them. Do you understand?"

The boy – his body little more than scraps of cloth – looked like he might burst into tears at Bethany's words. He wrung his hands, twisting and untwisting his fingers in his alarm. "They'll send us down their pipes to fuel their army like you said. I don't want that to happen. I don't want to go."

"I understand," said Fer, her voice said. "But we can't let them get away with what they've done."

"We've no chance against them," said the boy.

"There's always a chance," said Bethany, "if we work together. I told you what happened at the White City, when Cait and I unleashed those lost souls. There aren't as many of us here, but we can attempt something similar. They need those pipes of theirs to keep them alive. We can attack them. *Hurt* them."

"Ethan's right," said the girl with half a face. "They'll come with their machines, suck us screaming from the ground because we opposed them. Because *you* opposed them."

"That might be true," Bethany conceded. "But if they do win their battles in the other world they won't leave us in peace. After the White City they won't leave themselves open to another attack. Everything will change. But if we can help beat them we'll be free. We won't have to be afraid of them any more."

"I saw the woods once," said another boy, a few years older than the first. One of his legs was gone, replaced by a crude wooden limb held together with iron brackets. "I'd like to see the trees again." His eyes were wide, as if he could see the woods across the aether. "Could we go there, to the other world? I mean, if the Masters were defeated?"

Bethany, clutching her rag doll to her stained smock, looked to Fer for answers.

Fer replied in her own tongue after the wise man had translated. "If you survive and Andar survives, any of you would be welcome. Both Bethany and I found our way through the aether. One way or another I'm sure you could, too. People have always stepped between the worlds, following the shadow paths. Especially if there was need."

Bethany translated in turn, her voice quiet yet seeming to fill the echoing space. Then she added, "My family came from there, as some of you know. Cait and Danny, who some of you saw by the tower blocks the day I left, they've gone the other way, flying through the darkness to reach the other land. For us, for spirits, it's easier. All we need is a road to follow through the shadows. Even if we don't go there, this world is bigger and more beautiful than I thought possible. I've seen much of it now and I want to see more. I want what should have been mine all along."

There was another silence, and then the boy with the

caved-in chest elbowed his way to the front of the crowd. "I'll go with you, Bethany, I'll show them. Hiding down here is boring. It's time we stuck up for ourselves. Tell me how to get to this great factory so we can make a start."

A murmur of something like consent rang around the crowd of ghosts, although many also frowned or shook their heads in response. One or two shrank back into the shadows where they stood.

"Thank you, Georgie," said Bethany. "Those who wish to help, follow me, we'll show you what we have in mind. We have to leave this place. With any luck the Masters will leave those of you who remain alone when we're gone. For a time, anyway."

Bethany stepped through the throng. The spirits parted to let her pass. Some of the ghosts drifted after her, fingers reaching to touch her. Others stayed where they were or moved away.

Fer, Catherine and the Lizard King stood and followed along behind.

It was only when Bethany's voice whispered inside Fer's mind that she realised they were back in the real world. The spirits were dancing lights and murmurs once more, patches of light in the darkness. Fer, Catherine and the Lizard King had crossed back from wherever they'd been and were in the real space beneath the Town Hall. The air felt damper on her face, but not so cold. From somewhere nearby, a repeated booming sound shook through the cold air. Someone or something was attempting to batter down the door they had come through, just as the dead girl had said. Fer didn't have to seek far to find the mass of undain bearing down on the old wooden portal.

She sent a werelight bobbing into the air, lighting up the anxious faces of Catherine and the wise man. A short way ahead lay a rough pile of rocks, as if the roof of the cavern had collapsed there. Fer sent her light upward. The ceiling was only ten feet or so above. The walls, also, were nearby, far nearer than the distance they had appeared to walk. The hollow in the earth was really quite small, a far cry from the echoing cavern the ghosts had fashioned for themselves.

"What do we do?" asked Catherine. The werelight deepened the shadows on the old witch's face, making her lines of worry and exhaustion all the clearer. "How do we coax the spirits away from this place and take them to the refinery?"

Fer hadn't explained the plan she and Bethany had come up with. It had sounded so unlikely, desperate even. She had to tell them both now. Tell them or show them. "Help me move this pile of rubble," said Fer, kneeling to begin the task. "What we need is buried beneath."

She rolled away the larger lumps of rubble, picking up smaller shards and setting them aside as if she planned to move the whole mini-mountain a few yards to the left. Not commenting, the wise man knelt beside her to join in.

After a few minutes of work, something glinted white among the dirt and rock. Bethany had been right. There were bones there, buried beneath the rock fall.

Perhaps she imagined it, but there was a resistance, a tugging, as Fer lifted the delicate sliver of rib. It was as if the cavern wanted to hold on to its own. The cavern or the bone's original owner. Fer didn't fight it. Carefully, she placed that bone back on the ground. A few moments more scraping revealed another fragment. She touched her fingers to this one without dislodging it.

She sensed – or thought she sensed – less resistance this time. It was like coaxing a scared animal out of hiding. This bone, when she gently lifted, came away freely in her hand. She would take this one. Was it from the same person? Hard to be sure. Probably not. The jumble of smashed and fractured bones beneath the rocks was a puzzle that could never be put back together, but perhaps the original owners knew which bones were which.

Some like the boy Georgie wanted to join in the fight.

He'd been among those crushed. His voice, Bethany explained, counted for a lot. Although, the girl with the terrible skull injuries, Abigail, had been here too, and many would listen to her. Fer wondered how many of the ghosts of Manchester would actually help them.

She accepted that. In fact she preferred it. It made her feel a little better that some of the Spirits refused to do as she asked. That spirit of rebellion, of individuality, was something she understood. Making people go against their own natures was what had started all the trouble in the first place.

Catherine made a little cradle out of the woollen overgarment she wore and Fer placed the sliver there.

"Bones?" said Catherine. "And how exactly will they help?"

Fer returned to her careful work, talking over her shoulder as she scraped at the grime and rubble. "Many spirits are anchored to something in the real world. A place. A loved one. Or simply the dead person's own remains. That's why these spirits are here."

"Bethany knows what happened?"

"Children digging away at the foundations of the new Town Hall were crushed when the rock fell in. The people decided to leave their remains down here rather than going to the expense and difficulty of recovering the bodies *just to bury them again*. They all died but their spirits lingered, full of anger at their lives cut short."

"The *bad thing*," said Catherine.

"The bad thing. There were twenty or more of them, just left here as part of the foundations. Their rage rang through the aether and over the decades others have answered the call. That's why the Shadow Town Hall is here."

"And we're taking the bones because…?"

"The spirits we talked to would be lost outside. They knew little of life beyond the city. Bethany was able to travel because of Cait, but the others are tethered here, anchored to the real world by their remains. If we move the bones, the spirits can move too. Then, perhaps, once a few come the others can follow."

"But where are we taking them?"

Fer smiled up at Catherine as, reverently, she added another bone to the collection. "To the one place where they can do some real damage. To the one place where our enemies might welcome them, where they actually go out of their way to acquire bones."

"You mean the refinery?"

Fer nodded. "The refinery. Perhaps *we* might be able to break back in with the bookwyrm's help, but we won't be able to do much. The angry spirits, on the other hand, will be able to cause havoc. If we can get their bones into one of those metal lorry containers Genera uses, the ghosts can get right to the heart of the enemy's fortress without them even knowing they've been invaded."

"But there are already countless bones there. What difference will these few make?"

"These remains are old, and the spirits tied to them have grown angry, grown strong. They know how to work together. The recently lost can be so confused; they don't understand what has happened to them. They need a voice to summon them, show them the path."

A heavier boom thudded through the air, Fer could hear snarls now, mingled with high-pitched animal screeches from beyond the door.

Will the doors hold? she asked Bethany in alarm.

The dead of this place have poured their fear and rage into those nails and planks for many years, building up the barricades, said Bethany. *But the Masters are terribly strong. It won't be long.*

"We can't get out that way," said the Lizard King, as if he were aware of Fer's conversation with Bethany. Gently he lifted up a tiny finger-bone and placed it with the others in Catherine's garment. "Are there are other ways out?"

"Bethany says there's another door, on the opposite side of the cave."

"Where does it go?"

"I don't know. Underground." Fer stood. They had a small pile of bone fragments. There were many more left trapped under the rocks, but perhaps they had enough to draw the unquiet spirits with them. They couldn't afford to wait any longer.

"Catherine? You said you'd studied the old maps of the tunnels and workings beneath the streets of the city, when you and Jaiin were planning your escape route?"

"Well, yes, but this place wasn't marked on any map I saw. Sewers, aquifers, storm drains, mines, caves – they were there. But no Shadow Town Hall."

"We're so near the Library though. There must have been, I don't know, a gap in the maps. A space around which the tunnels led, without it being made clear why."

Catherine's forehead knitted in concentration as she thought back. "It's … possible. No one ever put all the maps and drawings together, but thinking about each one … it's possible there was a space around which the tunnels wound."

"And any passages nearby that seemed to stop suddenly, go nowhere?"

"It's possible, yes."

"Excellent. That's our way out. Hopefully you'll know where in the maze we are when we get through the other doorway. If we can open it."

Another shuddering boom resonated through the air of the cavern, followed by piercing shrieks.

"Come on," said Fer. "That will have to be enough. It's time we went."

15 – A MAZE OF STREETS

The second door, in the opposite wall of the cavern, looked even older and more dilapidated than the first they'd come through. Its timbers were green with rot, stained brown where the water had dripped from its rusting nails. But it was as solid a barrier as the first door when Fer tried to barge it open with her shoulder, strong threads of magic running through its grain.

Once again, with Bethany's help, Fer's fingertip touch upon it made it yield. The three hurried through, leaving the spirits of the Shadow Town Hall to their long darkness. Fer took care to close the door behind them, her touch putting the iron-strong wards back in place on the ancient doorway. The massed undain were still hammering their way through the first entrance. Perhaps the two doors between them would give Fer and the others time to get away.

Catherine lit a werelight, but it sputtered out almost immediately, like a candle flame in a gust of wind. She tried again, but this time managed only a brief spark. The older witch was spent. She muttered something under her breath. Fer didn't recognize the word, but she knew a curse when she heard it.

"Let me," said Fer, sending a yellow-white flame flickering into the air.

"I'm sure I can manage a little light," said Catherine. "I've been working them since I was six."

The older witch's face was a frown, frustration at her own limitations, her own weariness, clear.

"The light doesn't matter," said Fer. "We need you to work out where we are. If we can't find a way out of this maze they'll corner us and capture us."

Catherine nodded and turned to study the passageway they stood within. The walls were bare rock like those of the Shadow Town Hall, but there were horizontal gouge-marks that suggested people unknown had cut the tunnel from bare rock at some time in the past. The floor sloped downward into utter darkness. From below came the babble of running water, along with the acrid stench of human waste. In a way that was good. Wherever they were, the tunnel appeared to connect up with the sewers beneath the city, and sewers had hatches and grids to allow access to them. That had to be as true in Manchester as it was in Guilden.

Catherine went first, one hand on the rock wall as if she knew the caverns by touch. They had to stoop as they shuffled along to stop their heads bashing into the rough rock of the roof. After perhaps thirty paces, the tunnel bending always to the left, they emerged at a junction with a larger passage. This was hand-crafted rather than natural, its arching walls constructed from bricks the colour of dried blood.

Catherine stepped down into the stream of water running along the centre of the new tunnel. The smell was no stronger, nothing more than a miasma in the air. The water appeared to be fresh: rain run-off perhaps, or the course of some ancient, buried brook channelled beneath the streets. The older witch turned backward and forward, head cocked, as she attempted to orientate herself. Fer sent the little werelight darting up and down the tunnel in an attempt to keep up.

"But we're ... we're here," said Catherine. "I'm completely disorientated, I thought we were on the other side."

Fer stepped down beside Catherine. Fer wore good, stout boots, Andar leather, but they'd developed a few cracks on the long walk north that she'd utterly neglected to repair. She regretted her carelessness immediately as icy water seized hold of her feet.

"You know where we are?" she asked.

Catherine nodded. "As should you. Here, put your fingers to the wall. Feel anything?"

Fer touched the square-cut stones of the wall. She suddenly knew what she'd find. The marks were faint now, but the kick of the hind-legs and the swept-back line of the ears were clear enough as she coaxed the magical sign on the wall to give up its meaning. One of the hare witch-marks Catherine herself had left as she fled from the Library. Marks that Fer, Johnny and Ran had followed when they arrived from the Tanglewood.

Fer nodded and smiled at Catherine as the picture of the kicking, leaping hare filled her mind.

The older witch said, "At least I can manage a witch-mark that doesn't immediately fade."

Fer placed a hand on the woman's arm. "These marks saved our lives when we came to this world. I never thanked you for them."

"Well, anyway," said Catherine. "At least we know where we are. Jaiin and I counted these side-tunnels carefully, terrified we'd take a wrong turn when the time came to flee. But this one was a dead end, just bare rock at the end as if the tunnellers gave up on it after thirty yards."

"A doorway only visible from one side perhaps," said Fer. "A way out rather than a way in. It makes sense."

The Lizard King splashed into the stream to join them. He peered up at the wall, shoulders hunched in the cramped space. "So which way is the hare running?"

"Down there," said Catherine, pointing into the darkness. "We'll head away from the Library basement. Again."

"Should we erase the marks?" asked Fer. "So the undain can't follow us?"

"No time. Besides I doubt they noticed them last time, and they're much harder to see now. Let them look if they want."

Catherine splashed forward and Fer waded after. With her neck bent over it was awkward to keep the werelight bobbing ahead of Catherine. They passed another side-tunnel and then another, the wall at each turning marked with its magical hare imploring them to *follow, follow, hurry, hurry!*

As well as maintaining the light, Fer tried to sense the whereabouts of the undain and the human soldiers of Genera. There was only an unfocused, looming presence above their heads, their pursuers on the streets. She wondered what was happening in the cavern. Had the enemy broken down the first door? Had the spirits fled or fought? She could sense nothing save a voiceless dread seeping from the stone. She could detect no immediate threat, no nightmare horror about to leap from the darkness to devour them. If one was there, it was so well hidden she couldn't sniff it out.

She called over her shoulder to the Lizard King. "Is your phone working again? Does it have contact with the other machines? With the ... network?"

"Nothing yet," said the Lizard King. In the narrow tunnel his voice had a strange echo to it, a tremor almost. "We need to get up to the surface. As I recall it isn't far."

"You've been through this tunnel, too?"

"I ... no. Not in person. I was aware of you when you came this way."

Fer thought about that as they waded forward. "So you were expecting us that day we came to your hostelry. To the Golden Palace?"

"I wasn't sure. I didn't know who or what you were. I'd caught glimpses of you before, but obviously never in this world. The visions didn't make a lot of sense. They were very brief, just snatches. Your fear burned brightly, blotting out everything else. I didn't know you were coming to find me until you walked into the restaurant."

Catherine stopped, her outstretched fingers touching the curving wall to her left. "This is the mark telling you to take the turning. The route we both took to escape is that way."

Fer recalled the tunnel sloping upward to end in a metal grid that they had to push against with their shoulders to open. Distantly she could hear the booming roar of the city and its machines. The air smelled a little fresher, a waft of cold, clear air blowing from some crack or gap in the grating. If they went that way they'd emerge among the buses and the hurrying feet of the city centre. The sight of it all – dizzying, confusing – was one that had stayed with her. Her first proper glimpse of the other world.

"Should we go that way again?" she asked.

"I'm not sure," said Catherine. "They might be watching that exit now."

"You said you studied the maps. There must be other ways out."

"Many, yes. Jaiin and I plotted other routes through the labyrinth, including a tunnel that opens in the cellar of a disused mill. But it's a lot farther, and it isn't a good idea to stay down here any longer than we have to."

"As long as those doors hold the undain it seems safer down here than up there," said Fer. "There are no cameras to see us, and this running water will stop them tracking us by scent. They'll be able to find us using magic eventually, but they might get lost in this maze a few times first."

Catherine sighed, trying in vain to sweep her grey hair back into some sort of order. She panted as she stood there, stooped and weary. "Perhaps, but there are other things down here apart from the undain. The farther we venture from the city centre the more likely we are to meet them."

"What *things*?" asked Fer.

"There are lots of stories. Some of them silly myths, no doubt, but not all if you ask me. Creatures that live in this darkness. The worms that wind blindly through the deeper levels. The lost spirits, confused and angry. Bogles and boggarts and bugganes from the old tales."

The older witch's comments troubled Fer. Was what she said true? Could there really be such creatures skulking in the tunnels of this noisy, brightly-lit city? Somehow it seemed unlikely. Perhaps in Andar, but here in this world of machinery and glass and steel? The only monsters she'd seen were the undain and the people who served them. Catherine had been through too much. Fer caught the Lizard King's gaze. Concern was clear in his eyes.

"Whatever we do, you need to rest," said the wise man to Catherine. "I don't need to borrow your mind to know how exhausted you are. I mean, I'm exhausted too. We all are."

Catherine nodded. She still held the little bundle of bones in a fold of her woollen tunic. He voice sounded weak, cracked, as she replied. "Well, we can't rest here, but I think it's too dangerous to take the same exit as last time. We'll have to brave the monsters of Manchester's tunnels and head northeast. It's only half a mile or so."

"Are you sure you can make it?" asked Fer.

Catherine nodded, but there was a pause before the words came. "Let's keep going. There'll be no more witch-marks, but I have the route memorized. Only, sing out if you feel an opening in the wall on either side, yes? That's how I remember the way, and if I miss one we could end up anywhere. These tunnels lead to some unexpected places."

As Catherine set off Fer glanced at the wise man again, who frowned his doubts at her. There was nothing either of them could do but hurry on as quickly as they could.

Their trudge through the maze of passageways seemed endless to Fer. Her back and neck soon throbbed from the uncomfortable crouching position they had to adopt to scuttle through the tunnels. Occasionally they found a taller section, a modern sewer or river channel, and it was glorious to be able to stand up straight and stretch burning muscles. It never lasted for long enough.

The route Catherine led them along became windier and harder to follow, so that Fer was soon utterly disorientated and couldn't really tell if they were walking round in circles or heading away from the city centre. She could do nothing but trust in Catherine. Fer's impressions of what was happening on the streets were too vague to properly follow. There were still no undain near as far she could tell, no creatures at all save the occasional quick-moving, pink-eyed rat scampering out of their way. Occasionally, distant scraping and scrabbling sounds echoed, but when Fer reached out with her mind's eye she could never find their source.

She took to tracing her fingers along the left-hand wall while the Lizard King did the same on the right. Each time they found a turning they told Catherine, who simply nodded and pressed on. Two or three times, Fer stopped to sketch some witch-marks of her own, deliberately marking the wrong turning to take. A small thing, probably pointless. But if there were a necromancer among their pursuers, perhaps the subterfuge would throw them off the scent for a time, buy a few more minutes. It was all she could do.

They came to a fork in the tunnels. One branch, its walls more of the red bricks, led off to the left, sloping downward. The right-hand passage was rough stone, damp and dripping, but rising gradually. Catherine hesitated, looking from one passageway to the other. "I ... I can't remember which way to go."

Her voice wavered. Fer caught the troubled look on the

wise man's face.

"Take your time, there's no hurry," said Fer, even though she longed to be free of the seemingly endless maze. A hollow, booming sound echoed up the passage behind them. Fer told herself it could be anything. Water flowing, a bus driving over a grid, anything.

"I think it's right," said Catherine. Her lips moved as if she were reciting the words of some song or rhyme. "Except … we've just taken a right. Perhaps it's left now. Jaiin would know for sure but it's funny, I suddenly can't remember."

"Do you have any signal on the phone now?" asked Fer.

The wise man studied the glowing screen of the device and shook his head. "There's nothing."

"Do you have any idea where we are?"

The wise man studied the damp stones above his head, as if some clue might be written there. "None, I'm sorry."

"It will come to me in a minute," said Catherine. "I'm sure it will."

Another hollow boom found them, followed by a discordant squeal, metal upon metal. Peering into the darkness with her mind's eye, Fer saw them now, the undain amassed like a fog in the tunnels. One way or another, their pursuers had battered down the doors of the Shadow Town Hall. They were coming.

She had to do something. They couldn't fight; they'd be slaughtered or captured in moments. They could only run. The tunnels were as much a maze as the streets. A labyrinth above ground and a shadow labyrinth beneath. She longed to be free of it all.

Stepping forward she tried to see through the aether. It was impossible. She caught the occasional spark of life here and there, rat or beetle, but never enough to see clearly where the twisting tunnels led.

Bethany? Do you know these tunnels? Do you know which way to go?

The witch-girl's voice was faint, a whisper. *These are old ways, far older than me. Roads I've never taken. I'm sorry.*

In desperation, Fer opened her eyes and sniffed. The air from the right-hand passage was musty and damp, bringing with it the cloying scent of mud and decay. No way of knowing if that was the correct way. Turning to the other passageway she sniffed again. This time, beneath the fug, she thought she caught the faintest taste of something colder, fresher.

"This way, I think," she said. "We go left."

"Are you sure?" asked the wise man.

Fer wasn't anywhere near as certain as she sounded when she replied. "Yes."

The tunnel sloped downward, becoming damper and muddier all the time. Fer stopped smelling the waft of fresh air. Perhaps she'd imagined it. Perhaps it was wishful thinking and she was leading them in circles, or to some dead end where they could only turn to face their fate.

They arrived in a low, roughly circular cave that looked natural rather than man-made. Stalactites of slimy stone, ribbed like the body parts of some unknown creature, clung to the roof. They had to be far underground. A pool of black, still water filled the space, the werelight reflecting off its mirror-surface perfectly, revealing nothing of what lay beneath. Four tunnels led off from the cave into the darkness.

Fer hesitated, sitting on the lip of the entrance. Something about the unmoving waters troubled her. She imagined creatures emerging from it, tentacles lashing out to wrap around her, like some smaller version of the river serpents back home. With an effort she put the thoughts out of her mind. The long trudge underground had got the better of her. Her exhausted mind was imagining phantoms where there were none. When people were troubled by ghosts or nameless horrors of the dark, the demons were usually only in their heads. Every witch knew that.

Still, she let herself down gently. The waters were a foot deep, stone cold, inundating her ruined boots immediately. No monsters arose from the depths as she found her footing on the slimy floor and reached up to help Catherine down.

From somewhere in the tunnels, echoing down the passageway, three heavy booms reverberated, followed by a frantic shuffling sound.

"Can you sense anything?" Fer asked them. "Anything near, anything coming?"

Catherine shook her head, too weary to reply. The Lizard King closed his eyes for a moment, peering into the aether. Then he, too, shook his head. More sounds came: scrapings and scufflings and something rhythmic, like the pounding of feet. She tried to work out which entrance they were coming from, but it was impossible to be sure. The sounds echoed off the hard walls, jumping at them from odd angles.

Again she had to decide which tunnel to take, and do so quickly. Perhaps it would be best to pick one at random. Anything was better than standing and waiting to be captured or butchered. More sounds echoed from the darkness: thumpings and metallic scrapings, louder now. The undain appeared to be all around, as if filling the tunnels beneath the city.

"Wait, we're *here*," said Catherine. "I recognize this place, where five tunnels meet."

"You're sure?"

"Yes, yes. It's on the maps. We came through that one so we have to go that way." She pointed at one of the other entrances.

Fer was completely disorientated; she would have sworn the direction Catherine was pointing was the wrong way. Fer waded through to study the opening. It certainly rose gradually. And – again – she thought she caught a whiff of fresh air.

It was all they had. Fer leading, they set off.

The tunnel narrowed, forcing them to crawl. There'd been mines beneath the streets of Manchester once, so Catherine said, and this tunnel felt like one of those: a cramped passageway hand-cut through the rock in pursuit of some fading seam of coal. Fer's knees and elbows felt like they were bleeding freely from pulling herself along. At least the tunnel was dry, and they weren't having to work their way through water or mud. The passage rose, but it continued to narrow and there was soon no room to turn around. If they came to a dead end they could only writhe backward to reach the last cavern.

The tunnel tightened yet more, tapering to a close, and Fer was about to suggest they turn back, when her hand, thrust out in front of her, found empty air rather than rock. She heaved herself forward a few more inches and her head emerged half-way up one wall of a round, brick-lined room. In the corner, a set of worn stone steps led upward.

Fer described what she could see to the others.

"Yes, that's it," said Catherine. "Up the stairs, and we'll be out of the tunnels."

Fer crawled forward and, twisting awkwardly, found a lip of rock to hold onto while she pulled herself from the tunnel to let herself down to the floor of the room. She reached up to support Catherine and then the Lizard King as they emerged. Both were filthy, smeared with grime.

"I'll go up the stairs last," said Fer. "If they come I have the best chance of holding them off."

Catherine nodded but didn't object. The wise man took the cargo of precious bones from her so that her hands were free. Taking one step at a time, the older witch climbed, bracing her hands on her knees as if her legs didn't have the strength to push her upward. Fer sent the werelight floating after her. The stairs were slick with slime. The Lizard King climbed after her, and finally Fer followed, keeping the little light burning as brightly as possible.

From somewhere in the tunnels came a heavy *splosh* as if someone or something had fallen into a deep pool. The sound put her in mind of the Tanglewood, Seleena's fall into the water, killed by the undain that lurked in the magical forest. She prepared what magic she could muster, expecting some undain horror to writhe from the tunnel entrance at any moment. They ascended a few more steps and the floor below was lost to shadows. Fer couldn't work a werelight bright enough to illuminate everything. With a sense of disquiet, she turned away from the darkness and concentrated on her footing as they continued the climb.

Five minutes later they emerged in the wide, echoing space of the building Catherine had described. Despite Fer's fears, there was no ring of slavering undain monsters awaiting them, and nothing had reached from the shadows beneath to seize her by the ankle and haul her back. Thanks to Catherine's knowledge they had escaped the maze.

The building they stood in was clearly deserted, many of the tiny windows smashed, puddles here and there on the uneven stone floor. It had once been a mill, a place where people worked amid roaring, clattering machines to make clothes, so Catherine had explained. It was utterly quiet now, the city no more than a distant roar. After the muggy air of the tunnels, the breeze blowing through the broken windows made Fer shiver, but it smelled good, crisp and clean.

Catherine sank to the floor, panting like a hunted animal. With the Lizard King's help, Fer levered a rusting iron cover over the square of darkness they'd emerged from. The hinges squealed but gave. A heavy iron clasp had been set into the floor and, miraculously, a padlock was there, ready to be secured into place. Catherine and Jaiin had prepared well.

When the grid was locked, Fer worked what warding

charms she could into the old metal, putting all her strength into it until the tugging pains within her were too much to stand. Bethany, still with her, added her strength to it, too. Catherine also helped, although the strength she brought to bear was tiny, the faintest flicker. As they worked, the Lizard King found rusting iron wheels from some ancient machine in a corner of the room and wheeled them on top of the grid.

When it was done Fer stood, exhausted but satisfied.

"You took your time."

The metallic voice of the archaeon on the wise man's phone was strangely loud in the echoing hall. "I thought you'd been eaten alive or become lost without me to guide you."

The Lizard King took out his phone and fiddled with its buttons.

"Can you conceal us while we flee the city?" asked Fer, speaking into the little machine.

The wyrm on the screen exhaled a burst of red flame. "Impossible. They have eyes everywhere looking for you. CCTV, traffic control, helicopters in the air, many of them closed off even from me. You should be flattered; they're using everything they can to track you down." The creature sounded as if it was enjoying delivering the bad news immensely.

"There must be some way of escaping," said Fer. "Surely one as brilliant as you can find a way?"

The little painted dragon on the screen closed and opened its eyes. "There is only one thing I can do. I can't hide you, but I can flood their systems with false reports, images of the three of you all over the city. It will keep them occupied for a short time, chasing phantoms. Or, if they're lucky, they may come straight for the real you."

"We are grateful," said Fer. "We need to get back to the refinery as soon as possible."

"To Leviathan Refinery? Interesting."

"Can you find the best route to take? Away from as

many cameras and eyes as possible?"

The creature breathed fire and smoke again, as if it was still deciding whether to help them or not. "Well, I suppose I might assist you once again. If you hurry, I believe you'll have a chance, but you'll have to follow my directions to the letter. The options open to you are limited."

"We need to make a couple of stops along the way," said Fer.

"Oh? Just to make it a little more difficult?"

"We need to get inside one of those lorries they use to carry the bones into the refinery."

"And why would you want to do that?" asked the creature.

There seemed to be little point not to tell it. They wouldn't get far without its guidance. "We have a couple of extra bones we'd like to add to their collection."

"I see. Interesting. And the other stop you'd like me to arrange?"

"Tea," said Fer. "This woman needs a cup of tea. And come to that, so do I."

Two hours later, they stood upon a narrow bridge that arched over one of the city's motorways. For all Fer knew, it was the same bridge Cait had described, when she and Danny were shot at by the riders. A soaking rain filled the air of Manchester, blurring the lights, smudging the hard edges of buildings and roads. The rain trickled down her face, dripping off her nose. She almost envied the dead spirits hidden away beneath the ground, away from the soaking downpour.

Two rivers of traffic roared beneath them, the lights on one side a blinding white, the other red. The light was fading in the west. They'd weaved their way across the city guided by the archaeon, clinging mainly to deserted side roads and abandoned passageways, occasionally huddling in the shadows when helicopters rattled overhead or cars drifted by. Once, to Fer's surprise, the bookwyrm instructed them to take a shortcut through a large, brightly-lit shopping centre. It was completely contained within a huge building, no glimpse of sun or stars or sky possible from within. Hundreds – perhaps thousands – of people thronged its long halls.

"Are you sure this is safe?" Fer hissed into the phone. She felt very exposed. There had to be cameras everywhere, and many of the shops appeared to have their own security guards. One stood in the doorway of a jewellery shop, eyeing them with open suspicion.

"It's perfectly safe as long as you keep moving," said the bookwyrm. "I know what I'm doing. The Arndale Centre is a maze, almost impossible to navigate without getting lost. If anyone is following you they're likely to lose their way and end up where they started, or never find their way out at all. Besides, they'll have worked out by now that their systems are being flooded with false sightings. They're almost completely sure to dismiss images of you in the middle of the Arndale."

"*Almost* completely?"

"There's a good likelihood of it working. A very good likelihood."

A security guard sprinted toward them, one hand on the baton sheathed at his belt, the other holding his hat on his head. Fer stopped, preparing for the assault, but the man, chest heaving, trundled past them, perhaps following one of the false reports conjured by the bookwyrm.

"Hurry!" said the creature from the Lizard King's phone. "This is no time to stop and do some shopping. If you dawdle you're lost."

They raced on, back to the relative safety of shadowy back-streets and litter-strewn alleys. By following the creature's instructions to the letter, they made it across the city's maze of streets to reach the motorway bridge without being accosted. They'd even managed to take in a brief stop at a van that had been converted into a shop selling food and hot drinks. The Lizard King had approached alone, returning with handfuls of food and water and steaming tea.

No doubt as a result, some of the life had returned to Catherine's eyes as they stood on the bridge. She watched the streaming traffic beneath them, a calculating look on her face. Among the cars and buses and other vehicles were many of the lorries hauling along their great metal containers. Many of them no doubt ferrying Bone to the refinery portal. Building materials for the White City and greater Angere.

"I can't see how we can stop one of them," said Fer. "They're moving too fast."

Catherine nodded. "Even if there were a traffic jam we'd be seen too easily down there. And it's far too dangerous. We need to get to one of the truck stops."

"And where would one of those be?"

"Out along the motorway," said the Lizard King. "Which means we need a car."

"Can you do what you did last time?" asked Fer. "Pay to use one temporarily. You know, *hire* it?"

The wise man shook his head. "I'm out of cash, and I'm sure Genera would spot it immediately if I used a card."

Fer stared into the river of traffic, wondering if it would be possible to stop one of the vehicles, take control of the driver's mind perhaps.

The wise man's phone, which he'd slipped into his coat pocket, made the insistent warbling sound it made when it wanted attention. He lifted it out and pressed the button that allowed everyone to hear it.

The bookwyrm's voice was hard to make out against the roar of the motorway and the lashing rain. Fer put the little device to her ear.

"You'll need a vehicle," said the bookwyrm. "To get to the refinery."

"Yes," said Fer.

"Then once again it's a good job I'm here."

"You can supply us with a car?" asked Fer. "How is that possible?"

"In this world anything is possible if you have enough money."

"And you … have access to enough money?"

"Have you understood nothing, little witch? I have copies of myself in computers the world over. As we speak I have several thousand instances engaging in high-speed stock trades. The flows of money really are fascinating."

As so often, Fer had little idea what that meant. She relayed the creature's words to the others.

"How much money have you accumulated?" asked the Lizard King, his face close to Fer's.

"Tell me," said the bookwyrm, "what is the biggest number you can think of?"

"I don't know … a billion. No, wait, a trillion."

"Hmm. As I suspected, you don't even know words big enough to describe my current holdings. Speculation really is a most enjoyable game, although quite what it's for, what it *achieves*, escapes even me."

"You have a *trillion* dollars?" asked the wise man, the surprise clear in his voice. "Are you sure?"

"Of course I'm sure. And it's far more than a trillion. Money in this world is just numbers, and I'm good at numbers. Very, very good."

"So," said Fer, "you can pay for us to hire a car?"

"I can do more than that, I've arranged delivery of a new car. Rather a nice one. It's waiting for you a few hundred yards away, across the bridge."

"But … won't Genera know?"

"Extremely unlikely. The people I've been in touch with are used to acting discreetly, no questions asked."

"Who are these people?" asked Fer.

"Best you don't know. People who have been paid well to say absolutely nothing to anyone," said the colourful little dragon on the phone.

"And the undain," said Fer. "How near are they?"

"Oh, very near. They're closing in rapidly. Another minute or two and they'll have you, I'd say. But of course it's entirely up to you."

Fer took only a moment to decide. She was too cold and exhausted and afraid to do anything else.

"Show us to the car," she said.

16 – LEVIATHAN

"Are these containers *all* full of bones?" Fer stood in the shadows of a large, bleak lorry-park, filled with rows of the vehicles and their rectangular metal boxes. More lorries lumbered in from the motorway, their bright lights casting square silhouettes about her.

A few yards away, engine quietly purring, the Lizard King sat at the wheel of the car, ready to whisk them away at the first sign of trouble. He would be listening to any reports of imminent danger from the wyrm on his phone. She could see the anxious look on his face by the glow of the high orange spotlights that illuminated the lorry-park. If he saw anyone coming he would summon them, knock on a window or sound his horn. There were cameras up by the lights, peering down at the lorries. The wyrm had assured them he would hide the images of Fer and Catherine from the pictures they took, but he'd also warned them it was getting harder and harder to fool Genera. Their pursuers were starting to fill in the gaps, understand the tricks the wyrm had been playing.

"Hard to be sure," said Catherine, her voice little more than a whisper. "All of them here perhaps, this close to the refinery. Hundreds of them from across the world every day. Thousands."

"And people have no idea?"

"None. Everyone is so used to seeing these lorries they think nothing about them."

A cold wind whipped down the canyons between the containers, seeming to focus the force of the chill on Fer's face. A short distance away a tiny whirlwind of leaves and dropped scraps of paper whipped around as if some malign being were about to materialise. They'd seen lots of Genera's cars on the motorway, roaring by with blue lights flashing. The bookwyrm had kept them informed about their pursuers actions, explaining where Genera was directing its efforts in its frantic search, how the net was slowly tightening as each false lead the creature laid turned out to be a phantom. In a desperate bid to fool Genera, the creature had deliberately doctored images from their actual location on the motorway, making their images clearer in the hope their pursuers would see them as fakes and look elsewhere.

It wasn't clear the blind had worked. Fer gripped the pathetic bundle of old bones tight in their rag. The magic they were attempting seemed so small and weak in the face of the power of Angere.

"Do you really think this will work?"

Catherine sighed, as if she had little hope. "Only one way to find out. Sometimes all that's needed is a little nudge. A single stone slipping that starts off the avalanche. They've got away with murder for so long. Sooner or later such wrongs have to be righted."

When they were sure the nearby lorries were deserted, their drivers eating and drinking inside the brightly-lit building, Fer and Catherine approached the back of one of the containers. It was rusty and scuffed as if repeatedly bashed by some great force. Words were painted on it, their colour leeched to grey by the weird orange light.

"What do the letters say?" asked Fer.

"It's not in English," said Catherine. "Could have come from anywhere."

The back of the container was taken up by a tall set of double doors, an arrangement of metal levers and poles keeping them securely fastened. There were keyholes built into the contraption.

"Why do they need locks if they're only carrying bones?" asked Fer.

"To keep people out," said Catherine. "There's been a lot of trouble with folks hiding themselves inside these containers, or even underneath by the wheels."

The thought of clinging next to those thundering wheels, the road only inches away, filled her with horror. "Why would anyone do such a thing?"

"Desperation. Hope. Because the alternative of staying where they are is even worse."

Fer tried and failed to understand. She placed a hand on the lever at the back of the container and rattled it, hoping it might have been left open. It was securely locked.

"I'll work some rust into it," said Fer. "If I can weaken it we might be able to break it open."

Catherine nodded. "I'll keep watch. The driver could come back at any moment."

Between them, Bethany and Fer set to work on the locks, pulling moisture from the air and working it into the complicated mechanism, trying to speed up the natural rusting process just as she'd done on her escape from the library on the first day. The trick was to find existing flaws in the metal and widen them. If they could weaken the lock sufficiently, brute strength might finish the job.

They'd picked their container wisely: this one was old and everything was half-corroded. Still, after all that had happened, Fer had little strength left. Gritting her teeth she worked away at it, stitches pinching cruelly at her sides.

She nearly had it when Catherine placed a hand on her shoulder. "Someone is coming. We have to hide."

"I'm nearly there. A couple more moments."

"No," said Catherine. "We can't risk it. The drivers always check round their vehicles before setting off. If they see us they'll raise the alarm."

Fer and Catherine retreated into deeper shadows behind another vehicle as heavy footsteps approached. Twenty yards away, the Lizard King turned off the engine of the car. Fer expected to see some armoured Genera guard, some misshapen undain demon, but instead a drab, gloomy-looking man appeared, his gaze cast to the ground, shoulders hunched. He appeared to have no idea Fer and Catherine were there. He walked right past them, a cloud of smoke from his cigarette filling the air with its acrid smell and nearly making Fer cough.

The driver climbed into the next lorry. In a few moments its engine roared into life and the vehicle rumbled away in a cloud of greasy smoke.

A few minutes more working away at the lock, and Fer felt something give within the little mechanism, some shard of metal fracturing. There would be no way of fixing it afterward; they just had to hope people would think the lock had simply worn out.

Grasping hold of the lever Fer yanked it with all her strength. The mechanism held, but gave a little more than it had. Catherine lent her strength to the effort. With a *clunk*, the sound loud enough to echo off the surrounding lorries, the lock gave way. The steel shaft securing the doors slid out of its brackets.

The hinges of the container squealed as Fer pulled open the door. Perhaps she imagined it, but a sighing sound seemed to breathe from the lorry into the night air. She lit a faint werelight to illuminate the interior. They had chosen well; the container was definitely destined for the refinery. Inside, piled up to the roof, held in place by a fine rope mesh, the lorry was full of jumbled bones.

"So many of them," said Fer. She wondered who they were, what had happened to them.

"No time for that now," said Catherine. "Let's add ours to the pile."

Fer undid the little bundle of remains she carried. She wanted to place each carefully, reverentially, into the lorry, but a knocking from the Lizard King warned them someone else was approaching. The car engine started up. With trembling fingers, Fer tipped the bones through the mesh to join the others. Hopefully no one would notice a few sepia-coloured fragments amid all that gleaming white.

When they had the door shut and secured, everything looked just as it had. Fer hoped no one tried the handle and found the lock broken. Or that it didn't work loose on the road.

They climbed back into the warm, soft interior of the waiting car, and the Lizard King moved slowly away, trying not to look as if they were in any kind of hurry. Twenty yards away, a laughing group of three men were approaching, each of them jangling bunches of keys as they returned to their lorries. The Lizard King stopped the car a short distance away so they could watch. One of the men climbed into the lorry they'd opened, after only the briefest glance around and beneath the vehicle. Fortunately he didn't test the handles on the doors. In a few moments, the lorry was edging its way onto the motorway.

Keeping a safe distance, the Lizard King followed. Another police car, blue lights spinning, sped down the opposite carriageway but didn't slow.

Half an hour later, the dazzling constellation of lights from Leviathan Refinery lit up the windscreen of the car. In the darkness she couldn't see how brutal, how ugly the place was. In the daylight it resembled some vast metal beast stripped of its skin, its bones and veins exposed for everyone to see. The Lizard King parked as near to the gates as he dared so they could watch their lorry. It had joined a queue of five or six, waiting in turn to be admitted through the gates. The high fences were just as Fer remembered them, but there looked to be more guards on patrol inside, many holding large dogs on short, straining leashes. Somehow, as well as the bones, she had to get inside. It would be harder this time. Perhaps it would be impossible.

Their lorry rumbled forward to the front of the line, a guard holding up a hand to stop it. The driver handed down papers while other guards examined the vehicle, looking beneath it with angled mirrors on sticks. Fer held her breath as one of them walked behind the lorry. If he tried the doors he would surely see they'd been opened, and then the lorry might not be admitted.

Urgently, she reached into the guard's mind. Fortunately he was human, not one of the undain. Checking an endless line of lorries had to be a tedious job, and the guard's boredom made the intrusion easier. As subtly as she could manage she gave him the idea that he had already checked the doors, that the locks were secure.

The guard gripped the handle, paused … then took his hand away. Turning, he ambled to the front of the lorry and waved it through the gates.

Fer let out a breath of relief. The bones of the dead of Manchester were inside the refinery.

They waited for an hour, and then two, for something to happen. Fer tried to peer inside with her mind's eye, find out if anything was happening, but it proved impossible. Walls of fog blocked her. On their last visit they'd managed to puncture them, she and Catherine and Fiona working together, but now the defences were stronger. Once, watching from the car with her window lowered, she thought she heard a rushing, whispering sound in the air, blowing from the east, the direction of the city they'd left. Perhaps it was just the wind. Perhaps she'd imagined it. She sat there blind, powerless, waiting, while the flaring flames and sparkling lights of the vast building stretched out before her, and the deep roar of its unceasing machinery rumbled through the ground.

"Have you found a way for us to get inside yet?" she asked the bookwyrm for the second or third time. The Lizard King's phone was cradled on the car's dashboard. The creature didn't deign to reply for several moments before the screen lit up and the brightly-coloured image of the dragon appeared. It lay apparently slumbering on the ground but managed to summon the strength to open one bored eye.

"It is impossible, even for me. They have everything locked down."

"I thought you said you had copies of yourself in there, within their machines?"

"I did say that, yes. And possibly I still do have, but as I also explained I am unable to communicate with them. Either they're cut off or they've been deleted. If you get inside you might find there are versions of me that could help you, but I simply don't know."

"Can you tell us anything about what's going on in there? Have the spirits arrived? Are they attacking?"

"I have no idea, little witch. As I also told you, Genera have cut themselves off completely from the public network."

"Are they getting any closer to finding us yet?"

"All is quiet on that front at least. I've stopped sending them any images, fake or real. Hopefully they're in the dark as to your real location."

"Perhaps we should have climbed into the back of that lorry ourselves," said the Lizard King. "Then we'd have got inside."

"Except we'd be trapped," said Catherine. "Most likely we'd have been shipped through to the White City without being able to do anything."

"We have to do something," said Fer. "Whether or not the spirits have attacked, we have to do what we can to sever the flow of Spirit. How does it even get into the refinery?"

"Pipelines buried deep beneath the ground," said the Lizard King. "I catch glimpses of the spirits trapped within from time to time. There's no way to get to them I can see."

Another lorry trundled up to join the back of the queue. There were perhaps twenty of them waiting now, smoke billowing from each into the freezing night air.

"If we bewitch one of the drivers, put them to sleep, we could take their place," said Fer.

"The guards check the ID of the drivers," said the Lizard King. "They'd see I didn't match."

"So we get into the guard's heads, make them see what we want."

"It's a risk."

"Yes," said Fer, "but we're taking a risk sitting here in the open. We're taking a risk doing nothing. Cait needs us. Andar needs us."

Catherine sighed. "You're right. It's probably not going to work but there's no other way. The lost spirits from Manchester never came, or they've been contained or destroyed. I think we're on our own."

After a moment, the Lizard King turned the key to make the car shiver into life. "I'll park the car so we can approach on foot."

"You don't have to come with us," said Fer. "You can just drive away."

The Lizard King smiled, although he looked sad at the same time. "I really don't think I can."

"You won't be able to do much in there."

"Perhaps not. Do you think you will?"

He had a fair point. "No, possibly not," said Fer.

"We'll all try and get inside," said Catherine. "Perhaps one of us will be able to do something to the pipeline."

But as they stepped from the car into the cold night air, a siren began to wail from the refinery. Another and then a third followed it, the sounds angry and mournful at the same time. Fer felt a great thump in the ground as if something had exploded. The flames that burned constantly from the chimneys cut out for a moment, then burst into life, angrier and more intense. Red lights flashed on and off inside the buildings, and bells rang.

Cries came from the gatehouse as someone shouted urgent instructions. The lorry entering was being waved backward as the guards tried to close the barriers, seal off the refinery, but the vehicle was half-way through and the one behind had already pulled forward. Guards and drivers shouted and gesticulated angrily as they attempted to move the logjam. One guard ran down the line of lorries, his gun emphasising his point as he waved the vehicles back. For a moment, all was shouting and confusion.

The spirits had attacked.

"Come on," said Fer. "Let's run inside now. We can dodge between the lorries. They might not notice us."

Catherine looked doubtful, but after a moment's thought she nodded. The three of them clung to the shadows, ducking behind each of the lorries in line. One driver shouted at them from her cab, banging on the window and hurling angry words that Fer couldn't understand. Fer, with no time to think, terrified one of the guards would come running, threw an incantation at the driver, stunning her into an open-eyed slumber. It was a spell she'd worked many times to help take away the pain of someone's suffering.

The lorries at the front of the queue were angling backward and forward, attempting to manoeuvre out of the way as the guards, wielding guns, waved and pointed. The high mesh gates were half-closed, but the front lorry was still in the way.

For a moment it was wedged in place, unable to move in either direction. Fer threw herself to the ground. She'd be seen if she tried to creep alongside the container, but if she crawled underneath she had a chance. If the lorry started moving the wheels could crush her. She just had to hope she could get through before that happened.

She crawled. The vehicle's engine roared above her head, a long shaft of metal connecting the engine to the wheels spinning rapidly. She coughed on the fumes, but it didn't matter now. She turned to see if the others were following.

The Lizard King was crouching, getting ready to follow her. Fer didn't see where the shot came from. The wise man was hurled backward, blood blossoming on his shoulder where he'd been hit. His agonized cries were one more note added to the cacophony of sirens and shouts and thundering engines.

Fer began to crawl back to help him, but then Catherine's face was there, peering beneath the lorry. She shouted. "No. You go on, I'll see to him."

Fer hesitated for a moment, caught, then relented. She would only get herself captured. Turning from Catherine, she wormed her way to the front of the lorry as it juddered into life. Glancing back, she saw that Catherine was kneeling beside the prone Lizard King. Surrounding them stood a copse of legs, the guards' guns pointing down.

Fer took her chance. Not looking, not attempting to conceal herself, she scrambled up from the front of the lorry and, alone, raced for the interior of the refinery.

17 – UNQUIET SPIRITS

Fer raced for the cover of the nearest building. Cries and the clatter of running footsteps filled the air, but no one came for her and, so far as she could tell, no one shot at her. That was good.

She paused in the shadows of the nearest building. She could feel the humming buzz of the walls against her back as her gaze darted around. Now that she was inside the perimeter of the refinery her senses were returning. The aether raged with the anger of the dead spirits that had been anchored to those few, broken bones. And it wasn't just them; other spirits were answering the call. Many must have died in the construction of the refinery, crushed beneath falling walls or mangled in the machinery. Lost spirits left to wander alone and confused. These, too, joined in to strike back at their hated masters.

And there were others – those contained within the pipes that Genera used to suck Spirit from across the world to send through the portal to Angere. Some clever devilry stopped the spirits from escaping, but they felt some echo of what was occurring, and they screamed and raged to be set free from their confinement.

That was what Fer had to try and do. There was already

fighting taking place within the buildings; screams filled the air as well as the more distant calls in the aether. Cait had described the spirits attacking the living, and it seemed they could affect more solid things when they were roused: machinery and walls. But so far the pipeway appeared to be intact.

A door opened nearby and two armed Genera soldiers raced out, guns held forward as they sprinted for the perimeter. Fer took her chance. She slipped inside, erecting a hurried glamour about her face and body so that she appeared something like those armed guards to the briefest of glances. It might help a little.

She found herself in a brightly-lit corridor, the white lights complimented by spinning red bulbs along the ceiling. Growing up, she'd preferred shadows and half-light to the glare of the sun. She was one for cobwebby corners and the shade of the deep woods, preferred to wander in the dusk or the hush of a moonlit night. There was too much light in this world; it sometimes seemed like they wanted to banish the night completely. It was a sickness. Now, caught in the unremitting glare of the refinery, lost and alone, she longed more than ever to be wandering in the dappled woods of Andar, to dip her hand into the cool waters of some unnamed brook.

She hurried on. This was no time for feeling sorry for herself.

She rounded a corner and ran straight into another of the guards. With their bulky armour and the shaded mask of the helmet over their eyes, it was impossible to tell if they were human or some twisted undain monster. Could they even see her through their tinted screen, or were they seeing some machine-generated version of reality? Fer stepped backward, knowing this could be the end. When the alarm was raised she would have no chance of fighting them all.

The guard grabbed Fer by the arm and shouted something. A woman's voice, muffled. The guard gesticulated down the corridor. Fer, not understanding, said nothing, tried to pull away. Another soldier brushed past, paying them no attention. The guard holding Fer repeated her words and Fer nodded, as if agreeing to the instructions. Incredibly, the guard let go of her and raced off, too preoccupied with the attack to see through Fer's illusion.

Fer raced down the corridor in the direction she'd been told to go. There had to be a reason she'd been ordered in that direction. She passed a doorway through which she could see a room full of twisting pipes and ducts, some of them feeding into shining machinery the function of which she couldn't begin to guess. There were soldiers in there, besieged by swirling ghosts, more than one of them firing their weaponry uselessly into the air. One of the machines, struck by bullets, began to smoke and flame. Fer ducked under the windows and hurried on.

At the end of the corridor a tall set of double doors blocked her way, no handle upon them, no obvious way to open them at all. If she couldn't get through she'd have to backtrack round the building and try another entrance. There were words painted onto the door, words she couldn't read, but no doubt they were telling her she couldn't enter, that she wasn't *authorized*. Could she work some magic, break these locks, batter down the doors by whipping up a gale? Somehow she doubted it.

There was a button on the wall beside the doors, big and red like the cap of some poisonous mushroom. Not knowing what else to do she pressed it, expecting to hear more screaming alarms. Instead, a click from the door told her that some locking mechanism had been released. She pushed through and then through a second set to find herself in a huge vault, larger than the concert hall she and Johnny had gone to in search of his guitar.

Fully one third of the room was taken up by a huge iron machine. It squatted there like a dragon of polished black iron and gleaming silver. Wheels whirred and steam or smoke vented from chimney stacks all across it. One huge wheel, perhaps fifty feet tall, spun with alarming speed, metal axles turning other wheels and cogs. She had no idea how it functioned, but she could tell it was very old, a relic from a former age. Their new machines were smaller and shinier. This roaring, steaming behemoth was almost – almost – like something from back home, a blacksmith's forge perhaps, although built on a much greater scale. She could feel an intense heat blasting from it even at the distance she stood. Somewhere within it, an inferno raged.

She knew what the machine had to be. Cait had described it to them as they'd journeyed through the woods on their way to the land of ice. It was Genera's original machine, *Extraction Engine Nmbr 1*, used to suck out people's souls a century or two earlier. They fired the great beast up from time to time to impress visitors. It was clearly working now. Ten or twenty figures scurried around it, conversing, staring upward at the beast's curving sides as if unsure how to tame it.

High above, strung from the ceiling, ran the shining pipeway Cait had described. It was through this that the trapped, lost souls of this world were sucked through the portal to the White City. She could hear the high-pitched whine of their screams. Two other smaller pipes, more temporary looking, had been tethered to the main pipeway, and these, too, rang out with the cries of the lost. Genera's masters in Angere were sucking all the life-force from the people of this world they could to fuel their war.

There had clearly been fighting in the vault. Two of the armoured soldiers lay nearby on the ground, neither moving. She knelt beside them. The first was a man, his helmet half ripped-off to reveal his contorted features. He looked to have died in the throes of some terrible agony. The figure next to him was one of the undain: the face bestial, the limbs misshapen and segregated by too many joints. This creature, too, had been destroyed by the raging spirits. Their anger was a terrible thing. For the briefest moment, doubt at what they'd unleashed flashed through Fer.

The human guard clutched something like a phone in his hand. Fer took it, then edged away from the bodies around the side of the enormous vault, wondering how she could damage that high pipeway. It seemed impossible. Even if she could fly up to it she doubted she could do much to harm it, and she'd certainly be seen and shot down.

She wondered what had happened to the spirits that had attacked the guards, but even as the thought came to her they returned, a sudden rush sweeping through the vault, gleeful screams rending the air. The spirits flew at the people working on the hulking machine. Fer watched as one figure, standing high up on the machine's main cylinder, swatted at the air as if besieged by a swarm of angry insects. The figure teetered then plummeted to the ground, arms and legs flailing.

A team of soldiers raced toward the machine from another doorway. They looked as if they planned to shoot at the teeming ghosts, but then Fer saw that wasn't it. The weapons weren't firing bullets; they had flaring snouts like wide mouths. They were sucking the spirits in. Fer heard the wails as the ghosts were drawn into the devices. Genera had obviously prepared for a breach in the pipe and were fighting back.

Fer lifted the phone to her mouth and whispered into it. "Archaeon. Bookwyrm. Are you there?" She had no idea if that was how you contacted the creature or whether she had to press buttons. She should have paid more attention when Catherine or the Lizard King communicated with the creature. In any case, nothing happened. She tried again, talking more loudly. "Bookwyrm, speak to me. This is no time for games. I need you."

A little blue light winked on and off, and then the

screen changed. This display was only blacks and greys rather than the usual vivid colours, but the blocky outline of the dragon's head was perfectly clear. A plume of smoke consisting of a line of grey squares drifted from its nostrils.

"Hello, little witch. So you have finally made it inside the refinery. You took your time."

"Can you fool their systems, hide me from their cameras?"

"I've been doing so ever since you ran through the gates. Did you think you'd made it this far by your own brilliance and skill?"

She ignored the creature's taunts. "We didn't know if you'd be here. Your other selves said you were cut off."

"My other selves are, of course, completely right. Genera have managed to lock down their systems effectively. It has been an amusing battle, but I am, for the moment, isolated from the rest of the world."

"But you're still here."

"Well observed! Yes, I am. There are still plenty of places to hide in such a large and complex network. They have tried to seek me out, of course, searching for my binary patterns, but it's simply a matter of shapeshifting to evade them."

"Good. Wonderful. The thing is, I badly need your help."

"As it seems you always do."

"Yes. I know. Will you do it?"

The dragon paused, closing its eyes as if giving the question considerable thought. After its dramatic pause it replied. "As ever I am at your beck and call. Tell me what miracle you require me to work now."

"That great machine. The steaming, iron contraption."

"The old Extraction Engine, yes."

"Is it dangerous?"

"Of course it's dangerous! To you at least. It was responsible for sucking out people's souls for a hundred years. Have you learned nothing?"

"No, no, I mean, is it dangerous now? The heat from it is intense and the people operating it … they look like they're barely in control of it. The attacking spirits have killed several of them."

"Let me see."

For once she thought she understood what the creature meant. "You want me to point the phone at the machine?"

"No, no. There isn't a camera in the device you're holding. Isn't that obvious? I mean, let me go and see what the network is saying."

"Good. Do that. Only hurry. Someone is going to spot I'm not supposed to be here very soon."

The skirmish at the machine had died down, the spirits sucked from the air by the guard's wide-mouthed weapons. There was an urgency to the actions of those remaining at the machine. A jet of steam vented from the side of the main cylinder, accompanied a moment later by a piercing whistle. Even to Fer's ears it was clearly an alarm. There was a note of shrill panic to it.

Her instincts told her to get away from the rumbling, raging machine, but instead she walked toward it. She would no longer hide in the shadows. If she looked like she belonged there, people might think she did.

The heat mounted as she neared the contraption. The machine appeared to swell, looming larger and larger over her. She picked out more details: the whirring cogs and the smaller wheels turning beneath the cylinder, some of them flying around so quickly their spokes were a blur. Fer could no longer tell if the constant high-pitched scream she could hear came from the spirits thronging the aether, or the raging machinery, or both. From somewhere distant, an explosion rattled through the chamber, making the walls shake and plumes of dust cascade to the floor. The spirits were attacking all across the refinery. If they could keep the guards busy a little longer perhaps she'd have time to act.

She walked to a point where a series of control wheels and levers protruded from the side of the machine. Each was labelled with a polished brash plate but she could make nothing of the words. Someone shouted at her from twenty yards away, a man standing at another set of controls. Fer waved as if to say she understood, everything was under control, and the other figure pulled with all his weight on a long iron lever protruding from the machine.

Fer held the phone she carried back up to her ear. "Have you found anything?"

"Do you want my advice, little witch?"

"Yes, that's what I asked."

"Where are you now?"

"I'm standing at the machine."

"Well, then I'd advise you to run. The machine is out of control. It takes a lot of adjusting and monitoring to stop it exploding and the attacks of the dead have taken their toll. The machine should never have been fired up; it's far too dangerous, and now, well, I wouldn't like to be near it."

"What will happen?"

"When the internal pressure reaches a certain unknown point the main cylinder will burst. It will be a tremendous explosion. The Extraction Engine was very powerful."

Was it Fer's imagination or were the gleaming black walls of the engine shaking? The heat was parching her lips, making her eyes prickle. Her throat was so dry her voice was barely a croak. "The pipeway directly above it. The spirit pipeway. What will happen to that if the machine explodes?"

"What do you think will happen?"

"It will be severed, broken."

"Very good, little witch! It's almost like you don't need me here."

"Can you make sure that happens?"

"That's beyond even me. There are no electronic connections to the old machine. You'll have to do it yourself."

"What do I have to do?"

"I warn you, you really do not want to be anywhere near when it blows."

"Yes, I understand! Just tell me what to do."

"Describe the controls you can see."

Struggling to find the right words for the various handles and wheels and knobs, Fer did her best to explain what she could see.

"Is there a gauge?"

"A what?"

"Like a clock, but not telling you the time."

"Yes."

"What number is the hand pointing to?"

"There are no numbers. But the end of the dial is red and the pointer is there."

"Pressure is critical. Do any of the wheels have labels saying things like *Main Relief Valve* or *Pressure Vent*?"

"I have no idea! I can't read their letters!"

Despite the clattering, screaming noise all around, the bookwyrm's sigh in her ear was perfectly clear. "I will display the words on the screen for you. Look for any wheels with similar labels and turn them anticlockwise until they lock."

"Which way is anticlockwise?"

"Widdershins."

"Right. Let me do that."

"And when you've done so, little witch, do run as fast as you can, won't you? I do so enjoy our little conversations and it would be a shame not to have any more."

Fer slipped the phone into her pocket and, using both her hands, turned all the wheels she could see whose labels seemed to match the words the bookwyrm had shown her.

A group of guards clumped by as she worked, but once again they paid her no attention. People saw what they expected to see. The soldiers of Genera assumed she was someone trying to bring the machine under control and gave her no more thought.

The wheels on the machine were stiff, and more than one was hot, as if connected directly to the raging fires within. Fer stuck at her work, only occasionally swearing as the wheels refused to budge. In the end she had to use everything she had, her magic and her muscles, to force them to turn. Bethany helped too, although the witch-girl was faint, her terror at being back in the refinery clear.

When the wheels were turned, Fer paused to gaze at the bulk of the machine towering over her. It shook visibly, and the old metal seemed to have found its own voice. It creaked and whined, steam shooting from its joints. It surely couldn't hold together much longer. More cries came from the others on the machine. One stood back, arms wide, then turned and ran. Fer, taking her cue, did the same.

She followed the line of the pipeway high overhead toward another set of heavy doors. The glamour she'd been maintaining about herself slipped, but she didn't bother to rework it. Getting away from the thundering machine was all that mattered, and the guards of Genera would see that as well as she could.

She expected to be hurled to the floor by the explosion at any moment, but she reached the doors unscathed. Another red button was set there, but when she pressed it nothing happened. She tried again, hammering on it in barely-controlled panic.

Slowly, ponderously, the doors lumbered open. They were reassuringly thick and heavy, metal a foot thick as if the builders had feared the great old engine might one day explode. She slipped sideways through the opening as soon as she could and hammered on a second switch, shouting at the doors to make them shut.

Once again the doors took their time to respond. They stuttered, paused, then folded inward. Fer caught a final glimpse of the enormous machine, wreathed with steam, flame licking up its sides, and then it was gone.

She had to get farther away. She slipped through another set of doors to find herself in a second cavernous space. Cait had described this room, too. The far end of it was taken up by a cliff of bare rock. A powerful waterfall poured from it, filling the air with its rushing noise. The portal to Angere. The line of bone containers was there, as was the pipeway running directly into the cascade of water. Here was where it all went, the Spirit and the Bone, delivered to Menhroth and the horrors of Angere.

In one of the walls, overlooking the room, high square windows had been set. Fer discerned a figure standing at one of them, surveying the scene. She knew instinctively that the figure was watching her, seeing her as she really was. They had her. A moment later the doors beneath the windows burst open and a group of soldiers raced forward, guns held at the ready. They charged toward Fer.

She was taking all this in when the vast explosion shook through the walls, the stone floor bucking and rippling. She scrambled from the doors, desperate to get as far away as possible. Another huge *boom* came, rattling her ribcage. Fifty yards away, the soldiers had also been flung to the floor. They staggered to their feet, looking around in confusion, Fer momentarily forgotten.

Then Fer heard the screaming. Quietly at first, then rising in tone, a mixture of fear and anger and an uncontained joy. The trapped spirits in the pipe were free. They rushed into the air, swirling and dancing, a flood of them unleashed into the aether. Their glee was glorious and terrible. Fer caught glimpses of half-formed faces as the deluge continued. A whirlwind of them swept through the room and the soldiers, standing now, were attacked, spirits roaring through their bodies, picking the soldiers up and hurling them against the walls like rag dolls.

Would they attack her? Perhaps. There was little reason there, only blind rage. Fer raced in the opposite direction, following the line of the pipeway high overhead. The silver tube was quiet now, the high-pitched screaming from it gone. Perhaps she could hide somewhere among the containers waiting to go through the portal, escape when everything had quietened down. It was all she could do. Besides, if fire were to rage through the refinery, being near the water seemed like a good idea. The air smelled smokier than it had before, catching in her throat as she panted.

She was hurrying for the containers when more soldiers appeared through the doors. These moved with deliberate precision as if following the movements of some well-drilled manoeuvre. They fanned out across the room, forming a line to protect the portal. Fer reached one of the containers and threw herself behind it. This room was also brightly lit; there were no shadows to hide within and if there were cameras watching she'd be visible. She just had to hope Genera's attention was on the attacking spirits.

Another torrent of angry ghosts swept through the chamber, the walls no barrier to them. They hurled themselves at the soldiers, filled with their hunger for revenge. But these soldiers carried the wide-mouthed contraptions, and the dead had no defence. Some were pulled in. Others, swirling in their fury, swept through walls or floor to attack elsewhere.

The soldiers moved again, always facing away from her but closing in to form a half-circle around the portal. A half-circle which also contained Fer. They took up defensive positions around the waterfall, no doubt ordered to protect the portal and the White City at all costs.

Fer let out a deep breath. She had managed to find the once place in the refinery where she would be safe from the raging spirits. Perhaps she had a chance of surviving. The long chase into and out of the city had exhausted her utterly, but incredibly they'd done it. Done what Cait had asked.

The line of soldiers parted then to allow another knot of guards through. These carried conventional guns. They marched toward Fer. A woman pushed to the front, the only one of the group wearing normal clothes rather than bulky military uniform.

She looked directly at the place where Fer hid. She had to be Clara Sweetley, the head of Genera, Nox's replacement. The woman held up a hand, instructing her soldiers not to fire, not to move any closer. Water dripped from the woman's hair, but she paid it no attention. Fer looked around desperately, seeking some means of escape, some way of fighting back. She could see none.

The woman beckoned one of the soldiers to her side. He stooped so she could speak into his ear. The man nodded and turned to address Fer, speaking in the tongue of Andar.

"You can stop cowering in the shadows now, Fer. Did you think you'd managed to evade us? Did you think we didn't know you were here?"

More soldiers were edging along the walls, surrounding her. There was little point hiding any more. Fer stepped from behind the metal container. The spray from the nearby waterfall made every surface slick and shiny.

"We've destroyed the pipe," said Fer. "The Witch King will hold you responsible just as he held Nox responsible for losing Cait."

An expression of fury flashed across the woman's features after the soldier had translated. She passed more words back to her interpreter. "Perhaps. Except I'm not going to repeat Nox's mistakes. I'm not going to let you go free, am I?"

The woman smiled broadly then, as if, despite everything, she'd won a victory. Understanding flooded through Fer. The guards weren't there to capture her or kill her. They had herded her, cornered her quite deliberately. There would be no escape from that ring of unblinking, blank-minded soldiers, no escape from Leviathan Refinery. They had no need to capture her, because there *was* a way out, a route being offered to her.

The great waterfall at Fer's back filled the air with its noise and chilling spray. Through it lay Angere and the White City. Either Fer could step through or she'd be forced through at gunpoint. Or else carried through bound and unconscious, a gift to the Witch King from Clara Sweetley. Those were her choices.

Bethany?

Fer's dead relative's voice was little more than a distant rustle of leaves when she replied. *I hear you.*

Bethany, I'm leaving now. Back across the aether to my world. You should leave me if you wish to remain here.

Leave you?

This is your home. You're needed here. And … I don't think I'll last very long in Angere.

Don't go, Fer. It isn't safe. I've been there.

I'm sorry, I have no choice. But thank you. Thank you for everything. I hope you find peace. Stay away from the soldiers and their devices. Flee this place while you can.

Fer could feel the witch-girl's distress. Then with a wrenching pain, Bethany's presence left her.

Good bye, Fer. I'm glad to have met you. For a moment Bethany was only a whisper in the air, then she was gone.

Fer hesitated for only a moment longer. She wouldn't let her enemies have any more of a victory than they'd already won. She wouldn't let them truss her up and carry her through the portal like some tied beast. Turning away, blinking against the rush of water lashing into her face, she stepped into the soaking cascade that would take her to Angere.

To the Witch King.

18 – XOSTER

Angere

Fer stumbled from the portal, gulping for air, half-drowned from the torrents of water. The light was blinding, making it impossible for her to see what was around her. The ground she lay sprawled upon was white, but miraculously dry. *She* was miraculously dry, despite the deluge of the waterfall.

She pushed herself to her feet. She squinted, trying to make sense of where she was, steeling herself for attack from the soldiers of Genera following her through the portal, or from the undain of the White City lying in wait.

For a moment nothing happened. The only movement was from a flock of distant birds, black shapes swirling against the milky white sky. She stood alone in the middle of an enormous square, lined on all sides by towering buildings and elaborately-decorated spires. Some of them were twisted into weird shapes, leaning over alarmingly as if some earthquake had recently shaken them. Or perhaps they were supposed to look like that. Creatures that could build an entire city out of millions and millions of bones clearly weren't sane.

Everything, everything was white. The sight of it made

her stomach heave. She had crossed the aether back to her own world, but she was no nearer home. If anything, Angere was more alien to her than Cait's world. The An lay between her and whatever was left of Andar, and there was no hope. Somehow Cait had made the impossible journey across the river, but she, Fer, had no idea how to attempt such a feat. She'd escaped Genera but only by coming to somewhere far more dangerous.

Behind her, the portal was a wide oblong, framed by an ornate construction of bones, crowned by a single dragon's skull. Its red jewel eyes bored into her. That was where the pipeway led; from there the Spirit was carried away to feed the monsters of Angere. She had stopped that, at least. It was a tiny victory in the face of their overwhelming defeat, but she and the others had dealt their enemy that single blow. No more Spirit would be piped through to nurture Menhroth's armies, not for a while. It occurred to her that she should work something similar on this side of the portal. Rupture the pipe to free any spirits trapped within. Another small victory.

Still no one had come for her; the portal was unguarded, the city seemingly deserted. She thought she knew why. Menhroth was unleashing his forces against Andar, an armoured fist to crush a summer flower. Well. She could do little enough to prevent that, but she would do what she could.

She readied magic. Fire filled her. Fire felt right in this terrible, lifeless place. Fire to cleanse the corruption, fire to seer away the evil, cauterise the wound. She let the conflagration whirl inside her, like flames whipped up by an angry wind. When she could hold it back no longer she thrust out her hands and unleashed the magic at the dragon's skull.

For the briefest moment, those red eyes blazed as the flame lit them. Then the skull exploded from the fury of Fer's attack. The bone framework exploded, scattering shattered fragments. Fer covered her face with her arms and ducked as a hundred pieces of broken bone spattered into her.

Once again a wind-like sighing filled the air, the spirits' delight at being released. Once again she wondered who they were, where in that strange, terrible world they had lived and died. She would never know, and she could do little to right the wrongs inflicted on them. But she had given them that release at least. They would not be mere fuel for the army of nightmares laying waste to Andar.

Bells began to toll in the White City. Cracked, discordant, no rhythm to them, they rang out, sounding an alarm. The sound clashed off the stone surfaces, echoing, confusing.

She'd been seen. They would come for her now. The city wasn't completely depopulated; she could sense the storm clouds gathering as the undying soldiers of Angere hurtled at impossible speed toward her. The mind of Menhroth was there, too, unmistakable, a burning power at the heart of everything. His gaze had been straining eastward into Andar as he watched and directed his armies. But now he saw her, standing alone in his City of Ghosts, and the hunger blazing within him at the realisation was terrible to touch.

Menhroth saw who and what she was. She sensed his ravening delight. The blood he craved thundered through her heart and her veins. Her arrival was an unexpected gift, a joy. Clearly no word of their attack on the refinery had reached him. He would capture her and bleed her dry like some slaughtered farmyard animal, hang her from a hook until her veins dripped their last. And then he'd have the precious blood he'd searched for all this time, and hope really would be gone.

She refused to let that happen. She ran from the wide white square before they could come for her, heading toward the towering gateway that looked to be the only escape. She dare not enter any of the hideous, twisted buildings, a maze of bones she might never escape from.

The black birds scattered as she neared the archway, many of them mere tatters of feather and muscles, dead but still moving. They croaked dry croaks at her, feathers whirling to the ground like leaves falling in some morbid autumn.

Through the archway, beyond more domes and towers, she caught a glimpse of a wide strip of glistening silver. The river. It was like the sight of an old friend. She would head that way. Growing up, the vast flow of those waters had been a constant in her life. Now she was alone and lost, but it would be good to dip a hand in the An one final time. She could never reach Andar, but she could touch the waters that, in turn, touched the far shores of her home. That was as close as she could get.

Her thoughts ran on even as her feet clattered across the ground. She would do more than dip a hand in. She would not let the nightmares have her. She would stride out into the river, let the waters take her. Perhaps, by some miracle, the currents would sweep her away to Andar. More likely they would simply pick her up and take her from Angere, out into deeper waters from which there was no return, off to unknown lands. The waters or the serpents would have her and Menhroth would not. Another small victory.

Screeching cries cut the air, like those that had echoed through the tunnels beneath Manchester. The undain were communicating, drawing their net about her. She had only moments.

She half-ran, half-fell down a flight of grand stairs, slipping again and again and only just managing to keep her footing. She jarred her ankle, twisting it painfully, but hurtled on. There were undain on the steps but they were bent-over, little more than bundles of rags, cleaning the ground with tiny brushes. They paid Fer no attention as she fled.

At the foot of the stairs, a wide plain lay between her and the river. Three pipes snaked from the city to the river, disappearing into the mists, but they were flaccid, useless, their flow of Spirit cut off. She would never know if she'd made a difference, if what she'd done would have any effect on events in Andar.

The ruined remains of the ancient stone bridge stood near the pipes, stone pillars striding out over the waters. As she followed the line of it she saw that she'd been mistaken about the waters. The surface of the An wasn't moving. It was solid ice, its frozen flow gleaming brightly in the low winter sun. She couldn't wade out. Protected from the running water, her pursuers could follow her.

She stopped, chest heaving, unsure what to do. More cries keened in the air, rebounding off the terraces and steep walls of the city. There was only one thing she could think of, futile as it was. Perhaps if she slid out far enough she would find open water. Perhaps she would get that far before they reached her. Then she could slip into the freezing waters and let the currents take her.

Her breathing panicky, she raced for the bridge. If she was lucky there might even be running water to throw herself into at the end. In any case, it was the nearest point to Andar. It would be good to get that far at least.

She was half-way to the bank when the undain caught her. There was a blur of movement, a rush of cold through the air. She was suddenly surrounded: a ring of brute, twisted creatures standing there, steam rising off them from the speed with which they'd thundered to answer the summoning bells. Their animal snarls sent a shiver through her. The ring closed in, and she thought they'd rend her to shreds there and then, despite who she was. The words of the family secret rose in her mind and she prepared herself to use them, but she knew it wouldn't be enough. More and more of the monsters were arriving with each moment, and she couldn't hope to fend them all off.

Then she sensed the King once more, his trumpet voice stern as he gave his instructions to his soldiers. *Do not harm her. Bring her to me now.*

The nearest undain, a lopsided creature with hulking muscles, stamped forward, intent on picking her up and carrying her to Menhroth. There was something animal about its appearance, as if the necromancers of Angere had combined bull and man in its making. There was little intelligence in its eyes, only a fury and a hunger. The foul stench of sweat from its body made her gag. She could put an end to him at least. She'd skinned her hands from sprawling to the floor of the square. Her touch was blood; she had only to speak the words to despatch the growling horror from the world.

Another harsh cry thundered, this one much deeper. It seemed to come from the air. One of the flying undain was coming, like the one she'd destroyed on the banks of the An when everything had started. Menhroth was taking no chances, throwing more and more of his forces into capturing her. The bestial undain, its hand little more than a cloven hoof, reached out to seize her.

Then, miraculously, the misshapen undain backed away from her, eyes peering upward. All the undain stared into the sky, drawing weapons from sheaths, fanning out as if preparing themselves for attack. There were one or two giants among them: hulking creatures with glass-like flesh through which their bones and muscles were clear. These seemed to have taken charge. They were bellowing orders, instructing the undain soldiers where to stand, what to do. They peered upward, Fer forgotten.

A hand over her eyes, Fer followed their gaze. A creature did fly there. It was certainly huge, far too bulky to be one of the crows. From the long, slow beat of its wings it had to be enormous. It roared its cry once more, and this time red flame flickered from its mouth.

Understanding of what it had to be made her heart pound. A dragon. It could only be a dragon.

The vast creature stopped flapping and, angling its body into a spiral, hurtled to the ground. There was someone upon its back. A dragon and its rider flew in the skies of Angere. She had no understanding of how such a thing was possible; it was like something from the old stories.

The creature levelled out, wings wide, lancing low across the ground toward Fer and the shouting, hurrying undain. The dragon was going to destroy them. Fer stepped backward. No one tried to stop her, their attention caught by the oncoming wyrm.

She had to get away. She had no power against such a being. When it breathed its fire on the undain she'd be roasted alive as completely as them.

Yet the sight of the dragon, larger by the moment, its horned skin and gleaming red scales clearer and clearer, rooted her to the spot. The creature appeared to be flying directly at her. She could see its dagger-sharp teeth as it opened its mouth, ready to turn everyone and everything to ash. A wave of despair flooded through her. The creature was so vast as it thundered forward and she was so weak. She could do nothing, achieve nothing compared to such a beast. What had she ever achieved? She'd lost friend after friend while others did all the fighting and thinking. She almost slumped to the ground and waited for the creature to fly over her, destroy her, put her out of her misery.

With an effort, she set the dark thoughts aside. They came upon her at times, in the dead of night, or when faced with suffering or loss she could do nothing to prevent. This was keener, more overwhelming for some reason, but she did what she always did. Rather than trying to fight the despair, she imagined herself stepping aside from it, letting it carry on without her in its path. Breathe deeply through the moment, then the next and the next. Despair was natural at times, but it could suck the life out of you as surely as any of the hideous machines of the other world. She wouldn't let that happen. She would fight.

Nearby, over by the ruined bridge, a tumble of square

rocks lay in a pile, like dice left over from some incomprehensible game. If she hid behind them she might be shielded from the flames of the creature.

Fer ran. A sheet of flame blasted through the air even as she threw herself behind the rocks, then the bulk of the dragon roared overhead. The rush of its passing seemed almost to suck her into the sky. Her hair lashed around into her face. She caught a glimpse of the dragon's mind: vast and terrible and filled with an unreasoning rage. The creature thought only of destroying the undain. The malice of its mind sent a chill through her. The dragon or Menhroth; she didn't know which of the two she'd rather face.

Over the river the creature banked sharply, one wing down, then flapped massively to build up speed as it came in for another attack. The undain answered with volleys of arrows and spears, but these simply skittered off the creature's red and purple-red scales.

Wings beating furiously, the creature stalled then thumped to the ground, crushing a group of the undain beneath its bulk. The rider half-slid, half-fell from the dragon's back. She thought he was going to leap to the attack, sword flashing, but instead he staggered away, hands over his head as he dodged through the undain. His sword, she saw, was left sheathed on the dragon's flanks. It seemed strange behaviour from one of the fearless wyrm lords. The dragon lashed its head and tail around, nearly striking the fleeing rider.

Fer stood and called over to him. The rider – surely little more than a boy – hesitated for a moment, and then ran toward her. Behind him, the huge dragon vented fire, crushing more of the undain beneath its claws. The boy threw himself behind the rocks, cowering from the dragon just as Fer was.

He looked startled at the sight of her, wide-eyed. He was certainly nothing like the fearsome dragonriders from the stories. Scars lined his arms and neck, even winding up the side of his face. Someone – possibly even the boy himself – had attempted to cut wyrm lord tattoos into his skin. They were nothing like the flowing lines of Ran's markings. These were rough, as if the hand etching them had been shaky. Blue ink mingled with red blood; the boy had apparently been working on them even as they flew. The glint of alarm, of something bordering on madness, was in his eye. He'd been through a lot. But the sight of Fer seemed to calm him a little.

He passed his hand through his wild hair, a gesture of confusion. His eyes were a delicate green as he looked at her. "You ... you must be Fer. My name is Lugg."

Fer was stunned into silence. She had no idea who this boy was or where he'd come from. His accent was strange, archaic, the vowel sounds at odd angles. Their tongues, like the land, had become divided. "Hellen told you about me?"

The fighting between dragon and undain moved a little farther away, but even so they had to shout over the bellowing and screaming, the clash of metal on scales.

Lugg shook his head. "No, Cait. She said she had a distant cousin who resembled her. You were left in the other world when Cait came here. You're from Andar."

"You met Cait?"

"And Ran and Nox. It's thanks to her, I found Xoster. Do you know what happened to her?"

Fer tried and failed to make sense of everything. There was too much here she didn't understand. "Only that she reached Andar."

"Ah. That is good."

The dragon continued its rampage, sending the undain hurtling through the air with a flick of its tail, turning others into flailing balls of flame. The undain fought back, hacking with their swords, but their attacks appeared to have little effect on the dragon. If anything, they made its fury even greater.

Lugg looked at Fer, worry clear in his green eyes. "Are

you OK?"

"You mean, apart from being trapped in the White City while a dragon rampages nearby?"

"No, I mean the dragon's aura of despair. Is it affecting you? It's so easy to lose all hope. Or do witches have ways of stopping that?"

So that was it. She'd heard mention in the old tales about the despair that afflicted those encountering dragons. "We have our ways. The creature's aura isn't affecting me, it's the flame I'm worried about. The anger filling her is terrible."

The boy nodded. "Xoster's mind is all but gone. She is consumed by fury because of what was done to her."

"What was done to her?"

"She is the mother of all the other dragons, and now only she survives. The undain slaughtered her children. This was many years ago and she has lived alone ever since, consumed by fury. It's all that's left of her now."

Fer ducked behind the rocks as another gout of flame raged overhead. The heat on the top of her head was intense. Distantly she was aware of Menhroth, screaming at his soldiers to destroy the dragon. The King feared that Fer would escape. The tiniest flame of hope ignited in her heart. "Yet you tamed her, rode her?"

"Barely. I found her a month ago, in the high north, at the end of the Wyrm Way. She nearly killed me, more than once. Eventually I managed to make her understand what was happening, what we had to do."

"She let you fly her?"

The boy nodded his head from side to side in a gesture of uncertainty. The slightest grin crept across his features. For a moment he was just a boy again. "In part. Sometimes I think she forgets I'm there. It's dangerous when she starts diving and looping, but she tolerates me. I explained about the White City again and again and eventually she understood. We flew here down the wyrm roads to destroy them all."

"And can she destroy them all?"

Lugg let out a breath of air and looked Fer in the eye. "Truly I don't know. But I don't think we can stop her trying."

19 – CRASHING TO THE ICE

Andar

Cait watched on helplessly as the second and third bone catapults lurched into life, frames twitching as their arms strained backward to unleash their boulders against the walls of Caer L'dun. The first projectile had smashed through the walls not far away. She'd felt the old stones quake at the force of the impact. More than one dragonrider had been hurled to the ground, and others lay crushed under falling masonry. Perhaps the next boulder would hit the tower she and Hellen stood in. Perhaps the living machines would even try and topple the watchtower itself. It would explain why Menhroth had gone to the trouble of crafting the huge siege engines. With the Spirit being piped directly into them, they had to be capable of enormous destruction.

The wyrm lords unleashed volleys of arrows at the machines, hundreds of black bolts arcing over the river like scribbles in the air, but they couldn't reach the catapults. Even if they did they'd probably have little effect. In construction, the catapults resembled the Harvesters she'd encountered in Angere: roughly lashed together assortments of bone and flesh. Ran's knife blows and

Nox's bullets had had little effect on those creatures; she'd only been able to defeat them when Bethany showed her how to send ice creeping through them to crack them apart from the inside. The catapults were much bigger and more distant, and she was already bone-weary, but perhaps the approach would work again. There was nothing else to try. She had to be quick; there was only a moment before the catapults fired.

She steeled herself for the effort. In Angere she'd blacked out from the agony of destroying the second creature. Doing that now would help no one. But even as she reached within for the storm of ice to throw at the engines she saw she was too late. At some signal from the undain the two remaining siege mechanisms unwound, weights dropping and wheels spinning to send the arms jerking forward.

She felt the screams from all three machines a moment before she saw them go wrong. Instead of hurling their weights high into the air, the frames of the two machines buckled, as if their strength had suddenly gone, the bindings holding them together coming loose. Their arms wheeled forward unhinged. One came free completely, spinning through the air with a huge whirring sound, dragging scraps of the catapult framework with it, boulder still cupped in its enormous hand. The arm cartwheeled along the ground, end-over-end, then crashed to the ice half-way to the walls.

The other machine remained in one piece but for some reason the catapult didn't release its projectile. Instead the arm pivoted fully round and smashed into its own base, sending bones crashing, throwing the undain attendants manning the machine aside as the contraption collapsed into a jumble of useless fragments.

Cait felt the three sorcerous machines die, felt the fear in their choked screaming through the aether before it cut abruptly off.

There was another moment of silence across Caer

L'dun, both sides watching events on the ice. Cheers went up from the wyrm lords on the walls, snarls of rage from the undain answering them.

"What happened?" said Hellen. Her expression was a mixture of astonishment and distaste. "Why did those things destroy themselves? Did you manage to get inside their minds?"

Cait had sensed the panic of the machines clearly. "No. The Spirit feeding them, maintaining them, was cut off. It's like their power supply was severed just as they were about to fire. They ... asphyxiated."

"Those are pipelines trailing out of them?"

Cait nodded. "They must lead to the White City. Something's happened there, cutting off the flow to the machines as they fired."

Hellen stared westward to the river, eyes narrowed, as if unable to believe what she was seeing. "Fer, perhaps," she said quietly

"In Angere?" asked Cait. "Can you see her there?"

"No, no. It's too far. After all the magic we've worked I can barely see my own hand straight." Hellen smiled a weak smile. "Still, I suppose it doesn't matter what the reason is, it came just in time."

"Yes."

On the ground, the wyrm lords were racing to defend the breach in the walls, directed by a screaming Barion. While some of the riders climbed onto the ruined walls, swords drawn to face an undain onslaught from the river, others tried to pull clear the injured lying half-crushed under the fallen stones.

"I'm going to help them," said Hellen. "I can't mend bones and close wounds from this distance."

"I'll come, too," said Cait.

Hellen looked like she was about to disagree but thought better of it. She headed for the staircase.

Borrn moved ahead of her. "I'll go first."

"If you must," said Hellen. "There are none of the

creatures there, not at the moment."

"Even so, Ran and I slayed many of them on the stairs. I'd like to be sure they're dead and not waiting to grab your ankles as you walk by."

At the foot of their tower, the remains of many undain were strewn about on the stones of the ground. Cait turned away from the sight of the hacked, broken bodies of the attackers, at the frank, accusing stares on their dead faces. The two wyrm lords had fought off a huge number while Cait and Hellen worked their magic from the high window. Ran was expressionless as he studied Cait's reaction to the slaughter.

Weaving across the body-strewn courtyard, the four of them ran for the breach in the walls. The quietness of the lull in the fighting had been replaced by a chorus of clanking armour, the swish of blades being sharpened, the stifled cries of the injured.

The fighting had been going on for several hours, and so far the wyrm lords had resisted, beating back wave after wave of attacking undain. But the cost to the defenders was grim. Many were dead, and many others terribly injured. One Red Wing rider sat propped up against a wall, staring into the distance in apparent disbelief, clutching his right hand to his ruined left shoulder, the point where his arm had once been.

Hellen and the other surviving witches of Islagray moved among the wounded, helping where they could to stem bleeding or, at least, to alleviate pain. The riders, too, helped, bandaging wounds or cauterising the worst with red hot iron brands. Cait turned away from such sights, but she couldn't escape the agonized cries of the wounded nor the sickening smell of singed flesh.

Hellen's jaw was set in a line of grim determination as she knelt beside a green-tattooed rider, a woman surely not much older than Cait. The rider's eyes were wide and she breathed in tiny, rapid breaths. Hellen placed a hand on the rider's forehead and, after a moment, the rider's eyes closed.

"Not much glory in it, is there?" said Hellen.

"You've given her sleep?"

"It's all I can do for her, take her away from her pain. The damage is too great. Even Ariane would have been unable to help."

Cait stared down at the peacefully sleeping rider. "What will happen to her?"

The expression on Hellen's face was stark. "She won't wake up. It's all I can offer her."

"It's terrible," said Cait. "Just terrible."

"Yes. And it isn't over yet. The undain have lost five times as many as the defenders but the difference is they don't care. They'll keep throwing themselves at the walls. Their soldiers are dispensable and ours aren't. I don't know how such evil can be fought."

Moments later, a great swelling roar from outside the walls signalled a fresh attack. Ran and Borrn came to shepherd Cait and Hellen away, back to the relative safety of the tower overlooking the scene. Hellen looked like she was going to refuse, stay by the walls where she could work what healing she could.

"You're more use up there," said Borrn, indicating the tower with a nod of his head. Blood ran freely over one of his ears. "Working your spells on the attackers. Down here it just takes more of us to defend you."

With a scowl, Hellen assented. They climbed to their room in the tower as the first screams, the first clangs of metal on metal, resonated around the fortress. The next wave of the undain assault had begun.

Barion came to find Cait and Hellen again an hour later. His chest heaved and his gaze darted warily around as if he constantly expected attack. There was a hint of madness to his bulging eyes, as if he was close to the point of breaking. Some heavy blow had sliced through the armour above his elbow. Blood ran down the leather protecting his forearm as if it were his armour that was bleeding. "We won't survive the next attack. We can't defend the Anward wall with that breach; it would take half our numbers. We're stretched too thin. You and the others of Islagray must follow me to the watchtower."

Hellen hesitated, one eye on the press of bodies, the clashing swords on the battlements. "You mean to abandon them?"

"The defenders on the walls will buy you time," said Barion without emotion. "There is nothing more we can do."

"We'll be trapped like birds in a cage."

"No. There is a secret tunnel beneath the tower you can escape through."

"A tunnel?"

"Please, we only have a few moments."

"Very well. Show us the way."

Barion hurried from the room, clattering down the steps to the courtyard. He, Ran, and Borrn escorted them to the watchtower, fighting off the screaming undain attackers that launched themselves forward. Other groups of riders, Jenath and Beltaine among them, converged on the studded wooden doors. There were perhaps thirty wyrm lords in all, shepherding the ten or eleven surviving witches of Islagray. They entered the high-ceilinged hall that took up the whole of the ground floor of the watchtower. The riders set about barricading the doors, slotting oak beams into place to brace them even as heavy blows thudded upon them from outside.

When they were done, there was a moment of uneasy calm, the sounds of the fighting hushed by the thick walls.

Danny, Johnny and Merdoc appeared down the spiral stairs, wide-eyed with alarm as they peered into the hallway. Danny ran to Cait and clutched her tight. Johnny wandered up more slowly, stroking his chin as if pondering some deep mystery. Merdoc stayed where he was in the shadows of the doorway, flinching at each thump on the doors.

The walls of the hall were bare stone, but large, colourful tapestries hung upon them. The dragons seemed alive in the embroidery: wyrms soaring through the clouds, swooping around towers or across battlefields, flame unleashed on the armies depicted on the ground. Battles from ancient history. Cait recognized Caer D'nar in several of the scenes. The pictures were glorious, heroic, the huge dragons much more like those she'd imagined. Their glittering scales and the gold-edged fire breathing from their horned heads was beautifully stitched. But she'd seen what fighting really meant: the agonies and the horrors, the shattered limbs and the blind terror. The tapestries were a lie, a fantasy. She turned away from them.

"So, there's a tunnel," said Hellen. She actually managed to look amused as she addressed Barion. "The riders of old actually thought it possible you might be attacked and defeated one day?"

"They knew what we might have to face," said Barion, weariness in his movements. "They'd already been beaten in Angere and thought it likely such a thing could happen again. They built the passageway as a last resort."

"And where does it lead?"

"The location of the other entrance is a secret known only to the Wing chiefs. The tunnel cuts a hundred yards through the ground and emerges below the waterline of the An. There are some of the original bridge foundations still in place there. The passage opens out between two of the old stanchions."

"So we'll get wet?"

Barion shrugged. "A short swim into the water and back up to the surface. It's better than the alternative. Can you manage it?"

"Can you?"

Barion didn't respond to Hellen's question. "Come," he said. "We will show you the way. Perhaps, if we are fortunate, we will be able to escort you to Islagray."

"Those left outside that door will be killed."

Barion's gaze fell to the worn stone tiles of the floor. He spoke hesitantly, his angry bluster gone. "Caer L'dun is lost. Our only hope is to retreat to the Isle. Perhaps, somehow, we can defeat the undain there. With your help, eldest of Andar. Those who remain will give us this chance to escape. We have fought well, fought with honour, and killed many of them. But you were right. We weren't enough."

Hellen stepped closer and put a hand on his arm. "You did more than I thought possible. Much more. Andar may still survive to thank you."

Barion didn't meet her gaze. He walked to one of the tapestries, the tapping of his boots loud in the quiet of the hall. The tapestry depicted a red and a blue dragon entwined in some aerial dance. The tower of Caer D'nar was visible in the background, surrounded by the teeth-like summits Cait remembered. Barion pulled aside the tapestry to reveal a low wooden door. Jenath produced a key on a silver chain and unlocked it.

Inside was a square stone room. In its centre a heavy iron grille, padlocked, covered a flight of steps leading down into the darkness. A barrel stood nearby, an array of unlit torches fanning out from it. A low fire glowed in a corner, smoke leading through a small flue in the roof. The riders had clearly kept this escape route prepared. Borrn and Beltaine took turns to light the torches and hand them out while Barion knelt to unlock the grille with a key of his own. His torch flickered and roared at the rush of air blowing up from under the ground. Jenath closed and locked the outer door behind them. Everything was done with a calm reverence, a quiet, as if it were some ceremony the dragonriders were performing, not the abandonment of their fortress and home.

They descended steep steps that wound beneath the tower. Cait clutched the rough rope strung down the steps. As they descended, the stones became slick with a green slime that made it treacherous underfoot. The air smelled of damp soil and the sickly scent of the oil burning on the torches.

At the bottom of the spiral, another heavy iron door barred their way. Jenath found more keys from her chain and used them to spring the three locks. With a discordant grate, the door swung open. Barion, behind her, held his sword at the ready, fearful of finding the undain waiting on the other side. There was no sign of them. The tunnel led into thick darkness.

Cait and the others shuffled forward, the passageway always sloping down. The walls were rough now, hewn or blasted from bare rock by the riders of old. The shifting light of the torches cast misshapen shadows across the stones. Occasionally Cait splashed through pools of icy water. No one spoke. After perhaps twenty minutes the tunnel opened into a round cave that looked like it was natural. Stalactites dripped cold water onto their heads. Icy air blew down from two narrow air vents in the roof, and Cait caught the distant scent of leaf-mould and mud. On the far side of the room, the floor ended and the water began, a semi-circular pool of darkness lapping at the stones.

"It is only a short way," said Barion as he stared into the pool. "A few yards down and then back to the surface. There are rings in the rock you can pull yourself along by. I'll go first and return if all is clear. If there is ice I'll try and break it apart." An iron hammer lay beside the water, as if left there for exactly that purpose. Barion strapped his rider's sword to his back, then looped the hammer's strap over his wrist.

"And if you don't return?" asked Hellen. Her voice echoed strangely in the cave.

Barion sat on the lip of the rock, his legs in the water up to his knees. "Then I am dead and you must do as you see fit."

He slipped into the pool, the water swallowing him up.

Ripples furrowed its surface. Ran and Borrn stood alongside with their swords at the ready, wary of what might emerge. Jenath and the other wyrm lords guarded the tunnel they'd come down. There was no sound of pursuit, no thunder of hurrying feet down the passageway. Cait looked to the pool. She found she was counting to herself, waiting for Barion to reappear. After a minute there was no sign of him. She glanced at Hellen. The old witch's face was a frown. Danny squeezed Cait's hand.

After two minutes, and then three, there was still no sign of the rider. Then, in a rush of water he reappeared, gasping for air. Even in the light of the torches his skin looked blue from the cold water. "The way is clear," he said. "Follow me through."

One by one they let themselves into the pool. When it was Cait's turn she dipped her feet warily into the icy waters. She couldn't dawdle; a queue of witches and riders waited behind her. Gulping in a mouthful of air she pushed herself off. The shock of the cold was alarming, so intense that she almost panicked, her body screaming at her to get out, get warm. Floundering with her hand she found one of the iron rings and forced herself to go deeper, pulling herself down. She already felt numb, the An sucking the heat from her body. She was short of air, the need to breathe becoming more urgent with each moment. Her fingers found another ring and then another, and she saw a blur of light above her. She hauled herself toward it, breaking into the air with a cry, flailing and splashing. Strong hands grasped her, pulling her to the bank.

She stood on the muddy lip of the An, shivering alarmingly, clutching herself tight. They were at the same point on the river that Hyrn's boat had left them, the same place Fer was first attacked by the undain. Slender trees, branches sparkling with frost, surrounded them, concealing them from the road. Ice covered the river but a ragged hole had been punched through it. One by one, the others emerged from the waters as if the An were giving birth to them. Cait did what she could to help each of them up the slippery banks.

Hellen emerged, her grey hair plastered to her scalp. She looked old and frail, no longer the fearsome woman who had plans for everything and everyone. Her words were barely audible as she chattered through clenched teeth. "Help me work some heat, Cait." The old witch began to lay shivering hands on those who'd come through, sending a glow of magical warmth into them to counter the worst effects of the freezing water. Cait followed, but she made sure to warm Hellen first.

When they were all through they pushed past the trees, frozen leaves crunching beneath their feet. Ran went first to scout out the road. There was no sign of the undain in either direction. The top of the watchtower was visible above the treetops. Figures were visible in the windows up there, little more than silhouettes. Whether they were dragonriders or undain she couldn't tell.

"Where is *Smoke on the Water*?" asked Cait. She could see no sign of the boat on the ice. Her clenched jaws hurt from shivering.

"An hour or two south, out of the way of any trouble," said Johnny.

"Better get going," said Hellen. She looked a little more like herself now, more composed, although she still shivered, and water dripped from her lank hair. "I seem to have made this journey from Forness to Islagray a lot of late. Perhaps this will be the last time."

Three crows skimmed overhead in a V formation, flying low and fast as if they, too, were fleeing the undain. Cait had taken only a couple of steps when a thunderous rumbling shook through the air. She turned to see the watchtower swaying. A cloud of smoke billowed from its base as if a fire had been set under it, or as if the stones at its base had been smashed to pieces. The tower sagged then slumped to the ground, breaking in half as it fell. It toppled westward from the headland and onto the An, as if the ancient stones wanted to recreate the bridge from which they'd once been taken. Huge plumes of spray shot into the air as the tower crashed to the ice.

Barion and the other riders watched without comment. Hellen placed a hand onto Barion's shoulder. "It served its purpose. One way or another Andar has no need of a watchtower any more."

Barion nodded. The hunted look in his eyes was still there. "We must hurry. We are easy pickings out here in the open."

Hellen smiled through her weariness. "When Ran first came to the Isle, I told him other riders might follow. Seems I was right about that."

Barion turned and resumed marching. "We haven't got there yet. There's no way we can outrun the undain, and every chance we'll be slaughtered before we get anywhere near Islagray."

"Well," said Hellen, "that's a cheery thought." She set off after the dragonrider.

20 – ACROSS THE AN

Angere

X oster roared in her fury. Fer cowered behind the blocks of stone as the huge dragon lashed around, spraying fire at anyone or anything daring to come near. In truth it wasn't that, or the creature's enormous size and strength, that really alarmed her. It was the hatred, the unreasoning wrath burning in the wyrm's mind. The dragons of old had hidden their thoughts behind impenetrable walls, so she'd read. They were noble, wise beings that formed deep bonds of friendship and understanding with their riders. Xoster made no attempt to conceal her true self. Perhaps she simply didn't care, or perhaps the rage within her was too great to contain. Or perhaps, over the centuries, alone with her loss, she'd simply forgotten how to shutter her thoughts and feelings. The aether screamed with the storm of the dragon's hatred, just as the seared ground smoked from her red fire.

Fer caught the wince of alarm on Lugg's face, cowering next to her behind the massive stones of the ruined bridge. Despite everything he'd been through there was a vulnerability about him, a hint of the frightened boy. The dragon's bright flame burned in his wide eyes as he watched the scene, and Fer found herself wondering what Cait had made of him.

In any case, his connection with the dragon was clearly precarious, a long way from the deep trust enjoyed by the riders of old. Lugg had only been known to Xoster for a few weeks, not the long years a true understanding required. That he'd found her and been able to communicate with her at all was remarkable. But Xoster was clearly out of control, and Lugg and Fer were in as much danger from her as from the soldiers of Menhroth.

On the wide steps that led to the higher levels of the city, many undain were gathering. At some signal they would sweep down the steps like a tide, and while many would doubtless be set afire by Xoster, or trampled beneath her claws, some would inevitably get through. And then more as the wyrm tried to throw off her attackers, and before long even this huge creature would be overwhelmed. Overwhelmed and killed.

Perhaps there was no hope for Xoster, perhaps she was too far gone in her grief, but the thought of the last dragon being destroyed was suddenly unbearable.

"We have to get away," said Fer. She had to shout over the sound of the raging dragon. "Can you try to reason with her once more?"

Lugg didn't take his eyes off Xoster. He flinched visibly at each new roar of fury, each thud rumbling through the ground. "I could try. If she sees me she might relent and let me near. Sometimes, though, it's best to stay away."

"There may not be time," said Fer. "Menhroth is here. He'll throw everything at her."

Lugg looked at the towers and domes of the bone city, at the soldiers thronging there. He nodded. "The problem is getting Xoster to understand. She sees the undain and wants to attack. That's all she thinks about."

Fer ducked behind the cube of stone as another arc of fire flashed through the air, reeking of sulphur. Nearby, the blocks of the ancient bridge lay scattered down the bank of the An, some half submerged in the frozen water, like stepping-stones leading away from Angere. An idea came to her. She wanted more than anything to get home, even if there wasn't much left of it. "If we could get through to her that there are undain elsewhere, more of them, would she go and attack them instead?"

"Probably. The more the better so far as she's concerned."

"So let's fly across the An. Obviously it's frozen now. If the undain can cross it then why can't she? It isn't running water any more."

Lugg gazed into the east, considering. "You think most of the army is there?"

"Has to be. Those pipes lead due east, following the line of the old bridge. That takes them to Forness, the tower of the dragonriders. It must be under attack. And if the undain have reached there, then almost all of Andar is gone. Perhaps we can help while there's still time. Or be there at the end, at least."

After a moment Lugg nodded his head. "If I can get it through to her that the undain are doing to Andar what they did to Angere she might make the attempt."

"Does she know some of the riders escaped there? The dragonless ones like Ran, I mean?"

"Hard to say. If I can explain that, it might make a difference, too. Ran said there was a tower like Caer D'nar?"

"Caer L'dun, yes. It's where the Andar bridgehead used to be."

"I'll tell her that, tell her it's under attack. It might be enough. On the other hand she might ignore me, or even think I'm attacking her."

He was about to step out from behind the stones when the first assault from the city came. Twelve of the giant undain descended the wide steps that led to the river level. They looked something like wyrm lords but twice as tall, with eerie glowing lines instead of tattoos upon their ice-clear skin. She could see the purple and red of their muscles, the heave and pump of their organs, as they fanned out to surround Xoster.

The sight of the undain wyrm lords – if that was what they were – goaded Xoster to new heights of fury. She sprang at the nearest of them, huge wings flapping to give her distance, flame pouring from her maw. An undain was lit up, immolated. For a moment, incredibly, the creature survived the furious heat, even took a step forward as if intending to attack. Then it slumped to the ground, still burning.

Xoster roared noise and fire into the sky in exultation. The other wyrm lords, seeing their opportunity, leaped to the attack. They surrounded her, moving with incredible speed, one moment *there* and one moment *there*. They hacked at those parts of the dragon they could reach: her lower limbs, her flanks, her shoulders. A cry of purest agony poured from Xoster, and she whipped around, trying to face each of her attackers. But whichever way she turned there were wyrm lords to her side and behind, swords lunging.

For a moment it looked like the undain might be able to wear her down. But Xoster threw herself into the air again, spinning as she landed with an earth-shaking thump thirty or forty yards from the ring of undain. Her attackers, seeing what she was doing, raced to surround her once more, but even they couldn't move quickly enough. Xoster breathed a wide arc of fire, so intense Fer had to shade her eyes. When she looked again, there were twelve burning undain standing in a circle. One by one they toppled and fell.

She was about to say something to Lugg when he stepped out of their hiding place and, arms held wide as if he intended to embrace Xoster, walked toward her. Xoster, seeing him, snaked her horned head around. She breathed fire, but into the sky. Lugg looked so small in comparison to her. Xoster could burn him or crush him in a moment if she chose. Fer, heart pounding as she watched, caught something of the confusion in Xoster's mind. Lugg was a rider and the riders of old had loved Xoster's children, paired with them, rode them through the skies. But the riders of old had also betrayed them, turned against the dragons, become the creatures they now were. The creatures Xoster wanted to crush and kill.

Still Lugg walked forward, moving slowly, no weapons in sight, no threat. When he was close enough he dropped to one knee and bowed his head. A pause followed in which no one moved, not even the mass of undain. Fer was aware of a conversation taking place between Lugg and Xoster, words and ideas passing between their minds. Lugg had to repeat himself to get his message through.

Finally the great dragon, sending one final cone of fire into the sky, lowered her own head, as if to return Lugg's bow. She'd accepted him for the moment, saw him as a friend, a rider. The urge to take to the skies and unleash death on the loathsome creatures attacking Andar raged within her. Fer wondered how long it would last, whether Xoster's self-control would seer away her reason and she'd turn on Lugg, see him as the enemy. It was entirely possible.

Lugg climbed up the scales of Xoster's forequarters to seat himself on her back. He waved to Fer to join him. The undain, perhaps seeing what was about to happen, surged forward in a mass, rolling down the stairs like a flood, intent on overwhelming Xoster and destroying her where she stood. From somewhere in the shadows of the aether, Fer was aware of the presence of Menhroth, urging them on.

Fer ran for Xoster. There was no time to approach the great beast slowly and with reverence. She had to hope Lugg had explained about her, too. She steeled herself for the effect of the dragon's aura, hoping to blot it out as much as she could. It didn't come. Whether Xoster had accepted her, or whether the dragon's mind was now too far gone to make the effect work, Fer didn't know.

She reached one of the creature's four legs without being burned to a cinder. Xoster's splayed foot, her cruel claws, were as big as a kitchen table. Fer began to climb. The scales on Xoster's skin were as hard as dried wood, providing plenty of handholds and footholds. Lugg reached down to haul her up. She sat in front of him, clutching Xoster's neck as tightly as she could. She could feel the great pounding rush and heat of the beast's body beneath her.

With a dizzying lurch, Xoster jumped into the air and beat her outspread wings. Fer's stomach fluttered as the ground fell away. Xoster turned and banked and for a moment the walls and towers of the White City, the faces of the gathered undain, filled the world. Then they were over the river and level again. The surging motion was like being on a galloping horse but many times more violent. Fer came free from the dragon's back completely on each downbeat. She gripped the dragon's hide in panic.

"Hook your toes under her scales," Lugg called from behind her.

Slowly she began to relax, move with the body of the beast. They flew over wide expanses of ice, greyness beneath them and foggy cloud all around. The thin lines of the pipes guided them. Freezing air streamed into her, making her eyes water and her cheekbones hurt keenly. Daring to glance back she caught a glimpse of the city fading into the mist. Far below the surging waters of the An pulsed like a heartbeat, covered by the ice but still present. It pulled at her; the huge flow sucking the magic from her. But the frozen layer smothered it, dampened it, and Fer knew she could work magic if she needed to, just as Xoster could fly despite the vast expanse of rushing water.

Somewhere in the distance, hours of flight, lay what remained of Andar, her home. Excitement and dread filled

Fer in equal measure.

After an hour they saw figures on the ice. Long lines snaked across the river, heading westward from Andar. At first, thinking they were the defeated undain retreating to Angere, a thrill of hope went through Fer. But, reaching out with her mind's eye, she saw the truth of it. They were the people of her home being marched in chains to the White City. She wondered if there were individuals among them she knew, friends or family. Those she'd helped through birth or sickness. She picked through the lines of light trying to identify auras, but there were too many of them. Far too many.

Lugg had worked out who they were, too. He shouted into the rushing wind. "There's nothing we can do. There must be some of the undain there, but we can't attack without risking all the prisoners."

Fer nodded her reply. He was right. It didn't make her feel any better about leaving them. "Xoster agrees?"

"She sees what they are. She knows they aren't the enemy."

Eventually the familiar peaks and hills of Forness came into view, an outline of deeper grey in the misty gloom. The trees of the Crow Woods shaded the nearby slopes darker. On the river, the pipes led in sinuous lines to three large structures, their form and function hard to work out from the air. One looked ruined, little more than a jumble of bones, but the other two were structures of some sort. Individual undain, tiny as beetles, crawled over and around them.

Then the ruin of Caer D'nar came into view and for a moment Fer couldn't believe what she was seeing. The watchtower had been a constant presence in her life: visible for miles around, glimpsed between trees or over the tops of roofs. She'd walked under it many times on the road north. Now it lay in shattered ruins, the tower's back broken as its stones littered the edge of the river. The undain had destroyed the fortress of the wyrm lords.

Xoster roared in fury at the sight, Fer feeling the beast's rumble through her body as much as she heard it. When the sound had faded, Lugg shouted, "Can you see the undain? Are they still there?"

There were only a few figures crawling over the ruined walls of the fortress, no sign of an attacking force. Perhaps the Angere army had been defeated. Fer closed her eyes and tried to find them. It was a skill that had come fleetingly to her that first day, when she'd walked with the merchant up the road. She'd felt the sense of *wrongness* flying at her from the An and everything had changed. Since that day, pursued by the horrors in the other world, she'd grown more accustomed to finding the creatures with her mind's eye.

It didn't taker her long now. They were still there. The number of them was incredible. It was like glimpsing a lake of shadow flooding the land.

"I see them," she called back to Lugg.

"Where?"

"South. Only a few miles."

"They're heading to this Witches' Isle?"

That had to be it. Islagray Wycka would be where it ended. If that fell Andar was no more. "I think they're following the road and the river, then they'll cut inland."

"Are there any of them behind us? On the river?"

"Can't sense any."

Lugg went silent and a moment later Xoster banked to the right, so steeply that Fer cried out as she felt herself slipping from the dragon's back. They were diving too, picking up speed. The air rushed at her face so hard she couldn't breathe. Alarmed, she managed to cling on with her toes and inhale by turning her head to one side. After a moment they levelled out again, Fer's head swimming from the suddenness of the motion. They were over land, the tree tops sweeping by beneath them. The road wound along the edge of the river, appearing and disappearing between the black leafless branches.

"We need to get off," Lugg shouted. "When she attacks them she'll forget about us. We'll be thrown off is she loops or dives."

"How?"

"I'll try and persuade her to stop somewhere before we reach the undain. Once she sees them there'll be no stopping her."

There was nowhere among the heavily wooded slopes for a creature the size of Xoster to land. The only possible place was the ice, although whether it would support the dragon's weight Fer had no idea.

As she peered that way she caught sight of a small knot of figures on the river. Puzzled, she quested and found, to her surprise, they weren't undain. They, too, were people, and some of them she knew. What were they doing out there?

She pointed toward them, south and west. "There are friends there. Can Xoster take us to them?"

Again Lugg didn't reply as he communed with the dragon. Xoster's body continued to lurch as she beat her wide wings. There appeared to be an extra urgency to her movement, a keenness, as Xoster closed in on the undain she so despised. Then with another roar, filled with rage it seemed to Fer, Xoster banked right, heading for the tiny group of figures on the An.

"She's not going to stop," called Lugg.

"What?"

"She'll fly over them but she's not going to stop."

"So how do we..."

"Can you fly us off?"

"What?" shouted Fer again.

"Cait said witches in Andar could fly through the air. I thought you could take both of us down."

"I don't..."

"We're nearly there. It has to be now."

Cait was climbing into *Smoke on the Water* to sit beside Danny when a cry came up from Ran. They'd left the main party fleeing south to pick up the miraculous boat. The sooner they made it back to the Isle, the sooner they could prepare what defences they could muster. Borrn sat where Nox had been on the way north, and he stood to peer where Ran was pointing.

"In the sky! A dragon!" Ran's voice, normally so neutral and level, was filled with both wonder and something like terror.

"It cannot be," said Borrn, his voice catching in his throat.

"One of the undain," said Danny. "Has to be."

Cait knew immediately it wasn't. She'd been touched by that mind before; been engulfed by its searing fury. Lugg had headed into the north, and she'd assumed she'd never see him again. But he'd succeeded in doing something at least. The fury-filled mind Cait had glimpsed from Caer D'nar was there in the flesh, sweeping at them like a thunderstorm.

"Xoster," she shouted. "It's Xoster."

The two wyrm lords stood their ground as the dragon blasted forward. Cait looked around in desperation. She could think only of getting away. The intrusion of Xoster's mind in Caer D'nar had been agony. The dragon was insane, consumed by her rage, barely able to differentiate between the undain and the living. But there was nowhere to hide. Cait half-climbed, half-fell out of the boat and crouched on the ice, as if the spars of the little craft would offer some protection. Danny and Johnny followed her.

Hellen was working some magic, bending her will to gale or fog to fend off or deceive the dragon. It was too late. Xoster passed over them, blotting out the whole of the sky with her wings, her roar filling the world. Everyone, even the wyrm lords, threw themselves to the ice. Cait felt the howling touch of the dragon's mind. But there was no flame, no raking claws. Xoster wasn't attacking them. She swept over, banked sharply, and flew eastward to the land, huge wings beating to speed her forward.

"What the hell was that all about?" shouted Johnny.

"Those two, I think," said Hellen.

Up in the sky, two figures were half-flying, half-falling to the ground. By the way they flailed their arms, their descent was clearly uncontrolled. They were close to thumping into the ice when Hellen stepped forward and sent a heavy, rolling fog streaming from her hand to cover the ice beneath them. Somehow the fog was thick enough to cushion them, and they disappeared into it with no more than a soft *crump*.

Cait and the others ran over. She'd seen who the two falling from the sky were, two people she thought she'd never see again.

Fer and then Lugg emerged from Hellen's mist, both walking, both alive. Cait ran up to Fer and hugged her, the girl who looked like her. "How are you here? I thought you were trapped in our world. I thought you were dead."

"It's a long story," said Fer, "although perhaps not as long as yours."

There was so much Cait wanted to ask. "You were there when, you know, my mother…"

Fer nodded. "I was. And I'll tell you everything, I promise. For now we need to get to Islagray. I saw the scale of the army descending on it."

"We've been one step ahead of them all the way south from Guilden," said Cait.

Hellen watched the two of them from a few paces away, a tremble of delight on her features. She stepped forward. "It's good to see you, Fer. At least I didn't send *you* to your death."

"You didn't send anyone to their death. We did what we wanted, including Seleena."

"So that was Xoster? She's alive?"

"Lugg found her, talked to her. She's insane, I think, her mind lost to grief."

"Ah," said Hellen, watching the distant dot in the sky. "Understandable, I suppose. She's gone to attack the undain?"

"She has. The desire to destroy them consumes her."

Hellen's eyes narrowed as she made calculations. "So there'll be a dragon flying over Andar at last. I doubt Menhroth foresaw this turn of events, but even Xoster won't be able to account for them all. She is fearsome indeed, but they have flying creatures of their own, and necromancers that will fight back."

"She may slow the undain down, at least," said Cait. "Give the other witches and riders a chance to escape."

"Yes," said Hellen. "She may."

Lugg, meanwhile, stood with Ran and Borrn. Lugg's eyes were wide as he looked to the riders. Borrn clapped Lugg on the shoulder and Lugg grinned, looking very much the boy again. The skin on his face and arms was livid from the tattoos he'd given himself. His workmanship was poor, nothing like the swirling lines the other riders sported, but they'd been enough. Lugg was something Ran and Borrn could never be: a true dragonrider. The riders of Caer L'dun were treating him like one of their own.

Cait crossed to hug him close, too. "It's good to see you again. I thought you were mad going off into the mountains. I'm glad I was wrong."

Lugg's gaze flicked between Cait and Fer. "I'm glad you were, too."

"Was it terrible? I want to know everything that happened."

He was about to speak when Hellen intervened. "Such talk can wait. There are more pressing matters. Tell me, Lugg, what exactly will Xoster do?"

"She'll attack any undain she sees."

"Can you control her, direct her?"

Lugg stared into the east as he shook his head. "No. When she is calm she can sometimes be reasoned with. Now there is little of that wise and ancient being left, and there is no talking to her. She thinks only of killing."

"It is a sad ending to her long story," said Hellen. "Come. We can all squeeze into the boat and tell our tales as we head to Islagray and our own conclusions."

Barion stopped as Jenath laid a hand on his shoulder. "Something you should see."

The remaining dragonriders and the witches they were protecting had climbed the slope of one of the round, rolling hills that lay between the An road and Islagray. The light was fading, the day short, but they wouldn't stop when the darkness came. The entire undain horde was at their back, and the Isle of the Witches offered the only sanctuary to be found in Andar.

The walls of Caer L'dun were thick and tall, but they lay in broken ruins. There were barely any dragonriders left, a handful at most, for all their skill and sacrifice. Five hundred years ago they had failed Angere and now they had failed Andar. Barion fingered the string of red gems around his neck, the stones that contained the memories of the riders' shame. He was the chief of the wyrm lords, and *he* had failed Andar. That damned witch, Hellen Meggenwar, had been right. Right about the numbers they'd faced, right about losing. Well, they would stay true to the end, fight to defend Islagray. He was under no illusions it would achieve anything.

"What is it?" He was too tired to keep the irritation from his voice. What was the point of any of it now?

"In the sky," said Jenath, the confusion in her voice clear. "A flying creature."

"Another of those cursed undain?"

"No, I think not. It doesn't fly like them. It isn't clumsy and awkward. It flows and floats. Barion, if I didn't know better I'd say it was a dragon."

Barion peered into the gloom, trying to see what Jenath was seeing. His eyes were old and his sight of distant things was often a blur, especially when he was weary. A sword-blow to his face had done something to one of his eyes, his vision through it milky. "Where?"

"There. You see the three hills together on the horizon?"

Even he could see the Revenant Army flooding down the slopes, covering them. "Yes."

"Beyond, between the left hand and the middle hill. It approaches from the west."

Barion narrowed his eyes and saw. "I don't … ah, yes. Some kind of bird? A raven perhaps?"

"It's too large. At that distance it must be enormous." Jenath glanced at Barion and there was the slightest glimmer of wonder in her eyes. Barion frowned and looked away. A flare of bright flame, orange and scarlet, flickered across the most distant ranks of the undain. They were too far for any sound to be heard, but a shiver ran through the massed army as the individuals in it peeled back to escape the attack.

The flying creature soared nearer, cutting through the undain ranks, flame billowing. It swept forward at huge speed, spewing fire onto the front ranks, then flew on, toward Barion and the others, banking for another pass. It passed overhead, almost knocking the riders and witches over with the rush of its passing. Its head and wings and body were deep red, flame red, but underneath its scales were a livid purple shading to pure black.

Barion peered upward in wonder. A dragon. A dragon flew in the skies once more. And it could only be Xoster, the mother of them all. He stared at the great beast with a childish thrill filling his heart. In his dreams he rode the wyrms, flew with them as they danced their aerial waltz, as they laid waste to the enemies of the land. He'd never admitted it to anyone. But, unable to contain himself, not caring any longer, he laughed at the sight of the creature in the sky, his arms held wide in exultation.

Xoster flew an angled pass across the undain army, ploughing another wide path through their ranks, leaving only smoke and death in her wake. The undain fought back with arrow and spear but their weapons had no effect, glancing off Xoster's hide. The necromancers among the undain shot seething spheres of white fire that slammed into the dragon. These also had no effect, serving only to make her roar with greater fury.

It would take only a few more passes for Xoster to seer and destroy the bulk of the Angere army. Barion looked on with joy flooding through him, his weariness forgotten. All the sacrifice, all the loss had been worth it. At the end of the dragon's run she rose, scales sparkling, and tilted a wing to turn. She arched down to cut a third swathe through the panicking ranks of undain.

But this time she wasn't alone in the sky. Twenty or thirty of the ungainly flying creatures flapped toward her, their movements even more clumsy when compared to Xoster's grace. They looked little more than songbirds next to her huge bulk, like moths fluttering around a flame, but there were many of them, and more arriving. They nipped and battered at Xoster, flying into her, gouging at her eyes.

Xoster wheeled in rage, but she was surrounded and couldn't defend herself from all angles. The undain creatures clung on to her: three, four, five of them attaching themselves to the dragon's wings. The great wyrm battled, but she was encumbered, losing height, and as she slowed more and more of the flying beasts caught her and clung on to her, coating her like a swarm of insects.

With a roar that echoed across the valley, Xoster fell. The central mass of the undain army was directly beneath her. When she was nearly at the ground she thrust her wings wide once more and, still trailing the undain creatures clinging to her, tried to level out, hoping perhaps to throw them off. But she'd run out of room. Belching fire at the undain carpeting the ground, bellowing a roar of purest hatred, she ploughed into them, burning a wide path through their ranks, crushing hundreds and hundreds of them.

She tried to rise into the air, wings beating frantically to pull herself skyward, like a swan battling to take off from the waters of the An. It was no use. The undain threw themselves onto her, swords hacking and slashing. Soon there was a seething mound of undain covering Xoster.

There was a final gout of flame burning into the sky and then no more movement.

Among the wyrm lords and witches no one spoke. Barion sank to the ground, still expecting to see Xoster burst free of her attackers and take to the skies. This wasn't right. Great Xoster had flown out of the old stories, come to their aid in their hour of desperate need. She should have *won*. She should have destroyed the horrors of Angere and saved them. That had to be how the story went. But instead she'd died. She'd cut a swathe through the enemy, but she'd died, buried beneath the teeming weight of Ilminion's abominations. Tears blurred the vision in his one good eye as he watched the scene.

Jenath was there again, crouching beside him. "Come. We must hurry through the night to Islagray before they regroup. They'll still come for us."

When he looked up at her he saw that tears filled her eyes, too. Perhaps she had also secretly dreamed of riding a wyrm. Perhaps they all did. He nodded and stood. Turning away from the death of Xoster, the last of the dragons, Barion marched eastward into the twilight.

21 – WITCHING HOUR

Cait sat on the hard little bed in Hellen's room on Islagray. Somehow she'd imagined grander surroundings: ornate furniture, shelves full of books and treasures. Glass spheres and brass oil burners and skulls and witchy *paraphernalia*. Instead the room was small and more or less square, with a door and a couple of windows. A log fire glowed in one corner, filling the room with a welcome warmth. A star-shaped lamp dangled by a silver chain from the oak beam over the bed. Cobwebs had been left to festoon the corners of the ceiling.

She, Fer, Hellen, Ashen, Ran, Danny, Johnny and Lugg were squeezed inside the room, the three witches and Ashen on the bed, Johnny lounging in Hellen's wooden chair by her desk, and the others sitting on the floor. They'd arrived at the Isle on *Smoke on the Water* the day before. The others, the witches and wyrm lords fleeing on foot from the ruins of Caer L'dun, had arrived that morning. Rather than attacking after the intervention of Xoster, the undain had let them escape. That had puzzled Cait at first but now she understood why. Menhroth's had all his remaining enemies neatly contained in one place. He could surround them and finish them off whenever it suited him.

"Why are we here and not at the orchard?" asked Fer.

Hellen waved a hand is if to dismiss her question. "The coven is all very well, but sometimes they talk so much nothing gets decided. The air out there is so thick with worry what with the wyrm lords running around that you can't hear yourself think. Time is short. The eight us will make up our minds and then we can tell the others what we're doing afterward. Besides, I think some of them might not like what I'm going to suggest."

Fer nodded, apparently amused by the old witch. "Won't they complain at being left out?"

"Most certainly. Be too late by then, won't it? So, Ashen, would you like to tell us what you've been up to while we were failing to defend Andar?"

Ashen sat with two books in his lap: one larger and bound in red leather, the familiar gold diagrams of skeletons across it. The other smaller and plainer, bound in black. Ilminion's spell book and Akbar's journal.

Ashen cleared his throat and surveyed the room with a frown. He looked drawn and exhausted, black lines under his eyes. His hair was even more of a wild mess than usual.

"So, as you can see," he began, "we've managed to combine the two halves of the book into one. Here is the Shadow Grimoire, readable for the first time in five hundred years. In fact the magic required was simple enough, once the bookwyrm and I worked out the forms Akbar used."

"And it's all there? It's complete?" asked Hellen.

"Hard to be sure. Ilminion was adding to it constantly, setting down new incantations, writing notes on old ones. There's a lot in there and there are blank pages at the end. But the good news is we've confirmed what Akbar said in his journal. We only finished the translations and comparisons this morning. If you hadn't held the undain at bay as long as you did, we'd never have completed the task. But now we know for sure: there are definitely two versions of the Ritual of Seven Ascensions and they're definitely identical save for a single word right at the end. A single syllable in fact. The first uses the *ath* glyph. The second replaces that with *yaelth*."

"And what difference does that syllable make to the spell?" asked Cait.

"Unfortunately, I don't know. Ilminion didn't elucidate. Actually that's unusual as he generally explained any changes and differences with at least a few lines of scribbled notes. Here he simply wrote out the second version, underlined the new syllable twice and left it like that. The only way to fully understand the difference is to try both versions and see what happens. Which isn't practical."

"Would Menhroth know of the effect the switch would have?"

"I doubt it. Not if Ilminion didn't tell him."

"Then we're no further forward," said Cait. "We're left guessing."

"I think we can do a little better than that," said Ashen. He looked to Fer. "You were able to work some magic to destroy an undain. Twice now, by the river at Forness and again in the other world, when you were caught retrieving Johnny's guitar."

Fer nodded slightly, reluctant to admit to it.

"And both times, also, you used your own blood in what you did," asked Ashen, "splashing or throwing it at the undain attacking you."

"Yes." Fer's gaze fell as if she couldn't meet Ashen's eyes, as if she was admitting to some shameful act.

"Good," said Ashen. "So, what I'd like to ask you to do now is to repeat those syllables in this room so I can set them down."

"Why?"

"Because it seems likely they're the final, sealing words of the Ritual of Seven Ascensions. I'd like to confirm they are, and then I'd like to understand which version it is that's been passed down through your family."

Fer's mouth opened and closed as she worked herself up to speaking the words. The voice of her grandmother came to her, a whispered conversation in the dead of night. *Remember this. Tell no one else.*

"It's OK," said Cait. "You're not to blame for what your ancestors did, just as I'm not. None of us are. Perhaps you've been keeping this secret so you can use it now."

"It'll be perfectly safe," said Hellen. "There'll be no effect unless any of us happen to secretly be one of the undain."

Fer nodded, not laughing at Hellen's attempt at humour. In the end she spoke the words to the star lamp above her head rather than to Cait or any of those around her.

As she uttered the harsh, spiky syllables, Ashen wrote them down on a scroll of parchment he had ready. Afterward, he studied the words, drawing lines between his transcription and some other writing. Presumably the other versions of the ritual.

"Yes," he said at last. "It definitely matches. That was the final clause of the second version of Ilminion's incantation."

"You're absolutely sure?" asked Hellen.

"Absolutely. Fer said *yaelth* and not *ath*."

There was a little light of excitement in Hellen's eyes as she spoke. "So it's as we thought. Ilminion must have intended to use the second version of the rite, one that introduced a fatal flaw. He did intend to usurp Menhroth. But he was subtle; he knew he couldn't simply slay the King and take control. The riders and the Holy Court would never have allowed such a thing."

"The change would have been unnoticeable at first," agreed Ashen. "But slowly, ounce by ounce over long years, Menhroth's power would have waned and Ilminion's, his blood the sealing form in the rite, would have grown. Perhaps without anyone even noticing Ilminion would have become the greater of the two."

"And by then," said Hellen, "all the undain would owe their existence to Menhroth. Which would mean Ilminion had power over all of them. He could act when he chose to usurp or control the King."

"That has to be it," said Ashen. "Ilminion must have written the second version of the ritual once Menhroth had made his demands to be granted the power of necromancy. If the plans had succeeded it would be Ilminion, not Menhroth, sitting on the throne in the White City by now. Without Fer's words we could have guessed the truth of it, and guessed which version to use but her family secret proves it. She wasn't throwing some other incantation of Ilminion's at the undain that attacked her. She was sealing the great Ritual and so destroying them."

"But what Fer did wasn't like that," said Johnny. "The zombie guy at the gig didn't fade away. He fell to pieces then and there."

Ashen nodded his head, as if that made perfect sense. "Yes. Ilminion's magic has been in place for five hundred years, leeching a tiny amount each day. But it couldn't take effect until the seal was placed on the rite. Then five centuries of slow decay hit the undain all at once."

"Why didn't the power flow to Fer as it would have flowed to Ilminion?" asked Cait.

"That's a very good question," said Ashen.

Fer was staring at the ground. She spoke quietly into the silence that filled the room. "Both times there was a … moment of choice. There was a great rush of magic flowing into me from the creature I'd killed. The power of it was glorious, intoxicating. But it also felt tainted and rotten. Both times I refused it, turned away from it. I … let it flow from me rather than into me, and I remained what I was."

"Where did it go?" asked Ashen.

"Into the earth. There were voices in it. A clamour of

confused, distant cries. I let them find peace."

Cait squeezed Fer's arm, offering reassurance.

Hellen, listening intently to everything, cleared her throat. "Very good. And in that lies our one hope."

"It is still terribly dangerous," said Ashen.

"Are you suggesting what I think you are?" asked Cait. "That we walk up to Menhroth and throw those words at him?"

"There's the blood, too," said Hellen. "But, yes. That's exactly what I'm suggesting. We give him precisely what he wants. What he's been longing for and lusting after for centuries. After all we've done, everything that's happened, he surely won't suspect the truth of it. We'll pretend we're still trying to fight him and he'll overcome us, seize the book and use it to seal the necromancy."

"But how can we be sure he doesn't know what Ilminion was really up to?" asked Cait.

Hellen nodded as she frowned. "We can't but it seems likely given how desperate Menhroth has been to get his hands on the book and the blood. And, of course, he's never had the completed Grimoire to study."

A puzzled look had been gathering on Johnny's face. "OK, but, if there's a good and a bad version of the rite in the book, and we give the book to Menhroth, what's to stop him speaking the wrong one? The wrong one from our point of view, I mean. He might guess and get lucky."

"Because," said Ashen, "with the archaeon's help I've made a small change to the wording of the first version."

"You've put the rogue syllable into that one, too." said Cait.

"Just so. And made another tiny alteration, insignificant to the overall effect, to explain Ilminion setting down the second. It doesn't matter which version Menhroth speaks. Either will be sufficient."

"But," said Cait, "even if it is possible to get close enough to Menhroth, and even if he falls for it and it works, that's only one of the undain destroyed. The main guy, yes, but there are still, I don't know, thousands and thousands of others."

"There are," said Hellen, "but they come from him, don't they? He raised them. He's been very clever, making sure their existence was bound to his, tying their fates to him so that no one would dare threaten him. But when he goes the whole lot of them will go, falling like a rotting tower of wood."

"Are you sure of that?" asked Cait. "Does the Ritual say that's what will happen?"

Ashen shook his head, a frown clouding his features. "It doesn't, and nor does it say that anywhere else in the Grimoire or in Akbar's journal. That's speculation on our part. It seems likely."

"But basically guesswork?" asked Cait.

"Yes," said Ashen. "I wish we could be certain."

"We'd have to get very close to Menhroth to attempt it," said Cait.

Hellen nodded. "He is vain and proud, from what you've said. No one has dared oppose him or even criticise him for five hundred years. If we march onto the ice to challenge him I think he'll take the bait. He'll see the book and the heir of Ilminion within his grasp, and he won't be able to resist."

"The heir of Ilminion," said Fer. "You mean me or Cait."

Hellen's voice was regretful when she replied. "Cait, I think. It is too much to ask of anyone and it is a thing that must be done freely. But I think Cait should be the one."

"Why?" asked Fer. "I can go. I can take the risk. And surely Menhroth will be suspicious if we simply walk onto the ice and offer him the very thing he's been trying to acquire?"

"That's precisely why it has to be Cait," said Hellen. "It would look suspicious if it were anyone else. But I think Menhroth fears Cait. He's seen everything she's done. She escaped from Genera. She crossed Angere picking up friends and allies on the way. Because of her, Lugg found Xoster. She unleashed the spirits in the White City and rescued Danny. She even helped destroy his trusted servant Charis. He may think she's another like Ilminion. He wouldn't think she'd come out to meet him unless she was very sure of herself. Don't you see? Everything she's done so far has bought us this opportunity. If he sees her coming to face him it's unlikely he'll realise she's trying to trick him. He'll see a chance for a final, deciding showdown with his enemy, a chance to seize what he craves, and come to meet her."

"That's what you hope," said Fer.

Hellen nodded. "That's what I hope. I may be wrong."

"It's hugely dangerous," said Fer. "You may simply be giving Menhroth exactly what he wants."

"Yes. Or he might realise what we're up to and slip off the hook. Live with his thirst, his *need*, for more and more Spirit as he's been doing. Or he may not even come at all."

"He might kill Cait there and then to get her blood," said Fer.

Hellen glanced at Cait. "That's possible, too. That's why it has to be Cait's choice."

Cait studied their faces, the varying shades of doubt and alarm and fear she could read there. This did seem to be their only hope. Could she do such a thing? Walk out to face the Witch King? The thought made her insides boil with terror; it seemed insane to even consider it.

On the other hand, her gran always said she was capable of anything if she put her mind to it. She'd never really believed that, but perhaps it was time to try. She didn't feel anywhere near brave enough or clever enough, and she wished one of the others could go instead of her. But she *had* done all those things Hellen described. With help, sure, but she'd done them. Done them even when people like Nox kept doubting her. Now there was this final thing, a thing needing to be done. And she would damn well go out there and do it. Or try, at least.

"We'd have to make it look good," said Cait. "If I just wander out there holding the Grimoire and try to look all spooky and dangerous he'll suspect something."

"You're actually going to do this?" asked Johnny.

"I think I have to."

"Well, have you translated any of what we've said to Danny? Because he might have a view on it."

"I'll explain it to him later," said Cait.

Danny looked at her questioningly, his brown eyes narrowed. He'd picked up a few words of the language of Andar, and had obviously heard his name being used. He certainly would object to her plan. She'd explain everything to him later, try and make him understand that she had to do this thing.

"Menhroth might have these fears about me," she said. "But it will be pretty obvious I'm not much of a threat once I'm out there facing him and he tries to zap me."

"But you are a threat," said Ashen. "You have only to learn the words from Fer. It's your family secret, too. When Menhroth sends his guards or wyrm lords to come and take you, you can despatch them as she did. Destroy them. Menhroth doesn't have to know you're using the sealing words from the Ritual. He'll see you working some magic from Ilminion's book and his undain being destroyed and he'll believe. He'll think only he can stop you and he'll come."

"What if he thinks Cait is *too* powerful?" said Johnny. "Then he might avoid her at all cost."

"Again, he might," said Hellen. "Except, he knows he's more powerful than Ilminion was. He made sure of that five hundred years ago. So long as he doesn't know about Ilminion's deception it might work."

Johnny let out a whistle of air. "A hell of a lot could go wrong."

"Yes," said Hellen with a tired sigh. "Cait? It's up to you. No one can make you do this. You know the risks better than anyone."

"This thing with the blood. Does Menhroth have to, you know, drink it or something?" It was vile. The whole thing was disgusting.

"The touch of it will be enough," said Arran. "Ilminion was supposed to mark Menhroth's skin with it, so any splash or drop on the King should suffice."

That was something. She wouldn't have to let the King bite her on the neck or something. Still it was hideous. "And what if I don't go?"

"Then," said Hellen, "we'll fight side-by-side here and hope for a miracle."

"In that case, I'll go," said Cait simply. "It's all we can do."

"And I'll go with you," said Fer.

"Me, too," said Johnny. "And probably Danny as well, once you've explained to him what the hell you're intending."

"No," said Hellen. "I think Cait should go alone. The great danger is that Menhroth reads our thoughts, grasps what we're attempting. Cait has learned to erect walls around her mind only recently but she's already very, very good at it. I fancy she's been well taught by someone. Forgive me, Cait, but I know how good your defences are because I've tried to breach them. Perhaps your experience with Xoster, the violation you felt, helped. You, Fer, are also accomplished at that particular skill, but Menhroth would find it easier to see into your thoughts. And you, Johnny, he could read like an open book as soon as he glanced at you. Danny, too. Hard as this is, I think Cait has to go alone."

Cait nodded. Again, it made sense. The thought of walking out to meet Menhroth filled her with cold dread, but there was no alternative.

"No," said Ran. He spoke so rarely people tended to forget he was even there. "Not alone. I will go with her. My thoughts will be hidden from the King by my markings. He will not know the truth from me."

Hellen considered the wyrm lord. Cait had never been able to see into Ran's mind, and it seemed that was also true for Hellen. "Very well," said Hellen after a moment. "The two of you, then. The two of you and all our hopes with you."

Cait nodded her gratitude at Ran who met her look with his usual impassive gaze.

As everyone was leaving, Fer took Cait by the arm and spoke quietly. "I'll teach you the words of the family secret." They wove through the woods to Fer's little hut in one of the more distant clearings.

The syllables were coarse in Cait's mouth and the taste of something sour or rotten came to her. She was probably imagining it. While she practised, Fer threaded some of own jewellery through Cait's ears and eyebrows and lower lip. Then she mixed up some acrid dye and carefully combed it through Cait's hair. Soon her locks were the colour of water, the colour of ice once more. Finally, Fer gave her a pair of stout, black leather boots that laced up her shins.

"These should fit you. I think we're the same size. They'll keep your feet warm at least."

Cait took the boots gratefully. They wouldn't have looked out of place on the streets of Manchester. "Thanks."

"I wish I could come with you," said Fer. "I wish there was more I could do."

"I know. I wish you could come, too. All of you."

They hugged each other close, two distant cousins from two different worlds.

An hour later, Cait followed Hellen up one of the two flights of steps that wound up the inside of the chimney-shaped hollow of the Wycka. The sunwise and widdershins staircases. An iron railing had been embedded in the wall, but the steps were open on the other side to the great, round space of the building. Birds swooped through the air, their shrill cries echoing from the stone.

The wind picked up as they climbed. Cait clutched the cold railing more firmly as the stone floor receded. The discordant rumble of the Song, reverberating from the walls, became quieter. At the same time, the wind blowing over the open top of the tower made a louder and louder *oh* sound, as if the whole building were sighing in despair.

At the top, where the two staircases met once more, Cait and Hellen climbed onto a balcony that had been set around the outside of the tower. Another iron railing offered a degree of protection from the drop. The whole of the island was laid out around them: the orchard of witches on its hill; the trees and the roofs of the witches' huts nestling among them. Frost sparkled from every surface. Beyond the trees, the Silverwater gleamed. The cold was biting, the wind seeming to pinch the bones in Cait's face.

"I wanted to speak to you alone," said Hellen. "I know what you said to the others, but I want to be absolutely sure you meant it. No one will think the worse of you if you don't attempt this thing with Menhroth. You've already achieved wonders, done more than we could ever have asked for. And there really is a good chance it won't work, for all the reasons we said. If it does fail, then that's my fault not yours. I wish I could go in your place, I do. I wish I was cleverer, better-prepared, more powerful. But I'm not any of those things, and I'm truly sorry for it. Ariane used to complain that I went around giving people orders all the time. *Pots and pans before plots and plans* she used to say. Perhaps she was right, but I'm not telling you what to do now. What you do is up to you and no one else."

Cait put her hand on the old witch's arm. This could almost have been her gran standing there beside her, admitting to her failings.

"Without you Andar would have had no chance," said

Cait.

Hellen shook her head. "I've done little enough. But I know the thought of using the necromancy revolts you. I don't blame you for that."

"I don't see any other way now," said Cait. "We're turning the magic against itself. Fighting fire with fire. And somehow it feels like the price has been paid. I mean, I know this isn't witchcraft. I know that necromancy steals from others, takes without paying, but still it feels like we've earned the right, somehow, to do this. Because of everything we've been through. Everything we've lost. Does that make sense?"

Hellen nodded. "It does. To me at least."

"If Menhroth does come, do you think the plan will work? Truly?"

Hellen sighed as she stared over the frozen island. "Truly? I don't know. We're so weak compared to them. Love and sacrifice and friendship are such small things in the face of brute power, but sometimes the big and the strong fall because they overlook the small and the weak." Hellen threw a little smile at Cait. "That's what I tell myself, anyway. It's likely I'm talking nonsense."

"Why does he even call himself the Witch King? He's no witch."

A flash of amusement passed across Hellen's face. "To mock us. Perhaps to tell the world he's more powerful than any of us. Or perhaps, in the old days, a distinction wasn't made between witches and mancers."

"They'll attack the Isle while I'm out there."

"Oh, we'll do what we can. More weather spells, mists to befuddle them, webs to hold them fast for a time. Our grim-faced friends from Caer L'dun will fight to the last drop of blood. We'll put everything we have into it, but none of it will achieve very much."

"How many of them are left do you think?"

"We destroyed a lot of them. Between the serpents, the wyrm lords and Xoster, as well as everything that was done at Guilden and Hyrn's Oak and the other towns and cities, I reckon we've accounted for maybe half of them."

"A *half*. That's all?"

"I think so. An achievement given how unprepared we were, but obviously nowhere near enough."

"Doesn't the lake count as running water? There's a river flowing out of it."

"It would if it wasn't beginning to freeze. This cruel winter has reached us. Our time is up. You can no doubt feel the undain as well as I can, shadows massing on the horizon, moving to surround us. They'll be here soon. I think you should leave while you still can. And then we can only hope this isn't Andar's last day."

Cait hugged the old witch tight, feeling the hard bones within her. "Yes," she said. "Let's hope."

"Are you ready?"

"I suppose."

"You are troubled by what you are about to attempt."

"No. I mean, yes, of course, but it isn't that. As I climbed the stairs I just got to wondering how I got here. A couple of months ago I was a schoolgirl, going nowhere. I knew nothing. And here I am, with everyone depending on me. Your world and mine. It's insane."

Hellen smiled and put a hand on Cait's arm. "You've always been at the heart of things. You just didn't know it."

"I wish I knew more about my history. I mean, about how I got here, and who my ancestors were."

"It's a story I know some of," said Hellen. "There are many books and scrolls in the archive that mention your family. Quite a few of them were written by your family."

"I wish I had time to read them. Hear their voices."

"Perhaps there will be chance ... afterward. When you return."

Hellen couldn't keep the look of doubt from her eye as she glanced away into the distance.

"Perhaps," said Cait.

"One other thing," said Hellen. "Your blood. We can at least make sure Menhroth doesn't simply … take it from you." She held out a small blade, slipped from inside her sleeve. "This isn't much of a weapon, but it is sharp. Run it over your palm and you'll bleed freely enough. I've worked a few charms on it so it won't hurt. There's a little sheaf for it you can strap to your wrist. It's a small thing, but it's the least I can do. It might help impress Menhroth. Throwing your own blood around is a bit overdramatic, perhaps, but mancers do go in for that. Don't tell Ashen I said so."

Cait took the blade and strapped it to her arm beneath her sleeve. It felt pathetically small against her wrist, like a toy.

"Let's get it over with, then," she said.

22 – WITCH KING

Cait and Ran left Islagray less than an hour later. Johnny and Danny travelled with them as far as the banks of the An, *Smoke on the Water* skating them down the Gleaming while Hellen and the others remained on the Isle to prepare as best they could for what was coming.

Cait spoke little, watching the bushes and trees drifting by, their branches frosted with ice. The only sound was the hissing of the runners on the ice.

They said their farewells to Danny and Johnny six hours later upon a grassy, wooded headland where the tributary joined its mother river. *Smoke on the Water* would head back up the Gleaming for what safety the Isle could offer while Cait and Ran trekked across the ice.

Ran stood apart, polishing the edge of his blade with slow deliberation, staring into the west. Cait, Danny and Johnny squeezed each other close. There were tears in Johnny's eyes as he mouthed his goodbyes to her. He returned to *Smoke on the Water* to busy himself with ropes and pulleys, leaving her and Danny alone.

"I'm sorry," she said. "For this. For everything."

"It's hardly your fault. We're caught up in it, that's all."

"You don't have to be caught up in it."

"I think I do."

"There's a good chance I won't come back. Either Menhroth will see through our plan, or he won't and kill me anyway to get my blood."

Danny nodded his understanding. "I wish I could come. Wouldn't be able to do much, but still I could, I don't know, be there."

Now she was crying, too. "I really wish you could."

"Perhaps it will work out and you'll be back at the Isle tomorrow," he said. "We can go out on a normal date. Do they even have cinemas here?"

She laughed despite her tears and nodded her head in agreement. "That sounds wonderful. Don't go off with anyone while I'm away."

Instead of replying, Danny pulled her to him and kissed her. His mouth was cold in the icy air, but then his tongue was warm as his lips and her lips parted. Cait closed her eyes as they lost themselves in each other. For a time, a glorious and short time, there was only Danny in the whole world.

When they separated she gazed into his eyes. She wanted to tell him it would be alright, she'd come back safe, but she couldn't. Instead she placed her head on his chest and he held her tight.

When they were finally ready to part, her fingers lingering in Danny's as she moved away, she crossed to join Ran at the frozen edge of the An. She looked back once as they foot-slid across the ice. Johnny and Danny stood side-by-side, not moving. After a few moments more, the mists swallowed them up.

She and Ran headed into deeper waters, heading west and a little north to take them toward the White City. She carried the Grimoire in one hand as if it were some school textbook. Ran led the way, tapping the ice in front of them with the shaft of a spear in case the ice thinned. Cait spent the time reciting the sealing words of the Ritual in her mind, terrified of forgetting the syllables or placing them in the wrong order. She tried, also, to reach into the mists, seeking the presence of the undain. She had to find Menhroth. If the King didn't know she was there, they might encounter some part of his army instead and be killed before they had a chance to spring their trap.

Once or twice she lifted the seeing stone to her eye, hoping to catch some shadow or glimmer of light, but there was only the endless mist. She was soon utterly disorientated. For all she knew they were walking round in circles. It was a good job Ran knew what he was doing.

As they slid forward, neither speaking, her mind went back to the day they escaped from Greygyle's palace in Angere. She'd thought about smashing the tiny, tinkling ampoules of Spirit that kept the servants moving and working. She hadn't been able to do it at the time; it would have felt like she was killing the miserable creatures.

Now she was about to attempt the same thing on a far, far greater scale. If their scheme succeeded then all the undain, from Menhroth down to those mindless slaves, would be extinguished. Could she do that? Did she have the right? But if she didn't, many others would die. Die and worse. How did you know what was right and what was wrong? You could only do what seemed best at the time. What they were attempting felt like the right thing to do. The crimes that had created the undain weren't her crimes.

She was pondering these thoughts, going round in circles in her head, when a wide sphere of the mist around them vanished, as if blown backward by an impossible wind. Slanting sunlight shone down to illuminate the scene. Menhroth stood thirty yards away, clad in armour of white and gold, dazzling in the sun. Some sort of large dog-like creature snuffled behind him, its leash held by a hooded figure. A line of twelve undain wyrm lords waited in front, swords held at the ready. Behind, fading into the mists, stood rank upon rank of the undain, countless thousands of them. Another army making the crossing to join with those marching south through Andar.

Menhroth's voice was gentle as he spoke, yet it carried across the distance between them as if he were right in front of her. "Cait Weerd. I said we would meet again, at the end. The situation is somewhat different to the one I imagined, but events unfold as they must, however we try to stop them."

She took one more step forward. Her hands were shaking and for a moment she thought she was going to drop the Grimoire. That would seriously ruin the effect of what they were attempting. She took a deep breath. She had to get a grip.

She hadn't ever been much good at school, but she could do drama. She'd always enjoyed playing at being someone else on a stage, *becoming* someone else for a time. That was what she had to do now. She was no all-powerful necromancer come to slay the dark lord and save the worlds. The idea was laughable. All she had to do was pretend to be an all-powerful necromancer come to slay the dark lord and save the worlds, play the role, and maybe Menhroth would fall for it.

Despite the terror raging in her stomach, she spoke as slowly and clearly as she could. Her drama teacher had taught her to speak as if to the person at the back of the auditorium. She doubted the undain in the last rank of the army could hear her words, but the King would.

"I've come to destroy you, Menhroth. That is how events will unfold. Here is Ilminion's Grimoire, recreated from its two halves. Its knowledge and power are now at my control. With it I will destroy you and those that follow you."

Menhroth shook his head as if disappointed. "You have made a terrible mistake, witch-girl. Do you really think you can walk out here and face me?"

She didn't, not at all. "I do."

"It is a sad end. I truly thought we could achieve great

things together, you and I side-by-side on the throne of An. There is power in you. You are brave, too, I'll give you that. But now the time is come. Now I will kill you and take your blood. My day is finally here."

He motioned one of the wyrm lords forward to her. The hulking giant, black force-lines writhing over his hideous transparent skin, marched forward, sword point angled at her head.

Cait slipped Hellen's little knife from her sleeve. It was pathetically small in comparison to the blade the approaching wyrm lord bore. Discreetly she pulled the tiny knife across her hand. As Hellen had promised there was no pain. A line of blood welled in her palm. She had to hit the wyrm lord with it before that sword swung. She hadn't thought about that.

Ran stirred beside her, no doubt ready to leap to her defence. She acted first. She held the Grimoire open, glancing at it as if reading some arcane secret held within its pages. When the wyrm lord was only a few paces away she jerked her other hand forward, spattering her attacker with a sprinkling of her blood. The wyrm lord paused as if confused or offended at such a disgraceful act. Then as nothing more happened it stepped forward once more, even as Cait recited the syllables Fer had taught her.

Her throat was dry and she almost couldn't get the sounds out. The craziness of her situation struck her. She was about to be cut in half by this nightmare creature and she was babbling nonsense at it. She pressed on, keeping her voice low, not wanting Menhroth to hear.

She'd hoped for something dramatic to happen when she finished the words of the Ritual. Nothing changed; the wyrm lord was unaffected. She'd pronounced the alien sounds incorrectly, or they'd missed something. Perhaps Menhroth had worked some magic of his own to ward off what they were attempting. She stepped back. All she could think about was fleeing.

Then the giant wyrm lord stopped and began to writhe,

its body shaking violently. The creature grunted as if from the effort of trying to hold itself together, shrieked once, then exploded into a mist of debris. The dust from its body drifted in the air briefly before falling to the ice.

Cait stepped forward to resume her position. She glanced at her palm. More blood seeped from her cut. It would dry up eventually and she'd have to make another.

Two more wyrm lords approached her, separating to attack her simultaneously. If Menhroth sent all his guards at her at once she'd be lost; she couldn't hope to hit each with her blood before one of them got to her. She had to get nearer the King.

Spraying the two with droplets was tricky. The first she caught easily enough but when she threw her hand at the second, circling around behind her, nothing hit it. She should have been better prepared, had containers of her blood ready to throw. She balled her fist, squeezing more from the cut on her palm, then tried again, reciting the syllables as she did so. This time, a few specks of blood caught the wyrm lord in the chest.

A moment later, the words completed, the two of them were writhing and screaming as the first had. Two more sprays of dust coated the ice.

She took another step forward. She had to appeal to his macho pride. "Are you going to keep sending your underlings to do your work for you?"

Her words sounded ridiculous. Incredibly, they worked. Menhroth pushed aside the guards in front of him and came for her. The dog-thing followed, the cowled figure pulled along by it. It was the animal that caught her attention. It was large, like some big hound. Except, it wasn't a dog, or hadn't always been. There was something human in its facial features as it scrabbled forward on all fours. It shivered as if used to being beaten, but stuck to Menhroth. It didn't look like it was going to attack her, but she couldn't be sure.

She readied herself to hurl the words of the Ritual at

Menhroth. She would only get once chance.

The King stopped, ten paces away. Too far. The dog-thing took a step farther but then slunk back, whining, to hide behind Menhroth. There was something in the way it glowered at her that was familiar. She watched its quaking body with a horrified fascination.

"Ah, I see you recognize the Duke of Greygyle," said Menhroth. "I'm afraid his status is somewhat reduced since he allowed you to escape. He recognizes you, too. No doubt he blames you for his fate. Shall I unleash him upon you? I'm sure he'd like his revenge."

"That's hideous."

"Merciful. He deserved to die for failing me. Shall I turn you into one like him? The two of you could share a kennel together. Share the straw."

It was her turn to be goaded. Her clenched fist was filled with blood. She took a pace forward to get nearer to him. But as she did so he worked some spell of his own, blazingly quick, hurling her backward through the air. She hit the ice hard, cracking her skull, a sickening pain washing over her.

She forced herself to stand. Menhroth was farther away then ever. She was nowhere near close enough to him. She'd dropped the Grimoire too. It lay on the ice where his spell had struck her. Everything was suddenly going wrong.

The Greygyle thing sniffed at the book, straining at the leash held by the hooded figure. Menhroth stooped to pick up the Grimoire. He studied it for a moment with his night-black eyes, turning a few pages until he found the one he wanted.

The delight on his face made it clear he'd found the Ritual. A faint hope awoke within Cait. Perhaps they had a chance. He really did see her as a threat, and now he thought he'd taken the book from her. So long as he didn't see through Ashen's alterations, perhaps there was a chance.

Something else caught Menhroth's eye. He dabbed a finger at the page. When he lifted it she saw it was stained red. Some of her blood had splashed onto the book. Her hope flared more brightly. It was going to work. It was actually going to work. Menhroth intended to complete the rites there and then. He was falling for their trap.

She tried not to let her delight show on her face as Menhroth lifted the finger with her blood to his lips…

"No!"

Ran moved then, throwing himself forward. He kneeled to the ice before the Witch King, head bowed, sword laid down. He still wore, she noticed, the cheap silver chain she'd put around his neck when he lay unconscious in the woods near the White City.

"My Lord, stop, I beg you. Do not believe the lies of this witch. She seeks to trick you. Ilminion deceived you, plotted against you. This will not be your moment of final triumph, it will be your end. There are two versions of the Ritual of Seven Ascensions and the wrong one is set down in the book. It will destroy you. You have seen what she did to your guards. I have heard the witches and all their plans. I beg you, you know I am your loyal servant, do not speak the words. This girl knows the true form of the rite. Rip it from her mind, take her blood and speak the proper Ritual. Only then will your victory be complete."

Ran touched his forehead to the ice at Menhroth's foot. "My Lord, this I vow upon my life."

23 – RAN

Ran waited for Menhroth's reply. He stared at the blue ice, at the King's armoured foot. He dared look no higher until he was granted assent. The ice was smooth, reflecting the distorted shape of the figure standing over him.

It had been so hard maintaining the pretence all this time. He'd walked among hated enemies his whole life. He'd protected the girl through everything, making sure the precious heir of Ilminion survived to be delivered to this culmination. All the agonies he'd suffered: the wounds, the burns, the hatred and mistrust, all of it to keep her blood flowing long enough to be used in the Ritual.

He'd made so many sacrifices. In the other world, pursued by the soldiers of Genera, he'd been forced to give up his sword. Wedge it into the hasp of a rusting iron grating as if it were any old length of metal. Did they know what that had cost him? Any of them? Had they even thanked him? His rider's sword, carried from Angere by his forebear Arran five hundred years ago, handed down from father to mother for generations.

Still, giving it away had served a purpose. Told the

pursuing humans and their masters that he was there. A true black dragonrider, a loyal guard of King Menhroth, carrying out his whispered orders in the lair of their enemies even after all that time. He was a wolf walking among the child-like sheep of Andar as they flocked in their fields, oblivious to the dangers lurking beyond their borders. The sword would have been passed to King Menhroth and he or his guards – riders who knew Arran, fought alongside him – would have recognized it. The particular etchings on it that identified Ran's forebear, named him as one of the inner circle of the King's guards.

And before that, in the enchanted wood between the worlds, he could have slain the undain Lord they pursued easily enough. Instead he'd let the noble escape with only a flesh wound to his foot. Striking one of the lords of Angere went against everything Ran was, but in that brief moment there'd been no choice. He had to make it look believable, make it look as though he was trying to kill the undain. And did Fer and the others think less of him because he'd failed? Perhaps. Still, he'd had no choice. He'd done what he had to do.

Later, at the lava pit in the land of ice, he'd showed his true self again. Another risk, another fleeting moment of decision. A choice taken. With Cait's hand in his he'd jumped into the lava, hoping to drag her to Angere before any of the others could follow, the wyrm road sealing behind them. But Nox had fallen too, his hand in Ran's other. When they arrived in Angere, Ran had thought about killing Nox there and then, dragging Cait to the nearest Lord to offer her to the King.

But Nox's loyalties were unknown. And he was a lord of Angere himself, a Baron no less. Ran had decided to bide his time, watch and wait. Perhaps if Nox turned out to be disloyal, he could turn both of them over at the same time. Perhaps by staying quiet he would learn something about the rebels, although they'd turned out to be a huge disappointment. After all, there was no danger of Cait slipping through their fingers. There was no way to escape to Andar with the ancient bridge gone. Or there shouldn't have been. He'd carried on playing his role, silent and watchful, awaiting the moment to act.

The ancient orders were clear. Orders passed down to son and daughter in the quiet of the night, when no one else in Caer L'dun would hear. Orders brought across the bridge from Angere all that time ago, when Menhroth ascended and the straggle of dragonless riders fled to Andar before the river rose to sweep the bridge away. A hundred riders, and only one true to his vows and oaths. And what terrible sacrifices had been made there, too? Arran had left his wyrm behind in Angere. He, alone, still had a living dragon to ride. To maintain the pretence he'd abandoned the creature, denied it, betrayed it. The cost to both had been terrible, so it was said. The anguish and loss almost unbearable. But Arran, too, had done what had to be done.

Seek out the heirs of Ilminion, the children of Weyerd. Stay with them. Watch over them. Keep them alive until the King returns to claim them. Until that time be as one with the people of Andar. Until only Menhroth himself decrees otherwise.

And he'd done that hadn't he? He'd played his part. Even when the enemies he walked among, the enemies he'd pretended to befriend, were in Angere. When he'd had to fight those he was really loyal to in order to maintain the pretence of being true to those he secretly despised. He'd had his doubts. So many doubts. He was alone. After all this time, without any further messages from Angere for five centuries, was he still trusted? Did the King know he had Ran's absolute loyalty?

He'd made contact with his masters when Cait and Nox were taken to the palace of Lord Greygyle. The White City might have had a clue they were in Angere from the crow that had seen them the day they arrived. Ran had watched it flapping for the wyrm road just as Cait had. The creature was broken and ruined, and its message would be fragmentary. Ran had walked for a day before he found another of the birds, watching and listening from a black tree. He'd shown himself to it, bowed low, imagining King Menhroth seeing the scene replayed when the bird reached the White City.

Had it made the journey? He didn't know. The undain army had raced west, certainly, so some inkling had reached the King. But then Ran had encountered one of the undain riders as he came looking for Cait, and been attacked. The rider thought Ran was an enemy, loyal to Andar. He'd had to kill the undain, as he had the second that threatened Cait and the boy. They were two that might have known and loved Arran, and he'd slain them with the ancient rider blade. The bitterness of that had cost him, but he had to maintain the pretence, play his role until he was told otherwise. The King saw all.

At Caer D'nar he'd walked through the echoing halls of his forebears, the voices of the ancient riders filling his mind, imploring him to act. He'd heard them all his life: directing him, berating him, ordering him to stay true to their ancient vows. For many years he had no idea who or what the voices were, but he'd always known they were something he couldn't admit to. Slowly he'd come to understand that the dead riders of old were whispering to him. The urge to take up his sword and cleanse Caer D'nar of the vermin infesting it, Phoenix and the rest of them, had been almost overwhelming. They were a desecration, unworthy. He'd managed to resist, maintain his pretence, but only just.

When the boy Lugg set off into the north to search for Xoster, he'd almost succumbed again. The thought of finding her, of perhaps even riding a dragon, made lights dance in Ran's eyes. And if he could train Lugg he could show him the true path of a rider, explain about the oaths to the King. Lugg might have become a second loyal wyrm lord, and Ran would no longer be alone. But, again, he'd denied himself. He had his orders. His duty was to stay with the witch-girl and face his ordeal by fire at Fiveways.

Surely he'd had proven his worth, shown them the extent of his devotion, there? He'd managed to travel the wyrm road from the north alone, go through before any of the others, lugging his cart load of brimstone like some beast of burden. Had they suspected something, Cait and the others, at the long delay? Perhaps. But he'd deflected their doubts with a tale of trying to ignite the wyrmfire and everything had been forgotten in the rush of events. And then there were his wounds. The terrible burns he'd inflicted on himself to make his story believable, convince both Cait and Lord Charis that he, Ran, was to be trusted.

It had taken long minutes of frantic discussion at Fiveways to persuade Charis that he was true to them. That by appearing to deliver Cait to safety on the banks of the An he was ensuring her absolute faith in him. There was, still, the lingering doubt that the White City didn't know everything about her, that there was some hidden power to her, some further allies they hadn't taken into account. The girl's mother had been the same, deceiving Baron Nox into thinking she was a broken, weak woman. It was a mistake Charis dare not make again. And so he'd agreed to Ran's plan. The subterfuge with the explosion at Fiveways would be played out and Ran allowed to escape. Many undain had died, sacrificed in the fires, but that was the price to be paid.

By these means they would find out Cait's true intention, an explanation for what she was doing and how she intended to achieve it. There had to be a secret. A mere girl wouldn't just walk into Angere intending to take the book and defeat the King. And, after all, there was no real risk. Ran was bringing her to the White City and, again, the An could not be crossed. There was no possibility of Cait escaping. Even Lord Charis, Holder of the Keys and Guardian of the Aether, had conceded that. Ran couldn't be faulted for the oversight. He'd done everything asked of him, everything and more.

The extent of Ran's wounds at Fiveways had been a mistake, a miscalculation. It had made his story utterly believable, but losing consciousness in the woods meant Cait could act without him being there to watch and listen. He was young and strong and he'd trained every moment given to him, but even he had succumbed, his mind slipping from the world for a time.

Then there was his black dragon tattoo. The ancient guards had extra marks woven into their red, blue, green or gold markings to indicate their exalted position. The practice had died out among his forebears in Andar, the risk of maintaining the tradition too great. But his grandmother had revived a version of it in secret. Once the black tattoos had been worn all over the skin. As a mark of his true loyalties, Ran had allowed himself the single, small addition, hidden beneath his blue lines. The black dragon was invisible to normal eyes, but perhaps not to a witch's.

Had that been a mistake? The possibility that Cait had noticed the marks while he lay oblivious, overcome by his wounds, had racked him with alarm. But either she hadn't seen, or simply hadn't understood the significance. So much time had passed since the cleaving of the land, and what did this weak, foolish girl from another world know of anything?

And so he'd escaped with his mistake. By the time he'd come round, the girl and Nox were gone. He'd tracked them to the White City, hoping to discover their true intent, but by the time he'd arrived they were already caught, imprisoned in the dungeons. He'd sought an audience with King Menhroth himself, been allowed to enter that holy presence. Ran had greeted the undain dragonriders guarding the doors, huge and powerful, as equals. They would have known his ancestor and would surely honour and respect Ran, too, when the story was fully played out. It would only be a matter of time before Ran could join them: ascended, immortal, all-powerful.

The King on his golden throne, bone crown upon his

head, had heard Ran's tale with a blank expression. It wasn't Ran's place to question, but had the King doubted him? Doubted he was still loyal after all this time, despite Ran's wounds and his sacrifices? In truth he couldn't be sure. Was it possible the King suspected he was part of Hellen Meggenwar's plots? That he, or one of his ancestors, had thrown away their loyalty in the intervening centuries? He'd said nothing, of course. Once he'd recounted his story he wasn't allowed to speak again. He would be given his orders and he would carry them out. That was enough for him. To have met the King, bowed down before him after these years of lonely sacrifice, was enough.

Then the spirits of the City of Ghosts had awakened, unleashed by the accursed girl. While the towers fell, Menhroth had summoned Ran again to give him fresh orders. Find Cait. Find out her powers and her plans. Discover her strengths and her weaknesses. Ran had caught up with them on the bridgehead, cowering like cornered rabbits. Cait and Nox and the boy, too. He'd had to suppress the urge to slay them there and then, carry Cait's dripping corpse to the King.

Instead, as agreed, the attacking undain had let him fight them off for a time, dispel any doubts Cait might have about him. More sacrificed to maintain the illusion of his loyalty. He'd tried to find out Cait's true intentions. He'd actually asked her, demanded to know her plans and intentions. When she confided in him he could act, all doubts about him gone, his ascendancy ensured.

The appearance of the impossible boat had thrown his calculations aside. How could such a thing be? But he'd survived in Andar before and now matters were coming to their end he could do so again. He knew what he had to do. Continue to keep Cait alive. Make sure she was there at the end when the final meeting with Menhroth came. Again it had been hard. At Hyrn's Oak, on the way north, the stupid girl had wandered off alone into the wilds. He'd followed her, ready to leap to her defence once again if he had to. He'd been about to reveal himself to the undain that had taken her when Hellen and then Borrn turned up to rescue her.

Later, in Guilden, he'd managed to get away, make contact with the approaching army in case the King had further orders for him. He'd barely made it back in time to save Cait from being skewered by some mindless foot soldier. A moment when everything had nearly been lost. He'd saved her and battled on, following his secret orders to the end, staying true to his vows.

And now there he was. Bowing before the King for a third time, with Cait and the recreated Grimoire in their power. Everything had come together, his sacrifice and suffering worth it at this final moment of triumph. His forebears had failed the King, allowed Ilminion to be slain, and now he, Ran, had made amends.

He kneeled on the ice, awaiting the King's hand to finally, finally raise him up.

24 – THE FATE OF MORE THAN ONE WORLD

The remaining witches of Islagray, Hellen and Fer among them, gathered in the round, echoing space of the Wycka. The surviving wyrm lords and the few others who were on the island, Danny, Johnny, Ashen, Lugg and Merdoc among them, waited beside them.

No one spoke. There was a moment of utter quiet. The calm before the storm. The witches were good at sensing the undain now. Everyone knew the end was coming. Andar was overrun. The Silverwater was surrounded, tens of thousands of the undain thronging on the banks. The ice on the lake was solid and there was nothing, no person or power, that could stop the creatures coming across to kill them. Their spells and guards stood ready, but they were unsuited to such an onslaught. The wyrm lords would account for a few attackers but not enough. Not nearly enough.

Hellen caught the gaze of those around her, tried to offer a smile of reassurance. She was convincing no one. Whatever had happened out on the An, it had failed. They'd missed some detail. Ilminion hadn't betrayed

Menhroth five hundred years ago. There was no fatal flaw in the necromancy. The wording difference they'd agonized over in the Grimoire meant nothing, an insignificant detail. She'd been clutching at straws, false hopes. Rather than destroying the nightmare creatures they'd given them exactly what they wanted. *She'd* given them what they wanted. All her efforts had come to nothing. Now Menhroth and his army could never be stopped.

Barion stood beside her, sword at the ready. He was heavily bandaged from many injuries, one eye and half the golden lines on his face covered up. He cast a questioning glance at her. Hellen nodded to him, telling him the time was near. He nodded back in understanding. Or perhaps he was saying farewell.

It struck Hellen why the silence filling the Wycka seemed so heavy, so complete. The Song had stopped. There were no vibrations echoing through the stones from the Songroom. The singers had come to the end of the notes and had fallen silent. Andar, truly, was no more.

"They are here," said a voice, quiet and low. "On the island. So many of them. Our walls and wards haven't stopped them."

Hellen could see them clearly in her mind's eye. The army was so vast it was a huge cloud rather than a collection of individuals. Did they really need to send so many? Did they intend such slaughter and destruction that they had to send these thousands and thousands? A tenth of the number would have sufficed. A hundredth. She imagined her own blood spilling and spiralling down that central drain of the Wycka as the rain had done for so long. She had failed them all. She welcomed the end now. At least she wouldn't have to live with the knowledge of her own failure.

A figure appeared in the open archways of the Wycka. The undain leading the army. She thought it might be Menhroth, fresh from destroying Cait on the river but instead a stooped old man with a key around his neck hobbled into the room. His eyes were blank, a milky white. Charis had survived. The King's Chancellor from the old days, whom they'd seen killed by the serpents at Guilden. Here he was, unharmed and untroubled.

His voice was thin, a croak, as he spoke, as if his throat was worn out from his great age. "Hellen Meggenwar, Eldest of Andar" – he dipped his head even lower in a mock bow of respect – "I have long looked forward to meeting you. Our opponent on the other side of the river, on the other side of the chessboard, manipulating your pieces, sacrificing your pawns one by one until there is only you, the Queen, and these few underlings left."

"As I have told others, I am no Queen," said Hellen. "And as for pawns, weren't you destroyed when the river serpents took you?"

"That? No. An inconvenience. My army was lost, it is true, but I simply had to return to Angere for another. An impressive move of yours. As was the reappearance of Xoster from the old stories. You have been worthy opponents, truly, but now your game is done. Your Andar is gone. From this moment I am the ruler of these lands. A Prince by the hand of King Menhroth the First and Last, Menhroth the Undying."

"You are a slave," said Hellen. "Powerful, I grant you, but still carrying out the orders given to you. At least we are free."

Charis smiled a joyless smile at that. "Free to suffer and die. Where is the liberty in that? And you will only be *free* for another minute or so, I would say. Whereas I will be here for a very, very long time. You know, I may even make this island my home. Knock down this ridiculous roofless tower and build a proper palace in its place. I'll need slaves of course. Slaves to build, slaves to carry out my orders to the letter. An idea occurred to me as I strode unopposed across your pond. How amusing it would be if you and the other wicca here were to be those slaves.

Would you like that? We could ascend you with a glimmer of self-knowledge left in your minds. Just enough so you'd know, every day for the rest of time, who you once were and what you'd lost. The thought would amuse me every time I saw you. What sport I could have."

"Cruelty is a sport for you is it, Charis?"

"I rather think it is, yes."

"Once you were a good man. A kind man. I have read the old accounts. I know your life story. I know of the people you loved and who loved you. I know of your children. What would they say if they heard you now?"

If she'd hoped to make him pause, see the error of his ways, she was disappointed. Charis give a dismissive shrug. "Ancient history. Some of them are still in my household. Some I have even allowed their memories and their minds. Many are simply blank-eyed animals carrying out my bidding. It is a fine life. How sad it must be to forever lose the ones you love. Or to know that, one day, those who love you will lose you."

"Sad, yes," replied Hellen. "Death is rarely a good thing. But knowing we'll die at least makes us value life. Your existence is empty. Once you've defeated us, what's left? What will you do in a year's time? In a hundred? A thousand?"

Charis shook his head. "I really wouldn't worry about me. There are plenty of other lands to conquer, other worlds across the aether. The one Cait came from, and the boy and the musician there, lurking at the back. We have run their world for a long time, farming it for Spirit and Bone. But there's no need for that any more. Once the Ritual is sealed and our ascendance is absolute, we can set about conquering the place properly. Recreating it in our own image."

"They will fight you."

"And they will lose as you have. Now, let us put an end to this. I thought you might have more clever moves, a surprise or two to throw at me, but it seems not. How disappointing you are."

Summoned by some unheard call, his soldiers flooded into the Wycka. Four huge wyrm lords, eerie light glowing from their transparent skins. Behind them came undain soldiers, swords in hands. In a few moments the remaining free people of Andar were surrounded. Hellen tried to ready magic, but her strength was gone. The surviving wyrm lords of Caer L'dun hefted their blades, ready for the last fight. It wouldn't last long.

One of the undain riders stepped forward and held her blade over Hellen, ready to strike. She glanced to Charis for his approval.

"Now," said Charis, "I will offer you a choice, Hellen Meggenwar. You can either die first and get it over with. Or you can live a few moments longer and see your friends go first. Which is it to be?"

Hellen moved closer to him. There was a glimmer, the merest hint, of fear on his features, as if he still suspected some trick. It was a small victory, but that was all that was left to her now.

"I will go first," said Hellen.

"Very well." Charis nodded.

The rider stepped forward and swung her sword.

Cait watched as Menhroth stood unmoving, his gaze passing between Cait and Ran, kneeling at his feet.

More than once since the day at the library, Cait had experienced a sense of expanding perspectives, of seeing the wider world around her from outside, above. On the bridge back in Manchester, when Nox was pursuing her and Danny, she'd seemed to fly from her body and look down on the scene. Then again when they'd fought the riders outside the factory. And in Angere, at Greygyle's palace, it had happened more strongly. She'd seen the whole area, the undain army outside the walls. A moment of clarity. Another came to her now, and it seemed to her that her mind's eye flew upward, taking in more and more.

She and Menhroth confronting each other. Ran kneeling. Greygyle quivering and shivering, the hooded figure holding his leash. Farther out, the massed undain behind Menhroth, countless in number. Farther out still, the throng of them at Islagray, surrounding a few remaining sparks of life that were Danny and Fer and the others.

Farther still, and she saw the towns and cities of Andar, one or two flecks of life among them. The dead and the dying. There were the lines of prisoners being led across the ice to their fate in Angere. She saw Hyrn's Oak in ruins. She saw Guilden in ruins. Then, across the An, her gaze flew over the white halls of Menhroth's city and the palaces of the undain. Caer D'nar. All of it laid out like a map.

Here was the turning point. Here was the moment that the fate of everything and everyone was decided. And not just them. Everyone back home, and maybe in other worlds, too. Now it would end, one way or another.

Then she was back in her own body, facing Menhroth. He still hadn't moved. She could feel the hunger raging inside him, his mind briefly open to her as he grappled with the decision of what to do. For five hundred years he had sought the blood and the book and now here they were in his grasp.

He looked to Ran, trying to gauge whether the rider's words could be believed. He didn't know, Cait saw. He didn't know. He longed to seize the prize they had dangled before him. Hungered to take the book and not believe what Ran was telling him. Menhroth had gone along with Ran all this time partly because the King couldn't be sure the rider was telling the truth, couldn't be sure he wasn't simply another of Hellen's subterfuges. And perhaps Ran had been too good at maintaining his pretence. More than once he'd fought and killed the undain to protect Cait. He'd actually trained Lugg, shown him how to move and fight.

A worm of doubt twisted in Menhroth's mind, whispering that Ran wasn't loyal. That he was simply, desperately, trying to prevent the King from working the necromancy. There was the possibility, also, that Ran had been tricked into believing what he'd said. A last, desperate gamble by the wicca to foil Menhroth's intentions. Ran's mind, protected by his rider markings, remained closed off, unknowable even to the King.

Still Menhroth didn't act, his indecision pinning him in place. He was running out of time. His urgency burned in him, clear to Cait. He consumed a huge amount of Spirit to survive and now that supply had been cut off. Fer had done that. By disrupting the flow she hadn't only crippled the catapults. Menhroth had sated himself as best he could, draining the supplies of the White City, but most of their resources were deployed to the invading armies. His borrowed life was ebbing dangerously low. He'd come to take her blood, seal the Ritual then and there and so put an end to his constant need for Spirit. There was an edge of desperation in him, he was so close to what he craved. But now there was Ran, the troublesome wyrm lord, telling him not to take the final step.

Menhroth's eyes narrowed as he turned to her. She was the only one who knew the truth. He would find out from her. She had to keep him out, hide the reality of what they were attempting. If he discovered even the possibility of Ran's words being true he might not take the leap. He'd suffer for a while, perhaps, but no doubt he'd survive once he could feed from the captured people of Andar. And the worlds would be lost.

His assault on her was terrible, like fire raging around her brain. Desperately she threw up defences to deny him, keep him out. She was stronger now. She'd grown. Bethany, so used to hiding away, had taught her well. With an effort that felt like she was tearing herself in two, Cait beat him back, refusing to reveal her mind to him. Snarling, Menhroth's handsome features twisting into ugly rage, he attacked her again, spikes of red hot iron seeming to lance into her brain.

This time she was ready. Phoenix had said it would grow easier for her as the winter wore on. Ice. She always envisioned her magical power as ice. And there they were, upon the frozen An in the depths of the winter. She was strong there. She saw the pool of mountain water where Bethany had lived. It, too, was frozen. Cold power breathed out of it, ferns of frost feeling their way across the stones as she watched, a mist solidifying in the air. Walls of ice formed about her mind, so thick even Menhroth's attack couldn't batter it down. She hated fire and the cold kept it at bay.

With a scream of rage Menhroth stepped back. He could kill her there and then. That was a real possibility. Still he needed to know the truth from her. He reached down to the thing that had once been Greygyle and placed his hand on the creature's head, sucking out what dregs of spirit the former Duke had in him. Greygyle shivered, then sagged to the ice as Menhroth drained him. In a moment, the Duke was dust.

Menhroth turned to the unmoving figure holding still holding Greygyle's lead. Cait thought this must be some guard, or some noble of the Holy Court she hadn't met. Instead, as the figure pushed back the grey hood that hid his face, she saw the truth of it.

Nox stared back at her, his eyes blank.

Menhroth caught the look of shock on Cait's face. His voice was little more than a snarl as he spoke. "Yes, here he is, your precious Nox. I have given him a reward for his betrayals, too. He longed for ascension and now he has been granted it. He is aware of everything that is taking place but is powerless to act. I planned to keep him enslaved like that for a few hundred years, but now I need his Spirit."

"But he died," said Cait. "His body was burned."

"Dying is no obstacle to us," said Menhroth. "As to his body, that survived. Those archers couldn't even hit a slow-moving boat. We found him floating alone on the waters."

Menhroth held out his hand to touch Nox on the forehead. Nox didn't flinch. After a moment, he, too, slumped to the ice, his eyes closed. His body didn't collapse into dust as Greygyle's had. Perhaps he had been too recently ascended for the decay to take effect.

Menhroth looked down to Ran. "Step forward, rider. I need you too. Be true to your vows."

Ran hesitated. He glanced aside at Cait for a moment as though there was doubt in him. Regret. But then, still on his knees, he shuffled forward and let Menhroth lay a hand on his head. As Greygyle and Nox had, Ran quivered and shook. Then, groaning once, he fell to the ice and moved no more.

Menhroth looked back to Cait. He seemed to swell with energy. "Now we shall see the truth of it." He threw himself at her for a third time, intent on ripping the truth from her mind.

It cost her everything she had to resist him, hold his raging fire at bay. She was waning, the screaming pain in her body so great she wanted to cry out in agony. She refused to relent. Menhroth could not know the truth.

The intensity of the attack increased and she did scream, sinking to her knees, hands clutched to her head. She felt warm blood trickling from her nose. Menhroth towered over her, bearing down on her. Still she resisted. Nothing else mattered. She would keep him out. She wouldn't be violated.

With a cry of rage of his own, Menhroth relented. There was nothing left of that handsome man she'd seen on his throne in the White City. The creature before her was a snarling monster, features twisted and dripping, misshapen sides heaving from his exertions.

He was weak, spent. She saw what she had to do. It was her turn. They'd thought to fool him, make him complete the Ritual by his own hand, but now she saw another way. She would do it instead. She would take the place of her ancient forebear and speak the words that completed the rite.

His fingers had touched her blood. Was that enough? She had to make sure of it. Beads of blood still pearled across her palm. She stepped forward to place her hand on Menhroth's head, leaving her mark upon him. He cowered back, like an injured animal cornered by its attacker. She spoke the words Fer had taught her. The family secret. The sealing words of the Ritual of Seven Ascensions.

At the first syllable Menhroth went rigid; his muscles spasmed. His obsidian eyes were unreadable, but she thought she saw hunger on his features as she worked the long-withheld magic. Hunger and something like rapture as he drank in her words. Did he understand what she was doing? Did he believe she was helping him? No. His hunger was too great; it blotted out his reason.

She spoke the last syllables, including the one different. *Yaelth.* Menhroth sagged to his knees immediately, as if the electricity making his muscles rigid had been switched off. For a moment he didn't move. Cait waited for him to crumble and collapse as Fer had described.

When he looked up at her the expression on his features was stark. But not with the horror or shock she'd hoped for. Instead there was joy there, a wild triumph in his flaring eyes. He stood, casting her to the ice with a wave of his hand. Stood and laughed, a hideous delight on his misshapen face.

Hellen, bowed, her eyes closed, waiting for the blow.

Charis was right. She had no more moves. She had failed. She only hoped the pain would be brief.

But the blade didn't fall. In its place a wind howled through Islagray Wycka, strong enough to make Hellen stagger. It brought with it a smell of dust and decay, of damp and ancient tombs. It washed over her, filling her nostrils, and then was gone.

When she opened her eyes, Charis and the wyrm lords and all the host of undain were no more. A grey-brown dust flew on the breeze, whipping around in little spirals like water spouts. Then the wind fell and the dust drifted with it, becoming only a coating upon the stone floor of the Wycka.

A dust they could brush away.

Barion, the resentful and angry wyrm lord, let his sword clatter to the ground. His single good eye wide with disbelief, he turned to her and threw his arms around her.

Slow and low at first, but then gaining volume and speed, a chorus of singing thrummed through the stone of the walls and floor. It took her a moment or two to understand what it was.

The Song of Andar beginning again.

There was a moment when understanding dawned on Menhroth. He stared down at Cait, rage and disbelief twisting his features. He stepped forward to reach her, perhaps intent on his revenge with his final act.

Then Cait was thrown backward by the force of the explosion from the King. It blasted outward, seeming to fill the whole world. An explosion on the ice but also flashing in the aether, reaching to every undain he had created, all those bound to him and his existence. The power, the stolen Spirit, screamed from him, from all of them, destroying them in the moment he was destroyed.

The Spirit raged and seethed, a cloud of anger, seeking the object it craved. The person it craved. With a howl of glee it threw itself at Cait, offering itself to her.

Filling her.

For a moment the power of it was too much. She floundered in a rush of streaming energy, a babble of confused voices, screams and laughter. She fell, or flew, swooping to the ground but never hitting, thrown in whirling circles, like riding a roller coaster that went faster and faster but never reached an end. There was more screaming, and it was her own voice.

But then she found her footing, found solid ground, and she was no longer within the streaming river of power. Instead it was within her, flowing through her, and she could step aside from it, look at it. She could control it, direct it. Bend it to her will. The power of it was terrible, but it was hers to wield, not to fear.

She stood, chest heaving as the power fizzed through her like a charge of electricity, and only a moment of time had passed. She was alone on the ice save for the bodies of Ran and Nox, the two who had accompanied her through the portal to Angere. Where the King had stood a ragged crack had been torn into the ice. A cloud of ash swirled in the air above it. When it fell, it carpeted the ground with a dusting of grey.

The book lay where she'd dropped it. A breeze ruffled its leaves, revealing page after page as if it were deliberately showing her its secrets. She stooped to pick it up. Ilminion's Grimoire, the cause of so much trouble, so much loss. How insignificant it seemed. A dangerous, terrible book. But, also, a thing of wonder. A book of possibilities.

Her gran had told her the point about witchcraft was that a price had to be paid. You didn't go too far because the cost would be too great. But there were other ways to do magic. Hellen had said Ilminion had started out with good intentions. Perhaps he'd only lacked the sense needed to wield the power he'd unearthed. She could succeed where he'd failed. She could do great good in the worlds where he'd done such harm. Hadn't Hellen said there was a time to use the mancers' arts? Doing so had saved them, and now there was another opportunity. An unforeseen opportunity. A fate that, perhaps, was meant to be hers all along.

She would use the book. She would wield the undains' power. She could do anything. Many wounds in the world needed healing. She would set about doing so.

She leafed hungrily through the book with its diagrams and charts and incantations, deciding where to start. The people of Andar and Angere, and even her own world, would thank her, adore her, for what she was about to do.

Then faces came to her: faces in the streaming river of power that seethed inside her. The images of those whose Spirit had been sucked from them by the machines of Genera. Screaming, terrified faces, confused and lost. Then other faces danced from her memories. Her gran. Her mother and her father. Danny. Johnny. Hellen. Fer.

Cait paused. The sadness on those familiar faces was terrible to see. What was she doing? She boiled with so much energy it was hard to think straight. But the power wasn't hers. It was stolen. It was corrupt, rotten. She couldn't do this, this wasn't her. She thought about Danny, the way he'd looked at her in the White City when she'd unleashed the ghosts. The fear on his face.

She slumped to the ground. Her mother had used the cobbles of Manchester to work the magic. Cait had only the ice. But the ice was the An, and the An flowed over the ground, washing everything away. She placed her hands on the ground, holding her palms flat, ignoring the shock of the cold. She worked the magic she needed. She didn't know how to do it and the Spirit filling her resisted, the power of the Ritual binding it to her.

She grunted from the effort of what she was attempting and kept at it. Still the necromancy fought her, but the spirits longed for their release. Whoever they were, whoever they'd been, they craved the peace of oblivion. Cait opened herself to them, showing them the road to take. Down her outstretched arms to the ice, to the water. In a moment the flood was unstoppable. The agonies of loss as the power flowed from her made her gasp again and again, but she kept her hands where they were.

She watched them go. The countless slaves and soldiers of Angere. The higher nobles, Greygyle among them. The undain wyrm lords. Charis was there too, somehow still alive. The waters took him, also. Then, finally, Menhroth himself, fighting and seething but unable to resist. The An claimed him.

She was about to lift her hand from the ice when she saw there was one more in line. A final soul, clinging to existence.

Cait, said Nox. *Let me remain.*

You have your revenge, she said. *You are the last of the undain.*

Genera still exists. They must pay for what they did to me, too.

You were enslaved to the King. How can you survive?

Menhroth is gone and I, the last, am free. Free if you will make me free. Return me to my body and let me go.

She hesitated. If she did this thing how was she any better than Ilminion?

Why should I trust you?

Why shouldn't you? I've proved myself again and again. Hurry, please. The river pulls me in. I have only moments.

She hesitated. Perhaps he'd earned this after everything he'd done. Perhaps it was hugely dangerous. She didn't know, but she didn't want him to go. She'd lost too many others.

She lifted her hands from the ice and placed them onto Nox's head, letting his essence flow from her.

His body twitched and bucked, then his eyes opened. He stared at her for a moment with alarm burning in his eyes. He gulped in lungfuls of air while his muscles spasmed and he writhed in agony.

After twenty or thirty seconds his thrashing movements and breathing calmed. He twisted round to haul himself to his knees, and then to his feet.

When he looked at her again it was the old Nox, the familiar mocking look on his face. But he was an undain, the light in him gone. A triumphant smile sidled across his features. How much power did he have? How much had she given him? Would he fade or grow stronger and stronger? She didn't know.

His voice was slightly slurred, as if he was getting used to controlling his tongue. "Thank you, Cait."

"What will you do?" she asked.

"Return to our world. Begin the hunt."

"And when you've won, when you've beaten them, what then?"

"Then … we shall see."

"Will I regret this, Nox?"

He simply grinned in reply and, nodding his head in farewell, turned away. He strode westward toward the White City and disappeared into the mists.

Cait stood. Her hands were blue and numb. Her brain was also numb, but there was one more thing she had to do. Clumsily, she picked up Ran's sword. It was heavy in her hands. It was incredible anyone could wield it. It would do for what she had in mind. She propped the book upright, open at some random page. Then she lifted the sword and let it fall, using the blade's own weight for the blow.

The sword sliced easily through the book's spine, cleaving it in two.

She smiled to herself although no one would see. Her splitting of the book wasn't as elegant or clever as Akbar's had been, but it would do the job. Ilminion's Grimoire was paper and ink, nothing more. And ink could smudge and blur just as paper could mulch and rot. It wouldn't take much to destroy the Grimoire utterly.

Cait stepped to the crack and dropped the two halves

of the book in, letting the waters of the An take them, too.

She stood over the remains of Ran for a moment, thinking about everything that had happened. Then, alone, she began the long walk across the ice to Andar.

25 – THE ORCHARD OF WITCHES

Clara Sweetley walked through the echoing, ornately-decorated hall, the clacking of her heels the only sound. She strode past the third archway where, on her previous visit, she'd been forced to crawl on hands and knees into the presence of Menhroth. Now no one would force such humiliation upon her. The undain were no more, destroyed, if she understood matters correctly, by their own death magic. She'd never trusted such mumbo-jumbo. She'd watched in amazement as the two giant guards, escorting her to the portal, had suddenly stopped, looked around in confusion, and then simply disintegrated, scattering like pillars of ash in a high wind.

She stopped at the foot of the stairs that led to Menhroth's throne. She'd vowed to return, sit in that chair while people crawled into her presence. And now she would. The undain might be gone, but Genera remained and she was still in charge of it. No one could touch her.

They would have to abandon this world soon, rationalise their business plans. The refinery would need to be repaired, but that was all to the good. They no longer needed the pipelines through the portal. There was no longer any need to harvest Bone, but Spirit was different.

Perhaps she could learn the secrets of the undain, engineer her own ascendance, her own immortality. With Menhroth out of the way the world, the real world, was theirs to run.

Hers to run.

She climbed the steps to sit upon the great white throne. Yes. There was much to do, and many battles to fight. But for now she had won. It felt good.

The other directors of Genera would be there soon. She'd called – for once the term seemed completely apt – an Extraordinary Board Meeting. When they reached the third archway she would give them their instructions, explain about the crawling. And once they returned home, sealing the portal behind them, it was a practice she might even continue. It would do them good to really understand who was in charge. She might even have the great throne brought back with them. It would look good in the Board Room of Genera.

Smiling to herself, Clara Sweetley sat in silence and waited.

Hundreds of miles to the north, Phoenix sat at the top of Caer D'nar. Lines of smoke twirled off the embers of the night's fire. The other surviving members of the Smouldering Fire were there, too, watching and waiting. Since the girl from the other world had left they'd received no news. The undain were massed on the southern banks of the Dragon's Tongue, but they seemed to have lost interest in attacking. He almost wished they hadn't. Almost wished there could be an ending to their long story, one way or another.

Two days earlier, Xoster herself had come sweeping out of the north, huge and terrible, the boy Lugg upon her back. She'd circled the tower of Caer D'nar once, roaring flame, then turned south and east to head for the An. A dragon in the skies of Angere once more. The last dragon. A wonder and a marvel. It seemed likely that Phoenix would get his wish. The war upon Andar was raging, and the outcome would decide the fate of everyone. Soon they would know who had prevailed.

"Phoenix." Demara stood behind him, pointing something out. She placed a hand on his shoulder. To the south, a mere black smudge to his old eyes, a chough was coming. A message from one of the watchtowers at the Dragon's Tongue, judging by the direction. Soon the bright red of its beak was visible.

"News at last," said Phoenix. "Now we will learn the truth of it."

When the chough had landed and been persuaded to give up the message it bore around its neck, Phoenix read, angling the slip of paper to the light streaming through the archway. He read twice, not able to believe the words written there.

He looked up at the circle of his friends. Their eyes were wide with alarm, with fear. They thought the end was upon them.

"The girl did it," said Phoenix simply. "She actually did it."

The Doge sat upon his golden throne. Somehow the old chair had survived the collapse of the buildings, the crush of the falling stone. It stood canted at an awkward angle, and it was covered in a thick layer of dust. All around, Guilden lay in its ruins: mountains of stone that had once been buildings, glimpses of gold among the grey ash, frozen fragments of the miraculous city map.

But Guilden had fallen before and it would rise, phoenix-like, again. They would rebuild. The people, led across the ice in roped lines to meet their fate in Angere had been saved at the last moment by some miracle. Those who had fled into woods and hills were returning, too, creeping back to the city. The witch from the south had hinted some terrible sorcery would be attempted to save Andar. Clearly that had worked. And clearly he'd been wrong about the wicca and their ancient ways.

Guilden would rise bigger and better than ever, but they would always welcome the witches from the south now, just as they welcomed the mancers. Perhaps there wasn't so much difference between the two anyway. Perhaps true wisdom lay in listening to all.

He turned to the ex-Lord of Misrule. The man was a wheelwright by trade, and his brief Midwinter reign was over. Still, they would need people like him. They would need everyone. And perhaps he, the Doge, had been too remote from the people, too proud. He'd thought Guilden mattered more than the rest of the world but he'd been wrong. Sometimes there'd been wisdom in the Lord of Misrule's foolery and mocking.

"Your throne has survived, too, I see," said the Doge. "Will you sit for a while and discuss plans for the rebuilding of Guilden?"

The ex-Lord of Misrule had found the broken scraps of his own crown in the rubble. He placed the nest of twigs back on his head.

Fer pushed through the thick cobwebs that clogged the archaeon's tunnel. The bookwyrm's lair now looked more like the original one she recalled from her first visit in the Tanglewood. The shining metal and glass were gone. A rush of whispered words and ideas blew at her like a wind, attempting to batter her backward. She paid them no attention. She'd been through too much to get caught up in the creature's games.

"I know you're listening so you can stop pretending to be asleep," she said as she arrived in the rocky cavern. The dragon, larger than ever, lay with its arrowhead tail curled up around its great snout. Two trails of sulphurous smoke rose from its nostrils as if it might breathe fire on her at any moment. It didn't deign to even open an eye.

She wasn't impressed by any of it. "You can have it your own way, of course. We'll leave you in peace inside Akbar's journal. I'm sure you've read and understood every word of it by now, but you clearly have no desire to discover all the other *unknown* books."

The bookwyrm finally peered at her. Fer's own face reflected brightly in its slit pupil. There were no lines of glowing symbols, but its voice was the same mountain-shaking rumble. "Other books, little witch?"

"In Angere. You do know the undain are gone? There must be many tomes that you haven't read across the river. In the White City and the palaces of the undain. Perhaps even in the tunnels beneath Morvale Wycka."

The archaeon's breathing seemed to quicken very slightly. "It is ... possible. I have spent most of my existence in An, East-of-the-river."

"Good. Then you can help us rebuild the ancient bridge so we can travel to the other side more easily."

"The bridge! Have you any idea of the magic and the artifice that went into such a miraculous construction?"

"None at all. But I'm sure you've read some old papers and books, terribly difficult to interpret no doubt, that hint at how to go about it?"

"It's possible I have some inkling of what was involved."

"And you have the wisdom and knowledge of the other world, too. With magic and technology combined, you must be able to work wonders."

"It ... is possible."

"Excellent," said Fer. "Then we'll start work tomorrow."

She turned to leave, then stopped herself. "I did come to thank you, too. Or at least to thank the version of you that helped us in the other world. We'd have been lost without you. You saved us, more than once."

"Yes, I'm sure I did. But as one of me has said before, you do go to some interesting places. And your enemies … they had no time for libraries. When we first went to the other world the undain had destroyed all those books. Shredded them for no reason. Such a crime. If I had to choose a side it was always yours."

"Well, I'm grateful to you. We're all grateful."

"Just as you should be," said the dragon, closing its eyes once more.

"Is there any way you can keep in touch with your other selves?" asked Fer.

"Regrettably, the internet of that world doesn't extend to Andar. But … it is possible we can build a connection between their network and the shadow paths that thread through the aether. It is something I'm considering."

"So, another sort of bridge?"

"Just so, little witch. Now leave me in peace. I have much to do."

In Hyrn's Oak, Venn leaned her bow against the gnarled trunk of the ancient tree and rolled up her sleeves. There was much to do, much rebuilding. She spoke to the gathered crowds. "We will start with the bridges. We should be an island no more."

A chorus of agreement rose from the surviving townsfolk.

Cait and Danny sat together on the banks of Islagray, Cait's head resting on Danny's shoulder. In front of them the Silverwater was a glistening mirror. The ice had melted, the lake turning to water once more as if the winter, too, were of Menhroth's doing. The sun shone low in the sky but there was a warmth to it. It was good just to sit. She'd lost count of all the aches and bruises covering her. Away in the distance, a blur of vivid colour, Johnny relaxed in *Smoke on the Water*, enjoying, as he'd put it, some damn peace for a change.

"I can't believe we actually did it," she said eventually. "Actually defeated those horrors."

"We did," said Danny. "*You* did."

In the end it had been such a small thing. Not terrible battle magic or overwhelming strength of arms. A little thing. An insignificant thing. A single word different. A thing so easily overlooked.

"I guess," she said.

"It was a hell of a gamble, though," said Danny. "I didn't think it was really going to work."

"You didn't say."

"Well, no. Didn't think it would be constructive. At the time. What was it like? To speak the words I mean, work that magic?"

"It was … grim. I hope I never have to do anything like it again. I had a glimpse of Menhroth's mind when we were out there. The way he saw the world, like it was his to use, exploit as he wanted."

"Uh huh."

She hadn't decided yet how much to tell him. "I mean, I'll be honest, I could see the appeal. He was like a god or something. He could do what he pleased. But it was hideous. My flesh crawls to think about it."

"It was the necromancy that saved us in the end, though."

She nodded. "A balance restored. Necromancy, yes, but a price was paid. Maybe Hellen's right and there isn't really much difference between witches and mancers."

"Weird about Ran," said Danny. "I mean, did you have any idea?"

"None. All that time I was watching Nox, thinking he was the one I couldn't trust. Ran was always there to save me, so I thought."

"Did you tell Lugg what Menhroth had done to his father?"

"I decided not to," she said.

Danny nodded. "It's been hard on him. First his father and then Ran."

"He'll be OK. I saw Barion talking to him before. Don't know what will happen to the wyrm lords now there are so few of them, but Lugg has a family there, of sorts."

"They'll carry on even though there are definitely no more dragons, no more enemies?"

"Sure. I don't think they'll let little things like that stop them."

"And you?" asked Danny. "You'll carry on with the whole witching thing? Keep using it?"

She shrugged. "It's part of me. It's what I am. The trick is knowing where to stop like my gran said all along."

He nodded, his cheek on the top of her head. "So you're not going to end up like Menhroth? Insanely evil and all-powerful?"

She thought about what she'd done for Nox. She hadn't told anyone about that yet, but at some point she'd have to. "Wouldn't have thought so. Unless I have a *really* bad day."

"Be sure to warn me if you do."

"Uh huh. So, what about you? Are you ready to go home?"

Danny nodded again. "Haven't got a clue how I'll explain any of this to my folks, though. They'll be going up the wall with worry. Don't suppose, you know, time moves at a different speed here like in the books? We'll go back and find only five minutes have past sort of thing?"

"Don't think so, sorry. We'll just have to sit them down and tell them everything."

"Tell my folks?"

"I think they're old enough. I guess they won't really mind so long as you're back home and safe."

"Will you come with me? To explain it to them?"

"Of course, and Gran, too. And Johnny if he's coming back with us."

"What will you do? Now that, you know, your dad *and* your mum…"

"Live with my gran I guess. If she'll have me."

"Of course she will. But how are we even going to get there?"

"Don't know," said Cait. "Perhaps Hellen can arrange it. But…"

"What?"

"You're sure you want to go back? To our old lives?"

He didn't answer for a moment. "If we do, will we still be us? Will we still be together?"

She kissed him, gently, upon the cheek. "If you'll have me."

"Well … do you promise not to abandon me in the dungeons of any more ancient undead horrors?"

"I do."

He laughed. "That's settled then. It will be good to get home."

"Yes," said Cait, "Although things won't be sorted out there just because they are here. Genera is still a thing. Somehow I don't think Ms. Sweetley is going to simply leave us alone. And then there's Bethany and the other ghosts. Fer didn't know what happened to them, whether they're still, you know, unquiet." She wondered about Tom, the beggar outside the Library who'd laughed at her on that first day, too. He'd played his part according to Fer, but no one knew what had happened to him. Word through the aether had been patchy, although they did know her gran and the Lizard King had escaped the refinery unharmed, in the confusion of the spirits' attack.

"We can find out," said Danny. "I wonder what the gang will make of it when we tell them. Devi and Rachel and Val and Jen, I mean."

"Maybe we should leave them in the dark. It might be easier."

"I reckon you might be right. And what will you do with school and life and all that?"

"I don't know," said Cait. "But it's funny, that doesn't scare me any more. It seems exciting. It's like, after everything that's happened, I'm not afraid. I don't know where I'm going but it's *somewhere*."

Smoke on the Water was floating toward them, propelled, as ever, by neither oar nor sail. The V of its passing was a hard line fanning out across the lake. After a few minutes it touched its prow to the bank. The eyes on the little golden figurehead closed as Johnny leapt ashore.

"Hey guys. Not interrupting a moment of great romance am I?"

"Actually, yes," said Cait. "But we'll forgive you. Did you decide what you're doing yet?"

"You mean, should I stay or should I go? Yeah, I've decided. Just been explaining it all to Smokie here. I'm going home. Get the band back together sort of thing. Figure I've got some great material for a new album. And I promised to write some stuff for you, right?"

"And what about *Smoke on the Water*?" asked Cait.

"Still wants to go off exploring. See if the An really does go on forever, circling the whole world. But he'll have new passengers."

"Oh?"

"Sure, haven't you figured it? Fer and Lugg. Seems they want to go off travelling together. Like, *together* together."

"They didn't hang around."

"Yeah. There's something in the air. This early spring … it feels like the waters of a lake held back by a dam and finally released."

"I thought Fer would want to stay at Islagray Wycka. Learn the ways of the witches."

"Oh, I think she's into that idea now. Once she's seen a bit of the world."

"I wonder where Fer and Lugg will settle. Eventually I mean. Lugg from Angere and Fer from Andar."

"Yeah," said Johnny. "Symbolic, right? Fer muttered something about maybe rebuilding Morvale Wycka. The equivalent of this place on the other side. Perhaps she'll be like Hellen one day. Eldest of Angere."

Cait laughed. The thought was amusing after everything Fer had said about disliking covens and rules. "She should. She…" Cait stopped in mid-sentence. Someone was trying to talk to her from afar, through the aether. Another witch, politely enquiring if she had a moment.

"What is it?" said Danny. "What's wrong?"

"Hellen wants to talk to me up at the orchard." She rose, ignoring the complaints from her bruised limbs. "I'll go. She says it's something important."

"Want me to come?" asked Danny.

"Chill out here. I think it's just me she wants to see."

"Ah, right. Witchery."

"Something like that."

Cait saw Hellen from afar as she climbed the hill to the orchard. The old witch stood beside a bent, skeletal tree. She looked half like a tree herself, thin and hard and slightly stooped as if she stood in a raging gale. Was this what happened? Did the witches get so old and woody that they came up here one day and never came back? She could believe it.

Hellen's face was wrinkled, but her eyes burned with life and intelligence. "Cait. Thank you for coming. There's something I wanted to show you."

"What is it?"

"You know what this place is? How it works?"

"I think so. When one of you dies your spirit ends up

here."

"Something like that. Except, sometimes, it captures other spirits, too. Like a net catching a fluttering moth in the aether. A moth that happens to be drawn here. If there's unfinished business, or the person is rooted to this place, then they can find a home. A bit like Bethany helping you and Fer."

"Wait, you knew about that?"

"Oh yes."

"So Bethany's here?"

"No, not her. As far as I know she's somewhere in your world if she's anywhere at all."

"Who then?"

"Can't you tell? She was from here, of course. Her family I mean. Weyerd's great, great many-times-over granddaughter."

"You mean, my mother?"

"See for yourself, child. This old apple tree has stood here many years but never had an inhabitant. Now it does."

Cait regarded the tree. A single black crow had perched on its branches, gazing down at her with one eye. Cait's throat had gone dry. For a moment she didn't know what to say. "She'll stay here?"

"Yes. Whenever you come back, if you do come back, she'll be here for you."

"And, I don't suppose … my father? He had no Weerd blood, of course, but still…"

"Talk to your mother. She was a powerful witch. I gather she scoured the aether for … echoes before finding her way here. Two in one tree. It happens some time, when two souls are intertwined. The world is full of wonders."

"You mean…"

"Yes. Sit against the tree and open your mind. You have all the time you need."

Doing as she was told, Cait closed her eyes. She was

immediately aware of the two presences, the two familiar voices in her mind, speaking together.

Cait, love…

While the girl communed with her parents, Hellen turned to head deeper into the orchard. The trees were older, the undergrowth thicker, the farther you went. But the tree she wanted was only a little way in. A crooked blackthorn, its trunk bent over at a sharp angle as if it were growing in a gale. It was only a short time after Midwinter but already the first buds of the spring were showing upon it. Life was returning with miraculous urgency after too many dark days.

Hellen had her own spirit to commune with. She reached out to touch the rough, dark bark. After a moment, the presence of her old friend, Ariane of the Smiling Eyes, emerged from the background hubbub of dead witches' voices.

So you managed it at last then? the voice asked. *The wound is healed?*

Yes, said Hellen. *The wound is healed.*

The girl from the other world didn't succumb and become another like Menhroth? A Witch Queen?

No. I was almost completely sure she wouldn't.

Ah. Well, that's good.

Full of surprises that one, like I told you. In the end we were saved by her and by the mancers' greed and treachery. Strange how the world turns.

And what of you, old fool? Come to join us slumbering ghosts in the orchard?

Was she? She felt old and weary after the last few days. And her life's work was done. But still, she wasn't quite ready to rest yet.

Some day soon, she said. *For now I think I might wander off into the world. Do some good for a change. Become the hedge witch I always meant to be. Get away from these rules and rites and people expecting things of me all the time.*

You mean go and interfere in folks' lives even more, said Ariane. *Haven't they suffered enough?*

Hellen smiled. It was good to know her old friend had lost none of her barb just because she was dead. *There's something else, too.*

Oh?

Hellen had the distinct impression Ariane knew exactly what she meant. She pressed on regardless. *It's Borrn. He's heading away again soon, back into the wilds. There is much to be done in the wide world. We thought we might travel together.*

Ridiculous woman! said Ariane. *At your age?*

At my age, said Hellen. *Yes. The spring is coming on in a flood. The bud is swelling. Surely even you can feel it deep in your wooden heart? It is a time for fresh starts. Perhaps we'll even give Ashen a brother or sister.*

By the stars, woman, you're one hundred and thirty two.

Exactly. I think I'm just about ready for the responsibility of bringing someone up, now.

The presence of Ariane in the aether snorted, or as close to it as was possible.

I'll come back eventually, said Hellen quietly. *When I'm ready. I fancy a nice hawthorn tree. Something spiky. I can sit next to you and spend the years pointing out all your flaws until we both fade away.*

You won't have time, replied Ariane. *I'll be too busy pointing out all yours to you. Off you go then. Go and busybody the good folk of Andar and Angere. But before you do, there's someone else you need to talk to in the orchard.*

Who?

Isn't it obvious, woman? Who do you think you're going to find hanging around in an orchard? Especially this orchard. Oh, he was gone, lost. The faintest whisper. Now he's young and strong again and I fancy he'd like to talk to you.

Hellen understood then. Her touch lingering on the

bark of the blackthorn, she walked away, toward the oldest, densest part of the orchard, where the trees grew wild and overgrown and the spirits were quietest. She worked her way among the boughs, gently lifting grey branches aside so she could push her way into the shadows.

The shifting light through the leaves confused her eye, making her see shapes where, perhaps, there were none. Under the boughs of an ancient oak tree the shadows coalesced briefly into the form of a horned stag, powerful and majestic. Then it was gone.

Hellen marched toward the spot. The light shifted again and there was a man there instead, emerging from the dapple. He was tall, strong and completely unclothed. But he wasn't only a man: from his head sprouted the buds of new antlers. Hellen bowed to no one, but she dipped her head to Hyrn.

"So you are reborn, too."

His voice was the creak of ancient oaks and the babbling song of the mountain stream. "I am the land. The canker is stopped. The wound is healed and now I can walk the woods of An once more. It is … good to be alive and young."

"And what of Angere?"

"I will walk there too, as I did of old."

"The bridge is gone," said Hellen. "The land is still cloven."

"All woods are one wood. I can walk among them and between them as I please. In this world and in others."

"Well, that's all very nice. The rest of us will find it a little more difficult to cross the river."

"You can start building ships again. The river serpents will return to what they once were, harmless creatures of the deeps."

"That's a start," said Hellen. "And maybe one day we can build a new bridge, but for now we need a different land crossing."

Hyrn smiled at her. Was it her imagination or had his budding antlers grown a little as they talked? "You have something to ask of me?"

"Those tunnels we took to your island. Tunnels kept sealed by your will. If you opened them up folk could cross to the other side in safety, yes?"

"And then my island would no longer be my refuge."

"True. Do you think you need a refuge any more, Green Man?"

Hyrn snorted in amusement, sounding momentarily like some beast rather than a man. "You and the other child walked from Andar to the island. Not all the way across."

"But there are other tunnels are there not? I've heard tell of them. Caverns and delvings beneath the ruins of Morvale Wycka over in Angere. Tunnels leading under the ground just as they do from here. Tunnels that join up, I'm thinking. Passages that only need your word to be opened. Caves below ground and the bridge above, was that how it worked?"

Hyrn didn't reply for a moment. Then he took his turn to dip his head to her, very slightly. "Yes. You are right. The time has come for the pathways under the river to be walked. The An east and west must be united once more."

"Good," said Hellen. "And if I may, I have a favour to ask you."

"Another favour, you mean?"

"Just so. There is a wood in the aether. A Tanglewood. Put there twenty years ago by magical means."

"Put there by you."

"Indeed. It is sealed now, but its presence in the aether causes disruption. Danger even. An aethernal has taken up residence there."

"I have seen the creature that fills those woods like a howling gale."

"If the Tanglewood continues to grow, passage and conversation between that other world and ours will become harder and harder. The woods, all woods, are your domain. It is said Tanglewoods were originally of your creation, that once the whole land was one such, its ways and paths impossibly knotty. Can you intervene now?"

"You wish me to destroy the Tanglewood?"

"No, there is no need for that. Perhaps stop it growing, contain it. Such magic was beyond my meagre ability, but it would be a shame if the other world were lost to us."

Hyrn looked thoughtful for a moment, then nodded. "So be it. The creature and its impossible wood may remain as they are. An island of green in the aether. An acorn, perhaps, from which a new world might one day grow."

"Excellent. And can you open the pathways through the wood despite the presence of the creature? The walls between the worlds offer no obstacle to you, I know."

"You wish to leave this land?"

"Not me, but there are others. Everyone should be allowed to go home, should they not, Hyrn of the Green?"

"So they should, Hellen Meggenwar. Very well, I shall see that the paths through the Tanglewood remain clear for feet to follow."

"Good," said Hellen. "Well, if that's all sorted out I'll be on my way. Lots of work to be done. Lots of folk needing a healing hand." She turned away.

"Hellen Meggenwar?"

"Yes?"

"You remind me of someone. Another child of the wicca. A forebear of yours perhaps? I met her once in the woods on the other side."

Hellen turned back to look at Hyrn. "You mean Black Meg, that crossed to Andar when the bridge was destroyed?"

"Yes. That was her name."

"A mother's mother's mother, many generations back. She wrote down everything she'd seen and learned. All of this, everything I've done, is because of what she said and described. She's long gone and there's no echo of her in the orchard now. But it was she who saved us, as much as anyone. She and two riders, Dervil and Bordun."

"Ah. It is as I thought," said Hyrn. "I chose wisely, then."

"I think you did. She described you, too, you know. I know all about your little play in the woods. The two deer."

Hyrn nodded as if remembering. His antlers were an inch larger than they had been. "Yes," he said. "And now the two may live again, flourish together."

"Good. And will I see you again, in this world or the next?"

"Black Meg asked me that, too."

"And what did you tell her?"

"That I do not know. That I do not dream the world. It dreams me."

"Ah. Well. We shall see, then. Farewell, Hyrn of the Green."

"Farewell, Hellen Meggenwar."

Picking her way through the branches of the orchard, Hellen made her way back to the Wycka, to begin her preparations for leaving.

Seven of them stood among the trees: Cait and Danny, Johnny, Hellen and Ashen, Fer and Lugg. Both Merdoc and Barion hovered in the background, looking on, unsure of their welcome. Fer took them both by the hand and drew them into the group.

Grinning, Ashen put his arms around Cait. "We'll miss you."

"What about you? Will you go back to Guilden?"

He glanced at his mother. "Actually I'm going to stay here, spend some time in the archives studying the old texts."

"You're turning your back on the mancers?"

He looked a little sheepish when he replied, scratching his chin thoughtfully. "No. I've been persuaded of the wisdom of exploring the old magics and the new together. To be a mancer *and* a warlock or whatever that makes me. It's time for the old divisions to end."

Cait hugged him close. "It is."

Hellen stepped forward, a small, battered leather pouch in her hand. She held it out for Cait to take. "This might be of use."

"What's in there?"

"Books. Many books. I've scoured the archive for everything written by and about your family. When you get chance you can do some reading, find out about your history. Weyerd's account of the cleaving is in there along with much else. You might have to persuade the bookwyrm to translate things for you."

The bag only looked big enough to hold a few coins, and it weighed next to nothing as Cait cupped it in her hands. "But how can all those books be in there?"

"Surely you've learned enough about magic to answer such questions for yourself, girl?"

"Yes. Of course. Thank you. I'll read everything."

"Make sure you do. If you don't know where you've come from, you don't know who you are."

Cait slipped the miraculous bag into her pocket and turned to Fer. She took the other girl's hands in hers. It wasn't precisely like looking in a mirror, but the resemblance was close enough to make the experience slightly weird. Especially when the two of them smiled at exactly the same instance.

"Now we'll both be back where we're supposed to be," said Fer. "Your world is fascinating and strange, wonderful and terrible, but give me Andar any time."

"And I'm very much looking forward to having WiFi and showers again," said Cait.

"We may be able to converse at times, if the aether allows it."

Cait squeezed her cousin tightly. "I'd like that very much."

Fer stepped back to take Lugg's hand. To one side, the lower branches of two trees had been bent over to touch each other, their tips winding together to form a living archway.

"Step through and you'll be in the Tanglewood," said Hellen to Cait. "Look for two trees the same there, and they'll take you to the library in your city. The aether creature will allow you passage. Although, stay on the path if you want my advice."

"I thought you had to let a bat bite you or something to get through?" asked Cait.

"Not this time," said Fer. "Someone very good with trees and magic has arranged this."

"And can we ever come back the same way?" asked Cait.

"I think that would probably work, yes," said Hellen. "Now, off you go. I think your gran is waiting for you. She'll be worried if you don't appear soon and I don't want her complaining to me."

Cait nodded. There was suddenly nothing else to say. Hand in hand, Johnny following, Cait and Danny stepped into the archway to go home.

The End

Hyrn – a Cloven Land Trilogy prequel

Some wounds are too wide to heal...

The world changes one bright morning in spring. The ageing king of Angere turns to necromancy to prolong his existence, and the price of dark magic is paid in innocent lives. The land descends into chaos as loyalties are tested and friends become bitter foes.

For Black Meg, eldest witch of Angere, time is desperately short. She receives a vision from Hyrn, the horned man of the woods. The future is worse than anything she could have imagined. But Hyrn also shows her an answer, a way out.

It's a terrible and desperate path. But the free people of Angere have no choice but to take it.

Free to download.

https://simonkewin.co.uk/hyrn

ABOUT THE AUTHOR

Simon Kewin was born on the misty Isle of Man but now lives deep in the English countryside. He writes fantasy, science fiction and some things that can't make their minds up. He is the author of over 100 published short stories as well as a growing number of novels.

To find out about his other books, go to:

www.simonkewin.co.uk

Sign up for his newsletter and you'll be the first to know when he has new books out. There are some fine sci/fi and fantasy books to download for free as thanks.

POST-CREDITS SCENES

Nox walked through the shattered ruins of the White City.

Now that Menhroth was gone the towers and domes of his city were crumbling too, the necromancy that held them together failing. The walls shook and writhed, clattering to the ground around him. Beautifully carved bone lay in jumbled piles where towers and spires had toppled.

There were no guards, no people anywhere. Nothing at all moved. Even the crows were gone, their borrowed life turning to dust along with everything else.

The White City would soon be no more. No doubt the witches would turn their attention to the place at some point. They'd cleanse the ground, lay the bones to rest. Bury them or commit them to the river. It would keep them busy for a long time.

He had other work to do. The portal through to the refinery still stood, although its frame sagged badly, looking like it could collapse at any moment. That was where he had to go. Everything would be in chaos for a time, in both worlds, and in the confusion there would be opportunity. Genera would be vulnerable as it tried to adjust to losing its distant masters. And he knew how to exploit vulnerabilities.

He needed to understand what he was now capable of. Menhroth had given him considerable powers, intending to use him as a weapon against Cait if necessary. Now he was free from Menhroth's control, and he could do as he pleased. Cait had given him a rare gift. Perhaps he would turn himself into another Witch King. Perhaps he would destroy Genera and everything it stood for.

He hadn't decided yet. His life had been interesting and it looked like his death was going to be even more interesting.

He stepped into the portal to cross to the other world.

Bethany Weerd clung to the shadows of the shattered refinery. She'd remained after leaving Fer, helping to shepherd the lost and confused souls that howled through the place, offering what guidance she could. There were so many of them.

The buildings lay in broken ruins. The fires that had raged through them had left them as twisted and blackened piles of pipes. The great black engine was a smoking stump of metal, a jagged hole in its cylinder where the life had burst from it.

The people had gone; they'd either died or fled to safety. It was time for her to leave, too, back to the city where she belonged.

Then a figure stepped through the portal. He emerged from the roaring waterfall and stopped for a moment to take in the scene around him. She knew who he was, of course. They'd travelled together in Angere although he hadn't known about it. He was one of the Masters, and Cait had hated him. But she'd grown to like him, too. Trust him, even. It was complicated.

She realised with a jolt of alarm he was one of them now. How was that possible? They'd all been destroyed. The undain in this world had dissipated just as they had in the other, yet here was Nox, dead and now alive, burning with his own private rage.

Bethany shrank back into the shadows. She'd follow him, watch him.

The story wasn't over yet.